THE
Ultimate
Intimacy

THE
Ultimate
Intimacy

IVAN KLÍMA

Translated from the Czech by
A.G. Brain

Grove Press
New York

Originally published in Great Britain by Granta Books in 1997
Published simultaneously in Canada
Printed in the United States of America

FIRST GROVE PRESS PAPERBACK EDITION

Library of Congress Cataloging-in-Publication Data

Klíma, Ivan.
    [Poslední stupeň důvernosti. English]
    The ultimate intimacy / Ivan Klíma ; translated by A. G. Brain
        p.   cm.
    ISBN 0-8021-3601-X (pbk.)
    I. Brain, A. G.   II. Title.
    PG5039.21.L5P6413   1998
    891.8'6354—dc21   97-35481

Grove Press
841 Broadway
New York, NY 10003

99 00 01 02 10 9 8 7 6 5 4 3 2 1

Author's foreword

The statement that any resemblance between characters in a literary work and actual persons is purely coincidental generally tempts the reader to find real-life models for fictional characters.

The hero of this novel is a Protestant pastor, as the reader will immediately realize from its opening lines, and since I have a good number of friends among the Protestant clergy, whom I esteem for their social and moral stands, I should like to assure my readers that on this occasion it would be truly pointless to seek a model for my hero among their number. The same also applies, of course, to all the other characters in the book. After a lifetime's experience of prose writing, it is my considered opinion that the most authentic people and stories are those that emerge from the author's imagination.

THE
Ultimate
Intimacy

Chapter One

1

The light has grown dimmer in the chapel. Outside, seen through the narrow window, large flakes of March snow are falling. There are only two weeks left to Easter, so the chapel is almost full. Unless Daniel counts the three dozen or so loyal members of the congregation, people these days tend to come to church only around the traditional feast days.

'Christ,' Daniel says as he approaches the end of his sermon, 'crowned his work and teaching about the importance of love as the supreme expression of humanity with the most consequential of actions: he sacrificed his life for the love of people. The story of Jesus is also a message about God's new dispensation: original sin is erased. Sin brought forth evil. The penalty for sin and evil was death. Christ's death restores hope to mankind. It opens the way to good. Death is overcome and mankind is invited into God's presence.'

Reverend Daniel Vedra concludes his sermon, descends the two steps from the pulpit and sits down on a chair. His daughter Eva, the only child of his first marriage, once more takes her place at the harmonium. She plays well – very well. She has inherited his perfect pitch. The congregation on the other hand – in spite of all his efforts – sings badly, terribly in fact. Scarcely one in ten of those present has attended hymn practices.

> *Thine be the glory, risen, conquering Son,*
> *Endless is the victory thou o'er death hath won.*

How many of them truly believe the words they are now singing? But for the minister the words have a particular significance: his mother is dying. He has spent the entire previous night at her bedside

1

even though she probably didn't notice him; her soul was already preparing itself for the long journey into the unknown, the journey where she would meet Him. His mother believed this fervently while she was still capable of expressing her convictions.

Angels in bright raiment rolled the stone away,
Kept the folded grave-clothes, where thy body lay.

The minister looks around the gloomy chapel. He knows all of those present by name, he knows their life stories, their troubles, their jobs and the names of their children. But in the back row, at the side, an unknown woman dressed in strikingly colourful clothes has been sitting since the beginning of the service. She reminds him of Jitka, his first wife, with her long fair hair with its auburn sheen and her voice.

Jitka has been dead for almost eighteen years. Don't fret, she wrote to him several days before her death. Don't be sad. We'll meet again, won't we?

Yes, but in what form? In what form, Mummy?

Has death truly been vanquished? How long will it be before he finds out? How long before he discovers, unless there's nothing to discover at all.

No more we doubt thee, glorious Prince of Life;
Life is naught without thee: aid us in our strife.

What is stronger, faith without doubts, or faith that contends with doubts? 'I'd like to believe,' one of the prisoners he used to visit twice a month told him a year ago. 'How do I go about it, vicar?'

He was a young fellow who procured drugs for himself and others. He used to steal and take drugs because he didn't want to work and because he had no one to turn to. 'Pray, Petr. Confide in Him. Tell Him everything, even the most intimate things.' That did not convince him. How can you confide in someone you don't believe exists? But then, if you start to confide in someone, they start to exist. A heretical thought. Very heretical, in fact. Six months later Petr asked to be baptized.

He stands up and mounts the pulpit. Eva briefly continues improvising on the Handel tune. With a scraping of feet, rustling of clothes and coughing, the congregation rises to join him in prayer and, through his mediation, affirm their humility, confess their guilt and sinfulness and make supplication. *Jesus, who died for us on the cross, Lamb of God sacrificed for us sinners, You who suffered that we might have eternal life, have mercy on our weakness and give us the strength to believe. Be with those who believe in you and those who do not. Be with the powerful and the powerless. Be with prisoners and also with those who rule our country. Give our rulers wisdom and humility. And abide with those who are in any way unsure of the way ahead and seek a path to You. And do not forsake, we beseech You, either the sick or those who at this time are taking leave of this life in anxiety and in hope of Your mercy.*

Now the Lord's Prayer and the blessing: *The blessing of our Lord Jesus Christ be with you all. Amen.*

The closing hymn. He has chosen a short one. He is in a hurry and still has to take leave of each member of the congregation. He looks at them. His wife Hana is sitting in the front row in her old-fashioned Sunday clothes; beside her, their Magda, gazing at him devotedly through thick lenses.

He also notes that the unknown woman is leaving before the end of the hymn; one less to take leave of at least.

He walks up the aisle between the pews while the people wait in deference for him to leave first. The chapel is on the ground floor of a three-storey apartment house belonging to the congregation. On the first floor there is a library, an office and two guest rooms. He and his family live on the second floor. Now he stops outside the front door. A cold wind is blowing. The minister is too tall and thin, he looks as if any moment he might bend in the wind like the trees in the street. The wind can do little to dishevel the minister's already thinning hair, but it creeps under his black gown so that before long he will be chilled to the marrow. Fortunately he is used to it, having served for years in the Moravian Highlands where the cold months outnumbered the warm ones.

He grips an aged hand. 'It was very kind of you to come, Mr Houdek.'

'Why not, from time to time? It gives my wife pleasure and it does me no harm. And she is not up to it any more, much as she'd like to come. But you gave a good sermon, even for the likes of us pagans.' Mr Houdek owns a nursery that the Communists confiscated from him forty-five years ago, but he has lived to see it returned to him in his declining years. He probably does not believe in God but he occasionally comes to the service on account of his wife, who is unable to

3

make it here, just so that he can tell her what the sermon was about and who was at church.

'I'll drop by for a chat with your wife,' the minister promises. 'You sang splendidly, young Alois,' he says, turning to a lanky, red-headed lad. Alois used to be one of Petr's gang. He doesn't know who his father is, and his mother is in prison. He escaped a prison sentence; he didn't steal, apparently. Or that's what he maintains, at least. He admires Petr, which is why he turned up here and why he asked to be baptized. But he strikes the minister as more sincere than Petr these days. His wife has taken to the lad too and she recently suggested that he could come and live with them; the guest rooms are hardly used and Alois would get a taste of family life for the first time. Unless it was too late.

Admittedly, Daniel considered that at nearly seventeen it might be too late for the boy. He was also a little afraid for his own family, but agreed that they should trust in the essential goodness of their own children.

'Do you know they might release Petr next week?'

'I was expecting they might.'

'Do you think he'll keep it up outside as well?'

'He'll toe the line on your account, if for no other reason.'

Dr Wagner has a wide smile on his broad greyish face beneath a head of greyish hair.

'Good of you to come, Dr Wagner.'

Dr Wagner, by all accounts an excellent lawyer, has been coming to church since he failed to win a seat in parliament. He is an interesting man: well-read and thoughtful, but at the same time there is inside him a surprising emptiness that needs to be filled – through activity, through a career. When his career failed he turned to God. 'One has to draw some spiritual strength from somewhere.' And then he adds unexpectedly, 'It's something that often crosses my mind: there's something wrong with our society. It lacks a spiritual dimension. Nobody is guided by the Ten Commandments any more. And without them everything goes downhill.'

Elder Kodet approaches with his wife and two children. He shakes the minister's hand even more firmly than usual. 'Reverend, I have some good news for you.' He owns a real-estate firm and Daniel entrusted him with the sale of a house which has been returned to him as part of the restitution measures. It had belonged to his father and stood in a excellent location just behind the National Museum. Built

4

on art nouveau lines, it had even retained the original glass in two of its five balcony windows. He had been given back a house that he had never given a second thought to in his life, and had never hankered after.

'Shall I wait for you in the office?' Kodet asks.

He has no time for that now. He must rush to the airport to collect his sister and then take her to the hospital. Besides, doing business in the temple on a Sunday? In fact, the house frightens him somewhat. He fears that kind of good news. He has never owned a thing in his life and poverty strikes him as more honourable than a life of wealth. It is something he has often repeated in his sermons. Money, like power, deflects one from the essence of life. People who think about money tend to forget about the soul. These past few years have provided repeated evidence of that.

'No, I have to see my mother. I'll come and see you another time. When will you be in your office?'

'For you, any time, Reverend.'

The Soukups are among the last out. They have come without their children, who have no doubt been sent to the grandmother's. It strikes him that Máša's eyes are red from crying. He is concerned about the couple, or rather he is concerned about the husband, who has taken leave of his senses. The father of four small children, he has fallen in love like a teenager and wants a divorce. And Daniel always regarded him not only as wise but also as an ardent and devoted Christian. Even an ardent Christian can fall in love, of course; we are all human after all. But a father of four children ought not to lose his head. His wife is a good soul, evidently sensitive and gentle.

'I'm glad you both came, and together.'

'A fine sermon, Reverend,' Soukup says as he does every Sunday. His wife says nothing. Tears stream down her cheeks.

'Wouldn't you like to call on me some time?'

'Together?' the husband asks.

'I'd prefer to see you both together.'

'Fine.'

His wife merely nods and looks away as if ashamed and humiliated by her husband's infidelity.

While he is shaking her hand he adds, 'Be strong, Máša, and have faith that even if everyone were to let you down, the Lord will never abandon you.' He is excessively blunt. He shouldn't have taken the service today at all. Brother Kodet would have been only too glad to stand in for him. If he had asked his friend Martin Hájek or his wife, one of them would have preached in his place.

There is less than an hour until the plane lands, so he dashes off to the airport. He left it until last week, when his mother's condition suddenly took a turn for the worse, to call his sister in America. He put off breaking the bad news to her for too long and now he reproaches himself that Rút might not see her mother *compos mentis*.

Rút lives out in Oregon and they have seen each other just twice in the past twenty-five years. Until recently, they were only able to write about the most banal things, so they preferred not to write at all. But for years Rút used to send him a thousand dollars every Christmas, which amounted to more than his entire annual salary. Last year she even invited him to Oregon.

Rút was born two years before the beginning of the Second World War, while he arrived two years before its end. His sister could still remember air raids and their father's first arrest, whereas he is not sure he remembers his father's first release. He ascribes the difference in their characters to the different times into which each of them was born – or conceived, for that matter. His sister liked to laugh and her loud giggling accompanied his childhood years, whereas he tended to be serious. While his sister read pot-boilers and love stories, he chose *War and Peace* and *Madame Bovary*, as well as Plato, Bacon and Calvin's *Institutes*.

Both grew up in periods when hate was publicly proclaimed as something necessary, useful and unavoidable and when people acted accordingly. Rút refused to take account of it and shut her eyes to the reality. And when at last that was no longer possible, she fled the country. He decided he would challenge hate by choosing a lifestyle based on love. And being a person of conviction, he decided to study theology, at a time when he could be in no doubt that it would mean a life of poverty, with plenty of harassment into the bargain.

He manages to reach the airport on time and from the balcony overlooking the conveyor he catches sight of his sister waiting for her baggage.

When Rút at last appears in the exit, they hug each other, and he takes her travel bag. They then drive with great speed to the hospital.

He guides her to their mother's bed. She is asleep. As the nurses have removed her dentures, her bloodless, yellowing cheeks are deeply

6

sunken. Her thinning hair hangs in strands over her forehead. Some colourless fluid is flowing down a transparent plastic tube into a needle inserted in one of her veins.

Rút leans over her mother and speaks to her several times. Her mother does not stir. If she fails to come round, Daniel realizes in dismay, he will have wronged both his mother and his sister by preventing them taking leave of each other through his shilly-shallying.

But at that moment, his mother opens her eyes and says: 'Rút, my girl, where have you been gallivanting for so long? You haven't been to see me for at least a week!'

2

Diary excerpts

Shortly after she glimpsed Rút, Mother lapsed into unconsciousness. Hana said to me: 'Your mother's not aware of who's with her now anyway, go and get some sleep. Rutka and I won't stir from her.' So I went home but I didn't go to bed. I tried to think about something ordinary, to do everyday things. A copy of the Koran *was lying on my desk. By sheer chance I opened it at the Bee Sura: 'Your God is one God; as for those who do not believe in the hereafter, their hearts are ignorant and they are proud.'*

Last time I visited Petr he said to me: 'Reverend, I'm just beginning to realize I was in Satan's hands and you freed me.'

'That wasn't me, Petr,' I told him. 'All I did was tell you who could free you.'

He often speaks about his mother. At our first meeting he spoke ill of her, blaming her for divorcing and remarrying and for packing him off to the nursery school and playgroup for days at a time, and in the end she had done nothing to prevent them locking him away. Now he realizes how much he hurt her by the things he did and by the way he behaved. He is sorry and intends to make up for everything.

He really is beginning to examine his past without making excuses or justifying himself, and that's important. He has lots of good resolutions, I only hope he finds in himself the strength to act on some of them, at least.

Martin Hájek paid me a visit last week. He was remembering how they had refused to grant him a licence when he graduated from college and how, two years later, he received it for a remote parish in the Moravian Highlands. His fate was similar to mine. He wondered whether it didn't strike me occasionally that even in those frightful times we felt better than we do now?

We recalled how on the first Monday of every month we would hold a gathering of young people, some of them coming from very distant congregations. And we would often have discussions with people who were officially 'non-persons'. We talked for a while about how in those days we had a sense of mission. Or was it just a feeling of pride in our mission and our resistance? 'Do you know I met Berger in Jihlava?' Martin said. Berger had been the Secretary for Church Affairs for the two of us until a few years ago, but it seemed to me at that moment as if he belonged to another life altogether. 'What is he up to?' I asked.

'He's bought a pub, but he spent the whole time telling me about his ailments. I was expecting him to make some mention of what he used to do, that he'd maybe try to apologize for the way he treated us, but it didn't even occur to him to do anything of the sort. He behaved towards me as if we were old acquaintances or friends.'

'Humility is foreign to them, no one taught it to them,' I said.

Martin went on to ask about my mother and I told him her soul was growing wearier all the time. Then we talked about our children, and Martin remembered Jitka too. Generally everybody keeps quiet about her. It's not done to mention the departed, because it might upset those who remain. And the dead move further and further away from us until in the end we are unable to make out their shape.

I always find being close to death oppressive. I repeat to myself Paul's words: 'He has freed us from the very arms of death and will free us . . .' And also his message to the Romans: 'Yet the hope remains that the very Creation will be freed from the thraldom of death and be led into the freedom and glory of the Children of God.' And yet I feel anxious. More so than most other people perhaps. Most people follow Spinoza's dictum: Homer liber de nulla re minus quam de morte cogitat.

8

But a preacher expounding the Scriptures is in permanent contact with death – the issue of resurrection from the dead is the beginning and end of our message. A thought sometimes occurs to me: it wasn't just the Holy Spirit that ensured that, in spite of all the oppression, Christianity spread through the world and overcame all the pagan cults; the promise of eternal life also had a powerful effect. The moment we are freed from the clutches of death, from the law which binds all living things without exception, our entire being acquires a different perspective. The anxiety felt by every beast being led to the slaughter, or maybe even by the fly caught in the spider's web, is banished or at least attenuated. I reproach myself for my doubts. But were not the very apostles who witnessed the wonders that took place themselves prone to doubt sometimes? Didn't Thomas ask to touch Christ's wounds in order to believe?

And why did that wonder take place then, of all times; almost two thousand years ago, when the Jews fervently believed in the coming of the Messiah? Why, since then, has He only looked on in silence?

The Apostle Paul also wrote: 'And if Christ has not been raised your faith is futile; you are still in your sins. Then those also who have fallen asleep in Christ are lost. If only for this life we have hope in Christ, we are to be pitied more than all men.' (1 Corinthians 15: 17–19) I have read and even preached those three verses but none the less there is something that strikes me each time I read them. It's as if the apostle here was not referring to what happened but to how badly off we would be if it had not happened. As if faith ought not to be founded on the event, but that the event should be based on the fact that without it we would be simply wretched mortals like the rest of creation.

I ought to go to the hospital. I think about my mother all the time, but the awful thing is that even though she is still alive I think about her in the past tense. She was always severe but kind. She seldom kissed or hugged me but she was never unkind. I suppose she was just shy of showing her feelings. I take after her in that respect.

When they sent my father to prison they sacked her from the school where she was teaching and eventually she found a job with a bookbinder. She once brought me a beautifully bound book – a life of Comenius. She said: 'Nobody has been to collect this book for over a year.

They are either in prison or dead. You can read it for now.' It was not at all the sort of reading matter that appealed to me – I wasn't yet nine – but I loved that strange, captivating language. It sounded like music. And that musical language drew me to him. I have a picture of Comenius hanging in my office even though I have an aversion to worshipping saints of any kind.

I wanted Mother to move in with us but she refused. During the last six months I have visited her at least three times a week and taken care of her. I did her shopping, cooked for her and in the end even fed her. I used to tell her that I was praying for her, but I couldn't tell her I loved her. It's something I can't even say to Hana. It's as if inside me there is a rock face that I first have to scale. I managed to climb real rock faces with Jitka but this one beats me.

I am faithful but am incapable of being intimate. With Him still, maybe, but not with people. Not with my mother, nor the children nor with Hana. And intimacy is the first degree of fidelity, surely? Or is it the other way round: fidelity is the first degree of intimacy?

———⚬◯⚬———

One of my first memories. A pile of sand that had been tipped in front of the house (at the time we were still living in the villa in Střešovice which they moved us out of when they sent my father to prison). I was happy to have the chance to play in the sand. All of a sudden right in front of me there appeared an enormous cur with jaws half open and teeth bared. I was terror stricken and couldn't move. I expect I started to cry but I don't really remember. I just recall that primitive anxiety, a sense of menace that derived not from my own experience but the experience of our species. Then suddenly saving hands appeared – Mother's – and lifted me up high. Mother's soothing voice like music, like a prayer, like the song of angels. The assurance of safety and love.

It's ages since those hands were capable of lifting me up; on the contrary it is I who have been lifting Mother these past weeks and carrying her to the bathroom, or to her bed, or to the window to let her breathe a bit of fresh air. But even so, those hands – wrinkled and veined beyond recognition – still lived and could still caress. When they cease to live, the assurance of safety and the assurance of love will have gone.

When my father was near to death he lay in the hospital. Being a doctor he had his own ward and we could visit him whenever we liked. I would go and see him every day. We would talk about trivial things and avoid any mention of death. Father wanted to live but he knew that his heart would give out soon. One day I finally made up my mind and told him that his existence would not end with death, that the soul would not die but would live for ever.

He stared at me. He had very beautiful dark-blue eyes that age had not affected; not even his imminent death had dimmed them. He said nothing. I actually had the impression he was smiling. At first I assumed it was because, after all, he had heard some note of hope in my words, but then I realized that he was remaining silent simply out of a wish not to hurt me, in order, just before the end came, not to get into an argument with his grown-up son, whose opinions were to be respected.

I was intending to say something else about God's mercy but suddenly I became incapable of saying anything at all, so I also remained silent and just took Father's hand in mine and held it for a while.

Father closed his eyes and I felt him moving away from me into some unknown region. Then, without warning, he said: 'Eternity! What is eternity?'

I fell asleep where I sat. I slept for barely an hour but had a dream. I'll note it down quickly before I leave for the hospital: I was clambering up a steep rock which was partly covered in ice. The summit was close and the covering of ice glistened in the sunlight. I halted for a moment, flattened myself against the rock face and glanced back. In the depths I could see the dark-green bands of pine trees penetrating the stony moraine. No sign of life anywhere, I was here alone.

When I turned back to the rock face once more and looked upwards, it struck me that a strange glow was emanating from there. I carefully drove the ice-axe into the icy snow. I climbed with ease, as if I wasn't even climbing a rock face, but floating.

And then I caught sight of a being at the summit. How it had got there I couldn't tell, from heaven maybe. I had the impression that it was emitting light: so bright that I was unable to make out its features.

I stepped forward several paces – or rather I leaped the distance that still separated us. 'Who are you?' I asked.

'Daniel, don't you recognize me?'

'Mother, is that you? But how can you be here?'

'Don't ask, just believe!'

By now I could make out her features, but her face was as I remembered it from childhood, unmarked by old age and mental decline. Then she stretched out her arms as if to bless me, and I heard her say softly, 'You live right and you do right, I am pleased with you.' A wind suddenly arose and she started to dissolve beneath its gusts. All that remained on the mountain top was . . .

At this very moment, in other words at 11.15 p.m., 20 March, Hana phoned from the hospital. Mother passed away ten minutes ago. She lived seventy-eight years. Lord be merciful to her soul. 'I called you an hour ago,' Hana told me. 'Rút and I wanted you to come to the hospital, but no one answered the phone.'

3

It was drizzling on the day of the funeral. The suburban cemetery was on a hill and the clouds seemed to tumble and roll just above the pointed tops of the conifers. The freshly dug earth gave off a damp smell. Reverend Martin Hájek was now speaking about his friend Daniel's mother, how he had known her in the days when he was studying in Prague. He spoke about how he would visit Daniel's family and it felt as if this was his second home. 'Sister Vedrová was someone very special. I have known few women as kind or as patient as she was. She travelled through this life, which by our criteria was not an easy one, with a heart untrammelled by hatred or resentment; she travelled with courage and humility, always ready to listen to others, to understand them and lend them a hand.'

His mother had truly borne her fate with courage and if she had suffered she had done so in silence. Even though in her latter years her vascular illness had virtually prevented her from walking, she had not

12

complained. She would not speak about herself. Usually she would talk about Daniel and his worries and needs, or about the children and their requirements. When she retired sixteen years ago she used to ask him to bring her the manuscripts of samizdat books which she would then bind and with the proceeds she would buy clothes and toys for the children. She had even bought them a television set for his fortieth birthday.

The final prayer. He uttered the words of the Lord's Prayer without being aware of them. How many times had he repeated those same words in the course of his life? His kingdom had not come, but her spirit, so he hoped, now dwelt in it.

He watched as the gravediggers lowered the coffin suspended on thick ropes. For some people, such as his father, death was the last, irrevocable certainty. The certainty of an end. For others it meant the certainty, or at least the hope, that something new would begin for them, something definitely superior and less paltry than was offered by earthly existence. None the less he found both possibilities depressing. That new existence was veiled too thickly by the unknown. Unlike his first wife, he was incapable of envisaging the possibility of a future reunion.

On their return home they naturally talked together about the departed. Rút recalled experiences he could not have remembered. When the war was coming to an end, their mother had started looking for red and blue cloth as early as April. Not finding any, she dyed an old bed sheet, cut up two pairs of undershorts and sewed them into a Czechoslovak flag several days before the Prague Uprising. His sister also recalled their father's arrest four years after the war and how their mother had not wanted to let the officers of the state police enter their flat at five o'clock in the morning. She told them they were behaving like the Gestapo and amazingly enough nothing happened to her. 'You slept through the lot,' Rút told him. 'You were just six years old and were due to start in first class.' Then she reminded him of his schoolboy pranks. On one occasion, before the start of a Russian lesson, he had hidden some sort of letter full of Russian vulgarities in the class register. It had caused an enormous fuss, but he was not found out because he had resolutely denied it. His Russian had come in handy when the Soviets invaded the country ten years later, as it enabled him to write on the wall in Cyrillic: *Iditye domoi!* He had also tried to persuade the soldiers that they were being duped and manipulated and serving the devil instead of God. The trouble was they were obeying someone else's orders, not God's. That was if they had even heard of God.

'They're sure to have,' Daniel commented. 'And even if they hadn't, every human being has at least an inkling of His existence.'

'Isn't that awful,' Rút sighed. 'It looks as if Dan still believes that, after all he's been through! And that flag that Mother sewed during the war,' she recalled once more, 'Dan found it in the attic and carried it over his shoulder in the demonstration, shouting slogans. What was it we shouted, in fact?' she said, turning to her brother.

'I can't remember any more,' Daniel prevaricated. 'And yet come to think of it, it was "No traitors as legislators" or "Red brothers, get back to your reservations". And we pledged loyalty to those who showed no loyalty to us in the end. But that's the way it goes.'

His children listened with interest to the stories of their father's misdemeanours and patriotic deeds, and meanwhile their grandmother's death receded.

Rút was to fly home that same day as she had patients already waiting to see her. She refused to let him drive her to the airport, however. It was better to say their farewells here than in the airport departure lounge.

So he went off with his sister to call for a taxi and they found themselves alone for a moment in the passage. It occurred to him that there were important things they had not found time to talk about yet. They ought to speak about their father, the inheritance and their lives. But none of these were mentioned. There was no time, besides which protracted farewells wreck the slow progression towards intimacy and create a gulf which he, for one, was incapable of bridging. They embraced at least. And when she climbed into the taxi he stayed on the pavement waving until the car disappeared around the corner.

'Daddy, are we going to sing?' Magda wanted to know when he rejoined the others. 'Or perhaps we shouldn't after Granny's death?'

Now and again they would sing in the evening whenever there was time, or they would improvise a comedy which they made up themselves. It could be on a historical theme, or from their own everyday lives, or just some nonsense. He enjoyed thinking up absurd repartee and making crazy faces. The children liked it and it made them laugh.

A comedy was out of the question today, naturally. 'I'm sure Grandma wouldn't mind if we sang something. She enjoyed singing, after all.'

14

They went into the room where the piano was. He brought his guitar and Marek fetched his violin.

'Granny used to love "Sing the glad tidings!"' Eva suggested.

'And "By the waters of Babylon",' Magda recalled.

When he was small his mother had sung him lullabies and taught him simple little prayers. His father had most likely scorned them but kept his opinion to himself. Sometimes his parents would go out together in the evening and he would stay at home with his sister, frightened to go to sleep in case a robber came in the night. Death might even creep in.

By the waters of Babylon
we laid down and wept, and wept,
for Thee, Sion
we remember, we remember, we remember Thee, Sion.

At nine o'clock he said good-night to his children and went with Hana to the kitchen.

His wife ran water into the sink. 'Dan, you ought to go to bed, you look tired.'

'No. I wouldn't be able to sleep anyway.'

'I know it's hard on you, but it was the best thing as far as she was concerned. She had nothing but suffering to look forward to.'

'Don't worry, I will be able to sleep again.'

'We've got this journalist on our ward by the name of Volek,' she said, apparently changing the subject. 'He has just had a stomach resection and reminds me of someone, though I can't remember who. From time to time he comes into the nurses' station and keeps everyone entertained.' Hana related to him how the man had travelled a good part of the globe, had lived in China and spent time in New Zealand. He had told the nurses about the Maoris, and their belief that everyone who came into contact with the dead, even if only assisting in a burial, was forbidden to associate with people and was treated as a total outcast. Such a person is not even allowed to touch food, and has to be fed or eat without hands like a beast.

'There are some savages who believe that the spirit of the dead person envies them remaining alive,' Daniel explained, 'and therefore wants to do them harm. Even the ancient Jews considered the dead unclean, and anyone touching a corpse was forbidden to touch food.'

'But even those savages believe that the soul survives the body.'
'According to them, everything has a soul. Trees and animals alike. They will often beg the soul of a hunted animal to forgive them for what they have done.'

'It was the funeral that brought it back to mind. Here the people shook each other by the hand, whereas there nobody would be allowed to touch you.'

'Here they share your pain and distress, there they share your anxiety.'

'I share everything with you, Dan. The sadness, the distress and that anxiety.' She came over for him to hug her.

'Now you're all I have!' and he realized his oppressive loneliness. He consoled others in a similar situation with the thought that they had Jesus, who remained with them always, and he added quickly, 'As my nearest and dearest, I mean.'

In his workshop he had an unfinished carving of a woman covering her breasts with her hands. He had not touched the figure for at least a month. If it was successful, he was intending to call it 'Dignity'.

He had first taken the knife, chisel and limewood block in his hands on his return from Gustrow where he had seen Barlach's statues. Perhaps it was neither wise nor useful, but generally, whenever he set eyes on some work of art that enchanted or astounded him, he would fall prey to the temptation to try his hand at it also. And so he had tried painting, composing, and had even written poetry at one time. He played not only the piano and harmonium but also the guitar. So eventually he attempted to produce a human form from a piece of wood. For someone who was self-taught, the work exceeded all his expectations. Having seen some of the carvings, a gallery owner had recently offered him an exhibition, and after hesitation, Daniel had accepted. In fact, the offer had inspired him to work with greater concentration and responsibility.

He mostly carved female figures, giving his creations such names as 'Love', 'Sorrow', 'Longing' or 'Motherhood', but again and again the faces of those carved figures resembled the face of his first wife as it remained fixed in his memory from moments of love-making, when she would seem utterly transformed and more beautiful. Maybe that was why no one but he was able to recognize her in those carved faces.

From the waist downwards the figure would be covered only by a slightly gathered piece of cloth. That was how his first wife used to come to him every night, with a towel tied around her waist and covering her breasts with her arm. She never stopped being ashamed of her nakedness and always wanted to cuddle him in the dark or at least with the blinds down, and when she then spoke tender words to him she would whisper them as if fearing that someone else might hear her.

Perhaps she would have lost her shyness with the passage of years, but God had only granted them four years of life together – three years of health and one year of gradual dying which had been particularly cruel when the tumour painfully ate away her insides. So young, so kind, so considerate, so incapable of harming anyone. Why she of all people? But who has the right to judge God's will? Our earthly existence is no more than a blinking of His eye. The important thing is what comes after. Because what comes 'after' lasts for all eternity. All eternity close to Him – what meaning can any earthly delight have compared to that? Why then are we so attached to this earthly life? Is it because all that reaches us from over there is dogged silence? And the numbers of the doggedly silent swell all the time. It was curious how thinking about the death of his first wife, which had always dispirited him, seemed to take his mind off this fresh pain.

For a while he tried to make the shapes more precise but his hand shook and he felt too tired and unable to concentrate. Hana was right, he ought to go to bed.

At that moment he realized that light was still shining from another window on to the lawn outside.

Eva's small room was up in the attic.

He tapped on her door but entered too quickly and discovered his daughter trying to conceal a sheet of writing in the pages of a book.

'Who are you writing to?'

'No one in particular.'

'And I'm not supposed to see it?'

'No, it's not like that.'

'It's ages since we've talked together.'

'I don't like wasting your time. And you've been preoccupied with Grandma.'

'Grandma will have no more need of me now, besides which you'd hardly be wasting my time.'

'Mum said you had a lot on your mind. And then there were the prisoners.'

'The prisoners are important but not so important that we can't find time for each other.'

'We all have so little time. Mummy, Marek, and me too. All of us are rushing somewhere or chasing something. I sometimes get the feeling things are odd round here.'

'Odd in what way?'

She said nothing. Then she drew from her book the sheet of paper she had tried to conceal from him when he came in and handed it to him. It was a poem:

Somewhere inside us holy delusions flower
We snatch the blooms whose scent overpowers.
Somewhere inside us are flowers as pure as snow
In our dreams, at least, they are our pillow.

It struck him that there was something of his own nostalgia in the poem. His eldest daughter had inherited her mother's looks: the same colour hair and eyes, the long neck and the narrow shoulders. But in character she took after him: a fear of intimacy and therefore a sense of solitariness too. He stroked her hair. 'Tell me, is there something you'd really like?' He stopped short, realizing that what she wanted most of all she had just shown to him in the poem. 'I meant some *thing*, something nice.'

'You mean something to wear, for instance?'

'For instance.'

She brightened up. 'I did see this sweater, but it was awfully expensive.'

'Where did you see it?'

'You know that little boutique by the tram stop? But not now, not while we're in mourning.'

'I'm sure Grandma would like to give you a treat. What did the sweater look like?'

'It was green and had this design on it – white lilies. I don't really want it. It's only because you asked me.'

'Fine.' He stroked the hair again that reminded him so much of her mother. 'Any time you're feeling a bit sad and think I could help, do come and see me however busy you think I might be.'

He had converted the closet next to Eva's room into a study for himself with a small desk, a chair, a bookshelf and a filing cabinet full of old magazines, letters, newspaper cuttings and photographs.

He ought to sort out his letters. He took several bundles of envelopes out of the filing cabinet. Then he noticed one that was tied up with a red ribbon. They were letters he had written to Jitka in hospital and the ones she had written to him from there. He had not read them since it happened. He hesitated a moment, before putting the envelope one side and getting on with sorting his correspondence.

4

Hana

Hana was born in the last year but one of the war in a village not far from Litomyšl. She was named after her mother.

She could not remember the war, nor, for that matter, the collectivization of agriculture that had struck their village before she even started to go to school. The village had two churches, one Catholic, the other Protestant, but the age-old quarrels were now forgotten: believers were out of favour if they chose to acknowledge any other church but the Communist one.

Hana's parents used to attend the Protestant church, but not very regularly. Matters of faith were never discussed at home, grace was no longer said before meals and she had no one to encourage her to pray. When she tried asking how the world was made her father evaded her question, saying that it was something even people cleverer than he didn't know. Nevertheless as a child she regarded the pastor as the most venerable person walking the earth.

One was also required to respect one's teachers. At the primary school there was a kind woman comrade who taught her pupils not only to read and write and honour the working class and its vanguard, the Communist Party, but also took them on nature walks and picked the herbs they found and told them how to make their own herbarium. Hana enjoyed that and she learnt to draw flowers so well that they looked real and the teacher praised her for it. She even told her parents that Hana could study to be a painter.

Her parents considered it too outlandish an occupation and, above all, not practical enough, apart from the fact that Hana drew nothing but flowers and her gift was soon forgotten. She was the eldest of three children, although only one year older than her brother, who died when she was twelve. From early childhood Hana always looked older than her years, and this encouraged her parents to leave her in charge of her younger siblings at a time when she was still in need of someone to take care of her. She was not particularly attractive to look at, but she was well proportioned, and she let her dark hair grow as long as possible. Her most interesting feature was her eyes: they were large and dark, and in combination with her dusky complexion they seemed to suggest foreign forebears – Spanish, French or maybe Romany, although there was no mention of anything of the sort in the family history.

She was kind-hearted by nature and from a very young age she was brought up to be modest and taught that one came into the world chiefly to work. Her life was subject to the rhythms of village life – a rhythm dictated by the seasons of the year. Summer was the busiest time of all, even though it was the school holidays. It became less busy from autumn onwards. Best of all was the winter when the days were really short and they celebrated Christmas and skated on the village pond.

Once when she was skating, the ice cracked beneath her. Fortunately she was near the bank, so the icy water only reached up to her shoulders and they were able to pull her and two boys from her class out of the pond. A third boy disappeared beneath the ice and was not found until spring when the ice melted. She had not seen the corpse but they said it had been eaten away by the fish. It might not have been true, but the thought of lying helpless at the bottom of the pond, having her body eaten by fish that someone would then catch and eat, bedevilled her for years afterwards. She never went skating again and would not go near the pond even during the summer. She also refused to eat fish.

When she was finishing elementary school, she fell in love with a boy in her class. He lived in the neighbouring village and was half a head shorter than her. His figure seemed altogether shrunken, which probably explained why he was nicknamed Little Joe. He was not handsome by any means and his pale face was covered in freckles and pimples. In class he was ignored rather than admired by the other pupils. That might have been what attracted Hana to him. She always felt sympathy for the outcast, the weak or the handicapped.

Whenever they were standing together in some quiet corner (Hana made sure it was not too remote), Little Joe would say nothing at first, but then he would start to entertain her by telling her the plots of the stories he had been reading. They were few in number and mostly about Red Indians. Little Joe became so wrapped up in these stories it was almost as if he had been there himself. He would tell her how wild the mountains were and how broad the prairies. He would describe the beauty of the totem poles and the bravery of the chiefs, reciting their poetic names with affection. At home he made himself a bow and arrows that could actually hit a target. Hana did not find the Red Indian stories exciting but she was attracted to Little Joe's enthusiasm and his voice.

Their love did not go beyond kissing and cuddling. And now and then Little Joe would give her a ride on a tractor and bring her gingerbread hearts from the fair. Once he gave her a bunch of irises. Afterwards she drew them and framed the picture for him. She also baked him a cake and darned a rip in his shirt.

But in the summer holidays the tractor overturned with Little Joe in it and a few days later the lad died from his injuries. People came to his funeral from the surrounding villages; an accidental death always attracts greater attention than a natural one. Unless they belonged to the family of the deceased, children generally walked at the very end of the cortège, far from the grief and out of earshot of the weeping of relatives and friends. Hana, however, walked just behind Little Joe's nearest family and sobbed out loud.

Shortly afterwards she went off to Písek to study nursing. She was not entirely sure that she wanted to become a nurse but she knew of no other career she wanted to follow. After all, she had been brought up to regard helping others as the supreme meaning of life. She enjoyed life in the nurses' home even though she rather missed her village and her parents, and above all little Pavel, her youngest brother, a chubby five-year-old with straw-coloured hair and an eternally grubby face, who would run after her as if she were his mother. (Little did she imagine that one day her son would have the same hair and the same chubby figure.)

She still carried around Little Joe's photo in her purse, but the sight of it brought back fewer and fewer memories. In the end she left it where it was only because almost all of her fellow students carried photos of their boyfriends in their purses.

Water in any form seemed destined to be the cause of dreadful experiences in her life. Once when she was coming to the end of her second year at the school, she agreed to go swimming in the Otava River. Her friends left without her so she set off after them. Halfway there, a dirty, unkempt fellow leapt out at her from behind a tree. He put his hand over her mouth and dragged her off to nearby bushes. There he took his hand away from her mouth but hissed at her not to make a sound or he would strangle her.

She had often heard tell of such assaults and was even afraid to walk along the street on her own at night, but it had never occurred to her that something of the sort could really happen to her. Rapists were to be found only in stories, she had never met one in real life. She was so astounded and terrified in those first moments that she was scarcely able to resist. Then she tried with all her might to get free and even tore off the attacker's sleeve and scratched his face. But he was much stronger and twisted her arms until the tears sprang to her eyes. She stopped defending herself and then ceased to be fully aware of what was happening to her.

It all took only a few minutes. After telling her that if she spoke to anyone about it he would find her and kill her, the fellow ran off. For a while she remained lying half-naked in the flattened grass and then she started to groan aloud. A short while ago her principal fear was that she might die; now she had no notion of how she would go on living. She gathered up the tattered pieces of her clothing that lay scattered all around and returned to town.

She told no one what had happened. Not because she believed the rapist's threats but because she was terrified of people discussing how she had been dishonoured. And were it to reach the ears of her parents, the shame might be more than they could bear.

The fellow's unshaven face haunted her for many years afterwards. She would catch sight of it whenever she found herself in a crowd. Also from that time on she would dream again and again of being surrounded by a crowd of naked men with repulsively pink skin and hairy chests. They would dance around her and scream in rhythm at the orders of one unshaven one who would wave his enormous pink genitals. She realized that this was Satan himself trying to have power over her. She would resist him, but in the dream she would be aware of Satan's superior strength, so it wasn't a question of him overcoming her physically so much as taking possession of her soul and filling it with evil.

She toyed with the idea of taking vengeance on people for what one of their number had done to her, but this was foreign to her nature. Instead she simply turned against men from then on and shunned their touch. And when she went for her first job she asked to work on the gynaecology ward.

She was twenty-two and already living in Prague, when in spite of everything she fell in love with a doctor in the ward where she worked. He was seven years her senior and loved her too, or so he said, telling her all sorts of beautiful things and even reciting poetry while caressing her with the experienced touch of a man who had loved many women – something that was not apparent to her. But even though she enjoyed his caresses she never experienced real pleasure. They went out together for over a year and were already talking about getting married when out of the blue he announced to her he was going to marry another woman; that he had to because she was expecting his baby. At that moment she swore she would never again have anything to do with men. Nothing at all. If it had been possible she would have entered a convent.

So her life wore on between the hospital and the nurses' home where she lived. Lacking any distractions, she used to spend much more time at work than the others and usually did more than was required of her. Only on Sundays, unless she was on duty, she would go to church, though by no means regularly, and if she happened to have a few days off she would make the trip to see her parents and younger siblings. At that time she noticed that her father had started to become dangerously thin, losing all appetite for food. She urged him to see the doctor but her father, either from stubbornness or fear, refused to go, saying there was nothing wrong with him. When at last he let himself be persuaded, it was too late to operate. For a long time afterwards, she blamed herself for not having warned him forcefully enough, even though she had suspected the malignancy of the illness he refused to acknowledge.

When she was thirty-two, she met Daniel, who was the son of a doctor on her ward. It was shortly after Daniel's wife had died and Hana knew that he was now alone with a young daughter. One day when he brought his little girl to see his father in the hospital, Hana took the child to the nurses' station and looked after her there. The little girl had straw-coloured hair like her own youngest brother, and it touched her. As Daniel was leaving he thanked her and she told him truthfully how much she had enjoyed looking after the little girl.

23

In that case, he had said, I will bring her again. And he had indeed, leaving Eva in Hana's care several times after that and almost always chatting with her at each visit. He had asked Hana about her life and invited her to come to one of his church services. The following Sunday she had actually gone and when Daniel was saying goodbye to her at the end of the service and thanking her for coming, Hana had the feeling he shook her hand with particular warmth.

She didn't know whether she loved him, but she felt compassion for his situation, as well as a sense of security in his presence. This seemingly frail man with an honourable profession would never harm her, it occurred to her. All of a sudden she found herself considering the possibility of living with a man, taking care of him, having a family and maybe even having children of her own.

5

Even though Daniel used to visit the prison at least twice a month, he never managed to rid himself of a most unpleasant feeling each time the prison gate swung open in front of him. The guards always treated him in an obliging and even kindly fashion but in spite of that, the memories of his own recent interrogations would begin to come flooding back. The faces of the warders were so strongly reminiscent of the expressions of the officials and Secretaries for Church Affairs with whom he had been forced to endure lengthy and humiliating interviews.

The situation had changed, but not the people – or only slightly. And where there had been a change, he wasn't entirely sure if it was for the better. In fact he wasn't sure even in his own case.

Petr was brought in shortly after Daniel had taken a seat in the interview room.

'How are you, Petr?'

'Welcome to this cool place, Reverend.' The lad smiled. Whenever he smiled he looked almost childlike. Only the long scar on his left cheek testified to the fact that his past had not been so innocent. He also had a scar on his wrist, self-inflicted. 'I've tried killing myself at least five times,' he had told Daniel on their first meeting. 'With a razor, with pills, with water and with rum, and I also tried freezing myself to death. I went and lay down in the snow just in my pants and socks. But nothing worked!'

At that time he had been quite emaciated, with a sickly grey complexion; only his eyes had shown any real sign of life. But he had put on weight over the past three months and it struck Daniel that this lad who had never worked and had certainly never taken any exercise – who on the contrary had abused his body – had quite an athletic physique.

'Whenever you come it's like the sun coming out.'

'Come on, Petr, where did you read that?'

'In the Bible, of course, the one you left here for me: "His face shone like the sun", or something like that.'

'Everyone sends you greetings,' Daniel said, ignoring Petr's comparison of him with the Saviour. 'Alois too. He's earning money now. He's got a job with a building firm as a bricklayer.'

'Yeah. It's wicked how time flies. On the outside, at least.'

'I brought you some fruit. And my wife baked you a cake.'

'You are angels, the pair of you, Reverend.'

'Give the poetry a rest, Petr, you know I don't like it. It's quite possible that you won't even get a chance to eat it in here.'

'I bet I will. My lawyer told me they're postponing the hearing again. The court went and lost some papers apparently.'

'They've postponed the hearing?'

'For at least a month. They won't get here any sooner.'

'You'll put up with it for another month, seeing that you've put up with it for two years already.'

'I will, of course, but Reverend you have no idea what it's like when you're all ready to leave and then the moment is put off. Every day drags by and you suddenly feel what a hell hole this place is.'

'It's also up to us to decide whether we live in hell or not.'

'And also up to those who are with you here from morning to night. This place is swimming in evil as if you'd kicked over a bucket of it. And when you behave any differently they start to hate you. When they notice you praying, for instance, they either laugh at you or want to beat you up.'

'I know, Petr. I'll ask the lawyer if there is any way of speeding up the hearing.'

'And what if they don't release me?'

'They will. And if they don't, you'll have to put up with it.'

'With your help, I would.'

25

'You'd cope with it even without my help. If you have really changed inside you'll manage it because you know that the Lord Jesus will help you.'

'I tend to believe in your help, Reverend. The Lord Jesus is too far away.'

'He isn't, Petr. You only need to open the Bible.'

'Yeah, I know. But I haven't even got my copy any more. I lent it to that bright spark who shares my cell. He's half gypsy, or says he's only half. He's never read anything like it, but he's quite taken with the way Jesus performed miracles.'

'Petr, the miracles aren't the most important thing in scripture. What's more important is the message of love.'

'I know, Reverend. But what would a gypsy like him know about love?'

'So you tell him then.'

'Me? Hold on, Reverend . . . After all, I've lived like an animal all my life. An animal among animals. I can recall every kind word that was ever said to me, there were so few of them.'

'But there were some. Anyway it's good you're thinking this way. That you're thinking about yourself and not blaming everyone around you.'

'You're the one who taught me that, Reverend. Before then I used to do the same as everyone around me. I saw the splinter in other people's eyes but didn't notice the beam in my own.'

'Petr, I also wanted to tell you I'm trying to find you a job. Mr Houdek from our congregation has a garden centre and he's bound to have some kind of job for you.'

'Thank you, Reverend.' He didn't seem too enthusiastic at the prospect of a job in a garden centre. 'I've also done something for you.' He pulled out a large sheet of paper. On it was drawn a head with a crown of thorns. The face was so deformed that it looked almost cubist. 'I drew this for you. And for your wife.'

Daniel took the picture and thanked him for it. Then he wished him patience and strength. 'Christ can be with you anywhere,' he said to him as they parted. 'There is no place His love can't reach.'

On the way home, it occurred to him to call in at his mother's small flat at Červený vrch and collect a picture. His mother had moved there after his father's death. There had only been room for a few pieces of furniture from the old flat, and some pictures, most of which had been given to his father by women artists he had treated. There was one picture that Daniel liked. It depicted a young gypsy girl with a basket of flowers. She had a sweet face and big breasts that were just partly revealed. The painting wasn't signed but he didn't mind that; he liked the flower-girl. She had represented for him – during his adolescence at least – an ideal of beauty: dark eyes, a dusky complexion and big breasts. Maybe that was what he found attractive about Hana when he first set eyes on her.

He gazed at the picture for a while but could not make up his mind to take it down from the wall. Instead he opened the window. On the lawn below, someone had set up a low metal pylon and fixed vanes on top of it. It might have been a work of art, a child's construction or even part of a wind generator. He watched the vanes revolving quietly for a moment and then went back into the room and opened the wardrobe. All his mother's clothes were hanging there: her jumper with the darned sleeves, her worn overcoat and a few dresses, only one of which was worthy of the name of Sunday best. His mother wore it only on family birthdays, or for church on Sundays.

He was touched by the shabbiness of the things, even though possessions meant little to him. His mother couldn't afford to buy clothes and he didn't earn enough to give her anything towards them. It was only now that he could afford it, now that it was too late.

He wandered around the flat a little longer. He opened the refrigerator, which contained nothing but a half-empty bottle of ketchup and a tube of some ointment that had to be kept cool. It looked as if Hana had already taken away any food that might have gone bad.

On the armchair by the bed there lay a black-bound Bible in the Kralice translation; his mother had refused to abandon the language she had grown up with. There was a bookmark in the third chapter of John's Gospel and he noticed that his mother had drawn a faint line alongside three of the verses.

And this is the condemnation, that light came into the world, and men loved darkness rather than light, because their deeds were evil.

For every one that doeth evil hateth the light, neither cometh to the light, lest his deeds should be reproved.

But he that doeth truth cometh to the light, that his deeds may be made manifest, that they are wrought in God.

His mother strove to live in truth as revealed in scripture and as required by it, and she had brought him up to do likewise. She had believed he would manage it; she believed he would achieve something important, that he would leave his mark on this world.

When he failed to get into the grammar school because his father happened to be in prison at the time, branded as an enemy of the state and of the rotten system that held sway then, Daniel became despondent at the thought of having to become a trainee somewhere. At the time, his mother consoled him and assured him that everything that befell him would prove useful one day, and that as long as it was God's will that he should achieve something good and useful, there was no power on earth that could prevent it, and there was no reason why he should slacken his resolve.

In those days, he really did believe he was pre-destined for great deeds. Since he had no interest in technology, travel or politics, those deeds would have to be performed in other spheres. He used to have dreams – they might have been daydreams, but it was impossible to tell so many years on – in which he would appear dressed in a toga like a Greek philosopher, or a prophet even, and at such moments of enlightenment he would come up with all sorts of sentences that struck him as both wise and significant.

So he was enrolled on a booksellers' training course, but he didn't have a chance to qualify, as a year later his father returned home from eight years in prison, and strangely enough, Daniel was accepted into the grammar school.

Daniel naturally grew out of his adolescent dreams, but he always regarded his work as a mission and for a long time believed that moments of enlightenment would come again and that he would discover what was 'the truth' and find the answer to the most secret questions of being and non-being. And sometimes when he was talking to his first wife – who was capable of listening to him as no one had since – it would seem to him that he really would manage to get to the root of the mystery that veiled the manifestations of divine action in the world and discover the cause of human failings.

But when Jitka died, he seemed to dry up inside. He still strove to discharge conscientiously what he regarded as his mission; the question was what had he really accomplished – what, in retrospect, was there to show for it?

He had married several dozen couples, made sure the dead had a decent burial, and possibly given some of the living encouragement by convincing them that life had some purpose. During his period in the Moravian Highlands, there had been some Catholics who came to his sermons as well as some 'non-believers' on the odd occasion, but even so, the church – built in the eighteenth century, when the anti-Protestant laws were repealed – remained very empty, as most people in the village and its environs had no interest in his message.

Since the Velvet Revolution, he had suddenly been allowed to appear on television and visit prisons, and yet this wasn't quite what his mother had expected of him, or what he himself had once dreamt about. Moreover, he was no longer convinced that there existed any ideas that were sufficiently wise, noble or significant to influence people's behaviour. People's behaviour tended to be influenced by ideas that lacked both wisdom and nobility.

On the lowest shelf there stood some boxes full of papers. The outside of the boxes bore inscriptions in his mother's elegant school-mistress's hand: *Richard's letters. Letters to me. Letters from the children. Official correspondence. Miscellaneous. Photographs.*

What was he to do with these writings? Would he read them? Eva would most likely move into the flat. Before that happened, he would have to take away the letters. He would take them away unread and store them away somewhere in the cellar, where his children would find them after his death and dump them.

The photographs were also sorted into a whole lot of envelopes. He pulled one out. In a very amateurish, grey snapshot his mother was leaning against the fence of their villa in Střešovice holding a baby in her arms. The baby must have been him. The back of the photo bore the date: summer 1944. His mother was wearing a summer dress, which he could not recall, of course. The dress was shabby looking – it was the last year of the war. His father was in a concentration camp, his mother had been left on her own with the two children. Their father had returned only to be imprisoned again several years later. Their mother remained alone once more. No one even visited them. Only the old minister from their congregation called in from time to time and pressed a thousand-crown note on their mother towards the housekeeping. That minister was also long dead but he now discovered a photograph of him standing among a confirmation group. Daniel scarcely recognized himself, he was even thinner in those days and his forehead was partly obscured by hair.

And there were wedding photos of Jitka. They all stood there together. Only Rút was missing – she was already over the hills and far away. He turned over the photographs absentmindedly and returned them to their envelope: himself with Jitka with mountaineering ropes round their waists; his father; a coloured snap of Rút at the Yosemite Falls; the manse in Kamenice; a wedding photo with Hana. Another one with his mother sitting in her armchair bent slightly over some sewing. The armchair still stood here by the bed. He recalled how when his mother did any sewing she would generally prick her fingers until they bled. The blood would distress him, or maybe it was his mother's clumsiness that upset him. He became aware of the tears burning his throat. As if he only now realized that he would never again set eyes on his mother, either here in her armchair or anywhere else on this earth.

He stuffed the box back into the wardrobe and tried to dispel his gloom by thinking of their next meeting which had to occur one day, although there was no telling when, where or how. But no sense of relief came. *When they heard about the resurrection of the dead, some of them sneered, but others said, 'We want to hear you again on this subject.'* (Acts 17:32)

6

Matouš

Matouš Volek was born and grew up in Michle. His father had been a tailor's assistant – a very quiet and mild-mannered man. He died of belatedly diagnosed tuberculosis when Matouš was thirteen. A few days before his death, Matouš had observed above his father's head a strange glow that quickly grew pale before disappearing entirely. It had frightened the boy but he never told anyone what he had seen.

Matouš inherited his father's scrawny and rather stunted body, as well as his long-sightedness, diligence and meditative tendencies, not to mention pathological mood swings and a fear of women.

Matouš's mother had not remarried and the devotedness that was her main character trait was transferred from the ailing husband to the healthy son. She worked as a postwoman and her daily duties entailed doing the rounds of dozens of streets which at the time were mostly made up of low, temporary dwellings. In spite of this, she would manage to return home in time to prepare her son's lunch and chat to him about his problems. She even tried helping him with his studies by testing him on his school homework after quickly reading up the subject beforehand in his textbook. She wanted him to go to university so that he could be educated and learned, and respected by all, preferably becoming a doctor, or a civil engineer at least.

Matouš indeed went on to university, but to study something else entirely, namely, oriental languages at the Arts Faculty. Having a gift for languages and virtually no other interests (he didn't go out with girls, or rather none of them felt inclined to go out with him), he made full use of the opportunity and learnt Chinese. He acquainted himself with Chinese thinking, being attracted most of all to Taoism at that time, although, like the majority of Europeans, he only selected certain elements from it for his own lifestyle; he certainly proved incapable of freeing himself totally from his own self.

When, in 1968, Soviet troops invaded the Republic, Matouš was in his third year at university and like most of his fellow students he joined the street demonstrations to protest against the invasion. As the political situation deteriorated, however, he had to decide whether to go on protesting and thereby lose the opportunity to make his mark in the profession for which he had prepared himself, or to take the chance then offered for someone with no past. The prospect of losing his career didn't appeal to him. One of the wise sayings of Lao Tzu stressed that only the person capable of adapting to everyone would emerge the victor over all. 'Reserve your judgments and words and you maintain your influence.'

He therefore decided to coexist with the revamped *ancien régime*. This entailed joining the prescribed organizations, voting in the sham elections and not taking part in anything that might cast doubts on his loyalty, but also not getting involved in anything that would offend his own conscience. After all, the sage relies on the hidden life and non-action, in other words he argues with no one and thus avoids unnecessary quarrels. His best teachers were forced to leave the faculty but those who had reached the same decision as Matouš remained. There was no great change in the language teaching, but the associate professor purged the history syllabus of the most stimulating and also the most significant epochs in favour of the most recent Communist period. This did not worry him too much as he tended to seek knowledge in books which he had either acquired earlier, before they were removed from the libraries, or which he borrowed from the professors who had fallen out of favour.

He had counted on remaining in the faculty after graduating, or going to work at the Oriental Institute, but there was no vacancy for him in either place, and he was offered a job in the press agency instead. He regarded it as demotion, but in spite of his liking for Lao Tzu's teachings, the outside world held a deep attraction for him and he enjoyed travelling, observing and discovering, so he took the job. He also translated poetry and wrote verse himself: not about love, but about nature – the mood of a rainy day, about nostalgia and loneliness, about equanimity and spiritual calm. He wrote it in the style of ancient Chinese poetry or of the Japanese haiku:

> *October again.*
> *Leaves wilt.*
> *From the slate-grey sky, lethargy now falls.*

He managed to get several poems printed in magazines, although his efforts to have a collected edition published came to nothing. All the same he regarded himself as an artist; he believed he would make a name for himself one day as a poet. Then he would change his lifestyle, stop going out to work and devote himself to study and meditation, and maybe travel. However, for years he lacked everything necessary for such a lifestyle, namely, status, contacts, total freedom to travel – and money.

His visits to the nurses' station where he would tell the nurses all about his experiences in foreign parts were motivated more by loneliness than a desire to please. His illness depressed him, that and the fact that his wife Klára had left him.

When he first met her, Klára was a waitress in a little bistro where he would sometimes go for a meal. He found her physically attractive (although she was quite ordinary: bleached hair and varnished nails, and if she spoke for more than a minute it was tediously banal) but she had no sympathy for Chinese philosophy and poetry, and on the one occasion he had tried to explain to her the contrast between the forces of yin and yang she had fallen asleep. All the same, Klára herself set store by the fact that Matouš was a graduate and had seen a lot of the world. She was also taken by his flat, particularly the room in which the blades of a wooden fan rotated slowly beneath the ceiling and where there was a glass case and shelves full of the most unusual objects, such as purple-coloured receptacles for crickets, old-fashioned Chinese tiles or statues of the Buddha, some of them gilded. What most attracted Klára, who handled dozens of cups and saucers made of the cheapest and heaviest china, were the tiny tea cups of translucent porcelain decorated with exotic paintings of flowers and birds. When she first picked them up and felt their fragility, the very touch of them sent a thrill through her. They must have been not only rare but expensive too. Klára came to the conclusion that Matouš was wealthy as well as interesting.

Shortly before their first meeting, his mother had died unexpectedly (unexpectedly from the medical point of view, but as in the case of his father he had previously observed a fading aura above his mother's head), so he needed someone to take over the household duties and generally to attend to the practical questions of his existence. So he imprudently asked Klára if she would like to be his wife.

The marriage had lasted almost seven years. It continued now, in fact, as Klára had not divorced him and would put in an appearance at least once a month to ask him for money. He was always short of cash, and he could see no reason why he should pay her, as she didn't live with him and they had no children. The trouble was she would start to yell and heap reproaches on him until, in the end, she extracted some small sum from him.

Although he was nearly fifty, Klára was his first and only wife. He had lived with his mother until her death and during that time had had a few fleeting acquaintances with married women, all of them older than himself. Klára was different from them. Not only was she unmarried, she was also fifteen years his junior. She had been looking for a love affair, whereas he was hoping for a housekeeper rather than a lover. In his view, Klára was typical of the kind of modern women who looked after their own bodies first and foremost and wanted to dominate men. That was why they went after good-hearted fellows or preferably fools. Then they expected to be spoiled and supported, be given expensive gifts and lots of money to spend on new clothes and shoes, and later on with their lovers.

Even though little in Matouš's life turned out as planned, his marriage had turned out worst of all. But whose marriage ever turns out well anyway? He was determined that once he was divorced – which would definitely happen in the foreseeable future – he would not marry again, unless he happened to come across a woman that resembled his mother (should such a woman exist at all) or one who was rich and sufficiently generous to enable him to fulfil his plans to become an independent artist and philosopher. Never having met such a woman, he was able to talk non-committally to those in whom he had no interest, and even entertain them with interesting stories.

The hospital nurses genuinely enjoyed listening to him. His life seemed to teem with any number of exciting experiences, exotic cities, abrupt reversals of fortune, dust storms, fascinating encounters, Buddhist monasteries, oriental gambling dens, night-time hold-ups and other situations where it was a matter of life or death, or at least honour. Many of the stories in which he himself featured he had only heard or read about, or dreamt up. But he wasn't a liar, just an inveterate story-teller, and anyway he didn't attach any great importance to the stories (after all there was little difference between what actually happened and what could have happened) and as soon as he had borrowed them and retold them, he believed them himself. He definitely did not make it all up, however. During his life, he had travelled a good part of the globe and spent a total of more than two years in China. He had lived through the end of the Cultural Revolution, the death of Chairman Mao and the unexpected thaw at the end of the 1970s.

He found that great country quite different from the one he read about in the books of the ancient sages, yet at the same time he found much of what he expected: the Chinese theatre, music and drawing, and the regime and the government seemed to enjoy greater authority than what he was accustomed to back home. He found there curiosity, superstition, immense poverty and hospitality, as well as fanaticism and astonishing licence. There were lots of colourful costumes on festive occasions and drab uniform-like clothes on work days. He saw a good deal of the country: enormous cities, the valleys of great rivers and the mountains of the north, but there was much he did not see because, as a dog-eyed foreigner, he was not allowed to go everywhere, and besides, the country was too vast for anyone to visit the whole of it in a single lifetime.

He also managed to get as far as New Zealand, where he was able to hear the Maori tongue and to experience more than the average citizen of the free world, let alone of a country like Czechoslovakia where every foreign journey was a privilege, or at least an exception. His attitude to life's problems and to people was particularly influenced by his experiences in those countries where neither modern civilization nor Communist dictatorship had managed to wipe out traditional relationships and rituals.

From his travels he would send back stories to the illustrated magazines. In them he would argue that when civilization reached as far as the little islands in the South China Sea, it broke down traditional values without offering anything new in their place. Oriental thinking had always stressed that man was part of nature and was distrustful of theories that sought to separate man from the natural cycle. Christianity and Islam were seen to be retrograde steps in that respect, particularly since what vanquished the local traditions were not the values of the Ten Commandments, the Sermon on the Mount or the Sura of the Nocturnal Path, but the false values of consumerism. While missionaries, whether Christian or Muslim, arguably brought a spiritual message (though often they would have done better to accept it themselves rather than force it on others), the traders who came with them, or even preceded them, offered more attractive commodities – strictly for this life not the hereafter: transistor radios, televisions, cars and medicines that cured people the witch doctors or traditional medicine couldn't help. Admittedly all that was available only to a few, but the possibility was open to everyone. And the people paid for it with their countries' natural wealth and the traditions by which they had lived for thousands of years. Superficially it looked as if prosperity had come to those parts, whereas in fact they had been overrun by poverty, both material and spiritual.

His articles were cut and sentences were added, changing the sense of his message. He wrote about civilization violating old cultures but the editors substituted 'colonialism' and 'imperialist interests' for 'civilization'.

His hospitalization and stomach operation (his doctor had told him he had stomach ulcers but he suspected they were concealing the true diagnosis from him) had alarmed him. He had previously regarded death as part of life; dying was a force within us heading towards its goal. A person who died was simply someone who had returned. True life fulfilment could only be achieved by returning to the beginning. The living would never discover, Lao Tzu conjectured, what it was to be dead, and the dead would never know what it was to be alive. We had not known the thousands of generations who went before us, nor would we know those who came after. So what was the point of getting worked up about something we could not know?

So long as one has health and strength, it was possible to pride oneself on achieving discernment and peace of mind and self-knowledge. But when illness came, one realized one's mistake and saw that one was still wedded to the physical self. Anyway, Matouš had never achieved the equanimity he sometimes wrote about in his poems. In reality, he fluctuated between a state in which he possibly came close to seeing what was concealed from others, and one of hectic activity. In the first of them, which would sometimes last several days, he would abandon himself to inactivity or write his short poems, then he would throw himself into activity – travelling, writing articles and dreaming more about physical than spiritual pleasures.

What was bad about death, whichever way he looked at it, was that it would extinguish his self, the very thing that mattered most to him. Death would thereby deprive him of the chance to discover what direction the world would take subsequently, what the future would bring.

The thought of returning home filled him with desolation. Where was he to find someone who would chat to him in the evening and have a hot meal ready for him so he wouldn't have to traipse around pubs, or hold his hand when he was gripped by the fear that a malignant tumour was spreading in his stomach? There was nothing waiting for him at home that in the least resembled a living being, apart from the stuffed canary that his mother had left him.

The matron in the surgical ward where they had removed three-eighths of his stomach reminded him at least slightly of his mother on account of her kindness. On one occasion – it was when he had a particular attack of anxiety – she had appeared in the ward at his bedside and said to him: 'Don't be afraid, you'll be as right as rain again in a few days.' She had actually leant over and stroked his thinning hair. That touch remained fixed in his memory and it occurred to him that he would like to spend some time with such a woman occasionally, or at least converse with her.

Brother Kodet, who owned a real-estate company and was an elder of the church, shook Daniel vigorously by the hand. 'Please accept once more my deepest sympathy, Reverend.'

'Thank you for coming to pay your respects to my mother.'

'It was the least I could do. After all she was known and loved by everyone here. And she didn't have an easy life. I just regret she didn't live to see what we managed to obtain,' the real-estate agent said, coming to the point.

'Mother didn't want it. But you know that anyway.'

'She would have been pleased all the same, if only on your account.' He went to the filing cabinet and took out a file bearing the name of the street and the number of the house. He leafed through it for several moments and then began to discuss the situation and the offer. For a house that wasn't in the best condition and, furthermore, was full of tenants paying fixed rents – not enough, in other words, to cover the most essential costs – a German company was willing to pay him five and a half million crowns. While it was true that the price of apartment houses would rise when rents were deregulated, that moment was still far off, so it might be better to assume that prices would fall slightly for some time. But even if they remained unchanged, the condition of the house would deteriorate because repairs would require a lot of money, which Daniel did not have, and a house in disrepair would naturally fall in value.

Daniel listened in silence and could not bring himself to believe that it was his property and his money that was being discussed. Throughout his adult life he had been used to having to decide whether he could afford a new pair of shoes or to have his old pair resoled for the third time. He wore darned socks and grew his own lettuces, tomatoes and even mangolds in the manse garden. From early spring he and Hana would pick nettles which made an excellent soup. A million crowns had always been beyond his imagination, just like a million light years.

'So what do you say, Reverend?'

He had no yearning for property but it was true that his father had been attached to the house and the fact that he was a house-owner was one of the reasons why he had been regarded as a class enemy and fit for a show trial. He should hold on to the house on his father's account, but what would he do with it? On the other hand, what would he do with the money? 'And what about my sister, are you sure she has no right to it?'

'Not from the legal point of view. She is now a foreign national and has permanent residence abroad. But should you wish to compensate her in some way, no one can stop you.'

'Yes, of course.' He wanted to add that he didn't need it for himself, not even a fraction of that sum, but it struck him that it would be tactless to say it to this man, who was clearly proud of having found him a good buyer.

Should he agree, he could sign the purchase contract straight away. There were a few further formalities to attend to, but the firm's representative had left a small deposit which the minister could take charge of.

So he received a wad of thousand-crown notes in an envelope; the deposit alone was the biggest sum he had ever held in his hand. He thanked Kodet and put the money away in his breast pocket, causing it to bulge somewhat. He could leave now, but feeling rather sheepish that his purpose in coming had been entirely unspiritual, he steered the conversation around to church matters and also talked for a while about the prisoners he visited, one or two of whom seemed to be making a genuine effort to understand what was said to them. Most of them, though, had grown up in surroundings where there was never any mention of God, or of anything else that transcended the most basic interests for that matter and they probably only came to hear him because he offered them a slight change from the tedium of their daily routine. But in what respect did the ones behind bars differ from those who guarded them, or from those who were free to go where they liked?

And then at last he rose and took his leave.

It was only a short walk to the tram stop but he was unable to pay attention to where he was going. Then he realized he had been tapping the outside of his coat to make sure the money was still in his pocket.

They sold flowers at the kiosk by the tram stop. Although he had never been in the habit of bringing his wife flowers, he now asked for three dark-red roses, and as the bunch looked rather paltry, he asked for two more.

In the window of the boutique, he saw the green sweater with white lilies. The price took him aback, but then he realized how ludicrously little it was compared to the sum he had been talking about a moment ago, and he entered the shop.

When Simon saw that the spirit was given at the laying on of the apostles' hands, he offered them money and said, 'Give me also this ability so that everyone on whom I lay my hands may receive the Holy Spirit.' Peter answered: 'May your money perish with you because you thought you could buy the gift of God with money! You have no part or share in this ministry, because your heart is not right before God . . .' (Acts 8: 18–21)

He not only had perfect pitch, he also had almost perfect recall: the text that he had read many times was etched into his memory.

When he was almost home, it occurred to him that presents and flowers were usually offered for a birthday or some other celebratory occasion. But unearned gains were no cause for celebration.

So he went back and took a tram. He then changed on to a bus which took him out to the cemetery. The trees between the graves were still bare; only a solitary sallow by the cemetery wall was covered in silvery catkins.

He reached the family grave. The freshly turned earth was fragrant. The tombstone still bore only the names of his father and his first wife. The date of her death preceded even that of his father's. It was a long time ago, almost eighteen years. In recent times, cancer had become a more frequent cause of death, of young children as well, but in those days it was regarded as an old person's illness. He had found it almost impossible to believe when the doctor in the hospital told him his wife had an incurable disease. 'But we've got a little baby,' had been his totally illogical response at the time.

'That might have caused the tumour to come more quickly,' the doctor had replied, not understanding his comment on their fate, 'but it would most likely have happened anyway.'

Old people die and however distressing it is, it is part of the order which God has established for human life. But another component of that order is that none of the living ever knows the hour of his death. It is only pride that makes us think we have the right to some pre-ordained number of days.

A large jam-jar full of rainwater stood by the gravestone. His mother's body was still lying there, but what remained of the body that he had embraced twelve years before? And where do your souls now dwell, my loved ones?

He ought to buy a decent vase. He placed the jar in front of the

39

gravestone and arranged the roses in it in such a way that their heads rested against the marble. He then prayed for a long time in silence.

8

Letters

Dearest,

The little one has just gone off to sleep. You needn't worry about her. Your mother is staying here overnight now. Yesterday Evička called her 'Nanna'! I'm sitting in our room and ought to be writing a sermon but I can't concentrate. I keep on thinking about you. It's empty here without you, even though someone is always dropping in, and the place is often full of people. But I don't need to tell you that. And everyone asks about your health and is praying for you to get well soon.

And the Strakas told me about a healer in Stará Ves, a Mr Zástěra. He draws strength from the trees and then transmits it to people. Mrs Straková used to have that big lump on her face and the doctors said she'd need an operation to remove it, but then Zástěra laid his hands on her three times and the lump disappeared. They told me people come from Prague to see him, and from as far away as Brno and Olomouc. Even doctors visit him, apparently, and when they see the results they say they have no explanation for it. He even cures conditions which they regard as incurable. When you come back from hospital we'll go and see him.

This Sunday I intend to preach on Matthew 14, on the feeding of the five thousand, but what caught my attention in particular was a sentence that we don't tend to lay much stress on: 'And Jesus went forth and saw a great multitude and was moved with compassion toward them, and healed their sick.' I realized that it still applies, his power to heal anyone who arouses his compassion. And it can know no bounds, can it, since he's the embodiment of love? That's why he came among us mortals and died the way he did. It was to cure those of us who are sick and to give us life – here and beyond the grave – a life of love and hope. That's going to be the theme of my sermon and you know that above all I'll be speaking for you and about you, so that you'll get well.

I want you to know that I'm with you every moment of the day in my prayers and my thoughts, and at night in my dreams.

Last night I dreamt we were walking alongside the River Vltava at Zbraslav. It was a sunny summer's day and your hair glowed in the sun as if it was on fire. And you were completely well and you were laughing and I could hear your laughter. And then all of a sudden a boat arrived, a big river steamer full of happy passengers. We could hear music from on board and see the coloured lanterns. And . . .

Evička just called me, so I went and warmed her some semolina and she's sleeping again.

I won't continue with the dream. I'd better say cheerio, because I have to get on with my sermon. I'll pop the letter into the hospital for you tomorrow and the day after tomorrow is a visiting day again. I can't wait to see you and I hug you in my thoughts. Keep the faith. Don't lose hope. You know what he said: 'Take heart, daughter, your faith has made you well.'

Fondest love, Dan

---

18 November 76

My dearest Dan,

They've just brought me your letter and I'd sooner write straight back. I know you're coming tomorrow, but what if something happens in the meantime? I feel terribly weak, but that doesn't mean I've stopped hoping and believing. It's just that I can't ignore what awaits me. After all, you can see it too, can't you, and the reason you didn't tell me the end of your dream wasn't because Evička woke up but because you yourself got a shock. Because only I went on board the boat, even though you wanted to follow me. And the boat moved off and you didn't manage to get on board. That was the way it was, wasn't it, Dan? But the passengers were all cheerful. They weren't sorrowful even though they knew they would never return. That's the important thing, dearest. That boat isn't going to capsize, it's just going somewhere the two of us have not visited yet. But that's no reason to grieve, is it?

I won't be coming back to you, even though it makes me sad to think about it, Dan. I'm sad it all lasted such a short time, that I didn't get a chance to enjoy Evička, that I'm leaving the two of you on your own, even though I

41

don't want to. I don't want to leave you. You know I was happy with you. I don't know what made me write 'was' – I still am happy, of course.

But when that boat takes me away, don't grieve. You've got to go on living, Dan. You have a power within you that you'll be able to transmit to others: strength and wisdom and love. It has been a privilege to live with you. Maybe I won't be here tomorrow, but people will remain. Our little girl, all of them, are going to go on needing you and you will go on serving them. And even if we must part for a while, don't let it distress you, don't be sadder than you need be. We'll meet again one day, after all. In a place where nobody will ever separate us again.

Forgive me for writing this particular letter. It's not from lack of faith, it's just that I'm afraid of leaving without having said the most important thing.

All my love,

Your Jitka

———

28 November 76

Dear Rút,

Something terrible has happened. Jitka died. I don't know how I'm going to live. I'm trying in vain to find some consolation in scripture, from the thought that God's will is inscrutable. Evička will be six months old in two days' time.

I enclose the death announcement. That's as much as I can write.

Your Dan

———

3 April 1994

Dear Reverend, my friend and deliverer,

I must thank you most of all for your last visit. And also, of course, for the things you brought me, especially the fruit and bananas. I know you or your children don't even have everything you need. But you're the sort of person who makes sacrifices in order to give other people a treat. I've never met anyone else like you. Never. I've only ever known the sort of people who try to fleece the next fellow, to hurt him or even kill him. I used to get drunk with the gang, smoke grass and shoot dope. We used to have a laugh and

42

fool around with girls and boys. But what was good about it? Nothing except the fact we were all wallowing in the same muck. That's what we had in common. Nothing else. Except for getting involved in the same scams on the odd occasion. We used to share out what we took, but mostly it wasn't fair shares. The one who was strongest got the most. It stands to reason.

Dear Reverend, my friend and deliverer, I thank you most of all for the fact you talk to me as if I never did anything wrong. As if I was the same as you. You told me last time that I ought to think as much as possible about my future. You know that I've never really had a job in my life. I've spent the five years since I was fifteen either in here or loafing around bars where I had a good time. As they say. In other words I spent all I stole. I've no idea what I'll do outside. I've got no proper skills, have I? I could drive a car maybe, or some of the things they taught me in the can like raking leaves, digging and a bit of work on the lathe that I've already forgotten. I used to hate their methods. And all the time I was wanting to have no one over me. And you told me that he is over all of us. Jesus and his love. And I'm going to have debts to pay. And at the same time I'd like to live like a man and not a beast. By which I mean I don't want to drink, smoke or shoot up any more, but have something decent to eat at least. And find some nice girl and have kids. I'd like to be their breadwinner and look after them so they should never be in need. And Reverend, my friend and deliverer, I'd like to make up for the things I've done. And make it up to my Mum first off. I hurt her a lot and cost her a wad of money. And then some of the people I stole from. There was one old neighbour, she was eighty. I stole five hundred from her. That was nothing for me. The price of a bottle in a bar. But not for her. It could have been her dinner money. And I ought to pay back lots more. And give some thought to my future. Nothing definite, I'm afraid. I just know I'll never return again to Satan's world. No way. I'd sooner go and work in a hospital. Only I'd never earn enough there to do the things I've just been writing about. Dustmen are paid better. I don't know whether I'd be up to work like that. I'd like something more. But I've had no schooling and I doubt I'll ever catch up now. There's no time. There isn't the money. But I don't blame anyone. It's my fault the way I wasted my life like an idiot. Maybe you'll be able to advise me, and show me the way in this too. Or maybe he'll show me the way. You've told me so much about him that I'd never heard or dreamt of even. Who had compassion for the least of people? Who said: Ask and it will be given to you? Knock and the door will be opened to you. Another thing I have to tell you. He appeared to me himself.

It was some time in the night when I got this panic attack that I wouldn't keep it up, that there'll be too much for me to change or live up to, and at that moment I heard a voice. He whispered to me, don't be afraid, have faith. Your faith will save you. It wasn't a dream because I looked round the cell to see who'd whispered to me, but they were all asleep, and anyway none of them would say anything like that and then I caught sight of a face above me. It was terribly pale and nothing like the face of a living person. And the moment I set eyes on it it disappeared. Maybe they'll release me next month on probation for good behaviour. I enclose an invitation for you.

Best wishes, Petr Koubek

——— —

Dear Petr,

I was really pleased with your letter and am happy that you're sticking to the path you've decided to take.

I'm glad that in your mind at least you've found the path back to your mother. Always remember: 'A foolish son is a grief to his mother.' It also says in the book of Proverbs: 'Hear, my son, your father's instruction. And do not forsake your mother's teaching.' And right after that: 'My son, if sinners entice you, do not consent. If they say, "Come with us, let us lie in wait for blood, let us wantonly ambush the innocent . . . we shall find all precious goods, we shall fill our houses with spoil; throw in your lot among us, we will all have one purse" – my son, do not walk in the way with them, hold back your foot from their paths; for their feet run to evil, and they make haste to shed blood . . . but these men lie in wait for their own blood, they set an ambush for their own lives. Such are the ways of all who get gain by violence; it takes away the life of its possessors.'

You can look up the saying yourself, it is in the first chapter of Proverbs. There you are, already thousands of years ago people had the same worries and problems as we do. Some did their best to live as they should, others longed to get rich at any price and refused to see that the price was precisely their own souls. I believe that you, young Petr, have already grasped the essentials and have now left the paths of those who set murderous ambushes. I don't want to give you the idea that the path you are taking will be an easy one, but one thing I can promise you: you won't remain alone on that path, there are plenty of good people who will help you and support you when you grow weary. Maybe you won't fill your house with expensive goods, but instead you'll be able to invite the friends you'll make there.

Forgive me for being so brief, but I am giving a talk on television today. I'll be talking about our relations with those who are despised by people for no reason, purely on account of some prejudice.

May the love of Christ remain with you even in the place where you are now living.

With best wishes and congratulations,

Yours, Daniel

——— ——

Dear Daniel,

I was unable to come to the funeral as I was in bed with a fever. But I was thinking about you, dear Dan, and what you were probably going through and the pain you were feeling. We only have one mother, after all. She and I didn't see each other very often, but from the first I knew she was a good person, a fine and wise woman. I have never stopped thanking God that she brought up her son the way she did. It took someone very special to do that. My Hana will always be grateful to her too. After all, she had such a hard life, full of disappointments and but for you she would have grown bitter and spent her life in solitude. I am sure you'll be able to rely on her at this difficult time and even though she can't take a mother's place she can at least give you her love now and for the rest of her life. All of us who love you will do that too.

With love to you all, Granny Hana

——— ——

Dear Mum and Dad,

I'm only writing a postcard, because all the girls are only writing a card. The snow is wet but it's possible to ski. The Partridge said I was good. Apart from that we muck about terribly. We broke in a door and broke a window and hid the Partridge's skis. And we got drunk on wine, but I didn't. The

Partridge said we'll give her a heart attack, but before that she'll give us all black marks for misbehaviour. Last night I said my prayers, and I prayed for Grandma to like it in heaven. Best wishes to Eva and Marek.

Love, Magda

———

Dear Dan,

I had to stay at the hospital for the afternoon shift too. Things are quiet on the ward for a moment. I'd love to talk to you, but you're at the synod and will be coming in even later than me, so I thought I'd write to you. Anyway we have so little time to talk together these days and whenever we do, somehow we always seem to be in a hurry.

I realize that your grief over your mother's death comes on top of all the other things on your mind. I'd love to help you but I know that grief is something that words or pills can't dispel.

Two old ladies died on the ward today. One of them reminded me of your mother. She was also a small woman – quiet patient and devout. She received extreme unction the day before yesterday. It's something I've noticed over the years about people with a faith, even if they die unhappy, they have no anxiety and instead have hope. It's important that your mother left us in that way: with our love and her faith. As my father used to say: A believer now the Lord will endow. I still miss my father but one has to come to terms with it.

Nobody loves one as much as one's mother, nobody listens to one as well as she does, I'm aware of that. But whenever you're sad, Daniel, you've got me, even if I'm not able to tell you as well as your mum that I understand and share your feelings and I'm with you. Maybe it's precisely because I'm often unable to tell you and I'm shy of saying it out loud that I'm writing now to say I love you and that you're the only person for me, that you're mine.

Your Hana

Chapter Two

1

Every second Sunday, Daniel takes the service at the preaching station at Myslice, about thirty minutes' drive away. As the service in his own church ends around ten o'clock and the one at Myslice starts at half-past ten, he abandons his own congregation just before the final hymn. He generally has his old Škoda car parked in the nearest free space and he climbs into it without even removing his gown. On this second Sunday in April, he does all the usual things but the car refuses to start. Daniel leaps out and raises the bonnet. Whatever is wrong with the car, there is no time to attempt a repair.

The sound of singing can still be heard from inside the chapel. Daniel stares at the grimy motor and he is thinking less about what might be at fault than about which members of the congregation came by car and could possibly give him a lift. Then, although he heard no one approaching, a voice immediately behind him asks, 'May I be of any assistance, Reverend?'

He knows that soprano voice only from the hymn-singing in church. He looks around. The unknown woman, who has attended his service three times already but has always got up during the last hymn and disappeared before he can ask her anything, is now standing there with her head inclined forward slightly, as if stooping. Daniel notices that her neck is long and slender like his first wife's. She looks exotic in her brightly coloured knitted cardigan, compared to the other women of the congregation at least. 'My car is here if you need to get somewhere in a hurry.'

'I do, but I can hardly impose myself on you. It's a half-hour drive.'

'That doesn't matter, I'm not busy. My husband went off on a trip yesterday and my mother is looking after our little boy.' As they walk to her car, she tells him her name is Barbora Musilová but everyone calls her Bára. She has been attending his services for several weeks already. He tells her he noticed her the first time. Then he adds, 'The Sunday you first came was the day my mother died.'

'I'm sorry I brought you misfortune.'

'You? I'm not superstitious, I'm afraid. My mother would have died whether you had come or not.'

'My mother is still alive. But my father died a long time ago.' She unlocks his door first. 'The car belongs to my husband. He's obliged to show off – he likes to, in fact. So we've got this little Japanese thing with metallic paint. Not that I care about such things.'

'I'm very grateful for the lift, Sister Musilová.'

'But I don't belong to your church,' she says as they drive off.

'Did the word "sister" offend you?'

'No, why should it? There's nothing wrong with having a brother. Or having you as a brother for that matter. I just thought you ought to know.'

'Are you a Catholic?'

'No, I don't belong to any church.' Then she adds, 'My mother's Jewish but she has never attended synagogue. My father believed in communism when he was a young man. Then he stopped believing in anything, like my husband.'

'And did your mother survive the war?'

'She must have done to have me. I was born after the war, almost ten years after, in fact.'

'Of course. What I really meant was, how did she survive it?'

'She married my father before the war, when she was eighteen, a year younger than I was when I married. Fortunately she didn't get divorced, unlike me.'

'You were saying something about your husband, about him going off on a trip somewhere.'

'I remarried. Naturally enough, though God knows why. I'm sorry, I suppose I oughtn't to take the Lord's name in vain. Not in your presence, anyway.'

'Just speak the way you usually do.'

They pass the turn-off to the airport and leave the city limits. A nearby village is surrounded by flowering fruit trees. They are blossoming early this year after the warm winter. Only the past few days have been cold and at this moment clouds heavy with rain or snow are billowing along close to the ground.

'Thank you. I'm not used to talking to people like yourself.'

'But there's nothing particularly special about me.'

'I'm not used to talking to people who have a belief, and actually preach about it,' she said by way of explanation.

'Everyone believes in something.'

'Yes, I know. In a political programme or an association. Or in their career, like my husband. Or in the nation – there's nothing particularly wrong with that, is there?'

'What made you come to our church?'

'That's a good question.'

They now turn off on to a side road. The trees here are also in bloom and Říp Hill suddenly appears in the distance. It reminds him of driving along a highway over a year ago with Rút at the wheel. The road ran from Oregon to Nevada and he had the impression that everything around him was in bloom, including some trees and bushes that were unfamiliar to him. And on the horizon in place of Říp there loomed the massive, snowy volcano of Mount Rainier as if out of a dream. It was his first trip abroad and he strove to take in every single detail of the landscape, as he did every detail of the lives of the people that he met. His sister was extremely interested in how things were in the Republic and how his status had changed, even though she did not believe in Jesus Christ, and most likely didn't even believe that he, her younger brother, could truly believe either.

He really ought to concentrate on his sermon, but the woman at his side distracts him. She is nothing like his sister, more like his first wife. They were born, he realizes, at about the same time. But the image of his first wife has become fixed and unchanging. What would she have looked like if she'd lived to be forty? She'd certainly not have used eye make-up like this one. Or would she? And she would dress more soberly. She was unassuming and even a trifle ascetic. Maybe he was too. What is the point of dressing flamboyantly? Those who care too much for the outer covering are usually trying to conceal emptiness or sterility inside.

'It was most likely fear that brought me,' she eventually answers.

'Fear of what?'

'Of what? I can't really say. One doesn't have to be afraid of anything in particular, just afraid, that's all. Of people. Or of loneliness. Of life or death. Death mostly. Even though there are days when I don't feel like living at all.'

'Fear is human, Mrs Musilová.'

'Do you think so? My husband doesn't accept it. He can't stand it when I'm not in a good mood. He believes he's the only one with any right to have the blues.'

'Have you been married long?'

'Wait a second, I'll have to work it out. It's nearly fifteen years. With Samuel, that is. My husband has a biblical name. But it's the only saintly thing about him.'

'Samuel wasn't a saint. He was a judge and a prophet in ancient Israel.'

'No doubt. I wouldn't know such things. All I meant was that my husband has a character defect. But I expect I shouldn't have said anything, it's not polite to talk about the character defects of someone you don't know and who isn't present.'

A large farm office serves as a prayer room. In front of it there is already a huddle of old women waiting, as well as two men in their Sunday best, looking with some distrust at the luxurious foreign car.

He gets out. 'Thank you very much. And don't wait for me, I'll get home somehow.'

'I'll happily wait for you. I'll come and listen to your sermon, seeing that I'm here. Or are you going to preach the same one as in Prague?'

The room contains four rows of six chairs each, and even these are not filled. He writes the numbers of the hymns on a blackboard while greeting those who are gradually taking their places in the last two rows. There are nine in the congregation, including his companion, who remains standing by the door. Why? Maybe she feels out of place here. She is not dressed for a village service.

He sits down at the harmonium and plays a short improvisation. He concentrates. He has prepared an Easter sermon on a text from the Letter to the Romans. 'If we are united with him because we are involved in his death, we will certainly be involved in his resurrection also.' Quite unconsciously, he ends up speaking to his recent companion about her anxiety.

But he speaks less about resurrection, which has always somewhat disconcerted him, than about love that does not falter at any sacrifice, and about Jesus who, out of love for mankind, was crucified.

We speak of the miracle of resurrection after death, but we ought not to forget that living for love means resurrection during one's life. Several times during the sermon he looks in the direction of the unknown woman who brought him here. She is standing motionless by the door, cowering slightly, as if trying to protect herself from the cold or from his words.

When they get back into the car and drive off, she asks him: 'Do you truly believe that someone who is dead can rise again and walk? Someone who is long dead, I mean.'

'But it's a . . .'

'It's a myth,' she says. 'No, please don't explain anything. Not at the moment, at least. Do you think that the people sitting there understand you. Do they give any thought to what you told them?'

'I don't know. As far as they are concerned it is a ritual. They grew up with it. Besides, faith is not something you think about. You can reflect on God and many people have, but they've still not come up with anything. Even the psalmist complained: "I wondered what to make of it all and it seemed far from easy to me."'

'And you don't wonder about him?'

He hesitates for a moment, and then says, 'I do, of course.'

'But you know it's impossible to come up with anything. Is it also chiefly a ritual for you too?'

'No, I didn't grow up with it.'

'Your parents weren't believers?'

'My mother was. As for my father, I can't say. One doesn't have the right to judge whether or not another person believes, particularly when it is one's father.'

'My father wasn't a believer. I told you that already. He was a sort of – what the Russians call a "superfluous man". He did just one truly good and useful thing in his life: he married my mother and didn't divorce her, not even during the war. Even though he's bound to have two-timed her on many occasions afterwards.'

'My father was a doctor. But he spent many years in concentration camps. Under the Nazis and the Communists. What he went through in those camps shattered him. It is truly hard to reconcile those experiences with belief in a just and all-powerful God. Father didn't believe there was any higher justice. He didn't believe people have souls either. "Man has a brain," he used to say. "The brain is nature's greatest wonder, but it is terribly impermanent. The soul is the brain. When the brain perishes what remains of the soul?"' He checks himself.

'And in spite of that you chose your present career?'

'Maybe not in spite of but because. My father was a tolerant man.

He left it up to me to decide what I believed about the world, about people and their souls.'

'He died a long time ago?'

'Sixteen years ago. But he lived to see . . .' He checks himself again. 'A few days before his death he said to me, "What we have here on earth is neither God's nor Satan's creation. Heaven or Hell is what we create ourselves. Most of the time we create Hell."'

'Did you love him?'

'The way that everyone loves their father.'

Why is she asking him? Why does it interest her?

They are nearing Prague. The city is veiled in smoke. Human life veiled in mystery. And God's existence?

'I didn't love mine,' the woman breaks the silence. 'He used to come home, put his feet up on the table and demand to be waited on hand and foot by us. My mother, my sister and me. Mother would come in exhausted from work and had to put up with him. Whatever he earned he used to gamble. He seldom won, and when he did it was just used for more gambling. Mother used to support the lot of us. That's why I married so young. In order to get away from there. His shadow still hangs over me today. But he was tolerant as well, as far as I was concerned, at least. He let me study to be an actress even though I doubt if he'd ever set foot in a theatre in his life. I exaggerate. Apart from that he watched television.'

'And you're an actress?'

'No, I didn't finish the course. When I met Sam I switched to study architecture – not at the technical university, though, more the theory than the practical stuff. And these days I work as a kind of high-class secretary in his practice, or I design interiors for his buildings. I must admit, though, that I do act on the odd occasion when one of my former fellow students finds me a bit-part on TV.'

He notices that her shoulders are trembling as if she is on the verge of tears. 'Are you all right?'

'Yes. It's OK. I'm just cold. I got chilled to the bone there. Feel.' She is now holding the steering wheel with her left hand and stretching out her right to him. He notices a long reddish scar on her wrist. Petr has a similar one. He noticed it the first time he met him in prison. Petr's was redder, being more recent no doubt.

How did it happen?

Life wasn't fun any more.

Life isn't simply fun.

I thought it could be. And what's the point of living if it's not fun? The simplest questions are the hardest to answer.

But Petr lived. And this one is still living. He touches her hand. It really is cold.

'You could try warming it up,' she suggests. 'I can manage to drive with my left hand.'

She is clearly used to company of a different kind and doesn't realize that it is inappropriate for him to hold hands with a woman he doesn't really know. But he has no intention of refusing her request and so he holds her hand in his for a moment.

'Maybe I'm stupid,' the woman says, 'and you'll explain to me some time how it is that I will die, that my body will be burned to ashes or chewed to the bone by the larvae of some horrible beetles, but that one day it will be renewed and join with my soul which will never die. Have I got it right?'

'Yes and no.' He lets go of her hand but it is as if he can still feel the touch of her in his hand. 'It's not a question of resurrection of the body in material form. Not even Christ when he appeared to the Apostles had a material form, just a spiritual one.'

'You always manage to come up with some explanation,' she says. 'You preachers, I mean. Perhaps it's because you're wiser than the rest of us.'

'We certainly aren't.' He should never have travelled with this woman, and having accepted the lift should never have touched her at all.

2

Diary excerpts

The money from the house has come. Grandad built the house, Dad inherited it, but they took it away from him. And then when they jailed Dad, we lived in poverty. I remember at the time finding a crown coin in the street and thinking to myself that I could buy myself an ice-cream. It was an awful temptation. I even went as far as the sweet shop, but then I resisted and gave the crown to Mummy. It was enough for three bread rolls.

The interest on the sum in the bank amounts to more than ten times my pay. I've sent 50,000 to the Jerome Fund and Bosnia. I've also sent a contribution towards the children's oncology unit. Cancer took Jitka from me and made Eva lose her mummy. People in my family used to die of heart failure. That's how Grandad and Dad died anyway, they were still young at the time. I scarcely remember my grandfather. He was a master violin-maker. We used to have a violin at home that Dad would play when he had the time and wasn't in prison. I probably have Grandad to thank for my musical ear. They say he also used to play beautifully, but they didn't have tape recorders in those days and gramophone recordings would only be made of the greats: Hubermann, Szigeti or Kubelik.

The voices of the people and the violin sounds of those days have been engulfed by silence. These days everything can be preserved but will be forgotten anyway, like the tracts of the Middle Ages. Only those who have become symbols of their times will escape oblivion. But even they won't survive. And besides, what memory preserves are only gross distortions of reality.

I felt nothing when I sold the house, but I think it meant a lot to Grandad. An ordinary craftsman from a little village near Karlovy Vary, he had given his only son an education and left him a house in Prague. What will I leave my children?

From the memoirs of Colonel F. about an interrogation at the beginning of the fifties:

Once they drove me somewhere away from Dejvice. It might have been Ruzyně or somewhere else on the Prague outskirts. They staged a 'partisan trial' with me. They led me there as a 'spy' with a bag over my head and my hands tied . . . They put a noose around my neck and told me they'd hang me if I didn't confess. I didn't have anything to confess. They put a revolver to my temple. They'd shoot me if I didn't confess. I had nothing to confess. They fired, but it was only a signal pistol and I survived. It lasted several hours. I could hardly stand and was thirsty and probably had a fever. I asked them for water but they ignored my requests.

*Dad almost never talked about what he went through when the
Communists jailed him. He used to say it wasn't for the ears of women
or children. But they used to jail women too, and they even executed one
who was entirely innocent. Maybe Dad didn't want us to regard him as
a hero or a victim. Maybe he found it painful to think back on it. And
maybe he had other reasons.*

---

*Magda's class teacher called me in. Apparently Magda and her pal
Zuzana had climbed up on to the window-sill during break and poured
water on passers-by. She told me she would never have expected it of
Magda as she'd always been such a quiet child and she suggested she
ought to find another friend.*

*I asked Magda what sort of fun she thought it was to pour water over
people. She said she hadn't poured water on anyone, that she'd only
thrown spiders out of the window, and anyway they didn't fall on
anyone as they got caught somewhere on the way down.*

But you watched Zuzana tipping water on people.

*She didn't tip it on people, just on some old woman who's always
swearing at us for making a racket in the street.*

And some old woman isn't a human being?

But Daddy, she only poured it from a tiny little tablet bottle.

And she started to giggle as she remembered.

*I've realized that I've hardly been paying any attention to the children
recently. And the times I'm with them I'm either talking, praying or
telling them off. It's more of a routine. I don't share their troubles and
joys any more the way I still managed to do when Eva was small. I've
taken on too many responsibilities and I've also spent a lot of time with
Mummy, but there's no point in looking for external reasons, when it's
more likely to be as a result of something happening inside me.*

*If there ever was any flame burning inside me, and I believe there
was, it's going out now. I ought to do something about myself and I
definitely ought to pay greater attention to the children.*

---

*Not long ago I was reflecting on my capacity for intimacy. I'm
incapable of taking even my nearest and dearest into my confidence
and then all of a sudden I'm telling some strange woman about my*

55

father. I'm telling her things I wouldn't even tell Hana. Did I talk about them out of gratitude for the lift? Or because she reminded me of Jitka?

There was a moment when I was going to say that Dad lived long enough for me to make Hana's acquaintance at his hospital, but I stopped myself. Out of fear of taking her into my confidence, or because I didn't want to mention my wife?

I feel a need to talk about Dad ever since I found his name on the list. I was astounded when I read his name and date of birth among those of informers. My immediate reaction was that it had to be a mistake. How many people who found their close relatives or friends on it thought the same? What do we know of the private distress even of those who are closest to us? I believe he never consciously did anything dishonourable, not in that respect, at least, but I'm not sure that the others share my conviction. I have this idée fixe that they all know about it, that they read the list, noticed his name and are now looking at me and waiting for some explanation. It's up to me to defend him. But what am I supposed to tell them, when I myself hadn't suspected anything at all?

I also found some members of my congregation on the list. They included Brother Kodet who always used to smile at me so affably – just as he still does.

—⟨⟨⟨⟨⟩⟩⟩⟩—

*When I'm home alone
I finish a prayer
and cold wafts from the windows
my stove is old
I open its door
and in the flames I see
those dear faces
I shall see here no more
my first wife Dad
and now Mum as well
I listen to their silence
        until the fire goes out
        and I'm left alone
        in the cold again*

Yesterday I shouted at Hana because she wanted me to take out the rubbish when I happened to be writing my sermon. What's the point of preaching about God's love when I'm incapable of showing kindness to those nearest to me? We talk together so seldom nowadays. Maybe it's tiredness or not having enough time. Or my inability to be intimate? We have nothing to conceal from each other, at least as regards our behaviour. But at the same time it's as if we avoid mentioning anything fundamental about our lives. As if we never manage to stumble our way to it.

It took me almost a year before I could bring myself to tell her about finding Dad's name on the list. Whenever I am overcome with doubts about what I'm doing or what I believe, I never mention it to Hana. Maybe things that are fundamental to me she doesn't find important. She wants the children to be healthy and she's always dashing from one doctor to another with Magda on account of her eyes. Marek used to suffer from tonsillitis a lot when he was small and she'd get up and see to him several times a night, and the same thing with Eva whenever she was ill. She'd no doubt get up on account of me if it weren't for the fact I'm rarely ill. She treated my mother as if she were her own, particularly over this past year when Mum had become infirm, helping me to care for her as much as she possibly could. She brings the children up impeccably, to be hard-working, polite, truthful, modest and say their prayers. The children are the most important thing in her life. And I'm the next maybe. She makes sure I've got clean clothes to put on, that I'm never hungry, that I have a healthy diet and that I feel contented. She knows I love music and suggests we go to concerts together, even though she always falls asleep. If she sees me studying some book, she'll ask me what it's about, in the same way that she asks me what we talked about on the ministers' course. When I start to tell her, she hears me out but I get the feeling that she's not taking it in, that she just grasps individual words and sentences. The substance of what I'm saying doesn't interest her, it doesn't concern her, or it concerns her only on account of me. She is pleased when I like something and is distressed when I am distressed, even though she may be unfamiliar with the causes – so I quickly change the subject to something more familiar to her.

Jitka and I were in love with each other, body and soul. I love Hana and am grateful to her for always having shared the good and bad with me, and there were more bad, or at least difficult, times than good ones. Maybe it's all inside me: maybe I'm incapable of awakening in her what is concealed in every human being . . . Or maybe I'm incapable of awakening it in myself. Maybe I lack experience of women. Jitka's death took me unawares. It's as if it thrust me into some enclosed space that I couldn't get out of, not even when I met Hana, not even when I was already living with her. Maybe we got married before we had a chance to cross the barrier that separates people from each other, to discover true intimacy.

In the absence of intimacy – the ability to confide one's most secret fears or the thoughts that scare one and that one is reluctant even to admit or put into words for oneself – love wastes away.

⟶ ∘੭੮੭∘ ⟵

It looks as if they'll be releasing Petr on probation next week. So his lawyer tells me, at least. Petr is in a state of agitation about it. The last time I visited him he promised me he would start a completely new life when he came out. Steal? Never again, Reverend. I am a different person since you baptized me. Whoever is in Christ is born anew . . . What is old has passed. That's how you told me it, wasn't it? He has a good memory for quotations and the ability to smile like a little boy. He looks the very picture of innocence. I praised him and told him I was pleased with him, and that Jesus was sure to be pleased with him also.

I am aware of being proud of having possibly turned one person aside from the path that led to self-destruction and evil in general. I remind myself that I am at best only the intermediary, but we're not entirely responsible for our feelings. I even mentioned Petr on television when I was invited to do a religious broadcast. I gave him as an example of how one ought not to condemn anyone out of hand. Whenever we reject people on grounds of prejudice, as many reject not only those who have transgressed in some way, but also all Romanies solely because they are different, we banish them to where they can be the butt of our judgement and censure. Conversely, whenever we are able to accept and trust, and support what is good in people, we reduce the level of social evil.

An extremely vivid dream. I saw Dad standing as if in a pillory. He was naked and he had a barrel stuck on his head. The barrel was transparent so I could see that he was bleeding from the temple. Then a uniformed guard appeared and struck the barrel with a long stick. Dad started to sway and then fell down dead on the ground.

When I found his name on the list, I was determined to investigate all the circumstances. To find out whether it was a mistake, a police forgery or Dad's attempt to ease his lot somehow. Only by then he was dead and apparently no one else has the right to check the facts of the case. Maybe I should have done a bit more investigating off my own bat, but it would have taken up too much time and I had so little of it to spare then. I was also afraid of what I might discover. Now it occurs to me that what I feared most was discovering the truth on account of Mum. Could I tell her at all? And could I keep on visiting her and not tell her? But now she's dead it's only myself I'd be sparing. I have asked Dr Wagner to advise me what action I might take in this matter. One is obliged to bury one's relatives with all possible dignity, Antigone knew that a long time ago.

3

Daniel invited Petr to dinner the day after his release. Alois, whom he had also invited, welcomed Petr with a hug, Hana even kissed him. Yet whenever the conversation at table turned to prison she would quickly change the subject. She wanted to protect Magda at least from such talk. After dinner she preferred to take her out of the room.

After they had gone, Alois voiced a thought that he had apparently been mulling over for some time. 'There's a difference. Petr stole and they released him, Jesus was innocent and he was crucified.'

'I'd rather not compare the two,' Daniel interrupted him.

'All the same, what you were saying in your sermon on Sunday about Pilate offering the Jews the release of Jesus, I found that a bit odd.'

'What makes you think so?'

'The way I see it, the kind who rule don't ask people who they should release and who they should hang.'

'Crucify.'

'Whatever. But Pilate was in charge there. If he really did ask, it'd look as if he was frightened of the ones who were shouting.'

'Maybe he was. There was always the threat of an uprising in Judah at that time. But otherwise it's an interesting comment.'

Petr said, 'But everything's different these days compared to what it was then. Maybe Pilate suspected that it wasn't a man standing in front of him but the Saviour. These days they try villains and nobody cares about them so why should anyone ask people who they should release. And, besides, they don't hang people any more, they just lock them up until they go off their heads. But if anyone did ask the people, they'd say the best thing to do would be to hang all convicts straight off.'

'You're oversimplifying things a bit there, Petr,' Daniel said, unhappy with the direction the conversation was heading in.

'No way, Reverend. It's very cunningly thought out. Everyone thinks that it's all humane nowadays, but it could well be that things were better when they executed people straight off, than now when they just throw them in a dark hole to rot like old spuds or turnips.'

'But surely where there's life there's hope,' Eva spoke up.

Petr acknowledged that, but began to explain that bars weren't the worst things about prison, and it was even possible to get on with the warders sometimes. What destroyed you was constantly being surrounded by the same nutcases and perverts that there was no escape from. The same cons and the same talk: who had done what before they were sent down; the stupid mistakes they had made to end up inside; where money and pills could be obtained without trouble; where they could get women and how many they had had. Everyone would boast about all the things they would pull off when they eventually got out. But of course they never did those things and anyway they would be back inside before long. 'Thanks to you, my eyes were opened to that horror,' Petr said, turning to Daniel. 'I realized I was living in a world created by Satan.' He got more and more worked up as he spoke. Nobody could imagine what people were capable of. They tied a man, while still alive, to a metal beam and threw him in a lake. They would catch a girl, rape her and then cut off her breasts. And the money that circulated down there where people couldn't see! And when someone wanted to get rid of a guy they owed money to, they would just find a killer who would do him in for a couple of grand.

Petr was waving his hands as if trying to ward off the evil and shouting. His face underwent mild spasms and the scar on his cheek became livid. The lad felt a need to draw attention to himself and for that, like so many people, he needed evil. Either to practise it or to exorcise it. Daniel realized that the faces of his own children were unmarked in comparison – pure and childlike. As if the difference between Petr and Eva was not just a few years. If Petr was going to be coming here, and that would be desirable, there was going to be a new kind of authority in the house – certainly as far as Alois was concerned, and for his own children too, most likely. How could their life experiences compare with Petr's? Darkness was always tempting. The abyss, infidelity and sin were more attractive than the heights of fidelity and good works.

The best thing would be not to talk too much about Petr and let things return to their usual patterns as quickly as possible.

'Have you played yet today?' he asked Marek as soon as Petr left.

'How could I when we had visitors?' Marek said, shaking his head in astonishment at this question until his long blond hair hung over his face.

'Well, go and play now then!'

'Anyway my G string broke yesterday.'

'Paganini was capable of finishing a concerto on a single string.'

'I'm not Paganini, Dad.'

'But you've got three strings left.'

'Dad, we were told in physics today,' Marek said, changing the subject, 'that they recently discovered a quasar that shines like a thousand galaxies. And each of those has a hundred billion stars.'

'And you believe that?'

Marek shrugged. 'That's what the principal told us. He believes it. And each time he says "Just try to grasp how tiny we are!"'

'And you know what quasars are?'

Marek was very interested in astronomy. Maybe he also liked to be posed questions he couldn't answer. So that he could search in that infinite space for another God in place of the one who assumed human form.

'They are quasi-stellar radio sources,' his son informed him. 'They are moving away from us at almost the speed of light.'

'They must be a long way away already.'

'At least twelve billion light years.'

'Are you able to imagine that?'

'There are loads of things that people are unable to imagine,' Eva rose to her half-brother's defence.

'Is there anything else you want to know about quasars, Dad?'

'No, thank you. I don't know what use I'd have for the information.' Perhaps Marek was indeed interested in something that seemed unimportant or – more accurately – inconceivable to Daniel, something one simply had to take on faith, and he already had his faith. 'Or maybe some other time,' he added.

'Alois and I are going to make a telescope,' Marek went on to inform him.

'Where will you put it?'

'In the attic, of course!'

'Anyway, we haven't got a mirror,' Alois pointed out. 'We haven't got anything. Just two lenses and a plan of how to put it together.'

Then Eva wanted to know for her part whether Petr would be living with them like Alois, but Daniel said he had already arranged for Petr to stay at his older sister's.

'He'd be better off here,' Eva objected. 'His old gang could find him there.'

'Evička, if he takes it into his head to return to his former associates, nothing will stop him.'

Eva merely shrugged and he registered a kind of subconscious anxiety. No, it would be better not to have that lad in the house.

That evening, Daniel and his wife went for a walk.

The street was deserted. The cars by the kerb shone dully in the light of the street lamps and the clusters of forsythia glowed yellow in people's gardens. Hana linked her arm in his. 'I was dying for some fresh air. I feel I'm constantly indoors somewhere, like that lad who was in prison. And it's one problem after another at the hospital these days. There's no money for medicines, or blood, or even for bandages.' And then, as if she suddenly felt ashamed of complaining, she started to tell him again about the journalist who had a habit of visiting the nurses' station and telling them stories about China and other exotic countries he had lived in. In spite of her years in the city, Hana had remained a country woman. She loved stories. She would watch television sometimes, but she would get upset at the cruelty of almost everything that was broadcast. 'It must be interesting to see so many totally different countries and customs.'

'Would you like to see them too?'

'No, not really. No, it just crossed my mind when I was listening to those stories in the nurses' station.'

'We could take a trip together as a family.'

'Somewhere far away, you mean?'

'Why not? You said yourself that it must be interesting.'

'You're talking about it because now we can afford it?'

'And we've also the freedom to.'

'We'd better not. It wouldn't be deserved.'

'What makes you think you wouldn't have deserved it?'

'I wouldn't have done anything for it.'

'It could be instead of a present, say. Your birthday's coming up. And Eva's sitting her leaving exams in a few days' time. It would be an experience for the children too.'

'But the children don't even know their own country yet.'

'One never gets to know everything. But it's good for young people to get the chance at least once to take a look at their homeland from a distance.'

'Dan, you're crazy. You mean it seriously! Let the children go off when they're old enough to organize it themselves.'

'It needn't be China. I've always wanted to have a look at Jerusalem.'

'All right, Dan, if you think so, if you'd enjoy it, maybe yes, one day. But Eva hasn't yet done her leaving exams and I might never see my fiftieth birthday.'

He realized that he was irritated by her down-to-earth attitude that resisted any dreaming, any deviation from the daily routine. He gave her a hug so as to banish the feeling of annoyance and she held him close to her for a moment before quickly slipping out of his embrace. 'Not here on the street,' she whispered. 'What if someone saw us?'

4

Bára

Bára had gone to the church on the advice of her friend Ivana. She had been suffering from occasional bouts of depression. Although she had only just turned forty, she put it down to her age, as well as to her less-than-successful second marriage and the feeling that on the whole her life seemed an aimless slog.

The fact was she had suffered from mood swings and sporadic feelings of desperate hopelessness from early adolescence. When she was seventeen she slashed her right wrist in the bathroom at home. She didn't do it because of an unhappy love affair or for any precisely definable reason. Fortunately, her sister Katka found her while she still had a drop of blood in her veins. When they asked her at the mental hospital why she had done it she was unable to reply. She simply could see no reason for living when life led nowhere but to death, and there was no way of attaining the things one believed worthwhile. What do you consider of greatest worth? the psychiatrist had asked her. She had wanted to reply 'love', but the word was so hackneyed, so devalued by pop songs of all kinds, that it no longer corresponded to her conception of it. So she said nothing. But she promised the doctors and her mother that she would never do anything like it again, and she kept her word. Another spell in mental hospital, she maintained, and she definitely would go mad.

She really made the promise only to the doctors and her mother; she promised nothing to her father. She had no love for her father and in the last years of his life she scarcely talked to him. She considered her father ordinary: he wore grey clothes, worked as an insurance clerk, told silly risqué jokes, and if he read anything at all, it was detective stories. When she was still small, his relationship with her alternated between two extremes: either bringing her chocolate bars and custard puffs, or using death to scare her. Death would come for Bára if she was naughty, if she didn't clean her teeth, if she climbed on the window-sill, if she didn't look both ways before crossing the road, or if she cried because she didn't want to go to nursery.

'What's death?'

'Death is like the darkness,' her father explained. 'When death comes for you, you'll never see the sunrise again, the moon won't shine for you, not even a single star.'

'And can I really die?'

'We must all die,' her father said, visibly pleased that he had managed to frighten her.

'But you'll die before me,' she had told him, 'because you're old.' To her surprise, her prediction made her father laugh.

Apart from a feeling of aimlessness, Bára also suffered from a sense of her own inadequacy, and the paltriness of her pointless existence. There were no real reasons for her feelings: she was an exceptional woman to look at; her tall build and large breasts were the envy of most of her fellow pupils as far back as primary school. She had her father's fine hair which was of a fairly restrained blonde hue, but which, when the light caught it, acquired a deep coppery tint. She had her mother's eyes: set wide apart and the colour of forest honey. She had acting talent, a beautiful soprano voice, wit and a distaste for anything that could be regarded as humdrum and ordinary, whether in conversation, dress or art. She adored whimsical and outlandish pranks, like the time when she and her friends dressed themselves up in winter clothes on a sweltering summer day and, with woollen bobble caps jammed on their heads, they paraded through Prague with skis over their shoulders to the astonishment of passers-by. The very next day they were sunbathing half-naked by the windows of the classroom. She also enjoyed drinking. When she was hard up she made do with beer; as soon as she could afford it she preferred cheap wine, such as Portugal or Kadárka.

She had scarcely reached puberty, which happened around her thirteenth year, when she started to draw the attention of all kinds of men, from her own age group up to men old enough to be her father, but nothing convinced her that she was worthy of genuine interest, let alone love and admiration.

She married when she was nineteen. She tried to persuade herself it was because she was attracted to the man, but more likely it was because she wanted to leave home. Filip, her first husband, was closer to her father's generation, though he was nothing like her father, which was probably what attracted her to him most. He had an interesting and manly job – airline pilot – and spoke several languages, was a good tennis-player and an equally good dancer. Admittedly, he did have one thing in common with her father: he liked to talk about death, not hers but his own – one day his plane might crash. When he first told her this, she clasped him in her arms and begged him to give up flying as she was afraid for him. Her fear evidently excited him, as from then on he would take pleasure in recounting to her the disasters that had cost his colleagues their lives.

At the time of their marriage, she was in love with him and genuinely anxious about him, to the extent of going to meet him at the airport during the first few weeks. He loved her too and prided him-self on having such a young, beautiful and interesting wife. As he flew on overseas routes, he used to bring her expensive (and, to most people in the country, inaccessible) gifts. When in time he noticed that her devotion exceeded the level of affection he was accustomed to, he fell prey to the usual masculine vanity. Bára was his property, a mere accessory to his perfection. He started to treat her with increas-ing unkindness, constantly stressing all her faults: she wasn't punctual, she lacked purpose and didn't even pass muster either as a wife (she paid too much attention to studying instead of to him) or, later, as a mother. Little Saša screamed (because of her, naturally) often the whole night through, when he needed to sleep so as to be fresh for work the next day. He crushed the last remnants of any self-confidence she had. When she discovered that while she was spending her days and nights (or at least that was how it seemed to her) look-ing after him and his little boy, he was off making love to some air hostess, he explained to her that it was her fault for not creating a proper home.

She rushed straight back to her mother. Was it possible, she asked her, that men could be so mean, so blind to anything but themselves, so selfish, that they were incapable of seeing a true picture of the world or of their nearest and dearest? But her mother was too devoted to her own husband, who had actually saved her life, to accept such a gener-alization. She counselled Bára to be more patient, as she too had been patient.

Bára now began to think about doing away with herself after all, of entering the darkness for good and making a thorough job of it this time. The trouble was, things had changed: now she had a son to con-sider. So instead of killing herself she got a divorce. Shortly afterwards she fell in love with a man with a biblical name, a builder of Towers of Babel, as she used to call him. At that time, Saša was three and Samuel forty-three. He was actually two years older than her first husband, once divorced (he would divorce a second time on her account) and had a daughter from each of his marriages. She married him – she was convinced – out of love; she admired him and for a long time believed she had found the very best of men. She gave up her acting studies for him, and transferred to a course in architecture. Almost every day during the first months and even years after their marriage they would talk about the work that united them, mostly about his projects, which were surprisingly unconventional and liberal for their time. They would also pore over the specialized foreign journals that he was able to get hold of, and discuss – she with greater tolerance, he mostly with his own particular kind of haughtiness – all the various architectural and building projects around the globe.

When she had completed her studies, she realized that while they might share the same opinions about new materials and how the building of high-rise, pre-fabricated housing estates was a crime, on the most essential thing they would never agree: for her, the most important thing in life was the man she loved, whereas for him it was his work or rather success in his work – in other words his career. Compared to her first husband he was more cultured and well-mannered, but he increasingly required her to subordinate herself to the routine and lifestyle to which he had become accustomed. What this routine required from her was to minister to his comfort. Its aim was to ensure him peace and quiet for his work. For his wife and his own son there remained little time in his life and even less enthusiasm. For his stepson there was nothing at all; he should be content that he had a place at the table and a bed to sleep in. At first Bára strove to satisfy his requirements in an effort to wring out of him a recognition which she wrongly confused with love. There was never any acknowledgement; her acquiescence merely fed his sense of superiority. She soon realized that her second husband was also selfish and self-centred and she was merely an adjunct to his ego, simply a very young mother caring for an ageing child. Her relative youth just meant it was an even greater sacrifice.

And so, after a few years of marriage, Bára started once more to be troubled by the thought that her life was slowly slipping away and she was achieving none of the things she longed for. The dusk was gradually falling, the night was approaching and she got less and less chance to enjoy the sun.

At that time she started to imagine love with another man; for the time being he was indeterminate, and most likely non-existent and therefore unattainable: a kind, unselfish and wise person who would not genuflect with admiration before his own ego and not regard his wife as a mother to look after him. But these fantasies did little to help her, they were so utterly unattainable that they merely left her dejected and she began to suffer bouts of depression again. She resisted the temptation to be unfaithful not so much out of moral conviction but more out of fear of her husband killing her if he were to find out. He was jealous by nature and he grew more suspicious with age. Apart from that, she had no wish to harm someone with whom she had had many good times, with whom she had once been deeply in love and who had given her much.

At the onset of depression she would generally consult a tarot reader whose predictions contained much to raise her spirits: unexpected good fortune or a man who would steal her heart. She even predicted her a new marriage. When the depression was at its worst, Bára would lose all interest in life and be terrified of death. She would want to run away somewhere, put an end to something and start something afresh. What was there for her to start afresh, though? And she had nowhere to run to. Besides, she now had two sons and they needed her and she loved them.

In the course of her life she had acquired a number of woman friends. When she was in a good mood and managed to snatch a free evening for herself, she would call on Helena, a fellow student from her second period of study. Helena was the sort of person she could go to a wine bar with to drink wine and chat about nothing in particular. When she needed advice on child-rearing or consolation during desolate periods of marital vexation she would seek out Ivana, whom she had known since the time they were both studying acting at the Academy. Even though Bára abandoned the course after the third year and never returned to the Academy, the friendship remained. Ivana never went into acting but got married and had three children in five years. Her hobby was homoeopathy. Whenever Bára's anxiety states were at their height she would rush off to her friend who would prescribe for her anacardium or pulsatilla, although the remedies would never work. Either Bára didn't take them for long enough, or she didn't dilute them enough, or she and Ivana were simply not capable of determining her fundamental problem.

All the same, Bára was sure she could find a very precise name for her fundamental problem: lack of love.

What if she were to try going to church occasionally, it occurred to her friend at their last meeting. She didn't attend any church, did she?

It had been a long time since Bára had attended church.

Why?

Most of all because she had stopped believing in God, or at any rate in the one they preached about in church. When she was a little girl she had very much wanted to believe. Even when she was studying she had still tried; in those days to go to church not only meant admitting to one's faith, it was also a sign of opposition to those who forbade belief. And then it struck her that what they preached in churches was too rigid, it hadn't changed for a thousand years. The very symbol of a man or God dying in pain on the cross was an almost perverted emphasis on suffering and death.

On the contrary – her friend explained to her – the cross symbolizes the fact that death has been overcome. Even so, the cross was something like an execution block or the gallows, it would always symbolize for her a cruel and violent ending of life.

Ivana didn't feel well enough versed in theological questions to argue with her. But the minister at the church she attended was an excellent man, both wise and interesting. She always came home from his sermons with a sense of having been cleansed. He was a man of love, she said with unusual fervour. What's more, he had many talents – he sang, played the harmonium, wrote poetry, composed music and could do wood carving. And he had behaved with courage under the old regime; for several years he was banned from preaching at all in Prague. Perhaps he would be able to explain what she found inexplicable.

Bára did indeed attend the church the following Sunday. She didn't make her presence known to Ivana, however, and left during the final hymn. A week later, she did the same. When her friend asked her what she thought about the sermons, Bára replied that she had found them stimulating, but nevertheless she had the feeling she was incapable of believing. What people believed in was simply a dream about God coming down among people in order to conquer death. That was how she saw it anyway. It was a dream purporting to be reality. But death ruled the whole universe, after all. Nothing, no sacrifice, could end its sway.

Ivana thought it was possible that the minister's preaching wasn't up to his usual standard. He was absentminded these days. The first time Bára was there, his mother was dying. Most likely he hadn't got over it quite yet. Ivana also wanted to know why Bára always dashed off before the end.

How could she shake the minister's hand when she wasn't able to believe in what he preached?

But if she were to speak to the minister privately . . .

But he was in mourning, after all. She could hardly bother him at this time. Besides she was always in a rush; Sam would take it very hard if she were to neglect him on a Sunday morning. He always wanted her around him.

Did she think she wouldn't come next time then?

Bára said she wasn't sure. She concealed the fact she had already spoken to the minister, that she had given him a lift. She didn't even tell her how he had caught her imagination not only by the urgency with which he preached about the need for love, but also by the tenor of his voice and his gestures, which she suspected concealed some deep sadness or suppressed passion.

5

Daniel had been having disc trouble all that morning. The pain ran from his hip right down to the big toe of his right foot. He had first slipped the disc when he was climbing a rock in the Elbe Sandstone Mountains; he had lost his footing slightly and only realized that something had happened to him the next morning when he found he could not bend to put on his boots. Jitka had helped him to his feet and supported him as they went along in spite of his protests.

It might have been the pain or the weather – a blanket of smog lay over the city more reminiscent of autumn – but he had the impression that everyone he had met that day was either cursing or complaining. First thing that morning Magda had announced to him that she would most likely fail maths because she hadn't the first idea what it was about, 'and nobody,' she added reproachfully, 'is capable of explaining it to me'. Then Máša Soukupová telephoned and wept over her ruined marriage.

He ought to go and lie down. But before he could make up his mind Dr Wagner appeared, ostensibly to borrow some books from the library. It took them only a moment to choose the books, but instead of leaving, his visitor started to complain about society being bogged down in the basest materialism, and how life was dominated by money, brutality and vulgar sex. 'Fewer and fewer people believe in spiritual values – who has anything to offer now, apart from the church?'

Daniel could have pointed out that even the church was incapable of firing people's imaginations any longer. Only some crazy sect with a new saviour or at least Christ's Delegate at its head was likely to do that. For fanatics like these, people were prepared to give up all their property or even commit mass suicide. Instead, he merely said that the original church had expected Christ's coming and a pitiless judgment on all sinners. And were there so few sinners? But what people have a right to judge them?

Yes, that was his own view entirely, the lawyer agreed, particularly when they themselves were not judges and had simply stolen a list of names and printed them and thought that was enough to prove the guilt of those in question.

'I've been thinking about your father,' and Daniel finally realized the reason for his visit and why he was delaying his departure. 'In your situation I would let the matter rest. You'll never discover the truth after all these years anyway.'

'But there must be some files, some records, preserved still.'

'Not necessarily. And even if there were, what kind of truth do you expect to find in the sort of records *they* kept?'

'But I'd naturally like to find out something about the circumstances at least.'

'If you say so, Reverend.' In that case, Dr Wagner saw two options. Either to find someone in the Ministry and persuade them to look in the file – if it existed; this would probably not be free of charge. Alternatively, he could try to find some of the scoundrels who interrogated his father and had him on their books.

The idea of bribery was abhorrent to Daniel. And the thought of talking to such individuals even more so. But what he regarded as abhorrent was immaterial at this moment.

Dr Wagner was scarcely out the door when Alois burst into his office, still in his working clothes.

'Has something happened to you?'

'Me? No, not me!' He tried to brush the bits of lime off his overalls on to the carpet. 'But we had an accident at the building site. Fyodor, this young Russian guy, took a header off the scaffolding.'

'Was he killed?'

'No, not outright anyway, but he's in an awful mess.'

'Did you call an ambulance?'

'Of course, but they kicked up a stink about him having no insurance. He was working the way they do nowadays, on the black. A Russian nigger, know what I mean?'

'Which hospital did they take him to?'

'Your one. Where your wife works, I mean.'

'Do you want to phone there?'

Alois shrugged. 'The other fellows said they'll let him stew, seeing he isn't insured and he's a Russian anyway.'

'They wouldn't do that,' although Daniel wasn't entirely sure about this.

'He never spoiled anyone's fun. He didn't know Czech – that's true, apart from the sort of things you'd rather I didn't say here. And a few words he needed for the job. When he'd say words like "beer" or "buddy" it sounded Russian anyway. He said his father was here too, as a soldier.'

'When?'

'Couldn't tell you.'

'I think I can work it out.'

'I just thought it'd be better if you phoned, they'd just tell me to f—'

He wouldn't get to bed now. The lad wouldn't care about his back pain; he was waiting for him to do something. After all he'd preached to him about loving one's neighbour and the boy was now doing just that. He was showing concern even though he didn't have to.

He sent him to get changed while he limped off to get a painkiller.

They parked in front of the surgical block.

'What are you doing here?' Hana was always pleased when he dropped by unexpectedly. Then she led them to the ward where the injured fellow lay. Alois pulled a chair over to the bed and started to tell him something, more with gestures than words.

He looked at the foreigner whose father must have been one of those he had vainly told to go home twenty-six years before. It was better to come as a labourer than as a soldier; on the other hand the soldier had returned unscathed, whereas this lad lay here pale, covered in bandages, his lips drawn back with the pain, his blond hair soaked in sweat.

Was our fathers' iniquity truly visited on us after all? It certainly was a fact that here on earth we bore the consequences of their actions.

The orthopaedist that Hana took him to see, and that she had talked to Daniel about previously, asked: 'Do you have some connection with the labourer, Reverend?'

'No. A lad in our congregation is a workmate of his. I promised I'd enquire how he was,' Daniel said. 'Apparently he wasn't insured; does that complicate things for you?'

'Most definitely. I've just had the scoundrel he works for here. He was in a bit of a panic and so he offered to make a contribution but when he heard what an operation would cost he backed down. He'd sooner pay him the plane fare back to Kiev where he came from.'

'So you won't be operating?'

'It would be a fairly complicated operation.'

'And costly?'

'With the post-operative care, Reverend, about a quarter of a million. That's all. Because in this country a doctor still gets paid less than a bricklayer. The Germans would charge you at least three times that.'

'So you don't intend to operate on him?'

'We can't afford to, Reverend. The fellow who hired him as slave-labour should be locked up. But in this country they spend time badgering doctors to keep their costs down while villains like him do what they like. OK, let him pay the air fare, at least. In a couple of days he could be in a hospital in Kiev.'

'And can the operation be put off?'

'That's not the point; we've pinned his leg for the time being. It's more a question of what they'll do to him there. Have you any idea what medical care is like over there? Do you think they care whether or not he'll be a cripple for the rest of his days? They'll straighten it up a bit and slap it in plaster. And even then he'll be lucky.'

'And here you would operate on him so he could walk normally afterwards?'

'We'd do the maximum.'

'And what if someone were to pay for the operation?'

'I doubt that anyone would.'

'What if I were to pay for it, for instance?'

The doctor stared at him in amazement. 'Why would you do that for someone you don't even know?'

'You also help people you don't know.'

'But that's my job, Reverend. All right, I know what you're going to say: it's your job too. But just let me tell you something. Not long ago we had a fellow in here, about your age, with gangrene in his leg.

73

Abroad they have a drug to treat it that we don't have yet. It's expensive. About three thousand marks a shot. And you have to have a repeat dose every year. Here there are only two options. Amputation or death. That fellow didn't want to believe it and begged me to save his leg. So I told him about that drug and that he'd have to obtain it himself, and fast. He agreed. Then I told him the price and he burst into tears. He could never find that much.'

'So you amputated the leg?'

'There was no other way; he'd have died before he'd managed to get that amount of money together. The only reason I'm telling you this, Reverend, is so you understand that trying to play the good Samaritan in our business would break a Rothschild.'

The doctor was right, of course. It would take no more than a couple of minutes to give away all the money he had received out of the blue. It was enough to take a look round. People were suffering all over the world, all around them. All the same he said: 'I believe the right thing to do is for you to operate on him here, if you'll agree.'

'We always prefer to fix people up rather than kick them out somewhere else.' He added, 'I can't take it from you. Some of it maybe. We'll have to find the rest from somewhere.'

'We'll agree on the details later, but I wouldn't like anyone to know about it. Not even the lad concerned.'

The doctor shrugged. 'That will be no problem. No one would believe it anyway.'

6

Samuel

The architect Samuel Musil regarded himself as a capable and decent man, a good husband and even a good father to the children of his three marriages – or the last two, at least. The majority of people in his field had no doubts about his qualities as a professional, even though a number of his opponents branded his most famous and prestigious projects as crimes perpetrated on the capital. Lately, people had been blaming him for the skilful way he had operated under the old regime, but few had said so to his face and he was convinced that he had behaved no worse than most people would have done in his position and that he had never produced anything that was in any way at odds with his 'professional or human conscience' – or so he had claimed in a newspaper interview.

He had spent most of his life under the Communist regime. He used to start the biographical appendix to his personnel form with the sentence: 'I was born into the family of a poor peasant factory worker towards the end of the great economic crisis; after the war I joined the Union of Czech Youth and always sympathized with the policy of the Communist Party.' Admittedly, that sentence, covering the first eighteen years of his life, was not untrue, but in an interview with a newspaper on the occasion of his fifty-fifth birthday he did not repeat a single detail of it, but instead he recalled his years as a boy scout and the fact that his family never joined a co-operative and that his uncle was wounded in the battles on the Western Front. Fortunately, when he was setting up a practice after the fall of the old regime, nobody investigated either his origins or his convictions. All that was required was money, and it really didn't matter where it came from.

Samuel had no brothers or sisters. His mother had a tendency to depression and excessive mistrust, and even one child was an inordinate burden for her. There were days when she refused to speak to him, let alone caress or cuddle him. His father spent little time at home. He used to spend a lot of time at work and found little to entice him home; even in his looks, his son resembled too closely the wife who had embittered his life.

Samuel's schools had been terrible; he started primary school under the Protectorate and attended grammar school during the Stalinist years.

He graduated from university several years after Stalin's death, but even at that time the Kreshchatik in Kiev or the Lomonosov University in the Lenin Hills in Moscow were still regarded as notable achievements of progressive architecture. When he looked at them, however, the only thing that struck him was their bumptious ugliness. He wrote his thesis on the pre-war Soviet avant-garde. He emphasized the principles of the post-revolutionary Association of New Architects who had called for large unadorned surfaces and the construction of abstract geometric forms. These requirements, he maintained, had been the inspiration for Le Corbusier's purism.

He was also taken by the notion that whereas for the baroque the essential stylistic feature was the circle, in the case of revolutionary architecture it ought to be the spiral, as a form moving upwards to the Communist future of mankind. In his view, the avant-gardists had created a genuine revolutionary art which could be looked to for inspiration.

At first – like others of his generation – he had sincerely believed in progress and socialism. He had taken part in two youth building projects, and unlike most of the other participants he had managed to draw some benefit from them in career terms: not only was he able to try his hand at most building work but he also became familiar with architectural practice and soon realized the yawning gulf that existed in his profession between the reality on the ground and what was officially proclaimed.

At the second youth project he made the acquaintance of Katarína. She was a medical student from Slovakia. He managed to get her pregnant so soon that they were married four months after their return from the project. They never set up home together. For three years they barely saw each other twice a month except during the holidays, part of which they were able to spend together. When he got his first job with a design office he was assigned a flat and hoped that his wife would finally join him. She refused, having found another man in the meantime.

His second wife was called Kateřina and worked as a draughtsman. They were ill-matched socially. His wife was aware of it and tried to show her gratitude by her almost maternal care of him and unreserved recognition of his male supremacy. This suited him well and led him to regard his second marriage as successful.

As he grew older his tendency towards pedantry became more pronounced. He demanded order – from his employees at work and from his wife and daughter at home. Order in his terms meant punctuality and strict observance of all his instructions. He could not abide carelessly sketched plans, or to find a towel hung up sloppily in the bathroom in the morning – even a speck of cigarette ash on the table would spoil his mood for the remainder of the day. The sorts of things that ran counter to his idea of order were unplanned events, daydreaming, unexpected guests, dawdling and actions with unconsidered or even dangerous consequences.

Preserving this order enabled him to become an excellent organizer.

He could be relied on totally and because of this quality the directors of the design firms where he worked overlooked the fact that from time to time he would act with too much independence, and that he would always refuse jobs that he felt were beneath him.

Unlike many of his colleagues, who soon realized that nothing was required of an architect other than to build cheaply and not be inspired by anything that might come from the decadent West, he did not sit back but got hold of foreign journals and although he could not put any of the things he read into practice, at least he retained an awareness of what was being built around the world. As soon as the political thaw set in in the sixties, he managed to push through a number of interesting designs for exhibition pavilions.

When he met Bára, his first daughter had just married and the daughter from his second marriage was sixteen. By that time he had achieved recognition as a prominent architect who would be commissioned to design arts centres, Communist Party secretariats, experimental schools, and luxury holiday centres, or for the reconstruction of important historical buildings, rather than housing estates. At the age of only forty-three, he had already received a number of awards and even a state prize.

Although working within the regime, he never identified with it in spirit. Disillusioned with a government that had fulfilled so little of what it had once promised, he would read with unconcealed satisfaction articles in the foreign press unmasking its deceit and above all criticizing the government's uncreative and mostly hideous architecture. He skilfully contrived to avoid taking any post of political responsibility – not only because he was not sure how long the regime would survive, but also because he was afraid it might take him away from his work.

He was rich but lived abstemiously, not smoking and only taking the occasional drink, always remaining sober, since to get drunk would affect his competence at work the next day. He played tennis, and in the summer he would take a seaside holiday with his wife and daughter – in earlier years with both his daughters. Though of smallish build, he gave the impression of being bulky and even at the age of forty his hair had not started to go grey. His eyes were his most interesting feature: deep-set beneath thick eyebrows, and with golden-brown foxy irises. He had the ability to gaze at an interlocutor fixedly, so that he seemed to be listening intently, even when his mind was elsewhere. As a result, women who found him attractive, or who wanted to appeal to him, could be given the impression that he found them so captivating that he couldn't take his eyes off them, that his look actually betrayed his feelings for them. In reality nothing of the sort occurred to him.

Whereas he felt himself to be at the peak of his powers, his wife had aged prematurely. She had never shone intellectually, but as time went by she started to lose interest in anything that interested him or the society in which he moved. Whenever she spoke he felt ashamed of her. He preferred not to take her to social occasions where the majority of his colleagues and contemporaries had much younger and more interesting wives. And she genuinely made no objection.

But it was not he who first made a play for Bára. Bára herself was aroused by the thrill of the chase when she first chanced to meet him at the Architects' Club. And as she was interesting, beautiful and young, as well as game for anything, Samuel yielded. He exchanged a wife-mother for a wife-daughter in a move that was so radical it must have been the only significant change in his life that he never managed to come to terms with.

7

Daniel bought Hana a gold bracelet for her fiftieth birthday.

'But there's no way I can wear it,' she said when she opened its case.

'Why not?'

'So much gold. It doesn't suit me and I don't have any occasion to wear it.'

'You can wear it this evening. You know I've booked a table at the Chinese restaurant.'

'So you said, but it wasn't necessary. We could have had a lovely dinner at home.'

'We have dinner at home every evening.'

'Precisely, and restaurants are so expensive now.'

Hana refused to take their new-found wealth into account. He liked that about her, but at the same time he found her reluctance to accept change irritating.

'I'm looking forward to the restaurant,' Marek piped up.

'I don't want to go anywhere,' Magda grumbled. 'I've got to study. We've got a maths test tomorrow.'

'You're stupid. They give you fortune cookies after the meal.'

'Marek, fortune cookies are superstitious and stupid,' he rebuked his son.

'And now on top of everything else we're doing algorithms. If somebody doesn't explain them to me I won't be able to calculate a single row.'

'Algorithms? What are they?' Daniel asked, expressing interest.

'That's just what I'd like to know.'

'An algorithm is a procedure for solving specific problems by carrying out a precisely determined sequence of steps,' Marek quoted the definition. 'It's what computer programs are all based on,' he added. 'And you've got a computer in your office, Dad.'

'Indeed I do have a computer, but I haven't the foggiest idea what goes on inside it.'

'That's your loss.'

In the meantime Magda had rummaged out her textbook. 'That's what I have to calculate: make an algorithm to determine the numerical sum of the given natural number *a*. In determining each of the numerals you may use only arithmetical operations and whole-number division to determine the share and remainder.'

'I don't understand that at all.'

'You see, Daddy. Not even you understand it.'

'I don't have to, I don't go to school any more. It's curious that Eva never needed anyone to explain things to her. Not even now that she's about to take her final exams.'

'Because Eva's clever. Because Eva's always the best. Because her mother was . . .'

'Magda!' he snapped at her.

'I'll work through it with her,' Marek suggested. 'Even someone so utterly thick is bound to grasp it in half an hour.'

Hana had got changed in the meantime. She had put on the black dress she had last worn at his mother's funeral. It was plain and very old. She wore no make-up. She never did wear make-up, not even lipstick. Her shoes were carefully polished, that was true, but there was no hiding the fact that they pre-dated the Velvet Revolution. It struck him that gold genuinely didn't suit what his wife was wearing, maybe it

79

didn't suit her at all. He'd wanted to please her, but had only disconcerted her.

'Isn't that dress a bit funereal?' he wondered.

'Everyone wears black nowadays,' she said. 'Even very young girls go around in black. Haven't you noticed?'

'No, I expect I don't look at the girls enough.'

He was left alone in the room. He realized that he did not feel at all pleased with himself. He had neglected his children, he didn't know what algorithms were and Magda had the feeling that he favoured Eva. He gave his wife jewellery instead of giving her love. And even his attempt to restore the health of some unknown Russian displeased him. It struck him that the action had not come from the heart, that there had been something ostentatious about it: a gesture intended to convince an unknown doctor about Christian love, or more likely it had been a gesture intended for himself, to prove how he disdained money and how easily he could part with it.

Was it possible for one to uphold order in a world that was so disordered?

The telephone rang. He picked up the receiver reluctantly.

'Good afternoon, Reverend, this is Bára.' The woman's voice was slightly harsher on the phone than in real life. 'I'm not sure whether you'll remember me.'

'My memory's not that bad, even at my age.'

'Age is an awful thing. It horrifies me when I realize which year I was born in and I'm pleased when everyone immediately forgets it. I hope you're not offended that I didn't come last Sunday.'

'Church attendance is not compulsory for anyone. Besides, as you said, you are not of our faith.'

'Did I put it as stupidly as that? I apologize. At this time of year my husband is raring to go down to our country house. I don't know when I'll next manage to escape on a Sunday.'

'Is there no local church near your country place?'

'I've no idea. I've never enquired.' Then she said, 'There are plenty of churches everywhere, but it's your sermons that interest me.'

'Thank you. I'm pleased that you got something out of my sermons.'

'Sundays are not going to be easy from now on,' she said. 'But what I actually called you for was to let you know that I have a small role in a television play tonight. It's being shown on Channel One at ten past eight. But maybe you don't watch television.'

'Not usually, but I would certainly watch you. But I won't be home this evening.'

'Please don't be offended – I don't know what came over me. I just had the feeling I was somehow indebted to you.'

'I'm sure you aren't. On the contrary, I'm the one indebted to you – for that lift. I regret we won't be able to watch it, but we're having a birthday celebration today.'

'It's your birthday today?'

'No, my wife's.'

'So, do please wish her from me lots of love in her life. I expect it's just as well you won't be watching – it might have put you off me. You see, it's not a particularly attractive little role. Anyway, I'm sorry for taking up your time.'

'You haven't. And I look forward to your finding a moment to come and join us some Sunday.'

'Yes,' she said, 'I'll do my best, I truly will!'

8

Letters

Dear Reverend Vedra,

Everyone is asleep here at home, except that you don't know where my home is (where else but Hanspaulka?). I can't get to sleep, I'm down in the dumps. It could be the rotten weather or the fact that Samuel told me that I ruin his life, even though I do everything I can to make him feel contented at home. Samuel is my husband, in case you'd forgotten.

I've decided to write to you because you strike me as wise and kind, and I have the impression that you're someone who is capable of listening sympathetically not because it is in your job description but because you really are someone fired by the love that you preach about so fervently in your sermons. Of course it's possible just to talk about love and most people are capable of jabbering on about it *ad nauseam*. But one can feel that you mean it, which is why I looked forward to hearing you every Sunday. Now I miss your words and your voice. There are so many things I'd like to ask you about. Such as what one must do to live in love and freedom, when one is surrounded on every side by something else entirely: the pursuit of money, self-advancement and an awful lot of violence or at least selfishness, as well as male conceit and vanity, and men's craving to assert their own ego at the expense of their closest companions?

Now I'm astonished at my own effrontery, not only in writing to you but in burdening you with these questions, as a result of which I'm actually taking up your time. As if I couldn't make do with hearing you in church.

But if you could spare me a couple of lines I'd be eternally grateful.

Best wishes,

Yours admiringly,

Bára Musilová

——— —

Dear Mr Houdek,

Regarding our recent conversation about that young lad Petr Koubek, who has just been released from prison where he was baptized and who, I firmly believe, underwent a profound change of heart. You were so kind as to mention that he might be able to work in your splendid garden centre. He will therefore be coming to see you about a job next Monday. Working outdoors will do him good, after spending almost two years cooped up in prison. I am sure he'll show willingness, but I would entreat you none the less to be patient with him, in the beginning at least. When someone is in prison for such a lengthy period, his personality is bound to be affected, his reactions are often unpredictable and above all unreasonable. It is sometimes hard to take, but it is understandable when we consider the sort of surroundings he has moved in and the sort of people he could not help mixing with.

I do hope that Petr won't create any difficulties for you, but should any arise, don't hesitate to call me and I will try to intervene.

Please convey my best wishes to your wife and accept once again my thanks for your singular readiness to assist someone in need.

Yours sincerely, Daniel Vedra

——— —

Dear Mrs Musilová,

I do not merit the praise you heap on me. When I speak about love I do no more than pass on the most important thing about Christ's message.

The aim of what we do is to find real love. This was said most beautifully by St Paul: 'Love never fails. But where there are prophecies, they will cease; where there are tongues, they will be stilled; where there is knowledge, it will pass away. These three remain: faith, hope and love. But the greatest of these is love.'

What is one to do, you ask, in order to live in love and freedom, when there is so little of it around one? Do not expect me to speak as one possessed of understanding or capable of handing out prescriptions for how to live.

A life of love is, I suppose, the desire of anyone whose heart is in the right place. What was so terrible about the old regime was that hatred and struggle were regarded as so fundamental to life. To many this seemed to make sense because at first glance a life of love seems virtually unattainable. It is enough to turn on the television or read the newspaper headlines: terrorism, robbery, fraud, and all those killed in Bosnia or the Caucasus. And that is leaving aside our everyday life. Could we really hurt each other and quarrel the way we do every day if we lived in love? Could we hate people just because they have a different faith, or look different?

Our desires and expectations are often disappointed, however. Instead of striving once again to find love and put it into practice we invent all sorts of alternative goals. We build careers for ourselves and compete with each other, or on the contrary we waste time and fail to fill it with something that reaches out beyond ourselves. We often look for someone to blame for our dissatisfaction with our lives, not looking inside ourselves, but outside ourselves. We fetter our hearts with many injunctions, taboos and prejudices. Often they are so choked with these things that when an opportunity arises to fulfil something we've yearned for, we don't even notice it. So we just live, become cold, and replace love with apathy or even rancour.

You write about a world that is full of selfishness, money-grubbing, violence and male arrogance. That's what the world looks like to me sometimes. I've noticed that when people start a conversation with me it is in order to express some bitterness, not to say something kind. If I offer to carry a woman's shopping bag she becomes alarmed. She thinks that I want to rob her not lend a hand. But these are only superficial observations. Sometimes we can become outraged with those who are actually suffering.

I have no illusions about how difficult it is to live in today's world. Life has never been easy for those who expect it to fulfil their desires. Therefore every morning I try to reflect on what is really important for my life. If it continues to be a life of love then I will have to act and behave accordingly. It is not easy to enter the hearts of others. But wanting to love and to live in love means trying to do precisely that. Whether or not we try is solely a matter of our own determination, and this is precisely where our inalienable freedom lies: our inner freedom to determine our own actions.

I see I've gone on a bit – it's a preacher's failing, and yet I doubt whether I've said anything you didn't know already. I ought to add that real love should reach out somewhere. To Jesus, as I believe. That splendid theologian Karl Barth once wrote that 'human life has no meaning without belief in transcendental truth, justice and love which mankind is incapable of creating alone . . .'

My wish is that you will manage to live the way you would wish.

With best regards, Daniel Vedra

———————

Dear Reverend Vedra,

You can't know how pleased I was to receive your letter and how much it helped me. For me, love has always been the most important thing in my life even though I have seldom received much of it from others. No, that's unjust. My mother has always been marvellous and maybe the others would have treated me better if I hadn't messed things up myself.

I married my husband, who is successful and highly respected, out of love. I so earnestly wanted that love to last for ever, and still do, and want to remain true to this wish, true to my husband. And yet I watch with horror as that love fades and is replaced by recriminations, quarrels or cold silence. All that remains is a fixed routine: breakfast, shopping, cooking, housework and visiting people together, or even receptions with feigned smiles and bonhomie. I have two sons. Because of my own irresponsibility I deprived Saša of a father when he was very small. And I now know I must not deprive my little Aleš of his father.

Sometimes I wake up at night with a feeling of anxiety that I have difficulty in describing to you. It is a sense of wasting my life, my only life, my days, each of which is unrepeatable. Yet I spend them emptily, engaged in some duty or other which I mostly don't recognize as such, in a life without love and without devotion, even though I have long conversations about them at home with my husband.

There are times when I'd just like to take myself off somewhere or cuddle up to my husband and beg him to be with me, be mine, do something, save me. But he is asleep and if I did wake him he would tick me off for bothering him. I only interest him as a component. A component of the home where he takes refuge, where he needs me to look after and listen to him, as well as tidy and cook for him. But am I directing my request to the right person at this moment? You are happy because you have prayer and someone who listens to you, or at least so you believe. That's a comfort. That is hope.

There is also hope in what you wrote to me and the advice you gave, although I get the feeling that to live according to your advice one definitely needs enormous strength, patience and perseverance.

You have been so kind to me that I take the liberty to ask whether I might be able to come and talk to you about these things some time – whether I'm allowed to if I'm not a member of your church. I know that time is the most precious commodity that we have and were you to spare me a few minutes I would be eternally grateful.

Yours, Bára M.

Penned just before midnight on Wednesday in our fair, royal city which neither the Communists nor my husband have managed to disfigure.

——— ———

Vedra, you gypsy mouthpiece,

I watched your antics on television and it made me want to throw up. You literally called on us to be kind to 'poor' criminals and even gypsies! But do you share a house with them? I do. No sooner do you meet them than they're reaching for their knives. They get drunk and yell beneath your window. If it wasn't for the skinheads they'd have cut the throats of the lot of us. They will one day, anyway, when they outnumber us, and that won't be long. The only reason they haven't done it so far is because someone has to feed and clothe them. Have you already forgotten what you Christians have on your consciences? How many people did you burn at the stake just for saying the world was round, for instance? And what about when you used to bless weapons? Take your bloody love and stick it up your arse and don't come spreading it on the television where nobody could give a damn about you.

A viewer from Ústí

———•———

Dear Rút,

You know how terrible I am about writing letters. You're so far away that it seems inappropriate to let you know all the little details of our lives. And that leaves only the major events. One important event that affects both of us I've been keeping from you. Some time ago – it must be about two years already – a magazine here published a list of secret police informers. The list was obtained illegally and published without any official authentication. It contained over a hundred thousand names of people living and dead, some who signed to advance their careers and others who were forced to in prison. I found our father's name on the list: his real name, his code name and his date of birth. That's all. I have no other information and only the people on the list have the right to have it checked. If they died in the meantime, it can't be helped. You can imagine my feelings when I discovered Dad's name on the list. I wanted to spare you them. Besides, I've heard all sorts of conflicting reports about the matter over the past two years that I really don't know what to think. There is talk about people who found themselves mistakenly on the list because they happened to sign a bit of paper which they didn't think important and subsequently did nothing dishonourable. Now it seems to me that we ought to try to clear Dad's name if he was innocent, and knowing him and remembering him as I do, I just can't bring myself to believe he was capable of harming anyone in order to gain some advantage for himself or to spare himself some hardship. It struck me that you, as the older one, might know a bit more about him in those years when he returned from prison, that you might have noticed something that I was oblivious to, or even have heard something from him that he didn't feel he could tell me. This is the reason why I'm writing to you about it so belatedly.

I'm thinking of you. It's a pity we had to meet in the shadow of death and there was no opportunity for us really to spend some time together.

Love, Dan

Dear Mrs Bára Musilová,

Thank you for your frank letter. I welcome anyone who feels a need to talk to me about 'such things'. I enclose a card with the times you can catch me in my office – it is situated in the same building as the chapel.

And please don't speak in advance about gratitude before knowing what you'll receive.

Yours sincerely,

Daniel Vedra

Dear Reverend,

I thought I'd make it to church, but you know what we pagans are like – in the end we would rather do something else than help our souls. So I'm writing to you instead. I expect you can guess it is to do with that young man Petr Koubek that I hired on your recommendation and gave the job of driving the garden tractor. I've no complaints about the young man, it's just that he worries me a bit. To put it in a nutshell, he tries to do the job properly but his heart isn't in it. He has other ambitions. I suppose you might call them spiritual, but they seem to me inappropriate. As you know, he's a good-looking young fellow with an interesting face and a murky past. I mostly employ women, some of whom are still very young. Don't get the idea that he is tempting them to do anything wrong, anyway it would be quite normal if he happened to fancy some of them. No, he preaches to them, while they're hard at work and you can imagine that we have more than enough to do in the gardens at this time of year. He turns off the motor and, job or no job, he starts to tell them all about the life of the Holy Spirit in love and fellowship, saying that all people should be transformed. He feels that he is called on to start that transformation. The girls listen to him transfixed, and he enjoys that. But in the meantime the borders are overgrown with weeds and the carnations go unwatered. Maybe it would be a good idea for you to have a word with him, Reverend, and explain to him that he's in the garden to work and not to preach to the girls about the Holy Spirit.

Wishing you all the best,

Yours truly, Břetislav Houdek

Chapter Three

1

Brother Soukup has been sitting in his office for almost an hour and the conversation is getting nowhere. 'You condemn me, Reverend!'

'I never condemn anyone.'

'I know. But you think I'm behaving badly.'

'Irresponsibly perhaps.'

'Towards the children, you mean?'

'Towards everyone.'

'But you know I'm not an irresponsible person.' He has recently been elected chairman of the board of a printing company and he sets rather too much store by it. He wears only white shirts these days and even on this hot June day he has come dressed in a jacket and tie.

'It's possible to act responsibly at work and less so towards one's nearest and dearest.'

'If you only knew the sleepless nights I've had over it, Reverend Brother. You wouldn't believe how much soul-searching I've gone through before reaching this decision.'

'I believe you.'

'Máša was my first woman. I knew nothing about life.'

'At that time maybe, but now you're the father of four children.'

'But what am I supposed to do, Reverend Brother, now I don't love her any more?'

'It's up to oneself whom one does or doesn't love.'

'No, I can't any more. I simply can't stand her. When I see her looking shattered every morning, with tears in her eyes, it spoils my whole day.'

'But she's shattered because of you.'

'She's shattered on her own account. She's not built for today's world. Or any world, for that matter. She's like an old rag, if you'll excuse me, Reverend, for using the expression about the mother of my children.'

'Maybe you didn't give her enough support.'

'That's not true. I gave her everything she ever asked for.'

'Love too?'

'Love, too, while I could.'

'Don't you feel even a tiny bit of sympathy?'

'I did – while I could. But all I feel now is anger. That she's standing in the way of my life.'

'Those are very wicked words.'

'You're driving me to say them, Reverend. Because I feel you privately condemn me.'

'I never condemn anyone. And what about the children?'

'The children go around crying. And they're fearful of what's going to happen. The youngest one, the little mite, is always begging us not to quarrel! Do you think that's any sort of home for them? They'll be better off when I've taken them with me.'

'Without their mother?'

'She wasn't a good mother. Someone like her can't be good at anything.'

The phone rings. 'Excuse me,' he says to Soukup.

'This is Bára. Bára Musilová. Do you still remember me?'

'Of course.'

'You wrote that I could come and see you on Mondays or Wednesdays.'

It occurs to him that the woman is raising her voice needlessly; even the person sitting opposite him must hear every word. 'Of course,' he says, in as official a manner as possible.

'So that means today too?'

'How soon?' He glances at his watch.

'As long as it takes me to get from here to you.'

'All right, you'd better come then.' He hangs up before she has a chance to reply.

'I'll be going, Reverend. You won't understand me whatever I say.'

'Understanding is not the same as approving.'

'You condemn me.'

'I never condemn anyone,' he repeats wearily.

'I'm a home-breaker in your eyes. I've broken several commandments in one go.'

'We all break the commandments from time to time, but you can't expect me to be thrilled about it.'

'There are commandments that are worse to break.'

'It is not up to us to judge.'

'Yes, I know. But there are people capable of killing someone who gets in their way. Surely it is better to separate peacefully.'

'Certainly. And the best thing of all is to live in peace.'

'I can't any longer.'

'All right. Act according to your conscience. But be aware of one thing: this action is capable of turning against you one day.'

The man opposite thanks him and gets up from the armchair. He is pale and his thin lips are pursed so tightly that they are almost invisible.

Daniel recalls Soukup from the time he was still a member of the youth section. They met at summer camp. A fervent and even fanatical exponent of scripture, he once argued that people who did not obey the Ten Commandments could not be Christians. Martin Hájek had disputed this, saying that if that were so there would not be a single Christian left on earth. How many years ago was that? At least fifteen. People even forget what happened a week ago. Having a good memory tends to be a disadvantage.

It occurs to him that this man might actually commit murder one day. The worst thing would be that he would then demand that others should understand him. All he was doing was removing an obstacle in the way of his life.

Someone knocks and the woman architect enters. On this hot day she has decided to wear a short-sleeved blouse and a skirt that almost reaches down to her ankles. She is wearing slightly scuffed and down-at-heel canvas shoes. The skirt is black, the blouse white. She has a black fabric handbag slung across her shoulder.

She sits down in the armchair at the coffee table. 'So, here I am,' she announces. 'In a moment you'll be sorry you didn't say you weren't available.'

'It's not my habit to say I'm not available.'

'No, I suppose you can't really. You're not allowed to lie, are you. But you could have said you didn't have the time. Or told me that there was nothing for me to come here for. So I really am grateful.'

'Would you expect me to say: There's nothing for you to come here for?'

'No, I wouldn't.'

'So don't thank me. There's nothing to thank me for.'

'There is. Your own flock is big enough and you're bound to be tired of all the complaints they heap on you.' She takes a small white handkerchief out of her handbag and fiddles with it in her fingers. All the while she stares fixedly at him. She has large eyes the colour of dark honey; he would even call them Semitic. Her gaze unnerves him.

'There are more tiresome occupations. And I am doing this job of my own free will.'

'But it was not at all my intention to complain. I have an interesting occupation, a faithful husband, splendid children, fantastic friends and a dear old mother. I wanted to be an actress, but then I decided to practise architecture, which I now do, a bit, at least. I'm a "happy woman", in fact.'

'There aren't many happy people.'

'Aren't you happy?'

'I can't complain.'

'Sorry, it was a stupid question. All I meant to say was that a lot of people would be happy in my situation, and I realize that fate has mostly been good to me. I ought to say the Good Lord, as I'm sitting in the manse. Is that a picture of Comenius over there?'

'It is.' He also has two of his old wood carvings on the shelf. He is relieved that she seems not to have noticed them.

'Was he a member of your church?'

'No, but that's not really important, is it? I don't classify people according to the church they belong to.'

'So how do you classify them?'

'I endeavour not to classify them at all.'

She takes a packet of cigarettes out of her handbag. 'Would you like a cigarette?'

'I haven't smoked in a long time.'

'I thought not. Will it bother you if I smoke?'

'Not if it doesn't bother you.'

She lights a cigarette but exhales the smoke to one side. 'I'll ask you the question, then. When you wrote to me about love, what did you understand by the word?'

'There is no precise answer to that question. Everyone understands something different by the word.'

'But what do you understand by it?'

'Maybe the ability to sacrifice yourself for others. Or service. Or the ability to be with others when they need you.'

'That is also a service. But that kind of love is one-sided, isn't it? If everyone wanted to be self-sacrificing and serve, there'd be no one to sacrifice oneself for and no one to serve.'

'It's also a way to overcome anxiety.'

'Anxiety about what?'

'Loneliness. Death.'

'But you love God first and foremost. Christ. Or am I wrong?'

'It's rather that He loves us. And as regards our love, I give priority to love for people. I believe that Jesus did and does likewise.'

'What form does Jesus's love for us take?'

'Jesus sacrificed his life for people's salvation.'

'Lots of people sacrifice their lives. But that happened a long time ago. What form has it taken since then?'

'That sacrifice still applies and prevails as it did then.'

'How can you tell? After all, how many dreadful things have happened since then?'

'You're right. Some of them were so terrible they are beyond my imagination. I believe that love endures none the less.'

'And normal human love can endure an entire lifetime?'

'I believe it can.'

'And you also maintain that love manifests itself when we're with someone who needs us. I'd like to meet someone who is able to love that way.'

'You haven't met anyone like that yet?'

'No, I certainly haven't. Except my mother maybe. But I didn't meet her. Without her I wouldn't be here at all.'

'Are you glad you are?'

'Here and now, you mean?'

'I mean, in the world.'

'I'm glad I am here now – apart from that, I can't say. Or rather, sometimes yes, sometimes no. And there was one occasion when I decided to stop existing altogether. Am I keeping you?'

'No, I was expecting you, after all.'

She lights another cigarette. She has slender fingers: in that respect also she resembles his first wife.

'When I was seventeen I used to sing in a band. That's a long time ago. But I ought to start with something even longer ago than that.

When I was a very little girl, we used to spend the summer in a little village just outside Sedlčany, if you know that part of the world. It's not really important where it was. There was this hunchback living there, a dirty, crazy fellow who used to wear terribly muddy wellies and had black hairy arms like a gorilla. He used to kill small birds. Tiny redstarts, blackbirds, chaffinches and the like. Whenever he saw a nest in a tree he would climb up it, pull out the nestlings, wring their necks and throw them under the tree. I was terrified of him. Whenever I met him I would start to cry and my mother had to pick me up – at the age of five.'

'And the people there let him carry on?'

'It's conceivable that they forbade him to do it, but they couldn't lock him up for it, there was no law against it at the time. And maybe there isn't one even now, although there ought to be. But I don't expect he's doing it any more. He's probably dead. So when I was singing in that band – I don't want to take up too much of your time – one lad that used to play with us on the banjo travelled as far as Mexico and brought home with him some weird horrible thing – a mushroom. It was dried, and you could eat it or smoke it, or you could make it into a tea. It tasted bitter, not at all mushroom-like. We all took some of that mushroom and afterwards everyone had beautiful, colourful visions and the urge to make love – all except me. Instead I had the most horrible dream. I wasn't a human any more, but a nestling, and I saw that disgusting fellow climbing up towards me through the branches. And I began to be really terrified.'

Fear suddenly appears in her eyes. As she speaks she leans so near to him that he can smell her scent. Then abruptly she seizes him by the hand and squeezes it firmly, almost too tightly. 'Apparently I started to scream and there was no calming me down. That's how I spoiled their mushroom party. Why did I start telling you about it? Oh, yes. It was about me never finding it easy to be in the world. Well, it isn't, I tell you. That hunchback will suddenly jump up on to my breast and strangle me. I don't even have to eat any sort of mushroom any more. I simply have to wake up in the dead of night and I know that it'll happen one day. Death will come and wring my neck and no one, but no one will save me. Am I delaying you?'

Even now, it strikes Daniel, she might be under the influence of some drug. Maybe that is why she is squeezing his hand. People flee from death. He does too, except that he has chosen a different escape route.

'You're not delaying me. Is that why you came? On account of that anxiety?'

'Among other reasons. Don't be cross with me. My husband calls me hysterical. I am a bit. But only on the odd occasion. Tell me, what sense does it all make?' She finally releases his hand.

'What do you mean?'

'I mean life. The fact that we're here. No, don't tell me it's God's will. That that was the reason my father created me. And why do all those billions and billions of men father more and more children? That can't be God's will, can it? A God like that would have to have a computer in place of a head, except that a computer is incapable of love, so what use would such a God be?'

'Don't bother your head with questions like that. God is beyond our imagination, and so is his will.'

'And you know he exists, even though you can't imagine him, and even though you can't produce convincing proof of his existence?'

'There is so much in the world and the universe that is beyond our imagination, and yet we believe it exists. God is no more understandable than the universe, for instance, and the universe is no more understandable than God.'

'And do you think that's a good thing?'

'No, I wouldn't say so, but that's the way it is.'

'I'll give it some thought. I mustn't bother you with any more questions.'

'It's no bother. People are mostly afraid to ask frank questions.'

She gets up. 'You're not cross with me for taking up your time?'

'I've no reason to be.'

'Don't be so polite.' She shakes his hand.

'Did you come by car?'

'No, the car's my husband's. It was only when he took the firm's car on that trip that I had the use of the little Japanese one. I mostly travel by bus and tram.'

'If you'll permit me I'll drop you home. I owe you a long drive, don't forget.'

'You don't owe me a thing,' she says. 'On the contrary. You had the patience to listen to my hysterical questions.'

There is a flower stall at the tram stop. He pulls up and without even switching off the engine he goes and chooses three dark-red roses and returns to the car. 'Where do you live in Hanspaulka?'

'You still remember? At Baba, of course. But you only need to drop me at the bus stop. It will be better that way.' In the car she asks, 'Do you think I might be allowed to come and bother you again some time?'

He replies that if she finds it of some benefit, then of course she may.

'Thank you. And tell me also when it would be the least bother to you.'

'Come some day. Whenever it suits you.'

'Some time means never.'

'Monday week?'

'Yes, Monday's a good day. My husband usually has a meeting in the afternoon. At what time?'

'Whatever suits you.'

'Two o'clock, say,' she suggests. 'I oughtn't to accept them from you,' she says as he hands her the roses.

'I don't mean anything by it. It was just that – I had a kind of feeling of empathy when you were talking about your anxiety.'

'It's a long time since anyone gave me roses.' She leans towards him and gives him a quick kiss. 'Thank you. And don't forsake me!'

2

Diary excerpts

Petr brought the sister of one of his former gypsy fellow prisoners to the youth meeting. Her name is Marika and she must be about sixteen, although she looks at least twenty. She said almost nothing at the first meeting and she looked more at the floor than at the others. But when we started to sing she quickly caught the melody and sang without a single mistake, even though her voice sounded – I'm not sure how to put it – perhaps 'wild' might be the most accurate way to describe it.

I was apprehensive about how the others would take to her, but they treated her with consideration and praised her singing. When we were saying goodbye, young Kodet told her we looked forward to her coming again. I asked her how she felt about being with us and she said: fine.

Something has happened that I find impossible to comprehend or rather to accept. The moment Mrs Musilová walked in the door I became aware of an odd sense of anticipation that had nothing at all to do with the service or my vocation. I watched her sit down and my agitation grew. I said to myself: a black and white butterfly or moth. A death's head hawk moth. I bought her roses. Out of sympathy or in an effort to attract her attention? Or did I merely want to prove to myself that I could now scatter flowers all around me?

I have never been unfaithful, not in the real physical sense, at least. But unfaithful in spirit? I've tried to avoid that too, although I can't deny there have occasionally been other women I have found attractive. And seductive. There's Mrs Ivana Pokorná who has been attending our church for more than ten years now. I remember when she first entered the church I was bowled over by her appearance: there was something pure, spiritual and open about her, and the first time I spoke with her I was captivated by her voice.

I never touched her, but for several months I had the impression I was writing my sermon especially for her, and while I was preaching, I kept looking at the place where she was sitting. Worst of all, I had the feeling she found me attractive too, that she spoke differently to me than to other people. It's possible that someone else in my position would not have resisted. Was it my faith that prevented me? Or my position? Or quite simply the conviction that it would be unfair and mean to deceive Hana? I didn't try to embrace her, although I did several times in my dreams. I even dreamed of going to bed with her. When I awoke I felt ashamed, as if I had been in control of my own dreams. But then, what do dreams depict, apart from our hidden desires or anxieties?

And then there are day-dreams and the subconscious. A few days ago, when I started to carve the face of a new figure, I was surprised at the form it took. A narrow oblong face with sensuous lips, eyes set far apart, a high, backward-sloping forehead, a nose whose ridge was so straight it reminded me of the Cnidian Aphrodite. (In his Dialogues, Lucian calls this statue, which I only know from reproductions, 'the expression of perfect beauty'.) I was amazed to discover that the face did not resemble the faces of my previous figures; the features were those of the woman architect who had come to seek advice about love and when she left had made such an unusual request: Don't forsake me!

Eva is oddly dreamy. During our evening singing, she either remains silent or joins in as if her mind was elsewhere. She says she has to study for the leaving exam and indeed every evening when I enter her room she has a textbook open in front of her. But today I noticed that she was on the same page as yesterday.

She wore the sweater I gave her for several days and then stopped wearing it. It occurred to me to ask why. She blushed and said she'd lost it.

Where?

At school. In the gym.

I felt she was concealing something, but then I was ashamed of myself. She wouldn't do anything like that, would she? And since then we've not mentioned it.

Twelve billion light years, Marek said the other day. Does it ever occur to him how unimaginable that expanse of time is compared with the fraction of time we are on this earth? And two thousand years ago, a wonder happened: God sent his only son, part of himself. He delivered himself up to people. So long ago, so recently. A miracle on the scale of the universe or only here on a human scale? But in what proportion to eternity is our dimension? Are we dreaming a dream about God, who is eternal, or are we, on the contrary, his dream and therefore do not exist at all?

Marek wants to get to the bottom of time. Not through meditation or contemplation, but by means of observation. He and Alois have completed their telescope. It looks like a little anti-tank weapon or bazooka, but the boys are thrilled. Alois just loves model-making. He has several model planes on top of his wardrobe already, along with a model of the Apollo spacecraft. He impresses Marek. Both of them are more interested in things that are connected with matter than with the spirit. It is probably something to do with their age, although I recall that when I was fourteen I was buried in books. I even regarded mountain climbing as something that took one's mind off material considerations.

I cannot deny Marek's meditative spirit but at the same time he has a tendency to make snap judgements and he also displays excessive self-confidence. Once when he was barely eight years old I came upon him in the bathroom with a look of concentration on his face holding a watch in his hand. I asked him what he was doing.

He explained to me that he had filled the hand basin with hot water and submerged a glass of cold water in it. Now he was measuring how long it would take for the water in the glass to warm up.

I praised his inquisitiveness and he informed me that as soon as he had calculated it, he would send his results to the newspaper. Why to the newspaper, I was curious to know.

So that everyone should know about it.

I told him that his experiment was admittedly interesting but that the newspapers only wrote about big and important experiments.

But this is a big experiment, he objected. Not everyone's going to think of it.

More recently he has wavered between astronomy and ecology. He wants to know what I think about nuclear power stations, the hole in the ozone layer and the greenhouse effect. He is of the view that we oughtn't to buy anything in plastic packaging and that there is no need to have lights on in church. He protested when I told him of my intention to buy a new car.

I told him I'd hardly use the car, but that I needed it from time to time, for example, those Sundays when I have two services in close succession.

So don't have them in close succession, was his advice.

But I shouldn't just write about him critically. He goes with Alois to visit Fyodor. I asked him why he does it. 'He hasn't got anybody else,' he explained. The operation was successful apparently and Fyodor is happy. He was afraid he would be a cripple.

'Tell me, please, what's the Russian for cripple?' I asked.

'Kripel, of course,' he said, with his usual assuredness.

I went to check in the big Russian dictionary. The word doesn't exist in that language.

———— ❦ ————

At the theological faculty, most of my fellow students came from families with a Protestant tradition. Often they would be children of clergy.

In our home, Dad put up with Mum's faith because he was tolerant, but he made it plain that God was simply a human invention: man created God and not the other way round.

A lot of what my fellow students took for granted I had to figure out for myself. I would often obstinately silence within me Dad's sceptical voice. Anyway, I was never able to summon up interest in a range of questions that for centuries had agitated the Fathers of the Church and – to my astonishment – a number of my contemporaries. What point was there in arguing over whether fallen angels could atone for their guilt, whether mortality was a consequence of original sin, or whether man was subject to a single or a double judgement: judgement of the body and of the soul?

What excited me most of all was the figure of Jesus and his revolutionary message. At one time – I was barely twenty – I was determined to write a book about Jesus and started to seek out literature and study it. I was astounded at the amount of material written on the subject. The handful of facts recorded by the evangelists had given rise to thousands of parallel and quite contradictory interpretations. According to some, Jesus was God; according to others he had a dual nature and was therefore God-man. Some regarded him as a man, but endowed with a prophetic spirit; according to others, he was a messiah, or a leader of an ascetic religious sect, or alternatively a Jewish rebel. And of course I also read elsewhere that he did not live at all, or that the gospels had merged two different figures into one.

I perceived that I would not be capable of writing a real portrait of Jesus – nobody had yet and nobody ever would – and that the books I was reading told me more about their authors than about the subject matter. Only later did I realize that this was the fate of all books and films that try to deal with a real person. The essence of another person is unfathomable, and even more so when it is the Son of God, about whom information is not only fragmentary but also affected by prejudice, superstition or outdated beliefs.

For me in my younger years, belief was chiefly an alternative to the depressing lifestyle which then prevailed, an alternative to the miserable planned 'happiness' that depended solely on the number of things one could or was allowed to own. In the Bible I found passages that resonated with my own feelings and that filled me with satisfaction and helped me dispel my doubts and scepticism about its message.

When I informed Dad that I wanted to study at the theological faculty, he was stupefied. Then he asked me if I had given it proper thought. 'Yes,' I replied.

'If that's your decision,' is all he could say. But he went on to add that *it was necessary to weigh up one's decisions very carefully, but once one had taken them it was necessary to follow them through to their conclusion.*

I told him that it went without saying.

I went to a lecture by a German psychologist on 'Esoterica and Reincarnation'. In it he maintained that, according to the law of rhythm, which is the fundamental law of the universe, death alternates with life in the same way that waking and sleeping do – being alive and being dead are just two poles of the unbroken stream of life. So death was not unbeing but the opposite pole from being. When you die, you cross the boundary between two worlds, this one and the next. For the person who enters the next world, the next world becomes this world and our world becomes the next world for him until such a time as he again returns to it. Birth, the arrival in our world and hence the departure from that other, astral world, is regarded there as death. The speaker deduced that the soul brought with it from past lives a hidden memory and a knowledge which in this world takes the form of talent or curiosity. The lecturer talked of experiments in which patients had apparently been induced to recall not only what they had felt in their mother's womb, but also the life of their soul in the other world before their latest reincarnation. He even went so far as to speculate on the probable length of time between successive incarnations (apparently the period is getting shorter all the time and now lasts scarcely ten years) and whether a change of sex is possible in the process.

While I try to keep an open mind as regards the fate of the human soul during this life and after it, and am fully aware that Scripture expects not only the return of Jesus Christ but even of the Prophet Elijah, and that we all believe in the resurrection of the body, which assumes the continued existence of the soul beyond our world, I couldn't rid myself of the unpleasant feeling that I was listening to a charlatan.

I pray badly. I'm not talking about the prayers that I say aloud during services, but about the silent prayers in which I speak to God on my own behalf. I am incapable of being intimate even with Him. I remain silent about the most important things: my anxieties, my suppressed longings, my backsliding.

I do likewise in these notes. I am afraid that one day if someone reads them (although it's most unlikely; Dad left heaps of official bumf and notes – I brought home two full boxes when Mum died. I haven't opened them yet and I don't know if I ever will) they'll say to themselves: didn't anything bother him, did nothing drive him to despair, were there no moments when he was scared of nothingness and his vain attempts to elude it?

I mentioned to Martin my inability to be intimate enough in my prayers. 'That's something I'm aware of,' he said, 'all too well aware of, in fact. But prayer is itself a deeper level of intimacy.'

'What level?' I asked.

'At least the second,' he said and laughed.

'And which is the first?'

He reflected. 'When you tell your wife your dreams, say. Even the very intimate ones.'

I don't tell Hana my dreams. At best I write them in this notebook. I am at the first level of intimacy with my diary.

A dream about my mother. She was already old and infirm. She was lying in bed and I was sitting by her. Suddenly she said, I have to tell you something, Dan.

Go ahead, Mummy.

I've not told anyone about this, she said. Then she asked if I remembered how they had once built a new road not far from our cottage. I said I did. (We never lived in a cottage and no such road was ever built.) And did I still remember that young architect who lodged with us in that cottage? I didn't. It was when they sent Dad to prison, she insisted. I told her I now remembered.

He didn't want to live in a trailer, Mum explained, and the money came in handy, as it was already Dad's second year in prison. I took him in even though I knew that people would start rumours. He wasn't particularly young, but he was a fine man. He had eyes like the gamekeeper who seduced Viktoria. And so I had an affair with him, Dan. You know Dad got ten years, don't you? It never occurred to me he'd be released earlier. I used to write to him and send parcels, and *when they allowed visits I used to travel to see him. But I committed a sin, all the same. And I never told him about it.*

He'd forgive you, Mummy, I said in dismay, and the Lord will forgive you too.

He left anyway – that architect. He moved away six months later, and he wrote to me afterwards but I burned the letters.

Don't distress yourself, Mummy. You know what Christ said to those who brought him the woman caught in adultery and wanted to stone her? He said: Let he who is without sin cast the first stone. And when they heard this they left one by one. And then he asked her: Where are they who condemned you? Has no one condemned you? And she replied, No one, Lord. And what did our Lord say to her? Then neither do I condemn you. Go, and sin no more!

A peculiar dream. Was it about Mum or rather about me? How did that profession come into it: architect? Is it possible to go through life without betraying trust at least once? That's why he said: 'Then neither do I condemn you.'

3

Eva did fairly well in her leaving exams, but none the less Daniel had the feeling that she was changed somehow: dispirited, or more exactly, remote from everything around her.

'Glad you've got it over with?' he asked when she brought him the results.

'I suppose so.' She was due to start studying at the Conservatoire in the autumn. Then she added: 'It means you've got something behind you and something ahead of you. At least you know the thing you left behind.'

'And you're afraid of what you don't know?'

'No, I'm not afraid. I just don't know whether I'm looking forward to it.'

'That's just because you're tired out.'

She looked at him and said, 'I'm not tired out, Daddy. I just don't have anything to look forward to.'

'You'll have moments like that in your life. And afterwards you'll feel quite differently again.'

'Do you look forward to anything?'

'Of course. To seeing all of you, when we come together again this evening. To meeting people I like. To the things I have yet to discover in my life.'

'Yes,' she admitted, 'I do too.'

Early that evening, just as they were about to sit down to dinner, Petr arrived with an enormous bunch of roses for Eva.

'Petr, you're crazy. All these roses? We don't even have a vase big enough.'

'I was given them. When I told Mr Houdek they were for you.'

Petr had been working at Houdek's garden centre for four weeks now and he seemed to be enjoying the work. 'And I've got this too,' he said, taking from his pocket something wrapped in paper. 'I tried to make it for you.'

Eva took the gift and blushed. Wrapped in the paper was a little dove cut out of copper and hung on a leather thong.

'She only got one B,' Marek boasted on her behalf.

'If I were to have a leaving certificate,' Petr said, in an effort to speak grammatically, 'I would be in quite a different situation.'

'Exams are not all that important, Petr,' Hana said. 'It's possible to be a useful person without going to university.'

'What sort of job will they let you do these days without university? The best you can hope for is what I'm doing now. Sitting behind a wheel.'

'What would you like to do?' Eva asked.

'Preach. I'd like to tell people how terrible it is when they don't know Jesus and his love, when they land up in Satan's power. Do you know, Reverend, I caught a glimpse of him going by yesterday.'

'Of whom?'

'He was terribly tall, even taller than you. He had ginger hair like Alois. All of a sudden he appeared on the street when I was on the way to my sister's. Just under the bridge in Nusle, if you know where I mean. And he said to me: I know you from somewhere, pal. I never saw him in my life, Reverend. I remember everyone I ever met and I wouldn't have forgotten him, because he had a tattoo on his neck and stank like a kipper.'

'What did you say to him?' Eva asked with interest.

'I told him I didn't know him, and he starts to laugh and says: 'Peter, Peter, you may have denied the Lord Jesus, but you can't deny me.'

'He said that to you?' Daniel said, displeased with the story.

'On my oath, Reverend.'

'Save your oaths for something more important, Petr!'

'That was important for me, Reverend. The point is he asked me to go with him, saying he had a job for me, and if I didn't, I'd regret it. And I said to him: Get behind me, Satan, you monster from hell. And he laughs again. Then all of a sudden he wasn't there. Really, I swear it, Reverend. The pavement was all dug up for some pipes or other, so I even looked to see if he hadn't fallen down some hole. But he wasn't anywhere.'

Daniel noticed that Hana had followed Petr's story about Satan with interest. It matched her own worst experience. Perhaps that was why he commented, 'All sorts of strange things happen and sometimes it's difficult to find a rational explanation, but I wouldn't say you really met the devil.'

'So who was it, then?'

'Someone who'd heard about you from someone else, maybe.'

'And where did he disappear to?'

'I don't know, I wasn't there. Maybe he had a car parked nearby and got into it without you noticing.'

'Reverend, you forget where I've just come from. A real con has eyes in the back of his head, so I'd hardly miss someone climbing into an old banger right alongside me.'

'All right,' said Daniel, 'and you hadn't just happened to have had a few drinks?'

'Even if I had, I know what I saw. And I woke up in the middle of the night and it was as if someone was walking around the bedroom. So I switched the light on. There was nobody there, only I could smell that stink of kippers. And my shirt and trousers that I put on the chair the night before were lying all tangled on the floor. You may think that I dreamed it all up, Reverend, but I'd really love to preach to people about the danger they're in. Because I've seen it. I've seen it when someone's on a trip and he's in such a mess he thinks he won't find the way back, and how he's weak as water when he's coming out of it. I know what it is when someone has a wild beast inside them that just wants to booze, stuff itself with food and leap on a woman. The stuff they show on the telly, all them horror films and the cops and robbers – they're only fairy stories to frighten little children, even when they show someone eating a human liver. And I've seen someone do that too, but for real.'

The children – and Eva, in particular – were following what Petr said with almost too much attention. Daniel wasn't sure it was a good thing. He ought to send Magda off somewhere, at least.

Petr was a good speaker and there was no doubt he would be capable of winning people over to his ideas or plans. He'd proved that in the past, when he had been intent on doing evil, and he would no doubt be just as capable of doing it now – now that he had decided to do something useful, now that he had been given grace, as he hoped, to do so.

This gift should not be wasted. Nor should it be abused by people who might think they could use Petr to serve their own ends.

'We'll see, Petr,' he said, interrupting his preaching about evil. 'We'll find some way for you to tell people what you want to tell them. It might even be possible to fix something up with the schools.'

'Thank you, Reverend. But I didn't mean us to talk about me when we're celebrating Eva's exams.'

They all sat down to dinner together. In the middle of the table, in a five-litre gherkin jar, the fifteen roses gave off their scent. Eva hung the little dove around her neck and appeared at that moment contented, even happy.

4

Samuel

Samuel is leaving for Brno in the early evening to attend an important meeting first thing in the morning. There is a multimillion-crown sports complex project up for tender. There are always plenty of people interested in a contract like that, so if you don't take the initiative and aren't ready to pay 'a broker', then it's your own bad luck. For that reason, he needs to meet in advance at least some of the people who will be involved in the decision on the contract. Samuel is going reluctantly. He finds bribery distasteful and humiliating, and he begrudges the money, even though he knows he will make a good return on it. Moreover, he has not enjoyed travelling lately. It takes up too much time and exhausts him. Apart from that, he has to leave Bára in Prague and he knows her well enough to imagine what she'll do with her time the moment she's sure she won't bump into him wherever she goes and whatever she does with the one she happens to be with.

At least he is taking with him that architect Vondra who seems to him to flirt shamelessly with Bára. Samuel justifies taking him on the grounds that Vondra is a Moravian and knows the officials they will be dealing with. He is also taking his secretary Ljuba, both because she is capable and because he finds her attractive.

As always, Bára packs his overnight case carefully and goes out with him to the car. She gives him a hug and a kiss. Neither the kiss nor the hug have the warmth he used to feel. And she doesn't even put on a very good show of being sorry he is leaving, despite the fact that acting is her second profession. She cannot completely conceal her pleasure at getting rid of him for a short while at least. Samuel starts the car and takes a last look; Bára is standing on the edge of the footpath waving to him. She is still beautiful, she's tall and statuesque, and for a moment he feels a sharp pang of regret for something that is irrevocably lost, and sorry for himself that his life is constantly taking a different turn from the one he had imagined.

At the office he picks up the papers he needs and it occurs to him to ring home to see whether Bára picks up the phone, but he decides against it. Not because he would feel abashed but because he fears there would be no reply and the uncertainty – or rather the certainty – would play on his mind so much that he would be unable to concentrate on the negotiations.

He sits Ljuba next to him. She exudes a Gabriela Sabatini perfume (which he had also bought Bára) and youthfulness.

Once on the motorway, Ljuba tries to recount to him the latest episode of *M.A.S.H.* She wants to please him and has no inkling that he can think of few things that are a greater waste of time than listening to an account of a TV programme. Ljuba then proceeds to impart some bits of news, or rather gossip, about goings-on in the office – Samuel really couldn't care which of his staff are going out together, sleeping together, speaking together, or not speaking together. With one exception, of course: and about his wife no one will ever say a word, naturally, even if everyone knows what he doesn't, and might never know.

Vondra, for his part, talks about New York and Boston where he recently spent a whole month. He tells them about the musical, *Cats*, giving a passable rendition of Andrew Lloyd Webber's feline hit about the moon, before relating with considerable enthusiasm a meeting of the Krishna Consciousness Society. He learnt that in the next life, the sort of body people will receive will depend on the way they have lived in their previous incarnation. They could become demi-gods of which there are 33 million, or they could be born as a cat or as a pig and consume their own excrement. Our body is apparently like a bubble that forms on the surface of the water. In a while it bursts and is never seen again. Our soul simply moves from one bubble to another and we stupidly believe it to be the source of our happiness.

'What is the source of happiness, then?' Ljuba wants to know. She, no doubt, dreams of it like all women.

'Coalescence,' Vondra explains. 'Coalescence with Krishna. He's the Supreme Personality of Godhead, the incarnation of absolute truth.'

'Coalescence doesn't appeal to me,' Ljuba says.

Vondra assures her that she won't coalesce, but will definitely turn into some goddess when she dies. A goddess of love and beauty, naturally.

Samuel finds this sort of talk repellent. Young people nowadays have a tendency to make light of things beyond their comprehension, of anything they can't buy or misappropriate in some way.

But Vondra is winding up the topic anyway. 'If you're interested,' he turns once more to Ljuba, 'the Krishna people are supposed to be here in our country too. They could explain it to you much better than me.' And he turns to a subject he knows more about. With a certain disdain he talks about the work of the avant-garde, those intellectual Bolsheviks who fled to the States from Europe in the thirties and changed the face of most American city centres (Vondra actually uses the word 'downtowns'), and New York in particular. In his view, it was a baleful influence and transformed every major American city into one big cemetery with monumental concrete tombs poking up out of them. No, tombs is not the right word, because a tomb tends to be decorated at least, and have a dove or an angel, whereas these are more like gigantic gravestones: in place of carved letters, windows that don't open; in place of angels, television aerials.

One of the reasons why he is saying all this is to impress Ljuba, of course, but it is mainly to pique Samuel. Vondra knows he was a supporter of the avant-garde and that he strove, even in the worst times, to preserve and defend something of their principles.

Samuel could wipe the floor with the young know-all. He could draw his attention to dozens of buildings around the world where the avant-garde proved its prowess, but he doesn't feel like arguing, he doesn't feel like talking at all, in fact. He can feel one of his depressions coming on, and he is beginning to get a headache. He ought to take a tablet, but they are in his bag and his bag is behind him in the boot. He starts to drive faster, not because he is in a hurry, but more out of edginess or a desire to leave behind all that talk, that clichéd meandering from Broadway musical to transmigration of souls, and from incarnation to the Bauhaus.

It is possible to chatter away about all and sundry in the course of a single car journey, express a view on every topic, throw cold water on everything and feel high and mighty. In reality it's all much more complicated and mysterious, both life and death. How many times has he found himself in a place he has never visited before in his life and yet has known precisely what he is going to see! He was walking along a street towards the Herengracht in Amsterdam and all of a sudden he realized that if he were to cross the street and pass through the entrance of one of the buildings he would find a flea market there. How could he have known this, seeing this was his first visit to Amsterdam and nobody had ever spoken to him about a hidden flea market? Why was he born on the first of September like Dietzenhofer? In fact, the first time he came across his portrait in some book and pictured the face without the period wig with its artificial curls, he had marvelled at his resemblance to him. And when he first met Bára, her face seemed ominously familiar. He just didn't know – and only on that point was his prescience or memory hazy – whether it was a good or a bad omen.

As he approaches Jihlava, he recalls how at one time – as if in some other life – he used to hitch-hike to Bratislava to visit his first wife. Scarcely anyone would have imagined a motorway in those days, just as no one would have dreamt that the Republic would break up and Bratislava would be a foreign city. There were fewer cars then, of course, but they used to stop and he would often reach Bratislava more quickly than by train. He remembers making love all those years ago, the passionate embraces and then the sudden despair when he discovered he was no longer loved, no longer desired. And he lost his first daughter Linda before really getting to know her. Not long ago, about six months in fact, she called to see him in Prague. Not just a stranger, but actually a foreigner now. He hardly recognized her at first, but then he realized she had become more like him. Strange. And she called him *otecko*, Dad, in Slovak. That was strange too. He had not seen his second daughter Lída for a number of years and had met her husband only twice, maybe three times. They don't live in Prague. Two of his families have broken up and he didn't have the time, or the inclination maybe, to hold on to the children. And his third and last family? It is only self-deception, force of habit or lack of courage not to declare broken something that wrecked itself a long time ago. Nothing in life lasts. Life itself only lasts a moment – a bubble on the water – and it's curious how even for that moment one is incapable of maintaining some deeper feeling, loyalty or devotion. Maybe this depressing state of affairs is also affected by the general state of things. After all, there have been so many turbulent changes in the life of this country that spreads out each side of the motorway. The rich became poor and the poor rich, the powerful lost their power and sometimes their lives, and others took their place. Splendid old buildings fell into rack and ruin and ugly new ones were built. Everything took place at such a frenzied pace, in a mad dance, or a dance of madmen. One either joined in or fell out of the circle and straight into the abyss at whose brink the dance was held.

He didn't join in. He merely adjusted to it slightly, as a result of which he was able to create works that received recognition, and definitely much greater recognition than he receives now that young vultures are circling around devoid of scruples and intent on only one thing: making a fast buck. They will all end up in the next life as wild pigs, or tigers, more likely. A rather ludicrous and naive thought. Worse still, he is touching sixty. He is not as flexible as he used to be and he realizes he can't take the pace for much longer.

They skirt Velké Meziříčí. He once had a date here with his first wife, Katarína. They slept together in a little hotel on the square. Accommodation was so ludicrously cheap in those days, as was the price of a meal, although his salary had been ludicrously small too. But everything lay ahead of him then: all the projects, all the important buildings, the many journeys, the foreign countries, the interesting encounters, conferences, lectures, articles, receptions, recognition and conflict, not to mention two divorces, two more marriages and parenthood – he never seemed to find much time for the children, though he wasn't really such a bad father. Suddenly he is seized by an unexpected regret for times gone by, for his past life and even the old order

110

of things which, while he didn't like it and didn't think it was right, he had grown accustomed to, learning to manoeuvre and even excel in it; regret for his youth and his life as it gradually draws to its close. What is left for him? Scrabbling for contracts and offering bribes, because money means more than his name, his skills or his experience.

Besides, every new contract takes him nearer to the last one he'll ever receive, and to his own end. What sort of life has he had, really? What would his next rebirth be like, if something of the sort could happen in the mysterious order of life?

Out of the blue, the young vulture Vondra asks what sort of commission they should offer. Vondra thinks at least 13 per cent of the price. This strikes Samuel as excessive; it's shameless to demand several hundred thousand for nothing and therefore stupid and immoral to offer so much. But Vondra believes that everyone will offer 10 per cent and if they want to win it they will have to be generous. Generously immoral, he adds, and makes Ljuba laugh.

But no one will be offering a design like ours, Samuel points out. Vondra agrees, but the ones who will be taking the decision don't care about the quality of the design, only about their commission. That's the way it usually goes, and if things turn out differently, then so much the better.

They reach the Hotel Kontinental almost an hour before they are due to meet with the chairman of the sports club that is investing in the complex. Samuel takes leave of his travelling companions for a short while. The two of them go off together. They each have their own rooms but will most likely sleep together. A tiger and a pussy cat. He prefers not to think about such matters any more. He and Bára hardly ever make love now, and he fears other women because of AIDS and potentially emotional entanglements.

In his room, which is fairly luxurious, he removes the plans from his overnight case and looks them over once more to assure himself that they are original and interesting. The suspended cable construction of the roof might seem unnecessary for a small complex, but it creates a sense of vastness, of loftiness and originality. People yearn for originality. And even though it is no longer possible to come up with anything unique, there is no harm in a little surprise. He folds up the plans again. The time drags. There is still time for him to shower and change. He could even stretch out for a while.

There is a telephone on the bedside table. He ought to call home as

111

he always used to do whenever he went on a trip, and Bára would take it as an expression of love and concern. Now, though, she would think he was checking up on her and regard it as an expression of his jealousy and lack of trust. That's if she is at home and answers the telephone. Except that she's not at home at all, or if she is, she's not on her own; the phone won't give him any clue to the identity of her visitor anyway. She could be sitting on her lover's knee and begging Samuel down the phone to come home as soon as he can because she misses him so, and is afraid to be home on her own. Even a very bad actress can manage that. He suppresses an urge to get in the car and drive off home. Instead he takes a tablet of Imigran for his headache and another red capsule of Prothiaden. Then he goes down to the lobby and orders a glass of mineral water, since he can't mix the pills with alcohol, and with a sense of total desolation he awaits the arrival of those he is to bargain with, as well as those he is to bribe.

5

Daniel noticed that Eva was downcast rather than elated when she returned from her school-leavers' party. He felt like doing something to raise his eldest child's spirits. 'What would you say,' it occurred to him, 'if we were to go off on a trip somewhere together, now that you are an adult?'

'Just the two of us?'

'Just the two of us for once – that's if you could put up with my company.'

'We've never done anything like that before.'

'Maybe when you were very small. We might have been left on our own, but you wouldn't remember that.'

'And where would we go?'

'I was thinking maybe about the Prachov Rocks. It's beautiful there.'

'You and Mummy used to go climbing there, didn't you?'

'Yes. In fact something happened there that concerns you.'

'What was that?'

'Mummy and I were camping there exactly nine months before you were born.'

'I see. Do you think you'd still find the spot?'

'Definitely, although I've not been there since.'
'But I couldn't manage to climb the rocks.'
'We won't climb them. With my back I wouldn't go climbing anyway.'

Daniel found the spot easily – on a raised level area away from the Emperor's Passages and the other tourist trails. Several birch trees and two tall bushy larches pointed skywards, the colour of the leaves and grass were both soothing and hopefully spring-like. In the middle of a patch of sand were the traces of an old camp-fire. And on all sides there was a view of the many rock pillars, sheer rock faces and rock passages.
'Did you make a fire here?'
'I think so, but I expect there have been lots of other camp-fires here since.'
'Did Mummy enjoy rock climbing?'
'We both did. There was a good crowd of us. We even went abroad together, to Yugoslavia. It was still one country then and it was easier to get there than to the Alps. We climbed Bobotuv Kuk and several other rocks on Durmitor. I got stuck in a chimney there and I suddenly had the feeling I couldn't go up or down.'
'What did you do? Did you pray?'
'No, I certainly didn't. I was never one to believe that the Lord is there to help us out of sticky spots. Mummy was with me, or rather below me, and that helped me to keep my calm. In the end I climbed out like everyone else.'
'Was Mummy a good climber?'
'We all had to be, or we would never have reached the top together. Your Mummy had a very special affinity for the mountains. She used to say that rocks were ancient giants turned to stone who definitely lived once upon a time.'
'Did you try to talk her out of it?'
'Why should I have? Maybe she was right. Maybe they're still alive, but we are just unaware of their life because it takes place in a different dimension of time.'
'Daddy, you'd never say that in a sermon.'
'I suppose not,' he conceded. 'But it's a mistake.' Then he showed her some of the nearby rocks that he had either climbed or attempted to climb in vain, as well as some of the rocks her mother had scaled.
'I wouldn't manage that; Mummy must have been good.' Then she

added, 'It seems odd to me to be talking about her as my mum, seeing that I never saw her, that I don't recall seeing her.'

'But she can see you all the time.'

'Do you really think so?'

'Don't you?'

'I just can't imagine it: I can't imagine her seeing me without me seeing her.'

'I expect it's a different kind of seeing. It's beyond our imagination. But she's bound to be pleased with you.'

He looked towards one of the larches where the little blue tent stood. The blue had faded with time, the warmth had long ago evaporated from it and the canvas had gradually turned to tatters, like his memories. A lump came to his throat.

'No,' Eva blurted out, 'she can't be pleased if she sees everything. She's most likely weeping.'

'What makes you say such things?'

'Oh, nothing.' Eva resembled her mother in hair colour, figure and facial features. If he squinted slightly he could actually imagine it was his first wife standing there, untouched by time, that she had vaulted the abyss of years and just stepped out of the tent and was listening to the calm of the rocks. He ought to ask her what her 'Oh, nothing' concealed but he was strangely shy of his daughter.

'Shall I unpack the food?' she asked.

'OK.'

They sat down on a sun-warmed boulder and ate their bread.

'How did you and Mummy first meet?' she asked.

'It wasn't here. But it was on a climbing holiday. In the Tatras. I was already a vicar in Kamenice then. They used to call me "the climbing clergyman". Mummy was still studying at the Conservatoire. I found her very attractive.'

'But you waited a long time before you married.'

'We scarcely had time to see each other. She was studying in Prague and I was out in the Moravian Highlands. We used to meet a couple of times a month. We used to hitch-hike to get to see each other. We were poor.'

'If you'd got married, though, you could have been together earlier.'

'But Mummy had to finish her studies. But we spent longer together in the summer. When we first met, Mummy was just a bit older than you are now. She didn't say much, she sang beautifully, was a marvellous pianist and was nearly always smiling. With her eyes more than with her lips.'

'Maybe she only smiled like that at you.'

'We were in love,' he said, 'from the moment we met. How about you,' it occurred to him, 'have you fallen in love yet?'

'You're not serious, Daddy?'

'Yes I am. It's occurred to me on several occasions, but I've not wanted to ask.'

'I've fallen in love lots of times.'

'Lots?'

'But they didn't know about it. Those boys.'

'Not one of them knew about it?'

'Maybe one of them. Or two.'

'And where were they from?'

'From my class, some of them, or I knew them from St Saviour's. And I went to the Pentecostals a couple of times.'

'You didn't tell me.'

'I was afraid you'd be cross. Petr and I went to their youth meeting the other day.'

'Petr went?'

'He was awfully interested in them, so I took him. He was really mad about them. He told them about a feeling he had had of something coming down on him, that he couldn't describe. It was at night. He woke up and saw a strange light coming straight at him. He couldn't explain it, and then he realized that it could be the Holy Ghost.'

'An experience like that and he didn't even mention it to me.'

'You see, Dad, we think – he thinks,' she corrected herself, 'that you'd most likely start to talk him out of it.'

'I expect I would.' It struck him that Petr's experience of life had taught him how to speak in different situations in a way that gained him attention, recognition or even admiration.

'But something has really happened to him, Daddy. If only you could hear the way he talks about the way he used to live and how he has changed. Everyone listened to him with excitement. And at the end they asked him to say a prayer for everyone. And the way he prayed gave us all the shivers.'

'That's fine. So long as he prays sincerely, it's all right.'

'How else would he pray?'

'People can pray for all sorts of reasons, but I don't want to suspect him of anything.'

'He's interested in everything he's not experienced so far. He'd like to hear the Adventists and the Jehovah's Witnesses.'

'And you'd go with him?'

She shrugged. 'Surely there's nothing wrong with us wanting to know what other people believe, is there?'

'No, of course not.' Then he asked: 'Do you fancy Petr?'

She blushed and shook her head violently. 'It's not like that. I just find there's something special about him. He's completely different from the other boys.'

'That's for sure. Just think it over carefully, before falling in love with him.'

As if something like that could be thought over carefully.

6

Bára

Bára feels an unexpected flood of happiness. Samuel has gone off to Moravia for one of his business deals and is staying there overnight, so she has the whole evening free. She packed Samuel's overnight case, forgetting nothing, not even a single jar of tablets, and then accompanied her husband to the car. She hugged and kissed him, Samuel started the car and she finally waved him goodbye before going to phone her old college friend Helena and arranging to see her that evening. She takes Aleš over to her mother's, finishes a set design for a television adaptation of an Italian comedy – it's interesting how easy she finds the work when there's no one around clamouring for her attention.

Towards evening, she quickly gets dressed, putting on a white blouse and a long dark-green skirt – the colour goes well with her hair. She ties up her hair, which hangs halfway down her back, with a black ribbon, applies a bit of eye make-up, dons a straw hat, and sets off for town.

She is not due to meet Helena for another hour. She takes the bus to Dejvice and then the metro to the Small Quarter. She walks along Wallenstein Street and across Wallenstein Square. Everywhere teems with tourists, but she doesn't notice them. She notes with satisfaction that several houses in Thomas Street have been recently done up: the city of her birth is donning new clothes.

Then she walks up Neruda Street and on up as far as the Castle, where she notices she is already out of breath – she ought to cut down on her smoking, it's an awful habit. She then leans on the low stone wall that forms the eastern side of Hradčany Square and gazes at the city below. She is overcome with a spirit of generosity: she forgives those who have disfigured the city with the prefabricated grey of human rabbit coops, she forgives her husband who contributed several degenerate architectural monstrosities towards the general devastation, and it occurs to her that the beauty of her city as it was built up layer by layer over the centuries cannot be banished; maybe only a nuclear catastrophe could destroy it.

When at last she turns away from this elevated spectacle, she notices to her surprise that the telephone booth on the square is empty. She is seized by a sudden longing for an amorous conversation. She has lived so long without real love and has really experienced so little of it in her life. She goes over to the phone booth. She remembers the number although she has only called it once – she was a long time making up her mind on that occasion.

The minister's wife answers the phone, of course. Bára could hang up without saying anything or she could say that she wanted to speak to the minister, but instead she asks, 'Is that the television centre?'

'No, this is a Protestant manse.'

'That's silly. I need the television centre.'

'I expect you dialled the wrong number.'

'But this is the one they gave me!' And she gives the number of the manse. She has to repeat it three times before the woman, whom she only knows from sight at the church, concludes, 'They must have given you the wrong number.'

'It's so silly. I'm calling from a phone booth and there's no telephone directory. You wouldn't happen to know the number of the television centre, would you?'

That kind woman tells her to hold on a moment so that she can have a look in the directory, and Bára finally hangs up.

Half an hour later she is sitting with Helena at a small table in front of the Loreto and sipping something that purports to be vintage wine.

Helena is her age but looks older, having become stout and maternal although she only has one daughter. She has also held on to her first husband, some kind of civil engineer, who is in no way remarkable but earns good money at least.

For a while they chat about their husbands, trying to work out which of them is less self-reliant and more dependent on his wife and they come to the conclusion that those mummy's boys would most likely perish if their wives abandoned them. Bára complains that her husband increasingly neglects her, substituting conversation for sex and severity for tenderness. She only needs to arrive home half an hour later than he expects and he is already threatening to divorce her. Her friend reassures her that it's only talk. Bára is well aware of that, of course. Without her, Samuel would expire from one of his fifty ailments – his eternal migraines, the cramps in his intestines, his muscles, his gall bladder and his kidneys. His painful heart would have beaten its last long ago and he would most likely have taken an overdose or shot himself in one of his fits of total angst-ridden hopelessness. She is the one who keeps him alive, but why should she have to suffer for it beneath the lash of that slave-driver's nagging tongue?

Leave him then?

She can't leave him. She couldn't do that to her little mummy's boy. Nor could she deprive her real child of his home and his dad. She had done it once already and discovered that a new dad never becomes a real father. Poor Saša had already paid dearly for it.

When they have finished the bottle, they get up and set off in the direction of Střešovice. At Ořechovka, they come upon a little wine bar, where they order themselves a tasty snack and just a bottle of ordinary Frankovka this time.

Helena says that her silly ass of a husband doesn't nag. Instead he snivels and is sorry for himself. Sometimes he clears out and tries to get drunk on Smíchov light beer, but he never manages to. He just spends the night running out to piss and the next morning his poor old head aches.

Bára still feels happy. She has a whole free night ahead of her. As she puffs away, she tells her friend all about the pastor who doesn't even know how attractive he looks as he declaims about love from the pulpit. He speaks about the love of Jesus, who wants to forgive and free

118

people from the realm of death, while he obviously longs for ordinary human love. Those lofty phrases are just sublimated desire.

Helena wants to know if they have kissed yet. Bára says only once when they were saying goodbye, and gives the impression they have said goodbye more than once. 'But he's as shy as a little boy and has certain prejudices that such things are not done when the man and the woman are both married – that it is against God's commandments. All the same I get the feeling he is a good lover.'

Bára has aroused her companion's interest. 'It's his vocation that turns you on, isn't it?'

Bára admits this. 'And there's something about him; something totally out of the ordinary.'

'It always feels that way at the beginning.'

'No, not always. Almost never. Most of the time it's obvious at the outset that it'll be the same.' Bára bursts out laughing and then gets up and goes out into the passage. There she notices a public telephone.

This time the pastor himself answers the phone. Maybe his wife is already asleep. 'Daniel,' Bára says in a disguised voice, 'I love you.'

For a moment there is silence at the other end. Then the minister asks who is calling.

'Me, of course, Daniel. Don't you recognize me? That's a pity. I'm really sorry you don't recognize me.' Then she hangs up. She regrets she can't be with that man now, the one whose passion she senses, the one she suspects is a good lover.

When they leave the wine bar, they are both light-headed and jolly. They are not quite sure where they might go now and return to Pohořelec where, in front of the statue of Tycho de Brahe and Kepler, they catch sight of a large nocturnal gathering of tourists. The Germans are either drunk or lost or homesick. Bára cannot fathom how anyone could be homesick for Nuremberg or Hanover in the most beautiful city in the world and decides to raise their spirits a bit. She leans against the plinth of the statue and sings Rusalka's aria to the moon. She sings faultlessly, and astonishingly enough, even out here in the open, her voice sounds loud. When she finishes she passes her straw hat to Helena who does the rounds of the enlivened tourists who richly reward this unexpected experience.

When they turn the corner the two of them laugh long and loud and determine to give the money collected to the Bosnian refugees.

Helena suggests that they might still go back to her flat, as she lives on a housing estate not far away. Bára wants to know what her husband would say, but Helena assures her that he will have fallen asleep long ago and nothing will wake him.

It is already well past midnight when the taxi drops them right in front of the tower block on the seventh floor of which Helena's flat is located. The lift doesn't work so they both walk up the staircase. Bára is quite out of breath but looks forward to the view from the top. From Helena's room there is a good view of Prague, and a panorama of Hradčany all lit up. Bára goes over to the window, draws aside the curtain and gazes at the city which flickers in the mistiness of the small hours. Helena fetches a bottle of Frankovka from the larder and is pouring some into glasses. But Bára doesn't feel like drinking any more, besides which she is afraid of someone bursting into the room and spoiling the rest of the night. She would sooner look at the city, but feels that she is not high enough here, that the surrounding buildings block the view. What if they climbed up to the roof? If her memory serves her right, this type of building has a flat, tiled roof with access.

Helena agrees; there is a bench up there for them to sunbathe on. Marvellous – they'll sunbathe then. So they run up the remaining five staircases, Helena unlocks the iron door and they climb out on the roof. The moon up above them is just one day off being full and the roof is bathed in pale moonlight.

Helena goes over to the bench, but it is still not high enough. The terrace is surrounded on all sides by a waist-high concrete wall in place of a balcony. It is wide enough to climb on to. Bára suggests to Helena that they do so, but her friend is afraid. Beyond the wall looms a chasm and the twelve-storey drop frightens her. Admittedly, Bára has no head for heights, but at this moment it does not deter her – she must climb higher and higher. The moment one stops one's fall really begins.

She grips the wall and swings up on to it. She staggers momentarily but quickly regains her balance. 'Look at the city, rocking like a ship, and those lights above the water. You can keep your Venice and your Amsterdam, this is the most beautiful port in the world.'

'You're like a statue,' her friend comments admiringly. 'A pity I didn't bring my camera. But if you wait there I'll go and fetch it.'

'I won't!' Bára decides to walk all the way round along the wall. She stretches her arms out to the side like a tightrope walker and balances forward.

'Really like a ship, I can feel it rocking.' Helena prefers to sit down on the bench. 'I think I'm becoming sea-sick,' she announces and laughs at the thought of getting sea-sickness up here. Then she glances at Bára slowly tottering forward and advises her, 'Come down before you fall down.' But Bára laughs. 'But I have wings!' And indeed she has, for she can feel love entering her and love will give her wings, won't it? She reaches the end of the wall, and stops at the very edge, suddenly aware of the chasm before her and around her.

'I can't go on,' she complains. 'They've dug a hole in my way.'

'Come back, then!'

'How?'

'Turn round!'

'I can't turn round, the hole is all around me.' Bára stands motionless above the abyss, her legs suddenly turn to jelly and she knows she won't manage to turn round and therefore won't be able to return. She will remain standing here until the moment when suddenly an enormous wave rolls in and sets the vessels rocking, and her jelly legs will give way and she will tumble into the depths. She senses the waves breaking on the side of the ship; in a few moments, maybe, it will happen. She feels the floor rocking, she won't hold on much longer.

'Hold on, I'll go and fetch my civil engineer. He'll get you down.'

'Don't go anywhere!'

'Hold on, then, for heaven's sake!' Her friend calls to her from some distant shore and gets up from the bench on the dockside, but she is starting to stagger. 'Here comes the sea-sickness now, at last,' and instead of going to Bára, she heads for the harbour wall. She vomits.

Bára stands alone on the very edge. All of a sudden she feels like crying because she is standing here all alone, and nobody will come to help her. She would like to call out, Daddy! But her father is filling out his betting forms somewhere, or playing cards, or sitting at home with his feet up on the table staring at television. He doesn't care that his younger daughter has cut her wrists on his account and is now once more standing above the abyss, he doesn't care, because he skived off into the grave long ago, and even if he did manage to claw his way out of that grave he wouldn't come, he never did come when she needed him. The only one who ever came was her mummy, but her mummy is seventy-seven and she can't come, the lift's not working and she'd never climb up those twelve floors. Samuel won't come either; he's working hard on his career somewhere far away. She would come,

121

though, if it was him that was standing here, and she'd lift him down and bandage the cuts on his wrists and then comfort her poor little mummy's boy.

'You look like the statue of Aphrodite,' Helena calls to her from afar, 'just like a statue standing there. Now I know what's missing here: statues of Aphrodite and Hephaestus.' She vomits again.

And at that moment Bára remembers the pastor who looked at her in such a kind and shy way. He'd come, he'd be bound to come if she called him, because he already loves her, even though he hasn't allowed the idea to enter his head yet. And Bára suddenly feels relieved and is able to move once more. She turns towards the terrace and jumps down on to the tiles.

Helena says: 'You were beautiful. You looked just like the goddess of beauty.'

'I know I'm more beautiful than any goddess,' Bára says and bursts out laughing.

7

Daniel invited his friend Martin Hájek to speak to the young people of his congregation about sects. It was a topic that Martin had been studying for a long time. Why was it that people often found nonsensical ideas more attractive than the teachings of the church? Was it because the church was in a rut, that it wasn't looking for new ways of speaking to people, or perhaps that it had nothing to say?

Martin spoke first about each of the different sects and then tried to identify what they had in common. Most people wanted to feel they shared in some sort of exclusive destiny, that their particular faith marked them out from other mortals. They wanted to believe that in addition to the Saviour, who was long dead, they had found a new saviour, one who was alive, powerful, charismatic, and that he would lead them to what they yearned for; he would negotiate their journey to the heavenly kingdom and guide them along the path that would ensure them salvation and eternal life. Often such people would fall for simple-minded tricks and be taken in by confidence tricksters; they would be willing to give up their property and even their own minds, to leave their nearest and dearest and entrust their lives to the one they venerated. All the same, it had to be said that their experience was often both genuine and mystical, and possibly more profound than the experience of most Christians. What was typical for sects, therefore, was that they had a prophet who was unique among all the exponents of Christian scripture or any other holy book, and that the sect's members believed that the world would be transformed or end now, and not in some indefinite future. Some preached asceticism, others loose behaviour, some a life of love, others a life of hate. Some espoused exclusivity while others, on the contrary, believed they would become the one universal community. In none of the cases did they entertain any doubts about their path being the correct one.

Daniel regretted that Petr had not come. It was particularly on his account that he had invited Martin. On account of Petr and Eva. Admittedly, Eva was sitting here, but her thoughts seemed to be elsewhere. On the other hand, Marek and Alois, who had both come – as Marek had confided to him – because they found the topic 'really interesting', would whisper to each other every now and then during the talk.

When Martin finished and asked for questions, a customary silence ensued, and then Alois, who, if he attended such meetings was always silent, surprisingly raised his hand. Marek had probably egged him on.

What was the difference between the sects and the early church? In those days people had also believed in a miraculous Saviour. They also gave up their property and regarded their faith as the only right one, even though they were persecuted for it.

Martin conceded that every religion arose out of nothing, as it were, in that some chosen person heard God's voice and answered his call. At first glance, the similarities were striking, particularly as regards those who received a call and whose longing for faith, change, comfort and hope often blinded them. But when all was said and done, with a bit of effort we were able to distinguish the voice of the truly chosen from the voice of the charlatan who arrogantly convinces himself and others that he is the one and only infallible exponent of Scripture, the point being that he always chooses just the part of the message that suits his ends.

Daniel did not have the feeling that Alois found this answer convincing. It had not convinced him either, although he would probably have given the same answer in Martin's place. Over the centuries, we have come up with answers that seem to us acceptable even though we are unable to prove their truthfulness.

There were no further questions, so they sang another song, said a prayer and wound up the meeting.

At supper, Hana returned once more to the topic of the talk. Not long ago a young fellow had been admitted to their hospital with burns and wounds that had obviously been caused by flogging. He was said to be the victim of a satanic ritual. The lad was in such pain that they had been obliged to give him morphine, but when they asked him how he came by the injuries he either said nothing or claimed he couldn't remember.

'I expect he was doped when it happened,' Alois suggested as an explanation.

'Even if he was,' Martin objected, 'he is bound to have known where the black mass was held. Also he must have known that if he betrayed it, something even worse could happen to him. The sects don't generally countenance deserters. That is true not only of religious sects but also of most closed societies, whether it be the secret services or revolutionaries.'

After supper, Marek and Alois wanted to show the guests their telescope through which, they said, Saturn's rings were visible.

While Martin strove in vain to make out anything at all, Marek commented, 'If you ask me, you people don't really give a toss about science.'

'Who do you mean by "you people"?' Daniel asked.

'When you're preaching,' Marek explained. 'The people that wrote the Bible saw the world differently than we do nowadays.'

'They knew nothing about the galaxies, for instance?'

'For instance. And they believed people could be raised from the dead. And that there were evil spirits inside people and you could see angels.'

'Do you think those are the most important things in the Bible?'

'If they were wrong about one thing they could be wrong about others.'

'People have always been wrong about some things. But that doesn't mean they have been wrong about everything.'

Martin called out, 'I think I can see Saturn.'

'They didn't even know about telescopes in those days,' Alois added.

'Alois, a telescope won't help you to see the truth or God, for that matter.'

'That was below the belt, Dad,' Marek said, coming to his friend's defence.

'I apologize to you both,' Daniel said. 'I simply wanted to suggest that occasionally one may glimpse the essential even without a telescope. Too much clutter can sometimes prevent us from seeing the whole.'

'Galaxies are not clutter.'

'Maybe people didn't have an inkling about galaxies in the past, but it occurred to them nevertheless that man wasn't necessarily the most important and perfect thing in the entire universe.'

They left the lads to their telescope. Martin said, 'I know what they mean. We're too intent on defending the supernatural and fail to realize that there is no acceptable defence as far as they are concerned.'

'OK,' Daniel acknowledged. 'So away with Jesus's divinity, the resurrection, the Holy Spirit. What's left? God is supernatural too. Away with the Lord in whose name Jesus preached. But religion without a god is a nonsense. All you're left with is some -ism. Jesusism, like Buddhism.'

'The message of love is bound to remain. That's understood by all. Or almost all.'

Daniel recalled the lady architect who wanted to talk to him about love and was surprised to find the thought of her made him uneasy. 'Love is the essential thing in life, but there also has to be something above it. Even the Beatles had a message of love,' he remarked.

'The Beatles maybe; the church didn't always have much time for it.'

8

Letters

Dear Reverend,

I have the feeling I didn't thank you enough for those flowers. I have them on the table in front of me. As I look at them I think to myself what a special person you are. My husband asked who gave them to me. I said: Why you, of course, darling, you're always bringing me them. It's just that these days you're a bit forgetful about what you do. I think that nettled him.

Thank you also for the patient way you listen to the stories from my life and my inane questions. After all, preachers are there to preach not to listen, but you know how to listen and you make an effort to understand the other person. Last time you told me you thought true love could last an entire lifetime. Do you really think so? Is it something you believe in, or something you know for sure? And if it's something you know, then you're bound to know what one should do to achieve it. The way I see it, great love can only happen to people who manage to preserve complete freedom. You wrote to me about inner freedom, but what I have in mind is the freedom that we grant each other. It's not just preserving our own, it's also not begrudging the other person's. After all, it's not possible for a slave and a slave-driver to live together in true love.

It was something I discovered at home when I was small. My mother could never rid herself of the feeling that she owed her life to my father. I'm sure I told you that otherwise the Germans would have packed her off to Auschwitz – and how many survived that? Father was her rescuer and he accepted that role and played it to his lamentable end. I could never stand my mother's meek servility, I couldn't even stand my father for that matter, but that servility seems to have wormed its way into me. I can feel how it stifles all the better feelings in my soul, but still I serve my husband exactly the way my mother did my father, and Sam certainly didn't rescue me from anything, that's for sure. It's more likely me who rescues him – from his anxieties, before they totally unhinge him. But at least he's not like my father in that respect. He's reliable at his job and in his relations with me. I ought to value that, oughtn't I? And I do. I used to admire my husband. I considered him to be a remarkable individual, and still do, but that doesn't mean that I'm nothing, that I'm only here for him, simply a mirror for him to admire himself in.

Tell me, what must one do to preserve the most important things in one's life? To build them up instead of destroying them? Tell me: Is it at all possible? Why is it that all men – pardon the generalization, but it's not only my experience – why do they stamp around when they ought to go on tiptoe, strike when they ought to caress and cower when they ought to be offering support?

There, I've lumbered you with a pile of things again.

So don't be cross with me and don't forsake me.

Yours, Bára M.

———

Dear Daddy,

I arrived safely. Grandpa and Grandma were waiting at the station for me and as soon as she saw me Grandma cried out: 'You're the image of your mother.' Everything here is as it always was, nothing has changed since I was last here a year ago, apart from me, I suppose, but I don't see myself, except in that big mirror in the lobby, and luckily it's too dark there.

On Saturday, I borrowed Grandma's bike and cycled with Grandpa along the dike around Rožmberk. There are these enormous great oak trees there that must have been planted in the sixteenth century when Krčín was Regent. We stopped for a while and sat down underneath one of the oaks and looked at the water. Above it the mayflies hovered and a carp leaped out of it every now and then. Grandpa told me about how they take care of the fish ponds and then about Mummy when she was a little girl. It always makes me happy to hear about Mummy and at the same time I want to cry. I say to myself the way you do: it was God's will. But immediately it occurs to me: why? Why do some people die young and others are born deaf mute, blind or cruel? Why is there so little justice?

The other day I was walking past the church and I heard someone playing the organ inside. I went in. It was empty, but someone was playing Bach fugues on the organ – in a very special and beautiful way. There's no way of describing it because it's impossible to talk about music. I sat down and listened and had the feeling that life was endless. That's a silly way to put it. It just struck me that even though I was there on my own, God was with me because He is infinite and He is everywhere, that He finds it worth His while to be. I was curious to know who was playing so marvellously. So I got up and crept up to the organ loft, quietly so as not to be heard. Sitting at the organ was a tiny, grey-haired old lady and she was playing. She didn't notice I was there at all.

It was lovely of you, Daddy, to take me on that trip before I left. It was really nice and I keep on thinking about it. You're kind to me, you're all kind to me and I don't deserve it. I don't live the way I ought and even though I got my Cert I know I'm no good at anything and don't understand anything. How can I repay your kindness?

I always wanted to be like you, to be a bit remarkable in some way, to have faith, hope and love, to be kind to people, to know a little bit of what you know, to be good at something, maybe English, or sums like Marek, or putting together a telescope like Alois, or painting, or writing poems or songs. But I'm even hopeless at the harmonium – you must notice it most of all, except you pretend you don't because you don't want to hurt me, because you've always been sorry for me on account of Mummy. You always see her in me, but I'm not a bit like her. She was pure and good, I know that from you and from Grandma, whereas I'm . . .

Something else I want to say to you is that whenever I do something wrong now or in the future, it's entirely my fault and nobody else's, certainly not the fault of anyone at home at least, because you've always been much nicer to me than I have to you. Grandpa and Grandma send best wishes too.

Love, Eva

Dear Eva,

I'm pleased you're having a good time at Grandma and Grandpa's and having a little rest after your 'hard' studies. I understand what you meant about justice. Believe me, I've often had similar thoughts, even though I know that no one can understand divine dispensation. When your mummy died I was so full of bitterness that I even considered giving up preaching. (When people become bitter, they oughtn't to preach.)

At that time, it was Emanuel Rádl who helped me. In his *Consolation of Philosophy* he came to the realization that Christ brought direct guidance for mankind and that God acts the way that Christ did. He does not force anyone to do anything and so he is perfectly defenceless. He doesn't do miracles, doesn't send lightning or floods or plagues against people. He doesn't punish people in this world, he doesn't protect the wheat from the weeds that spread all over the field. In other words, to expect God to intervene directly in any matter whatsoever is to wait vainly for a miracle. But if God is a defenceless being, how does he operate in the world? He operates the way Jesus did. He loves people more than we can ever imagine and helps them

128

the way a defenceless person does: by teaching, by guidance, by praise, by example, by rebuke and by admonition. I am not telling you this as a lesson, but to let you know I understand.

But your letter also embarrassed me and worried me in fact. It embarrassed me because you praise me excessively. What worried me was the way you speak about yourself as if you were someone guilty of some great wrong. Your unfinished sentence: 'Whereas I'm . . .' startled me. I don't know of anything that you're guilty of, not that that is relevant of course. You're an adult now and have the right to your secrets. But if you have any, and they're a burden to you, you might be advised to share them. You know we'd never judge you. We know that it is not the role of people to judge others (Our Lord will judge us one day), but we'd try to understand you or help you somehow, should you need it and want it.

You must believe in yourself more, Evička. After all, you're only a beginner and no one expects anything from you but a willingness to live a decent life. And you have that. You've never done anything to harm any of us, leaving aside minor naughtiness or disobedience. And as far as faith is concerned, that's a gift for which we must be always grateful, it is a grace that we must ask for again and again. And, as you know, while grace can be refused, it can also be granted at the very last moment of life. And the Lord is good and will never ignore a sincere petition.

I am thinking of you and will continue to, and I'm already missing you. Give my best wishes to Grandma and Grandpa,

Daddy

P.S. Apart from the odd mistake you play the harmonium perfectly, and you know that as well as I, of course. And at the Conservatoire they'll give you the additional instruction to overcome what you perhaps regard at the moment as your lack of proficiency.

Dear Reverend,

I tried to call you before going off on holiday, but you weren't at home. I have some interesting news for you. I have managed to discover who had your father 'in his department' during the years sixty-three to sixty-eight. It was a certain Captain Bubník. After the Russian invasion, they kicked him out of the secret police. He earned his living for a while as a taxi driver and then worked as a warehouseman. That suggests to me that he was one of the more decent ones, and were you to approach him, he might tell you something about your father. Capt. Bubník is now a pensioner but earns some money on the side as a night-watchman for the Gross construction company. I enclose a list of all the necessary addresses and telephone numbers.

I wish you tranquillity and peace of mind during the holidays.

Yours, Dr M. Wagner

———

Dear Mrs Bára Musilová,

You sent me a nice letter with a number of questions, which I doubt I'll be able to answer as I don't want to give a preacher's answers and I'm not very good at any other kind. You ask not only about love and freedom, but also what we must do to build up our relationships instead of knocking them down.

I share your belief that love is the most important emotion in one's life; where it is absent, people are in a bad way, while on the other hand, where it is to be found, as Scripture tells us, it covers all offences. But love not only gives, it also makes demands and takes away. If nothing else, it gives the intimacy of a loved one and always takes away some of our freedom. (That also applies to the love of Christ.) These days people mostly choose freely to live together while promising at the same time that they will not freely enter into an intimate relationship with anyone else. In the modern world, that commitment bothers many people and they are not even particularly remorseful when they breach it or betray each other. I'm sometimes amazed at what a high value we set on freedom and how little we value responsibility or our faithfulness to our own promises.

I don't want you to think I don't understand what you say about freedom. If one truly loves another then one must not begrudge them their freedom, including the freedom to leave – for good, even. If one knows one may leave, it is easier to remain with another person, because there is no sense of anxiety at having entered a space from which there is no escape, and there is no sense of being a prisoner.

You also want to know what one may do to prevent one's emotions from

130

dying. It's hard to give an answer. One cannot see into another's heart, possibly only He can do that. I think that if one wants things to last one must constantly strive for a place in the life of one's companion and be for them the best of people. The only thing we have to bind another to us is love and understanding. All other bonds can be broken or feel like shackles.

And remember the words of Karl Barth that I quoted last time. There are boundaries that we will not cross on our own, while on the other hand there are chasms which lure us and can easily swallow us up. I don't want you to think I'm preaching to you impersonally; I too am confronted by these boundaries and chasms.

Yours sincerely, Daniel V.

———•———

Dear Reverend,

Thank you for your beautiful, wise and human letter. I am thinking of you. I would very much like to talk to you. But one cannot have everything. That's a precept I have to keep repeating over and over again, because I want to have almost everything. So far, I have almost always managed to obtain it, but I realize that I have to pay for this covetousness, by my services, work and good deeds. Thus I take care of my husband and fulfil his every wish. I comfort him when he is anxious, praise him when he doubts himself for a moment, I attend on him, I put up with his groundless fits of jealousy. I act as his wife, his secretary, his skivvy, and his nurse. And for what? To earn the right to spend a little time with my kind of people. How ludicrously tiresome: always wanting to earn something. I'm tired of all this 'earning' and would like something for nothing too: for no good reason, just for the fun of it, just for being me. I'd like time – time that doesn't rush madly away, the time and the freedom to make up to you for finding time for me, and to have the chance of taking up some more of your time maybe. Though I know that's something I can't expect, that I have no right to.

I don't know what I'm to do, don't know how to seek the truth, don't know how to manage to do all the things I want to do and I'm scared of time that keeps giving me menacing reminders. And I don't want to race through life, I want to live it: decently, properly, in love and kindness and hope. That's why I came to hear you preach, to hear what you would say about it.

I'd like to write something personal, but I am shy to put it down on a piece of paper that will go through the post. So instead I heap all my pitiful little anxieties on to you. One of the reasons I do so is to let you know I'm not cold, that I feel things: both pain and kindness, that I'm capable of being grateful for every kind word. I also want you to know that I can be happy too. Nowadays, the only time I'm happy is when I realize that you are there and that I might get to see you from time to time. I think about you, about how you spend your days, what you may be doing, what you may be thinking about, what is going on in your soul, because you have a soul, a beautiful one. You also have a kind and good heart and try to give so much with all of it.

There, I've heaped a load of stuff on you again. Forgive me and don't forsake me.

Yours, Bára

———————

Dear Mrs Bára Musilová,

I have thought a great deal about your last letter. It contains so much by way of feeling, pain, expectation and makes so many demands on life. I have been puzzling over what impels you to shower such praise on me, even though you do not know me at all. It struck me that you are in great need of something – or, more likely, someone – to believe in. Something good. Someone good. And from what you wrote about your husband I get the impression that you dream about a perfect man. But no man is perfect. People aren't perfect, only He is perfect. So you are always going to be disappointed, because only Jesus is incapable of disappointing us: he is the embodiment of love and understanding. The most that any of us can do is to seek in Him an example for our lives. You write: Do not forsake me! This is a plea that we address precisely to him. He alone is able never to forsake us because his love and his kindness are not restricted by time. The rest of us are here for just a short time, the length of a dream, and we do not know the moment when that dream will end.

We do not want to betray or forsake others. I know that I never want to forsake my wife as long as I live. I don't want to forsake any of the people who are near to me or who trust me. In that sense I do not wish to forsake you either. But what can I promise you? And so I simply beg you not to seek

God in people, apart from that of God which is in each of us. And try to find Him. He will never disappoint or forsake you.

I sense in you a great disquiet. I fear that it might send you hurtling off in a direction you don't want to go. One ought to strive to discern the consequences of one's actions.

I wish you success in your search for inner peace.

Yours, Daniel Vedra

———

Dear Reverend,

What a pagan I am that I never make it to church. And then the rheumatism has been troubling me just lately and I'm glad of a rest on Sunday. The gardens permitting, that is. And while I'm on the subject of the gardens, you know I'm not one to complain, but that young Koubek fellow, Petr, is going down in my estimation all the time. Two days last week he failed to turn up, and the next day he walked in bold as brass with no thought of excusing himself or anything. When he took his pay, and Reverend I don't pay badly, not when I think how much I had to slog every week when I was his age and what I'm giving him, he plays the lordship and sneers that it's not enough to buy a rope to hang himself. His very words. And this week he hasn't shown up at all and I've had to drive the tractor myself or ask Marie, and she's supposed to be in charge of the glass houses. So I'd be very glad if you'd let me know if I'm to count on him still or if I'm to find a replacement. I'm sorry to be the bringer of bad news.

Wishing you the best of health,

Yours truly, Břetislav Houdek

Chapter Four

1

Bára Musilová arrives as they agreed. She is only a few minutes late. 'You're not cross with me for keeping you waiting?' she apologizes breathlessly.

'But I'm at home.'

'I hate keeping people waiting.'

She is wearing the same black skirt as last time. And the ribbon that ties her hair is black as well. Her white blouse is open at the neck. It strikes him that as always there is something provocative in her appearance. Not so much in the way she dresses as in the way she moves, or rather in the way she looks at him. Daniel feels uneasy. 'Would you like a coffee?'

'I'd like a small glass of red wine if you have any, and a drop of water. It was stifling in the bus. But I don't know – maybe I'm holding you up?'

He brings wine and mineral water and two glasses for her.

'Won't you have a glass with me?'

'I'm not accustomed to at this time of day.'

'Nor am I. Nor am I accustomed to sitting in a manse – that's why I asked you for the wine.'

'That's perfectly all right. I'm accustomed to sitting in a manse.'

'But not with me.'

He gets up and goes to fetch another glass. He also brings a small plate of savoury biscuits and slices some salami to go with them.

'You're going to feed me too? You mustn't waste any time. I don't want to lose even one second of the time I can be with you.' But she reaches impatiently for the glass. 'So here's to our meeting and a successful afternoon. Is it all right to drink to such banal things? Here at the manse, I mean?'

He clinks glasses with her.

'On the journey here, all sorts of things occurred to me that I might ask you, though I don't think any of my questions are particularly original. I expect everyone asks you the same things.'

'I don't know what you have in mind.'

'Doubt about God's existence, for instance.'

'People don't usually ask. Either they have no doubts, or, more likely, if they do, they're ashamed to admit them to the minister.'

'And you personally, do you have doubts?' She stares fixedly at him. As if his reply really mattered to her. It occurs to him that her ancestors on her mother's side might well have been in that country that Jesus walked in, that they might have actually set eyes on Him and been struck with wonder by His deeds but turned away from Him when He died such a shameful death.

'I find it hard to imagine someone who wouldn't doubt from time to time.'

'I'm glad you replied that way. I was afraid you never doubted. I wanted to ask: Are you able to imagine the universe?'

That was not a question he had ever had to answer before. 'No, I'm not. My son is interested in astronomy. It's a pity he's not here; he might be able to give you a better answer.'

'It's just as well he's not here; it's your answer I'm interested in. Are you unable to imagine the universe because it's too big?'

'Partly.'

'How could God, who created all that, have assumed the form of a Jewish infant?'

'Jewish because God was fulfilling the promise made to Abraham. All the tribes of the Earth shall bless themselves in you.'

'No, you haven't understood me. I mean, how is it that someone who had the strength to create the universe could suddenly change into a human baby?'

'But God created with the Word. He didn't knock it together with his bare hands.'

'What does "created it with the Word" mean?'

'Let's call it "a command", then.'

'Like on a computer?'

'It's best not to compare God with anything. And I'd definitely not compare him to a computer.'

She sighs. 'I still don't understand. To create the universe and time and change himself into a baby that grows and ages until one day, in purely human time, some Roman bureaucrat has him executed. How does that differ from some Red Indian or Hindu myths?'

'I don't reject myths. They are rungs to understanding.'

'To understanding what?'

'To understanding existence. The beginning and the end.'

'And that myth of yours, is that just "a rung" too?'

'If you like.'

'You're very conciliatory. Or you're a doubter yourself.'

'No, a sinner.' He pours her more wine.

'You wrote to me that Jesus will not disappoint or forsake me. How can you tell? After all, he promised he would return during the life-times of those who were with him and lead them off to the Kingdom of Heaven. I've got that right, haven't I? And what can be worse than not to come when you promise to? And he's not given any news about himself since then, has he?'

'That expectation was premature. People took too literally one single remark of His. Times were different. People believed in miracles; they were expecting the end of the world. He, and the entire impact He had, is a mystery and will remain so. You can either accept it or reject it. It's a question of faith, the belief that what happened, happened as God's will to free mankind from the eternal law of birth and death. Or, to put it in today's language, God decided that man had reached the stage at which it was necessary to remove him from the effect of that law.'

'Why man, in particular?'

'Because man is made in His image. That is how he differs from all other creatures.'

'But you just have to believe all that. I expect you're happy,' she says, 'happy that you have something you can believe in, something that lasts for ever and ever, whereas for me everything is coming to an end when it's barely started and soon will end for good. But before it does, I'd still like to experience something nice. No, that's not the right word – something perfect. But I know that I'm not entitled to it, that I've lost my entitlement.'

'Why? Life does not end until the last breath – up till then every-thing is open.'

'Such as?'

'Such as grace and the love of Jesus.'

136

'Yes, we mentioned that. But what about the human sort?'

'There should be that too.'

'That was nice to hear. Thank you. And here you are sitting with me and listening to my talk.' She drinks up her wine and rises. Before leaving she takes another look around the room. 'You have some beautiful carvings here – I noticed them last time. Are they saints of some kind?'

'We don't venerate saints. No, I just do a bit of carving for fun sometimes.'

'You're a woodcarver as well?'

'No. My grandfather used to work with wood, though. He was a violin-maker. Before he died I used to go to his workshop sometimes and watch him working.'

'The faces on those two women are similar. As a matter of fact, they look more like young girls than grown-up women.'

'My first wife died before she reached twenty-five.'

'And those figures – they're supposed to be her?'

'You could put it that way.'

'You must have loved her a lot, then?'

'I did.'

'Forgive me for asking you like that. I didn't know your wife had died.'

He nodded. What she didn't know about him was a great deal more than she did know.

'Do you think you'll ever be capable of loving that much again?'

'But I remarried.'

'And do you carve figures of your second wife?'

He says nothing. This person makes him uneasy.

'Would you have to be deeply in love in order to carve the figure of another woman?'

'I don't know,' and it strikes him that it is fortunate she doesn't know about his latest carving. 'I don't know whether it has anything to do with love.'

'But surely all works of art have something to do with love.'

'I expect you'd know more about that than I.'

'But you know it too, don't you? In fact, you haven't answered my question. What I wanted to know was if it was possible, after losing someone you love a great deal, to experience a similar thing again or something even more powerful.'

'I really have no answer to that. I don't think love can be ranked,

and I actually find the idea of ranking people silly. But there are bound
to be people more qualified than I am – you'd better ask them.'

'And you wouldn't manage to?'

'Why does it interest you?'

'Maybe I'd like to know whether you'd be capable of loving me.'
She makes a short laugh. 'What will you say now? Don't say that we
are each of us married, just imagine for a moment that neither of us
are.'

She pours herself some wine. 'Now you're cross and remaining
silent. Remaining silent means you don't want to say "No" out loud.'

'Remaining silent means simply remaining silent,' he explains.

She quickly puts her cigarettes and lighter away in her handbag. 'Do
you think we'll see each other again? I don't mean in church, but like
this.' She stands opposite him, waiting. 'You are remaining silent.
Does remaining silent always mean remaining silent with you?'

2

Diary excerpts

Mrs Straková from Kamenice came to Prague and paid us a visit. I
hadn't seen her for years but she hasn't changed all that much. It always
gives me pleasure when someone turns up from those parts. From those
parts and from those days, someone who still remembers Jitka.

I enquired how things were with the congregation. She told me that
fewer and fewer people come to church on Sundays. No one's able to give
fine sermons like yours any more, she said, flattering me. Then she
complained about the decline in moral standards. They had had three
divorces in Kamenice in the past year. The men had lost their senses and
the women were taking leave of theirs, the young people only thought
about money and having fun. Mrs Straková laid the blame mostly at the
door of television. I couldn't get to sleep the other night, she said, so I
switched on the box, and Reverend, there were women running around
naked. It's worse than that Sodom you used to preach to us about and
that's a fact.

My visitor brought me a bag of dried apples and home-made buns.
When she left, it struck me that the world she had come from, and where

I too had lived for a time, was dying. I felt a twinge of nostalgia for it, in spite of its association for me with such dreadful times.

Shortly afterwards the phone rang. It was very late already, but I wasn't asleep as I was writing my sermon. Some woman's voice, it was a mezzo-soprano, called me by my Christian name and said: I love you. The voice struck me as somehow familiar and yet unknown. Once – it was precisely in those Kamenice days – someone rang me and abused me, calling me a creeping Jesus, a hooligan and – surprisingly enough – a Judas. But that abusive call surprised me less than this last one.

It can happen that someone in the middle of the night, just for their amusement, rings an unknown number and blurts something out. But that woman knew my Christian name. She could have found the number in the phone book, of course, or in the list in the church almanac.

—◦◦◦◦◦—

I had a visit last week from Mrs Ivana Pokorná of our congregation. She complained about the fact that there was a boy in her daughter's class who had shot his father. When I expressed astonishment that the lad was at liberty, she explained to me that he had committed the murder earlier, when he was under fifteen, and so he had escaped prosecution. He had been placed in a diagnostic institution but still attended school. Worst of all, she told me, the students in his class regarded him as a hero. Even the teachers. Why had he done it? His father used to beat him, she said, and had treated his mother brutally, and he might have had a mistress. So what was wrong with the son bumping him off?

I cited that case at the last meeting of the youth group as an example of moral cynicism. Ivana's daughter confirmed that the lad had no qualms of conscience. He declares that if he hadn't been successful that time he would have happily tried again.

We went on to talk at length about his action. Was it perversion, moral indifference or depravity, or was there perhaps another motive? How was it possible that a lad could kill his father and not even have qualms of conscience? I was surprised to find that the young people's opinions were much less unequivocal than I had expected. They explained that the son had obviously found his father's behaviour so despicable that he felt entitled to intervene. There's so much filth in the world and no justice, are you supposed to just look on all the time? Alois asked.

I conceded that parents often made mistakes as well. None the less one ought not forget that one of the fundamental principles on which society was founded reads: Honour your father and your mother, and that the Bible actually states: 'Anyone who curses his father or mother must be put to death.' (Exodus 21: 17)

Petr maintained that most criminals didn't feel guilty. On the contrary they regarded everyone around them as bad for not living up to their expectations. All of you, he said, turning to us, are too concerned about conscience and sin, but people don't give a toss about all that, apart from when someone steals something from them.

I agreed with him that our judgements of others are often categorical, while we tend to display much more indulgence when it comes to judging ourselves. Even so, murder was something that could never be condoned.

But that evening the thought occurred to me that the lad's action might actually have been prompted by desperation and a wounded or offended sense of justice. A wise son brings joy to his father, it says in Proverbs, but a foolish son brings grief to his mother. But what damage do an adulterous father or adulterous mother cause their son? And who nowadays will inform the son of a three-thousand-year-old law that says: Anyone who curses his father or mother deserves death?

The cynicism, hypocrisy and deceit that pervade the adult world burst with indignation over the cynicism of the children which they themselves helped bring into the world.

⊸◦⟨◦⟩◦⊸

After service on Sunday I had a word with Marika. (She didn't bring her siblings, but she is a regular attender. I don't know whether she follows the sermon but as soon as she hears the harmonium she enters into the singing heart and soul.) She loves her older brother and is convinced he's innocent. He fell victim to the gajos' revenge. When I asked her what he had done, she said: nothing. They locked him up over a fight in the pub, although he hadn't even been in the pub the night the fight broke out. It strikes me as unlikely but I don't think she's lying; she just believes in her brother's innocence. I am alarmed that the concept of what is just or even moral is being dangerously transformed. I get the same feeling when I think about the Soukups. He's determined to get divorced. He has fallen in love with a woman in the firm where he works. He has rejected the wife who loves him and serves him body and soul. He wants to deprive her of her children and she, in her despair, is incapable of defending herself. None the less, Brother Soukup considers himself a good Christian. He could have deceived his wife but he chose not to. He could have gone on living a life without love, but instead he gives preference to a life of love. How Christian it all is, and how weak and hypocritical at the same time.

Too many people run to Christ to fill their emptiness. When it doesn't work they start to fill it with something else – but the living Jesus, Jesus on the mountain, means nothing to them. The Ten Commandments? If He were to appear now and approach someone with the commandments, I doubt they'd follow Him. The Ten Commandments belong to another age. These days they call it a paradigm. We are seeking a new post-modern paradigm, we debate it in seminars. We argue about what is permitted these days and where the boundary is that must not be overstepped. We'll soon be asking whether any such boundary exists at all.

When she was on her way out, I told that architect woman she could stay longer if she liked. I don't know what made me say it. Well, actually I do. I find her presence thrilling in a strange kind of way. Even so, no sooner were the words out of my mouth than I took fright. What if she takes my words as an enticement? We sat for a further two hours almost. I think my behaviour was artificial. On the one hand I displayed an exaggerated interest in her life, asking her about her husband, even about the first one, as well as about her two sons, while on the other I was incapable of concentrating on her answers. I was thinking about those words she had spoken and which I had passed over in silence instead of categorically denying them: 'Maybe I'd like to know whether you'd be capable of loving me.' I had looked at her and realized what a beautiful and interesting woman she was.

For a short while she talked to me about her work and about modern architecture: about vaulted cubism and functionalism. She said tourists in Prague only look at the old buildings and fail to realize all the gems of modern architecture that are strewn around the place.

I know that's her speciality; I've never set eyes on anything she has created, but she talked with such enthusiasm that she enthused me as well.

141

Then I drove her right to her house. When I got back, I was happy I had resisted a foolish temptation but at the same time I was aware of a familiar sense of longing. That was how I used to feel years before when I would part from Jitka and the world would feel empty without her. Another thing that excited me about this woman was that she had Jewish antecedents. I realize that this is inverted prejudice, but I have always had the feeling that those who belong to the people of the covenant – even when they are totally unaware of the commitments it entails – have inherited something special. Surely somewhere within the consciousness of the entire lineage there must lie hidden the revolutionary insight that we are all made in God's image and an offence against God is therefore an offence against man, and in turn an offence against man is an offence against God.

⎯⎯⎯⎯⎯ ◦୨୧◦ ⎯⎯⎯⎯⎯

The things I brought back from Mum's included all sorts of old textbooks and other literature. To my astonishment I discovered among them a copy of the History of the Communist Party of the Soviet Union (Bolsheviks) *published in 1946. Dad must have bought it with the intention of learning the history of the country whose army had just liberated us. For a short while I leafed through it, finding in the margins my father's notes – sometimes only exclamation or question marks, in other places expressions of horror such as 'dreadful' or amazement – 'surely not'.*

On a couple of occasions I started to read some of the actual text and was astonished at the amount of lies, vulgarity, distortion and foul abuse. Dad had drawn wavy lines under them. The thought struck me: is it possible that people actually believed all this nonsense, all these fabrications and artful deceit, and that perhaps millions of people had believed it, even those who had lived through the events themselves, who had the opportunity to discover the truth and speak to eye-witnesses?

Fanaticism and the need to believe in an ideal blinker our vision. When can we be even halfway sure that what is proclaimed actually happened the way it is described, particularly when the news about it comes from people having blind allegiance to their faith?

The reliability of testimonies to past events is something that continues to fascinate me. Christ is the present and the future, we declare. But He is first and foremost the past. Whichever way I interpret

142

the Bible, I am dealing with events that happened and were recorded two thousand years ago. My gaze is therefore fixed on the past. Most people's gaze is fixed on some point in the distant future. No, that's an exaggeration. Most people gaze neither into the past nor the future, they explore neither truth nor lies, they gaze at the television.

❧

When we were still in Kamenice, our local Secretary for Church Affairs was a fellow named Berger, a former PE teacher. Maybe they had chosen him for his physical fitness and sobriety, in view of the fact that the previous incumbent had fallen asleep in a ditch when he was in a drunken stupor and frozen to death. I was required to apply in person to the Secretary every time I wanted to organize an activity that in any way went beyond my regular services. Sometimes he would make a personal visit. He would take a seat in my office, Jitka would bring him a coffee and he would start to persuade me that everything I did was a waste of time, as in the space of two generations there wouldn't be a single Christian left in our country, apart from a few crazy old grandmothers. He knew the content of all of my sermons and would warn me against any political allusions. I used to assure him that I had no interest in politics. 'I know full well what you mean when you talk about the Jews being taken into captivity and yet they never stopped believing in a Messiah who would free them.' When I objected that that was simply the way it was, he would say: 'Sometimes I really can't make up my mind whether you're a shrewd operator or just naive.'

When Jitka died he came to the funeral. 'Death is terrible, Reverend,' he said to me. 'You have my sympathy and I hope your faith helps ease your pain.'

A few days later I went to see him and mentioned that I desperately needed to return to Prague where my parents could help me take care of Eva who was six months old at the time.

He told me he understood my position and that it should be possible to arrange. I don't know whether it was really he who sorted it out but shortly afterwards the ban on my preaching in Prague was lifted, for a while at least.

❧

I'm writing about all and sundry in an effort to get that woman out of my mind, to avoid writing how I have yearned for her, how I have an urge to meet her again. An urge for love or for sin?

There was this quote from Martí in a recent issue of The Protestant: *'Religion and eroticism – a wild, but inseparable, couple. Even though they fight like cats and dogs, call each other names and curse one another, the one cannot last long without the other. Where religion is dying, eroticism wastes away and becomes simply sex. Where eroticism is dying, religion shrivels up into abstract metaphysics (as was once the case) or into arid ethics (as it is now).'*

I also recall what Balthazar the Cabalist says in Durrell's Justine: *'None of the great religions has done more than exclude, throw out a long range of prohibitions. But prohibitions create the desire they are intended to cure. We of this Cabal say: indulge but refine. We are enlisting everything in order to make man's wholeness match the wholeness of the universe – even pleasure, the destructive granulation of the mind in pleasure.'*

Where is the boundary between freedom and licence, between responsibility and self-denial that no longer serve life but inertia? Inertia that is one of the signs of death!

I've written nothing for almost a month. Have I lost the courage to be intimate with my diary? Or have I found a different form of intimacy?

I definitely don't have the courage to contemplate the consequences of what has happened. A month ago, B. called and asked if I could spare her a moment. There was a note of urgency in her voice and it struck me she had had some misfortune or other. I told her that I would of course find time for her, and straight away if necessary. She then asked if we might meet in the Small Quarter as she happened to have some business there at that moment. She described to me a bistro halfway along Carmelite Street where we could meet.

I arrived there in under half an hour and when I sat down at one of the small tables I could not rid myself of a sense of something unbecoming. Fortunately the bistro was empty, with just a sickly melody wafting from some unseen loudspeaker.

She arrived a little late. She started to apologize in her usual overstated fashion and thank me for coming. I ordered wine for the two of us and asked her if anything had happened to her.

She said she was suffering from depression, a feeling of anxiety that there was nothing permanent in this life, in her life, in people's lives, in the life of the Earth. Not even in the life of the universe, she added.

I pointed out that there was something permanent in life and the universe too.

'God, you mean,' she said and straight away objected that she didn't want any false consolation, that she'd sooner get drunk on wine than on some illusion. Then she spoke about her marriage. It was possible to put up with anything if one had a little support from one's partner. She maintained that she loved her husband but she had no support from him. On the contrary, she had to support him. 'You're different,' she told me, 'you're strong, you don't foist your burden off on to other people, you help them with theirs.'

Just as on the previous occasion, there were moments when I couldn't concentrate on what she was saying but instead simply registered the melody and tonal colour of her voice, and her appearance. I was also distracted by her fingers that involuntarily drummed the rhythm of the obtrusive muzak.

As we emerged from the bistro it was already getting dark. I wanted to say goodbye, but she detained me, saying that her mother lived a short way from there. Her mother was away at a spa and she had the keys to the flat. She had to go and water the house-plants; perhaps I might like to accompany her.

I remained silent and she asked if remaining silent always meant just remaining silent in my case. I continued to remain silent.

Her mother's flat is in an old Small Quarter house: just one room with a view on to a narrow little courtyard. Old furniture dating back to some time at the beginning of the century, a brass menorah on the high bookcase. On the couch lay a black cushion with a Star of David embroidered on it in white. The room was full of vegetation with a cheese plant in one corner and a dragon arum in a large flowerpot, while fuchsias and pelargoniums blossomed on the window-sills.

She went into the bathroom and filled the watering can. She asked if I was cross with her for bringing me there. I told her I wouldn't have come if I hadn't wanted to. While she was watering the plants she spoke to me continuously about how I was a remarkable person, the most remarkable person she had ever met. She said she could sense the goodness of my heart and also my wisdom, that there were words

145

concealed in me that I didn't dare speak. I told her she was remarkable too and that I sensed in her a passionate longing for understanding, compassion and love. I repeated what I had already written to her: that she sought God, but projected her search on to people.

She said: 'I'm just looking for a good man, a living man. I've been looking for you.' She came over to me and instead of backing away and making a quick departure, I took her in my arms.

It's strange how at that moment it struck me I'd first set eyes on her the day my mother died. Whose hand had thrust her into my destiny on that particular day?

Then we made love. I felt such ecstasy that I lost awareness of everything but her closeness and tenderness – and conceivably the long-forgotten tenderness that I used to feel with my first wife at such moments.

It was only when I had torn myself away from her that I was struck by the realization of what had just happened, of what I had done, and I was filled with horror and an overwhelming desire that it had all been just a dream from which I would awake into my usual innocence.

'Blessed is the man who endures trial, for when he has stood the test he will receive the crown of life which God has promised to those who love him. Let no one say when he is tempted, "I am tempted by God", for God cannot be tempted with evil and he himself tempts no one; but each person is tempted when he is lured and enticed by his own desire. Then desire when it has conceived gives birth to sin; and sin when it is full grown brings forth death.'

'Surely we have every right to,' she said, sensing my mood. 'Surely there can't be anything wrong in love, can there?' As we said goodbye, she asked when we would see each other again.

Instead of saying never, instead of saying we couldn't see each other like that any more, I asked her if she really wanted to see me.

'And don't you want to see me?' she said in astonishment.

I couldn't find the strength to say that I didn't.

We met there again on four further occasions while her mother was at the spa. More than once I wanted to tell her that we couldn't continue with what had happened, but the moment I set eyes on her I was incapable of saying anything that might separate me from her for good. Whenever we made love she said: 'Love can't be a sin – you know that, don't you?'

I think to myself, yes, but it depends what kind of love, in what

circumstances – but I am looking into those dark Jewish eyes, so full of
passion and anxiety and pain, and instead of all the things that burden
me at that moment I tell her that I love her.
The most terrible thing of all, it seems to me, is that it's true.
She would say: the most terrible and the most beautiful, because it
joins that which cannot be joined, and maybe that's exactly the way life
operates.

3

It was already dark as Daniel returned from the presbytery meeting.
From a distance he could make out the figure of a man leaning against
the lamp-post directly opposite the chapel.

'Waiting for me, Petr?' he asked when he reached him.

'Sort of, Reverend. But if you're busy, I can come back some other
time.'

'Come along in. I'm always glad when you turn up. Besides, you
haven't called on us for ages. Has anything happened?'

'No, apart from the fact that my sister's getting married.'

'That's good news, isn't it?'

'The guy she's marrying is decent enough, but I won't be able to stay
there any longer.'

'Oh, yes. I forgot you've been living there. Have you somewhere else
to go?'

'Not easy to find at the moment.'

'We'll come up with something. If you don't find anywhere, there's
still another guest room here. But I'd have to talk to the elders.'

'Thank you, Reverend. I knew you wouldn't leave me in a fix.'

As they climbed the staircase Petr staggered and Daniel only caught
him at the last moment. 'I had a couple of drinks at my sister's,' he said
by way of explanation.

'So long as you didn't do anything worse . . .'

'And I chucked in that job last week. I don't like gardening.'

'I suspected as much. Mr Houdek wrote to me about it. And can
you think of something you'd enjoy more?'

'It's not really a matter of enjoyment, Reverend. The thing is I'd like to achieve something and for that I need some education. And that means earning some money.'

'What would you like to achieve, Petr?'

'But I've already talked to you about it, Reverend. I'd like to preach. Like you, for instance. So that I can tell people they must turn away from the darkness towards the light. Reverend, you've got a bit of an inkling, but I've known it at first hand – the horror that people live in.'

'I have to congratulate you on that ambition, Petr. But do you have any notion what you might do to earn more?'

'Possibly. But I don't know whether you'd approve.'

'I'll approve anything that's above board.' He led him into the room with the piano. Hana and the children were most likely in bed asleep. So he went to make some tea. He suspected bad news. It was the job of clergy to receive bad news. Worst of all he was still concealing bad news within himself and there was no one who could relieve him of it.

He came back with the tea. 'So how are you going to make a living? If you don't mind my asking.'

He shrugged. 'I could be a dealer.'

'In what?'

'Whatever was around.'

'That sounds fascinating. And what if they catch you?'

'They won't.'

'You said that once before.'

'I was still wet behind the ears then. I was operating solo. Or rather with a gang that was as stupid as I was. And anyway it wasn't good. I used to steal as well.'

'Whereas now you've decided that you'll deal honestly in drugs.'

'I haven't decided anything, Reverend. I've decided I want to do something useful with my life, but if I'm to do it, as I explained to you Reverend, I need to earn something. You can't do anything without money these days.'

'Your news doesn't please me. I thought you'd opted for a different way of life.'

'But I have. I haven't done anything wrong so far, have I?'

'Not so far . . . Petr, try and recall what you used to say to me when I visited you there. That you never wanted to end up behind bars again. And just a moment ago you were telling me you wanted to preach.'

'Straight up. I really do.'

148

'If you really mean it, you oughtn't to be considering such plans.'

'I mean it seriously. But you yourself say nobody can be without sin.'

'There are sins and sins, Petr. A preacher who sold drugs wouldn't be a good preacher.' A preacher who preaches the Ten Commandments and does not live by them can't be a good preacher either.

'But nobody would ever find out about it. There are things that nobody ever finds out about. Except the Lord, and he is merciful.'

Daniel suddenly felt uncomfortable and the lad noticed. 'No, straight up, Reverend, there's much less risk in that than in what you're doing. It's run by fellows with experience. There are all sorts of fail-safe mechanisms.'

'What do you mean? What risks am I taking?'

'Preaching. It's not so long ago that you had all sorts of hassles. With the police, I mean.'

'They were a different sort of hassle. And the times were different.'

'Except who helped you in those days? Nowadays if they catch a guy there's always someone who'll see to it they let him off.'

'How do they "see to it"?'

'Reverend, you're such a saintly man; you know very, very little about life. Everything can be seen to, everything's for sale if the money's high enough.'

'I'm not saintly. The opposite, more likely. And as far as big money is concerned, that's definitely not your case, Petr.'

'Exactly. And if I go on pushing a wheelbarrow I'll spend my life paying off debts, and I'll achieve . . . I won't achieve anything.'

'I'll tell you something, Petr. To manage to lead a decent life is quite an achievement, believe me. And that applies to you and me alike.'

'Reverend, I haven't made any decision yet. But you know full well that I have to pay the bill for the time I was inside and I have just a month to clear out of my sister's place. And even if you let me stay here, I can't stay here for ever. I want to lead a decent and useful life. I'd like to see something of the world and help people who are in a bad spot like I was. Advise me, then, if you know of some other way of earning some money.'

All of a sudden he was struck with alarm by a connection that hadn't even occurred to him before. 'Haven't you in fact already started in a small way?'

'What do you mean?'

'I mean selling drugs.'

Petr gave a diplomatic answer: 'Virtually no.'

'And in reality?'

'I don't get what you mean?'

'Eva, for instance. Did you sell her something?'

'Oh, come on, Reverend, it'd be like selling something to you.'

'And would you sell me it?'

'No, never!'

'Not even give it?'

'That would depend on whether you wanted it.'

'And Eva did?'

Petr hesitated a moment. Then he said, 'No, she didn't.'

'She didn't even want to try it?'

'But everyone wants to try it at least once.'

'You louse.' Daniel took a step forward and raised his fist. Petr flinched and shielded his face with his arm. 'No, Reverend, don't ever think that of me. I talked her out of it!'

Daniel's fist remained clenched but he did not strike him.

'I really did talk her out of it, Reverend. I warned her off shooting speed. I gave her a bit of grass; that's less harmful than an ordinary ciggy.'

'And did you give any to Marek and Alois?'

'No, no one else. I swear, Reverend. I didn't offer it to anyone here. Eva asked me for it. She told me she'd already tripped on speed twice but she didn't have any money to buy herself another trip. I told her to quit messing about with speed and I gave her the grass just so she'd have something at least. I reckon I did the right thing.'

'Yes, a really good deed, Petr!'

'Reverend, if I hadn't given it her, someone else would have got it for her. They'd get her something harder that she'd end up hooked on, like me that time. You've no idea, Reverend, how quickly it takes a hold on you, and Eva doesn't know yet.'

'What a Good Samaritan you are, Petr.' The world was full of deceit: big words and shameful deeds. He felt an unexpected pain in his chest and his breathing seemed to falter. 'You'd better go, you louse. I don't want to talk to you any more!'

Petr got up and wished him good-night, but he stopped in the doorway and turned towards Daniel. 'The room you mentioned – I don't suppose the offer stands any more, does it?'

'It still stands,' he replied, resisting the temptation to agree with him, 'even though I'd sooner see you a million miles away.'

'Thank you, Reverend.'

'It stands on condition, of course, that you don't turn the manse into an opium den.'

'You can count on me, Reverend. And I genuinely did talk Eva out of it.'

4

Hana

The journalist who is being discharged that Friday brings Hana a bunch of purple irises. 'Whatever possessed you? Besides, I won't get a chance to enjoy them,' she protests. 'I'm off on holiday next week.'

'So you can leave them at home, or give them to someone. Flowers are not for returning!'

So Hana thanks him, and all of a sudden she realizes who the journalist reminds her of: a pity she has no photo. Little Joe has already been dead for thirty-five years but he too was a trifle stunted just like this journalist and would also tell her enthusiastically about far-off lands and their inhabitants. And he once picked her the same purple flowers: in those days they were most likely stolen, as they didn't grow them in the garden at home.

Past times rise up in front of Hana's eyes: her first kiss, the people she would never see alive again. She puts the flowers in a vase, but she hasn't time to enjoy them. Before she can leave she has a vast number of duties to perform, including drawing up the rotas for several weeks ahead and doing an inventory of the linen and medicines. Every year, at the beginning of the school holidays, she takes the children off to her mother's, although in previous years she would only go for a few days, saving up her leave in order to spend some of it together with Daniel. She never did use it all up anyway, preferring to take payment in lieu. Times had been hard and every crown used to come in handy. This year, Daniel had persuaded her to take an extra four weeks unpaid leave; after all, they didn't need the money and she needed a rest.

However, it was he more than anyone who could do with a rest. He

151

seemed somehow changed to Hana these past few weeks: frail, taciturn and preoccupied. She put this down to his not yet having got over his mother's death, but maybe the work-load he has taken on himself is wearing him out: running his church, preaching every Sunday, travelling to visit prisoners, speaking on radio and television, writing newspaper articles, organizing special days for the congregation and on top of it all preparing for an exhibition of his carvings. It is a fact that he has had to wait till now to do all the things they wouldn't let him do before.

She'd love to help in some way, but doesn't know how. She can never think of anything to talk to him about without delaying him, something to please him or interest him even. She suggested to him that he should take a holiday and make the trip with them. He admitted that he would like to go but didn't have the time at the moment.

Maybe he really didn't have the time, or maybe it was just that he didn't relish the thought of travelling with her. Hana has the impression that he has been avoiding her recently. Maybe he's stopped loving her. Every love grows weary in time, that's something she knows all too well. Besides, Daniel never did love her the way he did his first wife. It's true he still washes the dishes or takes care of the shopping and urges her to buy herself new clothes. In the evening he sits and chats for a while with her and the children, but Hana senses that even at those moments his thoughts are partly elsewhere. Sometimes it seems to her that although she was definitely a support for Daniel in the bad old days, he no longer has any need of her now, or if he does then it is only to cook his dinner or massage his aching back.

The irises in the vase smell sweetly and she conjures up the day she returned from the maternity hospital with Marek. The whole manse was decked out in flowers. Daniel said to her that day: 'I'll never ever repay you for this.' But that was a long time ago now. Much water had flowed under the bridge since Marek was a little boy and they moved from one manse to another, since the days when Daniel used to be called in for interrogations, and he was under permanent threat of losing his permit to preach, so that they would be shunted off to goodness knows where. Since then the bad times had become the good times but what did it mean as far as her life was concerned? It is possible to feel better in bad times than in the good kind. Tyranny binds people together whereas freedom distracts them by holding out opportunities to them.

Maybe Daniel never had needed her, just a mother for Eva, and that was the reason he had taken her into his life. But his heart belonged to the one who had died. Hana recalls how, when she moved into the manse, she found traces of Jitka everywhere: her clothes in the wardrobes, two pairs of ladies' shoes by the front door, her photograph in a frame on Daniel's desk and above the child's cot a paper dove whose wings flapped in the draught. 'Jitka was already in hospital when she made that,' Daniel had explained and was at a loss what to do with the clothes and shoes, as he could hardly throw away things that reminded him of the woman he had loved. So Hana had to live for a while with the effects of the departed and for the whole time with the memory of her. Daniel never spoke about Jitka and Eva called Hana 'Mummy'. In fact, until she was eight, she had not known that her real mother was no longer alive.

Now Eva was grown up and could cope without her; so could Daniel, in fact. Who needs you, when you are not even needed by your nearest and dearest? Probably nobody – and that's a difficult realization to live with.

It's almost two o'clock and Hana quickly writes out the most urgent instructions for the afternoon shift. *Feed Mr Lagrin!*

A week ago they had moved a Romany youth on to the ward. Skinheads had thrown him off the cliff at Šárka. He had survived the fall but had suffered multiple fractures and concussion. This morning they had taken him off artificial feeding on the grounds that he should be able to feed himself by now. When she went on to the ward she discovered he had not touched any of his food. She asked him why.

'I cannot hold the spoon.' And he showed her how his hands were shaking.

'But we would have fed you.'

'I did ask, but the sister she told me that on her wages she would not feed me.'

Later she asked in the nurses' station who had had the nerve to say such a thing, but naturally no one owned up. But even if the nurse had owned up she couldn't throw her out, as she'd never find a replacement.

Hana needs a holiday. She feels tired out. Not so much from work as from life in general. Her life admittedly has its regular routine but there is nothing in it that she really looks forward to. It doesn't offer any enticing prospects. And the heavenly kingdom that Daniel so often talks about with such enthusiasm has never assumed any definite form in her mind and she has never imagined what might await her beyond its gates. She is almost ashamed of the fact and feels ordinary and down-to-earth compared to Daniel. Maybe she too would be capable of elevated thoughts and deeper contemplation about God and His plans, but how can you have elevated thoughts when two nurses this month have already handed in their notice. One of them she considered the best on the ward; now she has found a job as a hotel waitress.

'And won't you be sorry to be dashing around somewhere with dishes when here you could be doing a job for which only you are qualified?'

'But they pay three times as much.'

Where will she find new nurses now, with nothing to offer them? For the time being they will just have to share out the duties among themselves and that could well cause others to leave. What will happen then she prefers not to contemplate. This is a ward where the slightest neglect or inattention means death; and it can happen that several post-operative incidents or complications can easily occur at the same time. Now she is left with only one nurse for the night shift and she won't manage everything even if she splits herself down the middle. And then there was the holiday; she probably shouldn't have listened to Daniel and taken four weeks extra leave.

It is already two thirty; Hana has finished taking stock of the medicines and is on her way to the changing room. She has not managed to account for all the analgesics and the ephedrine preparations; someone is stealing them for their own use or making some extra money by selling them. Everything comes down to money these days. Everyone wants to get rich quick and the essential things in life are ignored.

What are the essential things in life?

Faith, hope and love.

Except that faith is dying and hope is therefore also on the decline. And what people now regard as love has little in common with it. It tends to be no more than a mutual encounter of bodies and at best a few trite saccharine phrases. She doesn't know them from personal experience, but has picked them up from television serials or from listening to the girls in the nurses' station.

They often confide in Hana, perhaps on account of her motherly appearance, or because she's a pastor's wife, or simply because she's a patient listener. She is unshockable, understanding and ready to give advice. She tends to advise patience and warn against excessive trustfulness and impulsive decisions guided by feelings rather than prudence.

Sometimes, when she sees that passion, that total surrender to expectations of love, or when she detects the unconcealable tremor in the voice, she realizes that deep down in her there is also a hidden longing or perhaps an anticipation of some vague change, some action that will carry her out of this current that sweeps her along monotonously between the same banks.

It could well be that when she is giving her young subordinates a talking-to and warning them against foolish outbursts, she is addressing and rebuking herself too. She warns others against imprudence, never having been aware of imprudence under her own roof. Thanks to her job, she has heard more about drug addiction than Daniel. In this country every other person is a drug addict without knowing it. Grandparents are used to swallowing a whole tube of tablets each day, unable to imagine life without them. They would die of anxiety at the emptiness. They don't have a god so they stuff themselves with anadin, Valium and anti-depressants. Maybe that's permissible at the end of a life, but what will happen to the ones who start it at age eighteen? Her step-daughter is at risk and Daniel is too good-hearted – naive, she'd say – to give Eva a proper talking-to, let alone punish her. He believes she'll come to her senses on her own. But how many drug addicts ever came to their senses on their own? The only outcome of such a kindly and understanding approach to child-rearing would be that Marek and Magda would end up being tempted too. Marek seems to be sensible enough but Magda is attracted by anything she sees as forbidden or sinful. Not long ago Hana found a box of matches in her school bag. 'What are you carrying matches around with you for?'

'No particular reason. In case I needed to see something when it gets dark.'

'So long as you're not thinking of smoking.'

'Oh, Mummy, whatever makes you say such a thing?'

Her astonishment did not sound in the least convincing.

Those two young criminals that Daniel was so proud of reforming, and that he spoiled more than his own children, wouldn't come into the house if Hana had her way. Even if they have been baptized and they feign piety, there is no reason for them to be friendly with their children.

If only Daniel had more time for them to talk together. If only he would find a moment to tell her he loves her.

Hana leaves the hospital in a bad mood. Outside the front entrance she bumps into the journalist who has just given her a bunch of flowers and so reminded her of her first love. His name is Volek. He greets her with a rather unconventional bow. She had mentioned she was going on her holiday. It occurred to him he would probably not see her again so he would like to thank her for all the care he has received and invite her for a coffee, at least.

'No, thank you. I have to get home. My husband and children are expecting me.'

'How old are your children?'

'Twelve and fourteen.'

'You can't be serious, Matron!'

'I also have a step-daughter who is eighteen. Why do you ask?'

'I just wondered whether they might cope for a while without you.'

'That's not the point. You've already given me these flowers. It wouldn't be right for me to accept an invitation from you as well.'

'But I'm only inviting you for a coffee.'

Hana cannot understand the reason for the invitation but it will help take her mind off things. He is an entertaining man, and in spite of his profession he seems quite trustworthy.

The little bar is right next door to the hospital. There are only a few people seated at the small round tables, but the background music is a bit too loud. She doesn't feel at all at ease but she will have to put up with it, having accepted the invitation.

The journalist orders two Turkish coffees.

'That's not really the best thing for your stomach,' she scolds him.

'There you go; I didn't realize you knew my case notes.'

'People mostly take the advice we give them with a pinch of salt. We discharge them and they're back in a twinkling.'

'Actually I don't like coffee,' he admits. 'At home I only drink tea, but real tea, not the sort of thing they offer you in a pub here. When you go into a tea-house out east,' he says, indicating with his arm somewhere a long way off, 'it is not just a ceremony, but something else as well, something for you to taste and smell and see. For instance, they can drop in your teapot a small ball that some dear little Chinese ladies have woven from tea leaves up on some plantation in the

156

mountains. And that ball starts to swell and turn into a flower that unfolds while at the same time imparting to the water the taste and scent of tea, such as you'll never encounter here. Whenever I'm abroad I stock up on teas. Should you ever happen to have the time or inclination to call on me, I would make you Dragon's Fountain, say, or Snowflake.'

'And you make tea all by yourself?' Hana asks, disregarding his invitation and realizing that she has never seen his wife during visiting hours, though from his notes she saw he was married.

'Yes. I would never entrust anyone else with tea-making.' And for a while he describes the proper way to make tea. Water may be poured on the tea three times: the first time for strength, the second time for taste, the third time for thirst. But in China when you arrive in the evening for a tea session, they just sprinkle tea in the pot and then simply pour on hot water. 'You see, it's my conviction,' he adds, 'that the person who knows how to drink tea also knows how to forget the din and bustle of everyday life.'

Hana then asks about his wife and what she does, but the journalist brushes the question aside. Klára works in a bar, finishing quite late at night and sleeping through the day, so they scarcely see each other.

Apparently he does not enjoy talking about his wife; maybe there's something not quite as it should be between them and that was why she did not even come to see him. Perhaps that was the reason for his illness; Hana recognized long ago that most illnesses have their origin in mental not physical pain.

And what does her husband do, the journalist wants to know.

Her husband is a pastor.

'I've never taken coffee with a pastor's wife. Nor with a pastor, for that matter. My people were unbelievers and I take after them. I must have been in more pagodas than churches. But I only visited them because I was interested in statues of the Buddha.'

'Do you think it's possible to live without a faith? Live well, I mean.'

'The way I see it, Matron, what is more important than faith is to have a good heart. I met a lot of people like that in China. They had no faith, just a good heart. And you're exactly that sort of person, and that's why you are able to take loving care of total strangers.'

'We are all carers.' Hana is at a loss; she is not used to chatting with men.

'Of course. But you're different. I'm sure you're kind to good and bad alike. Because you can't help being kind. You remind me a bit of my mother. When she was still very young,' he quickly adds. 'She was the best person in the world.'

'That's what everyone thinks about their mother.'

'But she really was an exceptional woman. And I have known both exceptional and selfless women.' Again he recalls some Chinese women he once met when he first arrived in that country. Their husbands had been jailed or had been sent for re-education to some commune a thousand kilometres away and everything had fallen on those women: caring for their families and earning a living so that their children did not die of hunger. And in China, particularly for women, that meant working until they dropped. But they did not complain and bore their fate with humility and courage.

'Maybe they were ashamed of complaining in front of you, a foreigner.'

'Maybe,' he concedes. 'But all the same, their patience and composure was remarkable. And they waited loyally for their husbands.'

He then goes on to tell her about a massive flood he once witnessed on the Yellow River. The water got into the houses and barns, carrying away livestock, chattels and even people. The women behaved just like the men. They would carry a hundredweight of earth in baskets on their backs, those little women, to help repair the dikes and save what could be saved. It was impossible to save anything anyway, as water is such a mighty element and in that plain there wasn't even the tiniest mound you could climb up above the water.

Hana listens to him with interest. She likes the way he speaks nicely about women, even if they were women from a country she will never set eyes on.

'And weren't you afraid?' she asks him and says that she is afraid of water; water has always played a baneful role in her life, and almost killed her once.

Matouš starts to apologize for bringing water into his narrative but China is all water: rivers, enormous rivers flowing across the plains and between weird-shaped cliffs. And canals and rice paddies. In their paintings and songs, the surface of the water glistens in the moonlight. The trigram 'k'an' denotes water, rain and also danger. As to whether he was afraid, at such a moment one thinks of what one ought to do, not about the danger. The same thing applies to an earthquake. But during an earthquake everything happens so fast that one doesn't even have time to be afraid. One either lives or not. Perhaps if he were trapped somewhere under rubble he might be afraid. He goes on to tell Hana about a volcanic eruption he witnessed during his one and only visit to Washington State. The volcano had a beautiful name – Helena – but what he saw was terrifying. It looked just like an atomic explosion. The entire mountain top blew off. He just stared at it and in those first seconds it didn't even occur to him that his life was at risk. It looked like a fantastic film effect. It finally came home to him when the cloud of ash and smoke started to drift towards him. All of a sudden he realized he couldn't breathe. And it started to turn dark in the middle of the day.

While Matouš is telling stories, he draws in the air with his finger: the plain, the water, the river winding through the rocks, and the mountain top flying off. Hana notices he has a pretty hand with fine, almost feminine fingers.

'But do you know what I found most astonishing of all was not the darkness at noon, nor the solidifying lava, nor the burning trees, but the silence. Not the cheep of a bird, not the chirp of a cricket – not even the buzz of a fly. Most of the people around me found it horrifying but for me it brought back the words of the Chinese sage: In the sky symbols arise, on the earth shapes are formed. And also: What first rises to the sky must fall to earth. And instead of being horrified, I was aware of the greatness of nature.' Matouš relates terrible experiences yet smiles all the while at Hana. When Hana expresses surprise at his smile, he explains that when he experiences something of that kind he is actually happy: that he survived and that he has enriched his life, his experience. And that was something he always longed for, particularly while he was young – to experience something, to understand something and then tell people about it.

'Tell them what?' Daniel was possessed by that need too. It is a male characteristic. Daniel retells an ancient message, trying to inflame even the hearts of those who seemed bent on taking the opposite view. Because of it they had lived in poverty and had to live for a time in a remote village. And they had not been allowed to travel at all.

'That's not easy to answer in a few words. At one time I had an urge to tell people at least something about the world they were not allowed to see: what it looked like, how the people behaved, the way they thought, what customs they had. You see, the world was divided into two in those days. Our part was good, the other part was bad: now it's the other way round, in a sense. Nevertheless there is only one world and it is both good and bad. Most important of all, it is threatened by what we do in it. We rush forward somewhere without looking to right or left. That's something you become aware of in that place, where, since time immemorial, they have acknowledged values other than just progress and the pursuit of success and change. When you return you are bound to ask: where will it all end? And your answer is: in the end we will destroy ourselves and life in general.'

'People always expect catastrophe,' Hana says. 'At one time people actually expected the end of the world. My husband often talks about it in sermons: how the sun will turn black, the moon will run blood, the stars start to fall to earth and the skies disappear. It's a horrifying thought.'

'That's true,' the journalist admits, and he excitedly starts to tell her how these used to be only nightmares. The beast rising out of the sea had seven heads and ten horns. The Hindus believe that when the age of Kali arrives, the gods will massacre each other, the earth will be engulfed by fire and water, and there will be a return to the chaos that reigned before Creation. The Persians believed that life would perish in the convulsions of the earth, after which would come fire, flood and the fall of the heavens. It was always something that would come irrevocably by a higher will. Nowadays we are preparing our destruction ourselves because we are too attached to material things. Man should fix his mind on other values. He should seek the love that sees and is wise, as well as harmony and the fundamentals of the order that rules the universe.

'My husband says everything happens by the will of God. Without it, not a hair will grow, or fall from the head. But he also appeals for love.' It is odd how easy she finds it to talk to this man. She would never dare broach such subjects in front of Daniel. Daniel was too learned, serious, genuine and responsible. She would be afraid of blurting out in front of him something that would betray her ignorance. She finishes her coffee. 'Thank you for inviting me,' she says, 'and for the coffee.'

He asks her then where her husband preaches, and she tells him.

'I must come and hear him some time. Maybe I'd get to see you at the same time.'

She takes her leave of him. She can't fathom out why he should want to see her again, but when she emerges from the smoky and noisy

160

room she realizes her mood has improved, and she actually feels vaguely pleased. Someone has felt it worth his while to spend some time with her.

5

Captain Bubník lived in a four-storeyed house in Vokovice. As Daniel mounted the staircase he was unable to dispel a queasy feeling in the pit of his stomach. He always used to feel something similar when he was summoned to an interrogation or to the office of the Secretary for Church Affairs.

The State Security was no more, even the police uniforms had changed, but the incidents and experiences of the past had not disappeared, they remained – indelibly – lodged in people's memories.

He rang a doorbell on the third floor. The door was opened by a little grey-haired old lady in a flowery apron.

He introduced himself and she said she knew who he was and that her husband was expecting him. Then she asked if he preferred coffee, tea or beer, maybe. He refused everything, still obedient to the old wisdom that it was better not to accept anything from such people. By now a man appeared in the doorway, and having overcome all his distaste and embarrassment, Daniel announced himself.

'Is that the pastor?' A slightly corpulent seventy-year-old with a grey deadpan face, rather gingery eyebrows and senilely expressionless eyes behind cheap spectacles stepped towards him. 'You're very welcome.' The man shook his hand firmly like an old friend he was meeting after many years. He led Daniel into the room which looked 100 per cent mass-produced, from the carpet on the floor to the pictures on the walls and the ceiling lamp.

'Pastor,' he repeated when they were seated at the chipboard table. 'That's an honourable calling, caring for souls and their salvation. I've been retired for thirteen years now. I always used to say what a treat it would be not to have to get up in the morning, except that these days I wake up at 4 a.m. and I'm not able to go back to sleep. More aches and pains, fewer joys and pleasures. You mentioned your father in your letter, didn't you?'

'I understand you,' he said when he had heard him out, 'those

161

pirate lists caused a lot of harm. And above all among the survivors, because they weren't able to seek redress. Where they had been wronged.'

'Were they often?'

'It depends what you mean by wronged, Reverend.'

'Wronged is probably not the right word. Duped or misled would be more accurate, seeing that people were often included on the list without their knowledge.'

'I shouldn't think so, Reverend. And anyway it's neither here nor there. Some didn't sign and even made things up; others signed and you didn't get anything important from them anyway.'

'And my father?'

'Your father, your father. He was a doctor, you say. Dr Vedra?'

He looked as if he was trying to call the name to mind. Then he shook his head. 'I've got a bad memory for names. There was a time when I could remember all sorts of things, I knew all the Sparta football team line-ups for the previous twenty years, but nowadays – you know what it's like for old people.'

'I've brought a photograph.' Daniel took an envelope containing two likenesses out of his bag. As he passed it across he had the impression of doing something dishonourable. As if it was he, now, who was acting as an informer by offering a picture of his own father.

'Yes,' said the man opposite, 'the face is familiar. At least I think so. On the other hand, nothing definite comes to my mind. After all, it's thirty-five years ago or thereabouts. Are you able to remember people you dealt with thirty-five years ago?'

'I used to deal with people in a different fashion. And yes, I do remember the people who attended church.'

'You've got a good memory, and you're younger. But I will tell you one thing: the fact I don't remember means your father was totally insignificant. From the point of view of being of any use, I mean. The big fish – the ones that really meant something – you remember them even after all those years.'

'Can't you recall even a single interview?'

'No I can't, really. Don't forget that I was given the boot from there. After that you try to forget it all. I had other worries. The only ones that stuck in my memory were those that stood out in some way. From the intelligence point of view, I mean. As well, of course, as the ones we pumped regularly. They were the ones that yielded a lot. Your father was definitely not one of them.' He leaned over towards Daniel and said, 'There's no sense in investigating it like this. You must know best of all the sort of person your father was. Even if there were some files still around and you got access to them, you wouldn't learn much from them because everything was far more complicated than anything you might read there.'

'Thank you. I expect you're right.'

'Your see, people these days over-dramatize everything. They've got the idea that it was only scoundrels, brutes and fanatics who worked with us. But we were normal people. At the beginning we believed, like a lot of others, that socialism would bring something better than what we had. Anyone who resisted it seemed to us like an enemy. But when you started to analyse things, you soon lost your enthusiasm. We only did as much as we had to.'

'I also had some encounters with some of your people,' said Daniel. 'It's possible that the people who dealt with me only did what they had to, but it was plenty, I assure you. But that is neither here nor there at this moment.'

'Yes, you're a pastor. The way the church was treated was crazy, absolutely mindless. We are all reaping the dire consequences of that now. People nowadays only believe in property, money and their careers.'

He was unable to fathom whether the man was putting it on, or whether he was saying what he truly felt.

Then Daniel realized that this man had once sat at a desk with portraits of the murderer Stalin and his local Czech satrap on the wall behind him, while his father had sat facing him, the indelible experience of eight years in the camps imprinted on his mind, and an understandable feeling of tension. His father would have known he had to give some sort of answer, and whether he left the room a relatively free person was entirely up to the person who now sat opposite his son Daniel with a friendly expression on his face, talking to him as if they were jointly engaged in the struggle against present-day materialism. The man could not recall his father, he had just been one of the many they had summoned whenever they needed them. Whereas his father, if he were still alive, would certainly have remembered him. This captain had been one of just a few of those who had attached themselves like leeches to his father's life. Later this man had disgraced himself and maybe then some other captains had latched on to him, so that he now felt justified in bemoaning his reduced state. Any sense of humility, let alone repentance, was foreign to such people. And by coming to see him, he, Daniel, had bolstered the man's feelings that he was one of the just, one of the victims, someone worthy of honour, praise and trust.

Suddenly he felt disgusted at his action in coming here and the fact that he was meekly sitting and listening and scarcely taking issue. He stood up, saying he had no wish to stay any longer, thanked him and prepared to leave.

'Should you ever need any advice,' said the erstwhile captain, 'or just feel like dropping in for a chat, you'll be very welcome!'

6

Matouš

Matouš Volek is not in particularly good form. His appetite is not returning and his stomach hurts from time to time. He can't go to the pub or to any of the offices of the journals he works for. This is the third day he has been entirely alone and to cap it all it is Sunday morning and holy days have always depressed him. He spends a little while playing with the seven tangram dice but fails to build any interesting picture. So he tries to call up a number of friends but nobody answers the phone. They are probably at their weekend country places or at the seaside.

It's hot. Matouš gets up and puts on the big ceiling fan. The fan whines, which Matouš finds irritating, but at the same time its noise and the movement of the hot air remind him of cheap hotels in China or Singapore. He searches among his CDs for the one with Chinese music with its sense of the unusual that always soothes him. While listening to the 'Moon Mirrored in the Waters' he makes himself a pot of red tea and then goes to sit in the old armchair with its worn leather cover.

A white screen and behind it the lively gestures of the puppets. Gongs and Mongolian fiddles. Wooden clappers. The somersaults of the actors in their pure silk costumes. Wu-tan in a red robe and wielding a sword.

Pagodas in parks, the red walls of the Imperial Palace, gates with yellow roofs. The fish market and bicycles flashing past like a shoal of fish. Those under sentence of death being hauled off to execution on a cart; rebellious intellectuals and con men, smugglers, corrupt officials and murderers. The ever curious crowd goggling at those who are about to die. When the crowd becomes enraged, it hurls books into the flames. Brainwashed children burn the works of old Chinese masters along with those of foreign devils, or goad an old man along: they thrust a four-sided hat on his head and hang a sign around his neck saying 'STINKING TEACHER CHANG PREACHING THE CAPITALIST ROAD'. They make him kneel before a portrait of Mao and recite from memory some of the dictator's articles. Then they dance the Dance of Loyalty and hang a wall-poster of loyalty on the wall. They all sing 'The East is Red'; all in the name of some senseless, self-destructive revolution, all in a country where until recently the old were esteemed as nowhere else in the world.

The Yellow River and in it Mao, the fat, ugly and cruel unifier of the country. Even on the day before he died millions of brainwashed children and old people were shouting: May he live a thousand years!

How many years, how many months, how many days does Matouš have left? He would like to leave his burrow behind, leave behind the world of screeching tramcars, a world well-disposed to con men, loose women, cancer and bad poets, whose works mostly did not get burned, and find a place of silence wherein he would hear nothing but his own breathing. But the fan whines and the solitude presses on his brain and all he can see and hear are mindlessly roaring crowds.

If only his bad wife were to look in; she regularly drops by for money. It is two months since she was last here. She was probably too ashamed to come to the hospital, or else she knew he had no money there. But at this moment he would give her whatever she asked for, provided he had enough. Maybe she would make it up with him and stay till the end.

Matouš believes he is endowed with a special gift of perceiving the aura that surrounds every individual, so that at moments of clairvoyance he is able to discern when the aura is so weakened that the person no longer has enough strength to live. But he is incapable of seeing his own aura and this fact does not help his peace of mind.

He knows he ought to rise above all the cares that flow from his awareness of his own self, cut the umbilical cord that connects him to the outside world. Instead of succumbing to anxiety, he ought to advance with equanimity towards the Great Coalescence. Except that he spent the whole of yesterday gawping at the television in order to dispel his loneliness, distract his thoughts and not miss what life had to offer for the brief moment that fate still granted him. But on Sunday mornings there are only children's programmes on television. So he pours himself a glass of wine and some lines of poetry come to him:

> *Drink wine, anyway,*
> *do nothing*
> *Float away*
> *Fathomless longing.*

In his stomach the wine is instantly transformed into boiling lead that rises back into his throat.

The eyes of a jade Buddha stare at him from the glass case opposite his bed. *Oh, monks, this, then, is the noble truth about suffering: birth is suffering, old age is suffering, sickness is suffering, death is suffering, contact with unpleasant things is suffering, when one does not attain what one wishes it is suffering . . .*

Suddenly he makes up his mind. It's Sunday, he'll go and hear the husband of that motherly matron preach. Maybe his sermon will cheer him up.

He enters the chapel after the service has started. The place seems half-empty to him. Perhaps it's always like this, or perhaps it's because the holidays are beginning. All the same, Matouš does not sit down but stands behind the last row of pews trying to make out whether the pastor's wife is also in church.

Shortly after his own arrival, another woman enters. She is strikingly attired and her long hair with its faintly Titian red hue hangs halfway down her back. She stands alongside him, opens the hymnal and when she has found the hymn, joins in the chorus.

Matouš doesn't join in the singing; he doesn't know the melody and the text seems to him imbued with a belief in something he finds utterly foreign.

The pastor's wife is sitting right in the first row. He easily recognizes her plump figure and the slightly greying hair which, instead of being hidden under a nurse's cap, is combed up high into a bun. Matouš's mother wore her hair the same way.

The pastor is too tall and gaunt and it seems to Matouš that there is something ascetic about his appearance, or maybe something intense. He emphasizes each of the words he now reads from the Scripture as though wanting to attest that each word was a stone in a foundation or an unshakeable rock. *Do not lay up for yourselves treasures on earth, where moth and rust consume and where thieves break in and steal, but lay up for yourselves treasures in heaven, where neither moth nor rust consumes and where thieves do not break in and steal. For where your treasure is, there will your heart be also.*

It's interesting that even in those far-off times people didn't have anywhere to hide their treasures from thieves. Confucius also lived in a time of wars, discord and crime, but believed that in some earlier age harmony, justice and wisdom had reigned, and we must return to those values if we wish to remedy the way things are.

The pastor continues with his reading. The text emphasizes that people should not worry about their future or fear that they will have nothing to eat or wear. Then the minister starts to interpret the text. In his opinion, people have become plunderers, always wanting to own something. Nothing of what they already have seems enough to them and in a way they turn into bandits, taking where they can, plundering anything that cannot protect itself, whether it be someone weak and helpless, an animal, a tree, any living thing. They even plunder the dead resources of the earth and transform them into enormous quantities of things which soon turn into piles of waste.

Matouš senses agitation welling up from within him. It is a state he is familiar with. Sometimes he can engender it when he has drunk several pots of strong green tea. At such moments, objects start to become transparent; plants and all living things become surrounded with an aura of gentle colours and he is able to discern the traces of past contacts and the outline of imminent death, decay and putrefaction. And at that moment he realizes that the pastor's aura is fading; it appears and then disappears like the twinkling light of a distant star. The pastor has not long to live. Maybe he suspects as much; Matouš can detect nervous anxiety in his words. It is also odd that whenever the pastor looks towards the place where Matouš is standing, his speech seems to falter and it is as if he has lost his thread. Only when he turns away does he continue with possibly even greater emphasis.

During the last hymn, the pastor hurries out and so does the woman at Matouš's side. His agitation gradually recedes.

A middle-aged man stands outside the door shaking everyone by the hand. He also greets Matouš. 'You're here for the first time today, aren't you?'

He confirms this and explains that he was in hospital and the pastor's wife invited him.

'It's nice of you to have come,' the man says with pleasure. 'I hope you have enjoyed being with us.'

The pastor's wife also notices him. 'You really did come then, Mr Volek?'

'I said to myself it would do me no harm to go to church once. But actually I was only looking for an excuse to see you again.'

'There's not much to see,' she says. 'But my husband will be pleased if you come more frequently.'

'I actually agreed with quite a lot of his sermon,' he says, chiefly to please her.

'Really? You ought to tell him. He'd be happy to hear it.'

'I don't know when I would have the opportunity.'

'If you like, and if you have no particular plans, you can join us now,' she suggests. 'You can have lunch with us. My husband will be back at noon; he has another service today. And our children will enjoy listening to you. I have spoken about you at home.'

Her invitation takes him aback. Could he really have captivated this woman? He protests that he could not be such an inconvenience. But the pastor's wife dismisses his protests. They are always having someone home for lunch.

And so he manages to enter the flat in the manse.

In fact, it is a very long time since anyone has invited him to lunch. He has no friends, only acquaintances, and he tends to meet them in pubs or wine bars.

Stepping into the front hall, he certainly does not have the impression of entering a manse. The walls of the front hall are hung with posters: Michael Jackson; alongside him some space rocket on course for Saturn; and below that the open jaws of an enormous salmon begging to be protected.

'Marek and Magda hung all of them there. The poster with the salmon was sent to us by my husband's sister. She lives in America,' the pastor's nice little wife explains and leads him into the living room where normal pictures hang on the walls. On the piano stands a vase of purple irises. 'You see? I have really nice patients who bring me flowers,' she says with approval. 'If you like you could take a seat here – there are lots of books on the shelves, or you could play the piano, unless you'd prefer to take a walk in the garden. I have to get on with the cooking.'

He follows her out, of course, and even suggests that if she had some French beans, dried mushrooms, soy sauce, pepper and something he could use to make a meat broth, he could cook a piquant Chinese soup.

To his surprise the pastor's wife accepts his offer and brings him everything he has requested and also lends him an apron. 'We are used to our guests making themselves at home,' she explains. 'If you didn't enjoy it, you wouldn't have offered. And you really will be helping me, as I still have my packing to do.'

So he prepares the meat broth while the good wife at his side scrapes the potatoes. He has no objection to such a division of labour here, he senses the relaxed, homely atmosphere – a good home. When they were still living together Klára would refuse to cook. He had to cook for himself or they would go to the pub. She said to him once: 'When you buy a car I'll cook you what the Queen of England has for dinner.' But he could never afford a car and she never even cooked him the handful of rice that the Chinese ricksaw driver has for supper.

A freckled little girl with glasses bursts into the kitchen. The pastor's wife says it's their Magda, and he loses his composure slightly, being unused to dealing with children and aware that it would be a good idea to entertain the little girl somehow. He recalls the fable of the giant leviathan that could appear in the form of fish or fowl and as a bird could rise to a height of ninety thousand miles, in other words higher than any satellite or rocket. The trouble is, the fable does not really have a plot and turns into a morality story, unsuitable for telling, least of all to children.

Happily, Magda ignores him and takes a banana from the fruit basket, asking whether she ought to pack Eva's old black swimming costume or take her own old one. When Mrs Vedra suggests they go out the next day to buy a new one, Magda exclaims that that would be super and dashes out again.

'You have a pretty daughter.'

'Except for the glasses. Her eyes are getting worse all the time.'

'I've worn glasses since I was ten. My eyes won't get any worse now.'

'The doctor promised me it will stop when she reaches puberty.'

'You said you had two children of your own and one step-child, Matron. If it's not too bold a question, was your husband divorced?'

'The very idea!' There was a note of amazement or even offence in her voice. 'His wife died when Eva was just a baby.'

'And did you always work in a hospital?'

'Yes. After the Charter they wouldn't let my husband remain in Prague. He was only allowed a little church in the highlands. It took me almost an hour to get to work from there.'

'And did you have no option?'

'My husband had a really tiny salary. Admittedly people would make us gifts of food, but I realized the congregation was too small to support us.'

'And now you wouldn't need to?'

She shrugs. Then she says, 'No, not any more. My husband got back an apartment house in Vinohrady in the restitution and sold it for a lot of money. But I wouldn't like to be stuck at home.'

'And what would you like to do?'

The pastor's wife again shrugs, seemingly unsure of what she would like to do.

'You could find something nice to spend your time on.'

'What do you have in mind?'

'There are so many opportunities nowadays.'

The matron shakes her head and he quickly adds: 'I don't mean having fun, but doing something where you'd be your own boss.'

'I'm hardly going to start a business somewhere. I wouldn't know how, anyway.'

'I could easily imagine you managing some trust to assist disabled children. Or lonely grandmothers.'

The pastor's wife ponders his words. She neither says anything, nor protests. Maybe she could make a contribution towards the publication of his poetry. 'And what plans do you have for your money?'

'I don't concern myself with it. We bought the children new clothes. And my husband bought himself a car. He needs it, since he also has the charge of a congregation in the country.'

'But it must be an interesting feeling to come into wealth all of a sudden.'

'No, I prefer not to think about it.'

He observes this woman. Her hair is already greying, but the skin on her arms is still smooth and her round face is almost free of wrinkles. If she were to dye her hair she would look younger. But it would seem she has no desire to, in the same way she has no desire for money. That is, if it were possible for a woman not to have any desire for money. How much could they have received from the house sale? How much is a lot of money? Money interests Matouš; it would help him lead an independent existence. But he had had nothing to demand back in the restitution, his forebears had been ordinary peasants or workers. One of his grandfathers had been a gamekeeper and he could have asked for his shotgun back if it had actually been his own.

And did returned property also belong equally to the spouse? Probably not – at least not during the life of the recipient. If this good wife were to divorce she'd remain poor, she'd only be rich when that preacher-sermonizer of hers died and returned to the Lord, which shouldn't be long by the look of it. Unless he divorced her first. But pastors probably don't divorce, and certainly not very often. But what about their wives? He hasn't any notion of how pastors' wives behave. Most probably just like any other woman in our part of the world; you can win their favour so long as you find the right way to their hearts. But that was an art he had never mastered.

When the soup is cooked, he mentions that he not only has oriental cookbooks at home but also Chinese and Japanese prints and a collection of interesting objects and some figurines, mostly of the Buddha. 'When you pay me a visit I'll be happy to show them to you.'

The matron remains silent for a moment, and then says, 'I'm sure my husband would find that interesting. He is a very good carver himself. Though not of Buddhas.'

And so, despite using her husband's interest as an excuse, she actually accepts his invitation.

7

Daniel was waiting at the Smíchov bus station to drive Eva home. He had always waited for her like this ever since she was small and would come home from different camps. He had waited for her even when there was no longer any real need for him to do so, and when in fact it was no longer appropriate. But seeing that he always came to meet her half-brother and half-sister he was afraid his eldest child might feel neglected. Maybe – even though he didn't like to admit it – he wanted to make sure no one else was waiting for her. Also he was worried where she might go if he left her a free choice.

Eva was the very last to appear in the door of the bus. 'You've come to meet me, Daddy?'

'And why wouldn't I?'

'I thought you were cross with me.'

'What made you think so?'

'You know very well. Petr wrote and told me that he admitted to you I had asked him for speed. But he talked me out of it. It was given to me by some other people.'

'Given or sold?'

'They wanted something for it.'

'You talk about it as if you were buying a hot-dog.'

'But I only bought it a couple of times and then Petr talked me out of it.'

'We won't talk about it now.'

'I'm really sorry. I ought to have talked to you about it, but I was afraid you'd be upset.'

He felt he ought to point out that he was upset about what had happened and not about the fact she hadn't told him about it, but he'd first have to make the same comment about his own actions. It needs a lot of courage to admit to an action that one is ashamed of and knows to be wrong. One's reluctance to hurt someone else is just an excuse; in fact it is a lack of courage.

'What's new at home?' Eva asked.

'Mum has gone off to Grandma's with Magda and Marek. And Marek has started to read like mad. The last few days before they left he moved into the library and started to devour books. Mostly about astronomy and nature, but also my theological writings. And before I forget, we discovered that our daughter had started taking drugs!'

They reached the car. 'We've got a new car?' she said in surprise. 'And you didn't tell me in your letter.'

'Didn't I? Maybe I didn't think you'd be interested. The next time we buy a car I'll let you know.'

'I've been reading too,' Eva said. 'Grandad has an interesting book about Bach. And I played the piano a lot.'

'How much is a lot?'

'About three hours.'

'During the entire stay?'

'No, every day, of course!'

'That's good. One mustn't neglect one's talent.'

'Agreed,' she said, ' – if one has talent. Unlike me.'

'Listen,' he said, 'what about finding somewhere to sit down together, seeing that we haven't seen each other for so long and you've been practising the piano so diligently?'

'Like a pub, you mean?'

'If you like.'

'But we can just as easily go home.'

'At home there's always some disturbance or other – the phone or visitors, you know how it is.'

In the Small Quarter they found a garden restaurant. There were a few locals in the tap-room, but in the garden they found a free table beneath a red sunshade advertising Coca-Cola. In the shade of an old ash tree it seemed cool.

'What will you have?'

'Could I have a Coke?'

'You can have whatever you fancy.' His elder daughter was sitting opposite him, slightly red in the face. Like her mother, she didn't tan, just went red. Anyway they had stopped recommending sunbathing just recently. Why had he really invited his daughter to the pub? Certainly not because the telephone would disturb them at home. Most likely because that was how he invited the other one out. He'd spent more time with her these past weeks than with his own daughter, whom he had neglected to such an extent that he had failed to notice how far she had wandered off. Now he was trying to make up for it. As if he could get back the time that he had wasted so rashly, as if there were any way of rectifying what had happened.

'And wine?' she asked.

'You can have wine too.'

He ordered them each a glass of wine. Not even her arms were tanned; they were just freshly covered in lots of freckles. He pictured to himself a hypodermic syringe and a needle puncturing that skin, heaven knows what kind of needle. The very thought was nightmarish – surely it couldn't happen to the little girl opposite, his little girl.

It was a fact that he seldom found the time to talk to his daughter, to ask about her worries, her pals, to hear some of the things she thought about, what her concerns were, whether the poem she had shown him was her only one or whether she wrote verse more frequently, and who she showed it to. Admittedly he saw her every evening at the dinner table and at the Sunday service, and was endlessly giving her orders, making sure she prayed, taking note of the marks on her school reports and the names of her teachers, studying literary and general history with her, and even telling her about those things that were either deliberately omitted from the curriculum or lied about. But she herself was so unknown to him that at the moment when she clearly needed him, he sat here as if with a strange young woman. He was incapable of intimacy even with his own daughter.

'How are you planning to spend the rest of the holidays?'

'I expect I'll go and spend a week with Mum. And then Marek and I were thinking of going for a couple of days to protest against the Temelín nuclear power station.' She sat rather stiffly and answered him like a model pupil or a model daughter.

'I don't know whether that's a particularly good idea, whether Marek would be capable of protecting you if the need arose.'

'You keep on staring at me as if I've committed a terrible sin, Daddy.'

'It's not a question of sin, just the fact you could completely ruin yourself!' He knew about her failings, she didn't know about his. Which of them was ruining themselves more? What was more excusable, or understandable, at least? 'And I'd also like to know if you intend to give it up!' It was possible, or probable in fact, that if one deceived those around one, one influenced them even if they knew nothing about one's deceit. Because people who deceive behave differently from those who have nothing to hide.

'I wanted to tell you that it's not Petr's fault. He tried to talk me out of it.'

'Why are you always talking about Petr and not about yourself?'

'I don't want you to do Petr an injustice.'

'I don't intend to. But you must realize that I'm more concerned about you than about Petr. But while we're on the subject – am I supposed to be grateful to him for teaching you another bad habit?'

'He didn't start it. And he persuaded me not to inject anything. After I'd got hold of the hypo myself.'

'Where did you get it?'

'At school, of course.'

'But you haven't answered my question about whether you intend to give it up.'

'I already have, thanks to Petr.'

'Thanks to Petr, who in place of one bad habit taught you another?' He was having trouble suppressing his anger.

'Daddy, you don't know anything about it. Petr isn't wicked. On the contrary, he wants to help people. And he talked me out of speed because I might get hooked on it. Marijuana isn't addictive. And anyway I've given that up too. Down at Grandma's I only drank milk and ate vitamins.'

'What made you start it at all?'

'I just wanted to try it. I sold that sweater you gave me on account of it. Are you cross with me?'

'On account of the sweater?'

'It was a present from you.'

'To hell with the sweater,' he said, unable to control himself. 'What made you go looking for the muck in school?'

'Because almost everyone in our class had tried it.'

'That's an exaggeration.'

'And they also drink, smoke cigarettes and marijuana, and all of them have a steady. Almost all the girls have slept with someone,' she explained.

'But surely you don't have to do everything you see the others doing.'

'Not everything, but at least something. Particularly when . . .' She checked herself.

'Particularly when your father is a pastor?'

'Everybody looks at me as if I was made from something else.'

'I regret that, but have you chosen the best way to prove you're made from the same stuff?'

'I chose the worst way – deliberately,' she said, with a sudden display of wilfulness.

'I have no doubt that it upset you the way the others looked at you, but I'm sure that they didn't all look at you that way. I'm sure that you had friends in your class too. So that probably wasn't the main reason.'

She raised the glass of wine and slowly sipped it. 'But I told you not long ago – the reason.'

'You did?'

'Emptiness.'

'Yes, I know. Emptiness at home with us.'

175

'And in myself.'

'I'm sorry. I'd hoped – I'd imagined that we were giving you something to fill that emptiness. More than some drug.'

'That didn't fill it either. You just forgot about it for a while.'

'How?'

'You really want to know?'

'What do you forget about? The emptiness?'

'Everything. Yourself. That you're lonely, for instance. Speed becomes your friend. And I also felt stronger after it, that I could do all sorts of things.'

'What, for instance?'

'Be good at school. Be good to people. To love them. I had the feeling I'd be able to do anything I tried. Such as being able to carve a figure like you. Playing the piano the way you expect me to. And after grass, I had the feeling that time almost stood still, and that when time stands still you won't ever die. And I had this incredible urge to laugh at everything. I found that beautiful: that I could laugh. And I thought up tunes and poems. Really, fantastic poems.'

'Did you write them down?'

'No, that seemed totally pointless. Why write? I was just happy I had thought them up.'

'Happier than you'd feel normally?'

'Differently. But without it I never have felt very happy anyway.'

'I'm sorry to hear that.'

'It's not your fault. It's no one's fault. It's just the way I am.'

'Evička, you know yourself that it won't make you happy. And there's an awful price to pay for that brief moment of happiness.'

'I know, Daddy. I've already given it up. I really have.'

8

Letters

Dear Dan,

I've arrived safely with Magda and Marek. As usual, we are occupying the little bedroom at the top of the house under the roof. It has a beautiful view of the countryside with all three ponds clearly visible. Such splendid peace prevails everywhere. And then in the evening I was watching television and they showed the hospital where they had just admitted a little girl whose arm had been torn off and other people mutilated in the conflict and I began to be ashamed of indulging myself here, and of taking an extra month off, and it occurred to me that I could offer my services to them during this month. Apparently they have a shortage of doctors and medical staff of any kind. What do you think?

It would seem only right to me, but I was mentioning it to Mother and Magda overheard. She leapt on me and started to wail: Mummy, I'm not going to let you go anywhere. You'd get killed!

Magda is a good girl but she is incredibly lazy. When I ask her to pop to the shop for some yeast she looks at me as if I'd asked her to load a wagon with bricks. Today she slept in until ten thirty and was even astonished that I'd woken her. Yesterday a hornet flew into our room and she was so terrified she started to yell like a mad woman and crept under her bed. She stayed there until I had got rid of it. Marek, on the other hand, has mowed Mother's entire garden and whitewashed her pantry. Apart from that he has his head stuck in that thick book about the universe. When I happened to open it, I discovered some indecent pictures cut out from somewhere. I know there are nude pictures all over the place: on the television and on calendars, but even so, I'm disappointed in Marek. I haven't said anything to him, but perhaps you should have a talk with him and explain to him that it's not a good way to look at women. I know he argues with you sometimes, but you're the person he sets most store by. He'll be coming home in a few days' time as he wants to go with Eva to the protest camp near that nuclear power station. I don't know whether it's a sensible thing to do.

It's so difficult, Dan, to know what to make of today's world, to know what is right and what isn't, what is good for people and what is harmful. Mother finds it very hard to walk and her rheumatism is worse. How's your back? I left you some Brufen tablets – 400 mgs – in the medicine cupboard, just in case you get an attack.

Our young Pavel came and spent a day with us. As you know, he's bought himself a shop in the village and run himself into debt. Now he's worried and even opens up on Sundays. But what's the point, he won't sell more than people are able to buy from him. I also talked to him about Bosnia. His view is: They made their bed, now they've got to lie on it! I recalled where it says in the Scriptures: Judge not lest ye be judged and also: Harden not your hearts lest misfortune befall ye – but my little brother just said that he has enough troubles of his own and can see no reason why he should also bother his head about people shooting at each other somewhere in foreign parts. Sorry for lumbering you with this chatter, I'd better finish.

Dan, please don't forget to water the house-plants – all of them, please! And if this dreadful heat wave continues (apparently you had 34 degrees in Prague), don't forget to spray the garden.

We still have more than a fortnight of our stay here left, but I'm already missing you terribly. I'm not accustomed to such long holidays, and I was a bit worried when we were leaving because I sensed you were having a hard time. Should you need me, just call and I'll come at once. You know you're the person I hold dearest.

Best wishes from Mother and me.

With all my love, Hana

Dear Dad,

We're having a super time. We go swimming and for walks and muck about with the girls from the village. Grandma baked some curd and poppy-seed buns and they were the bestest and biggest in the whole world. Mum also said only Grandma knows how to bake buns like that. We've got five little angora bunnies, they look like fluffy tennis balls with red eyes. We say our prayers every night and we're all going to church on Sunday. I'm sending you a great big kiss, Love Magda.

P.S. Mum said she wrote and told you I'm lazy. Dad, I'm not lazy, I'm *on holiday*, that's all. You write too, please. I know you don't say bestest, but when I'm on holiday I can write what I like, can't I?

July 94

Dear Dan,

This is the beginning of my last week at this spa where Sam is being treated for one of his many conditions. I'm being a good wife and putting up with the boredom here, accompanying my husband to treatments, taking walks in the colonnade, and talking to him about architecture and his health problems. When he takes his afternoon nap I slip away for a few moments to the little park in front of the hotel and yearn to be with you. I miss you so much, my darling, so very, very much!

You are a revelation for me, one that has grown from meeting to meeting. It has grown from nothing, by which I mean I never thought that someone like you could live among people. It would be bold of me to tell you who you are, because I don't know you, but I fear that my boldness would only be the vanity of someone who never doubts her judgement. But I'll try anyway. You're kind, you're good-hearted and you're strong, even though you're a real man. You're generous. You don't hurt people. You place life above success, knowing that the only real success is to lead a good life. You think that it is your faith that guides you, but I think you're guided by your heart. I also think that you're not one to criticize or reprimand people over little things, what you want chiefly is for them to be kind and live in love, like you yourself. I agree with that, because love is the thing my heart demands, what my soul cries out for. I could be surrounded by the best people in the world but if my heart was cold nothing would happen. My need for love comes from my fear that life has no meaning, that everything comes to an end, that nothing that I want to last ever lasts more than a few moments. It is a defence against the chilling universe. Sometimes when I'm falling asleep I can hear my heart suddenly start to thump wildly, because I abuse it even though I know it doesn't deserve it, that it's a good heart. You haven't abused yours, my darling, you've only refused to hear it. You've convinced it that a good life consists of being loyal to an old vow instead of to your own heart.

I'm thinking of you. After so many years of my life, I've started to like myself. That's a gift from you. I look at myself and tell myself I'm beautiful and desirable when someone like you can love me. When you can love me even when you try desperately not to. I can sense that, of course, my darling. I look at myself and know I'm a feeble, imperfect woman, that I'm impatient and selfish. Since you don't have me for your entire life there's no need for it to worry you.

But please keep me in your warm love for a few more days at least, no, a few more weeks, no, a few more months, please. Don't forsake me, even when I'm awful sometimes.

Love, Bára

My dear Hana,

Your long letter really cheered me up. I was moved and even shamed by your determination to go and lend your help in those places where people are murdering each other, misled by false prophets and criminal leaders.

I don't agree with your brother. However far away people may be, I think we must regard them as our neighbours, and therefore perceive their pain and suffering. The trouble is there are so many people. The people who suffer outnumber those who don't, and the weight of suffering, if it was all added together, would make a crater deeper than the deepest pit of the ocean, so it is too heavy for us to bear. I expect the most we can do is help in those places that we can see and reach.

But Magda is right to say she wouldn't let you go to a place where there is shooting. I don't think such places are made for children or their mothers – they should leave those places, not seek them out. And the children need you – even Eva, who I thought would be able to fend for herself by now. She does in fact, but in a way that terrifies me, and I firmly believe that your experience and wisdom will help us rescue her from that poisonous whirlpool before it drags her to the bottom.

Don't worry about having a peaceful time and a rest, you deserve both. You've done enough for others in your life and had enough of your own suffering.

And don't have any worries about me. I'm feeling fine and my work-load is somewhat less now, so I have a bit of time to do some reading and a spot of wood carving.

I'm thinking of you all and looking forward to seeing you.

Love, Dan

Hi Dad,

We're having a fantastic time and it's fantastic here, the people, I mean, because in other ways it's like in a sci-fi film, those cooling towers that stare down at you from high above. All that concrete. There's enough to build an entire enormous city. A dreadful concrete city, that is. We go to lectures and have discussions in Czech and English and our meals here are cooked by Dutch vegetarians. They travel every summer to protest against nuclear power stations wherever they are being built. Except that they've almost stopped building them anywhere else, only here. Yesterday we projected on to the towers portraits of the politicians who dreamt up this place. It was stupendous. Now we're preparing a non-violent action. A blockade, in fact. Maybe we'll tie ourselves together and lie down in front of the gates. We're still discussing it. I like the fact that the people here are thinking about the future and are unwilling to let television pull the wool over their eyes. Eva has just gone off to the villages to persuade people to save energy and insulate their windows instead. I expect she won't be back till this evening.

Are Mum and Magda back yet? If they are, give them our love. And love to you too. We're both well.

Wouldn't you like to come and visit us? A few famous people have been here already, singers mostly. They share our views. You could talk to the people too and let them know you agree with us and that Jesus, if he only had the slightest idea about nuclear power stations, would be here with us too.

So write to us soon. And pay us a visit. You can sleep in our tent.

Marek

———

Dearest Bára,

Last night was unusually hot. I couldn't get to sleep, so I got dressed again and went out into the garden and looked at the stars. My son looks at them almost every evening whenever he's at home and then asks me questions to try and catch me out. You tried to do the same about the size of the universe. Yes, there are distances that are unimaginable and insuperable, but I was always more interested in the distances that separate people, distances that are infinitesimal compared to the universe but which often seem equally insuperable.

You write lovely things about me, I've told you not to more than once, and you write beautiful things about love. I agree with you, even though I am frightened of what has happened and is happening – between us. At the same time, I am grateful for what happened and is happening. I sense the possibility of a great love between us and through it the intimacy I have yearned for, something I experienced or started to experience with my first wife, but which I only associated with her. I had stopped believing that I could ever experience anything similar ever again. Have I the right? Have we the right?

Even though I ask these questions, I am grateful to you for the short time you have been in my life. And that gratitude remains, though I shudder to say it. You write 'nothing that I want to last ever lasts more than a few moments'. It strikes me, on the contrary, that if people so desire there is no such thing as 'nothing ever', that it is something that only death can say, and not even death need say it precisely the way you feel it. But human folly is capable of anticipating death by entire decades. Often 'nothing ever' is something we create for ourselves, through our weakness, selfishness, or ignorance. Or our desperation.

What are we going to do?

I also want to let you know that you are a special, exceptional individual. You have a greater yearning for love and wholeness than I have ever encountered in another human being. I feel near despair because what there is between us can never be whole. Or can it? What would we have to abandon for it to be so? How many people would we have to hurt?

And so we lurch, you and I, between a yearning for completeness and the anxiety of 'never ever'. It's a very imperfect situation and therefore very human.

I feel an enormous love for you. I couldn't recant it at this moment, even if I tried.

Love, Dan

———

Dear Reverend,

I apologize deeply to you for all the bad things I have done. I only told you all those things the time I got drunk because I was miserable, because I had to move out of my sister's. It's not true that I could be a dealer. It's just that I need to earn more money because that's the way things are nowadays. I am now searching for the truth. About life and about the Lord Jesus, because I've found out that everyone sees him differently. Such as the Jehovah's Witnesses or the Roman Catholics. The way they honour the Virgin

Mary, for instance. The other day one of their priests gave me a leaflet with a prayer by St Louis which actually states: it is thy privilege to hold absolute sway over angels, men and demons; it is thy privilege to dispose of all the gifts of God, just as thou willest. What do you say about that, Reverend? Isn't it almost blasphemy against the Lord? Or take the Pentecostals. They maintain that everything of any importance comes from the Holy Spirit and we have to believe in its power and not yield to Satan. That seems to me right, because the Holy Spirit was poured out on the apostles, after all. I'd also like to ask your forgiveness, Reverend, over Eva. I didn't mean her any harm. I just wanted to get her out of the clutches of those rotten speed dealers. Marijuana doesn't do you any harm, Reverend. But I ought to have talked to you first, and so I now beg you for forgiveness.

I prayed that you and the Lord God will forgive me.

Yours, Petr

Darling Dan,

I don't know what I'm to do with you. A double life destroys one, unless one totally abandons the need to be a complete whole. Forgive me. Forgive me for destroying you. But unless one gives up the need for love, I suppose there is nothing for it, in certain situations, but to lead a double life. In today's world, at least, and with our morality. One can fool the brain, but not the heart. The heart is a compass, you know that, don't you? You know how to read it. From the very beginning, from the first moment I heard you, I knew I could trust you, that I could place my head in your jaws and be sure that you would not harm me. Taking a chance with you is not just placing my head in your jaws, it's also needing completeness without an escape route. But I'm leaving myself an escape route anyway: the way home, back to my husband and my sons. Except that my home is also a place of peril. I'm constantly on my guard here and there is no loving embrace for me. Instead there is a man who demands my embrace while keeping his arms behind his back. Admittedly I try to accommodate him. I look cheerful and smile, but deep down inside me something that can never be renewed is being burnt away. There is something dead inside me, something I can't bring back to life. My cheerfulness here is awfully superficial, I feel it and so does Sam who is always complaining about me. He distrusts me and suffocates me. I can't get closer to him and I can't leave him. I am stuck here and I'm unhappy. The atmosphere here is not one of blissful ignorance that conceals everything. It is an awareness of ruin. It destroys me because I need joy for my life to have meaning. I don't want to live without joy and without love. I'd sooner not live at all. I don't want my life to be merely a succession of duties. I don't want to save the world with duties but with joy. I long to leave, to disappear, to turn my back on everything, free myself, dissolve, be no longer. I talk about myself as if I didn't think about the others. In my daily life I constantly have to think about others, I have no time to remember myself. It's thinking about you that has made me remember myself. When I'm with you I feel that I may think about myself too. You are someone who doesn't intimidate me, or blackmail me, threaten me or ridicule my craziness. You're someone who really loves me, not because I'm particularly worthy of love but because you're overflowing with it. I feel an enormous gratitude towards you. I have never really encountered anything like you.

And now I feel like crying because you're somewhere far away, all too far away. I don't have you near me as my salvation, my dearest of all men, my real man, the one I trust, the one who won't let me perish, to whom I can admit to being weak, incapable and pathetic and yet he won't reject me.

And now I lament that I have found the kind-hearted man I longed for and he is not for me, won't ever be for me. I know it. I have found that man and can thank God that he let me know you at all.

It surprises you that I write about God and you think I'm doing it to ingratiate myself with you. But I don't want to go against the Ten Commandments. I understand them and respect them – apart from the one about not coveting my neighbour's husband. I understand that life requires order and that morality is good so long as it is not hypocrisy.

I really have made a proper mess of my life, but at this moment I'm happy, so happy in fact, I could easily die. But I don't want to, I want to be with you for a long, long, long time – at least one whole night.

I love you so terribly much, that I can't see how to survive it. We return in three days time, will I see you?

Bára (with love)

———

Dear Marek and Eva,

I'm glad you like it at the camp. It's splendid that we now live in a society in which people can say freely what they don't agree with. That was something I could hardly do when I was your age, and certainly not freely. Thank you also for the invitation but I won't be coming. The thing is, I'm not sure who is in the right in this argument. I do believe that people ought to live more frugally, and indeed I preach about it often enough. I believe they should show greater consideration towards nature and life and weigh the consequences of their actions. But it's not easy to convince them. That's something I've discovered. Most people are more attracted to wealth than to frugal living. In that respect, people nowadays would seem to be worse than in centuries past because it's easier to get rich and anybody who would voluntarily live in poverty risks ridicule. That's why electricity will be produced. After all, you use it too and life without it is difficult to conceive now. And whether it is better to obtain electricity from coal, oil or nuclear fission is something I am unable to judge. I don't understand it, in the same way I don't understand mathematical sets, and don't know what to make of black holes or quasars. And Marek, I'd only ask you not to fall prey too easily to over-simplified judgements, but instead to weigh up the pros and cons. Now and in the future. Because the moment you stop making up your own mind you risk being taken advantage of. I was taken by your idea that the Lord Jesus would be with you if he were on earth. Jesus would certainly be on the side of those who managed to live frugally, and whose actions were governed by love and humility before the majesty of God. Even so, I don't think we should draw Him into our own all too mundane – or even political – disputes. Instead, Jesus should open the gate to what is above us, what lends meaning to our lives and its values, what transcends our brief lives. Because without that, all that remains is the cold universe full of the galaxies that you so often speak about. In such a universe it matters little how electricity is made or what from.

Best wishes to both of you.

Love, Dad

Chapter Five

1

He was already asleep when the phone rang. 'It's me, Dan. You're not cross with me for calling so late?'

'I've no idea of the time. It must be midnight, isn't it?'

'I don't know either. I dashed out without my watch. I need to have a talk with you, but I don't suppose you'd be able to.'

'I'm alone at home. My wife is still in the country.'

'Do you think you could come and meet me somewhere?'

'Are you crying?'

'Maybe. I'm awfully upset.'

'Has something happened? Is it the children?'

'No, the children are asleep. Everyone's at home in the warm, only I'm out here freezing in the phone-box at the bus stop. It's like being in a glass coffin. But I'd sooner be in a wooden one. Seeing nothing, knowing nothing and then being pushed into the flames where it would be warm at least.'

'I'll come then.'

Half-past midnight. Outside, an unseasonal July chill and the wind chasing clouds across the sky, their edges pallid in the light of the moon.

He catches sight of her in the distance standing at the bus stop, long after the last bus has gone. She is huddled up in a short blue-and-yellow mottled coat.

He pulls up right in front of the bus stop and opens the door.

'I've got cold hands again,' Bára says, 'and feet too. I'm cold all over and you've come in spite of that.'

He asks her what has happened.

'I ran away. He threw a ruler at me.'

'Your husband?'

186

'Who else? We were having a row. Over Saša. But I don't want us to sit like this in the car.'

'I don't know where we could go.'

'So just drive on!'

'All right. Will you tell me what happened?'

'You don't mind the muck spilling on to you?'

'That's why I've come, isn't it? So you could tell me what happened.'

'Didn't you come because you love me?'

'It's one and the same.'

'I know. So take my hand.'

Her hand is as cold as that time she drove him. How long ago was that?

'He can't stand Saša,' she says of her husband. 'He's always bossing him about, forbidding him things. Calling him a good-for-nothing idler who does no studying and comes in late. And today he yelled at him that he needn't think he'd be going on to university, that he'd maintained him long enough. And I said I'm the one who maintains him anyway, he's my son, and Sam started yelling at both of us that we're layabouts. I sent Saša away and told Sam that he mustn't dare do that to me. It flabbergasted him that I should have the gall to stand up to him, because after all he is someone whereas I am no more than a flea that has crept into his clothes, a dustbin in which he chucks all his foul moods. He grabbed the steel ruler and hurled it at me. If I hadn't dodged, he could have killed me. Oh God, it's so vile, forgive me, I dashed out of the flat but I had nowhere to go. I would have gone to Mum's, but it was too late and she would have had a fright, so I called you.'

'I'm glad you called me.'

'I'll never forget you came for me, that you didn't leave me in that phone-box. And now, instead of getting a night's sleep . . . Where are you taking me? To the airport?'

'No, I'm just driving along.'

'I'd fly somewhere with you. Somewhere far away. Somewhere overseas. Somewhere that's warm. Barcelona, say. They're bound to have warm weather there, and Gaudi too. But wherever I am with you it's warm, your heart gives out warmth. Don't worry, I don't intend to drag you off somewhere or throw myself on you. I'm going home. No, don't stop. Bear with me for a while still. Drive me somewhere, just for a short while.'

So at Červený vrch he turns off the main road. He draws up in front of one of the tower blocks. 'There's an empty flat up there. It belonged to my mother.'

'Your mum died that same day. I know.'

When he unlocks the door he looks up and down the passage, as if fearful someone might see him. But they are all asleep at this hour.

Inside the flat, he is aware of the familiar odour that has still not disappeared even in the five months that his mother has not been here.

He helps Bára out of her coat and they sit down opposite each other. Bára fixes on him a look of total devotion, or at least that is what it seems like to him and he realizes he is pleased; instead of wasting time sleeping he can spend it with her.

'I don't suppose you'd have a drop of wine here?'

'There's not a thing to eat or drink here. Nothing but ketchup.'

'It doesn't matter. Why did you sit down so far away from me?'

'I'm sitting quite close.'

'I want you to sit closer.'

He moves his chair so that their knees touch.

'There was a time when he really did maintain us,' she said, 'when Aleš was small. But I was the one who looked after them. He didn't have to lift a finger at home. And what's more, in the evenings I would help him with tracing plans. But since the revolution I do as much work as him, maybe more, because I drudge for him at the office, play the occasional bit part on television, and also do the housework. So tell me, what sort of layabout am I? How can he say he maintains my son?'

'I don't consider you a layabout, do I?'

'But he does.'

'I doubt that even he does, really.'

'So what makes him say it?'

'I don't know. I don't know him. Maybe he just wanted to hit out at you somehow. The pain of a slap passes quickly, the pain of injustice lasts longer.'

'But tell me why, why he should want to cause me pain? Why?'

'Maybe he's jealous of your son.'

'Why should he be jealous of my child?'

'You give him love he would like for himself.'

'And don't you find that horrible?'

'It's human.'

'And would you be jealous of my Saša too?'

'No. No one has the right to deprive another of his share of love.'

'I know. You definitely wouldn't torture me.'

'I've done all sorts of bad things in my time, but so far I don't think I've been cruel to anyone.'

'You've done lots of bad things? There is only one that I know of. Tell me, why didn't you come for me long ago?'

'How could I come for you when I didn't know you?'

'Exactly. You weren't interested in any old Bára. You happily left me to the mercies of a fellow who hurls steel rulers at me.'

'Don't think about it any more.'

'You're right. I'm sorry. Here I am with you and I spend the time talking about another man. Tell me, do you still remember your first wife?'

'How do you mean?'

'Can you still bring her to mind?'

'Of course.'

'Often?'

'It depends what you mean by often. Less now than years ago. But most frequently I remember some situation when we were really happy or, on the contrary, when we hurt each other.'

'You're able to hurt someone too?'

'Such as when I didn't do something she wanted or didn't protect her enough. When we were going out together, we lived a long distance apart, several hours' journey. There were times when I didn't bother to make the trip because I didn't feel like trudging all that way. And once – it was when she was already expecting Eva – she was summoned to an interrogation. And I let her go there and didn't even wait for her outside the office because there were other things I had to do. Whenever I remember that, I feel regret that I didn't stand by her then.'

'But it only bothers you because she is dead.'

'Yes, I can't make up for it any more.'

'You can make up for it with the living.'

'I've tried to ever since.' Then he says, 'And you remind me of her.'

'Do you think I resemble her?'

'No. It's more a sense of familiarity, a sort of intimacy.'

'It must have been awful for you when she died. Tell me, did it ever strike you as unjust?'

'It's not the business of death to be just, is it?'

'And how about God?'

'God is just, but his justice is not the same as human justice.'

'Do you think there can be two sorts of justice?'

'It's not the question of a different sort, but of a different dimension.'

'You believe in the fourth dimension?'

'I mean the dimension in which God moves.'

'When my sister died I felt it to be an injustice. Why her, of all people?'

'Your sister died? You didn't tell me.'

'It's ten years ago now. I don't like speaking about it.'

'She was the one who found you when you wanted to kill yourself?'

'I only had one sister. Katka was so kind to me. The kindest of all next to Mum.'

'What was she suffering from?'

'Nothing. She got into a skid when she was driving her car. For five days she was conscious and they just thought she would never walk again. Then she lapsed into unconsciousness. They kept her for six more weeks on a life-support machine. When they switched it off, that was that. When does the soul leave the body? When they turn off the machine, or before?'

'I couldn't tell you.'

'Do you think it's fair that good young people should die?'

'Good and bad people die. We all must die.'

'Yes. Ever since then I've known that I can say cheerio in the morning to someone I love and I may never see them alive again. Or they me. It's sad. It's a sad arrangement, don't you think so?'

'And how would you like it to be? How would you have life arranged?'

'I'd like to know I have a few days left. For living. For loving you.'

'You're sure to have.'

'How can you tell?'

'I'll pray for it.'

'You'll pray for me not to die yet?'

He nods.

'I prayed for my sister too, that time. But it didn't help.'

'Don't think of death any more.'

'You're right. Don't be cross with me. Here I am with you and I'm talking about death. It's just the mood I'm in. Tell me, will you lie

190

down with me, or are you in too much of a hurry?' She gets up and finds the door to the bathroom without difficulty.

He hears water running. It is most likely rusty. It has been months since he ran any water here. He was unable to forget his first wife. Particularly during the first years after her death. Maybe that was the reason he was never able to be completely close to Hana. He was grateful to his second wife and he loved her. But he was incapable of loving her like his first wife. It seemed natural to him, in fact, that one could give oneself fully only to one person in a lifetime. What is it that he feels now? Real love? Or has he yielded to some comforting self-deception?

When Bára returns she is wrapped in a towel, in the same way his first wife used to wrap herself. 'I took it,' she says, referring to the towel. 'It belonged to your mum, but she would have been sure to lend it if she knew I was here with you and I loved you.' Then she asks him to turn off the light in the room, but to leave the one in the lobby burning as she is scared of the dark.

They make love on the old ottoman that he still remembers from his childhood. 'My darling,' Bára whispers, 'I love it when you put your arms around me. You're so attractive: I love your mouth, your teeth, your eyes. They're a greyish blue like the Prague sky. If I didn't have you, if you hadn't come to meet me, maybe I wouldn't be living now. I need love to live and without it I'd die. Without you I'd die.'

She groans in ecstasy and begs, 'Save me. You will save me, won't you?'

'From what?'

'From all evil. From cruelty. From the world. From me. From death. You can. You can do it. You can do anything.'

'I don't have that power, sweetheart. But I love you.'

'There you are. You have the power of love.'

The light from the lobby falls on her face that seems pale. But her hair has a coppery sheen and her eyes are dark.

'I've already told you I'm not God.'

'One doesn't need God for love, though. Love is in the human heart. In mine and in yours.'

What time can it be? How did he come to be here? Is it a sin? Is he betraying those he loves? Is he betraying himself? Or, on the contrary, would he be betraying himself if he weren't here, if he had renounced this moment when the love he feels overwhelms everything?

She puts her arms around him. 'Tell me you don't mind I dragged you out at night.'

'I'm glad.'

'We've never been together at night before. And never the whole night. And we won't be tonight either. But I'd love to wake up in the morning at your side. At least once.'

'So would I.'

'Would you go somewhere with me and spend a whole day and a night with me?'

He looks at her and into her honey-coloured eyes, and she says, 'Yes, it's me!'

'I'd go with you for a night and a day and a night and a day and . . .'

'No, you know yourself it will never happen. And besides, when you woke in the morning you'd notice I had wrinkles, you'd notice I'm old.'

'But you're not old.'

'I'll be forty-one next month. Do you realize how dreadful that is?'

'No, that's not dreadful.' He sits up. The light from the street enters the room. What is dreadful is to live a lie, to deceive one's next of kin – this is what occurs to him, but all he says is that she is still a little girl compared to him.

Bára stretches out her arms as if wanting to draw him to her, but she too sits up. 'You want to go already? All right, I know, we have to.' She embraces him again. 'Don't forsake me!'

'I won't.'

'But you will. You will in the end. Just now you were thinking what a problem I am for you.'

'No, what was actually going through my mind is that I am deceiving my wife and you're deceiving your husband.' He gets up and goes over to the window. The windmill below the window turns silently.

'I know it bothers you. And already I feel a chill down my spine at the thought of what awaits me at home.' She dresses rapidly. 'Maybe he'll kill me one of these days and you won't even find out! And you'll go on preaching how important it is for us all to love each other!'

2

Diary excerpts

I talk to Eva in a friendly way, I don't reproach her with anything and I act as if everything was all right. But I can't dispel the fear that I've neglected something, that I've messed something up. I always wanted to set a good example to my children, not to speak about truth and love, but to be truthful and live in love. But what if the way I behaved, the way I acted and the way I treated her, only tended to increase her sense of inferiority and inadequacy? Young people are prone either to excessive belief or excessive disbelief. It depends on their character and the people they model themselves on. As a child I scarcely knew my father. He was in prison. When at last he came home he was my hero, but his behaviour was so natural and earthy, and he tried so 'sinfully' to enjoy life, that I sometimes found him hard to take. Maybe it would be better for the children if I were to swear sometimes, or play cards, or at least get drunk from time to time. But what if they were to discover what I'm really doing?

It is well known how hard it is to be the child of famous parents. Clergy aren't usually famous people, but their children don't tend to have an easy time either. Exemplary behaviour is expected both from the parents and from the children. But should any of them fail, they are the butt of scorn and their disgrace is the subject of general satisfaction.

My thoughts are in a tangle, just as my life is. And I look for excuses for my actions.

I have definitely fallen far short of being a perfect example for my children. I have simply tried to live in accordance with what I preached. And I have never exalted myself over anyone, and that includes my own children. I've never saddled them with any burden of responsibility. At most I've reminded them of the words of Ecclesiastes that always struck me as wise:

Come now, I will make a test of pleasure; enjoy yourself. But behold, this also was vanity . . .
I searched with my mind how to cheer my body with wine – my mind still guiding me with wisdom – and how to lay hold on folly, till I might see what was good for the sons of men to do under heaven during the few days of their life . . .

*I also gathered for myself silver and gold and the treasure of kings
and provinces; I got singers, both men and women, and many con-
cubines, man's delight.*

*And whatever my eyes desired I did not keep from them; I kept my
heart from no pleasure . . .*

*Then I considered all that my hands had done and the toil I had
spent in doing it, and behold, all was vanity and a striving after
wind, and there was nothing to be gained under the sun.*

*I'm not sure whether they were capable of understanding the text.
And what about me? Am I still capable of accepting its wisdom? If I am,
I'll preach on it. No, if I still accept it, I'll live by it.*

———⚬◦⚬———

*I was invited to take part in a radio phone-in on what was supposed to
be a topical issue: Why are people losing confidence in the church. Apart
from me, there was a parish priest, Father M., a tolerant and big-
hearted man, plus some sociologist and an editor. The listeners who
phoned in mostly attacked the Catholics, accusing them of hankering
after property, of wanting to take possession of the national cathedral,
and of having used power to force their beliefs on people and burn the
innocent at the stake. I kept on waiting for someone to raise some serious
objection, such as calling into question Christ's divinity or Mary's
virginity, saying that everything we preach is based on a faith that is an
insult to the intelligence of people nowadays, but nobody voiced anything
of the sort. I left at the end with the galling feeling that the human
mind just flitters on the surface, fascinated with property, violence and
old grievances. As Comenius writes in his own biography: 'For I have
observed that people do not speak at all, but only mouth things, i.e. they
do not transfer a thing or the meaning of a thing from one mind to
another, but instead they exchange among themselves words that are
misunderstood, or understood insufficiently and wrongly. And this is
done not merely by the populace, but also by the semi-learned crowd . . .'*

———⚬◦⚬———

*From the last letter of Mrs Milada Horáková, written a few hours before
her execution on 27 June 1950:*

'I'm completely calm and prepared. The minister has been here, and even though Dr Kučera couldn't come, I found it a great support – I begged him also to help you above all. Rely on all of those who can and want to support you. Live! Live! . . . There are so many of you – I'm alone and also have to cope.

'I never doubted your strength, but you have surprised me. It will be painful for a while, but the pain will gradually diminish. Go out into the meadows and the woods, you'll find a little bit of me there in the scent of the flowers. Go into the fields, look at all the beauty and everywhere we'll be together. Look at the people around you and I'll be reflected in each of them in some way. I'm not at my wit's end or in despair – I'm not putting it on, I'm so peaceful inside because my conscience is clear.

'. . . During these last moments everything has seemed so unreal to me, but in fact I have only minutes left to count. It's not so bad – you're the ones that matter now, not me any more. Be strong! I love you so much and a love like this can't be lost or just evaporate, can it? Nothing in the world is ever lost, everything goes on growing somehow and is renewed again. Follow only the things that are close to life. Cling on to each other and support one another!

'I repeat it once more: the new life that is now approaching has brought me incredible peace of mind. The play is over for me and the curtain's coming down, but a new play is beginning . . . Maybe I played my part badly, but it was an honest attempt. You can take my word for it. I meekly submit to the will of God – he set me this test and I accept it with just one ambition: to obey God's laws and preserve my good name as a human being.'

What would I write in such a situation? And to whom would I address my last letter?

Bára and I meet in Mother's old flat. We don't see each other more than twice a week and always briefly. We have no time. She talks to me about her work and her life. Several times she has brought a letter she wrote to me in the meantime. But she hasn't wanted me to read it at once. 'You're not going to waste the time you could be with me!' I find her letters almost spellbinding, although I know I must not accept the praise she heaps on me.

I told her that should her husband refuse to support her son's university study, she could rely on me. She said that such a thing was out of the question, but it is important for her that I say it.

Apparently, for several days her husband treated her and even his stepson with more consideration. I asked her if he had apologized for throwing the ruler at her.

'Apologize? To me? That's something he'd never do. In his eyes I'm not a fully developed human. I'm just a woman, aren't I?'

I also confided in her the news that I had found Dad's name on the list of police informers.

She asked if it distressed me very much.

I told her I would like to know the truth.

'But you'll never discover the truth,' she objected.

I said that if truth could not be discovered then there could be no justice on earth.

'And there isn't any,' she said. 'There truly isn't any justice.'

⁂

It's fascinating how Marika, the gypsy girl, takes for granted the accounts of Jesus's miracles. For her, miracles are still part and parcel of life. Unclean spirits move amongst us and the seriously ill can be healed by the touch of a hand and a stormy sea can be calmed by a single command. Her grandmother knew how to exorcise evil spirits and her blind girlfriend was visited in a dream by her late father who prophesied that she would see.

'And did she see?'

'Yes, of course.'

In her world, the dead move about and still live together as they did in life. They are invisible to us, the living, but they can visit us in dreams. She believes it is possible to charm or to offend the sun, the moon and the wind. Am I to explain to her that this is all superstition and error, that only our Lord was able to perform miraculous deeds, because he was the Son of God? Or am I, on the contrary, to tell myself that the message of Scripture can only be accepted fully and unselfconsciously by people such as she?

Marek and Alois took her to visit the Pentecostals in Libeň. They came back in high spirits as they had experienced something out of the ordinary — even speaking in tongues and, as Marek put it, 'genuine piety'. Their enthusiasm did not please me. Something is happening to

196

people: they are turning outwards instead of inwards. I remember watching a televised service of the Apostolic Church when I was visiting Rút in Oregon, although it looked less like a church service than a television show. The preacher dashed here and there on an enormous stage, yelling, crying and laughing, telling stories from the lives of basketball players and racing drivers, singing and invoking the Holy Spirit, which played some crucial role at the end of each of his stories. He had a pile of paper napkins to hand which he used to wipe the sweat from his brow and then threw them away all over the stage. I told the boys that speaking in tongues was not so much an expression of faith as an expression of confused minds, which leads them into a state of false ecstasy so that they believe they are speaking to our Lord. Wherever the conscious mind is absent, anything can gain a foothold, and mostly it is something bad, not something good.

Petr hasn't shown up for several weeks now. I asked Marek and Alois if they had any news of him and where he was actually living. Alois hadn't a clue, and Marek seemed to me to hesitate before replying – as if he knew something and was frightened to confide in me. I felt like shouting at him but I stopped myself. Distrust is worming its way into our family and I myself am not without blame in this regard.

***

I had a talk with Marek about love and the beauty of the female body. I told him that the really beautiful woman is the one that you love. And suddenly I realized that all the while I was thinking of Bára, and I thought to myself, what right have I to preach to Marek?

Almost every night I wake up with an oppressive awareness of the lie I am living. I ought to give up preaching (not just to my children). How am I supposed to talk about morality, love and honour when the way I live denies them all?

Bára believes that white lies are merciful precisely to those whom we deceive. I won't leave my husband who hurls rulers at me, she told me, and you won't leave your wife, who looks after you, who brought up your daughter, bore you two more children and loves you. So everything will stay the way it is, I'm sure of it. So why cause them pain?

It's a philosophy I can't accept, but on the other hand I am unable – and too craven – to suggest anything else.

B. rang me this morning to say she's ill. She was with her husband at their country place at the weekend and it looks as if she slipped a disc when she was digging the flower bed. She managed the homeward journey, but this morning she was unable to get out of bed. Fortunately, her husband stayed in the country, as he wanted to do some drawing in peace. She told the boys to go to their grandmother's after school and now she's lying at home like an invalid.

I told her it was a pain I was familiar with and had some tablets I could bring her.

She doesn't want tablets, she hates tablets, but if I wanted to, if I were to find a moment and come over, I could find out where and how she lives.

I bought a bunch of roses and a small glass vase from Nový Bor.

'You're crazy,' she said when she opened the door. 'You mustn't go wasting time rushing around the shops.' She was wearing some faded sweater and tattered jeans. 'I'm lying down,' she announced. 'You won't mind that I first invited you to our house on the very day I'm unable to stand upright?'

We walked (or in her case, limped) through a spacious lounge in which stood several flower pots containing miniature citrus trees as well as a fig tree that almost touched the ceiling.

I certainly have had little occasion to visit houses of that kind, and I was taken aback by the luxuriousness of the Finnish furniture and the emotional vacuity of the abstract paintings intended to embellish the white walls. She noticed and asked whether I disliked modern art. I replied that I found some works disconcerting and had the impression that some of their creators had no wish other than to be original, whereas I was always looking for some message.

You're a pastor, she said, you have to look for a message in everything. It's good enough for me if they make me happy or I enjoy the colours. Then she added that she accepted no responsibility for the furniture. Although she was an interior designer, the entire arrangement of the house, apart from her own room, had been Samuel's choice, as he couldn't bear to live in anything that was not organized according to his scheme of things.

Then we arrived at her own room. I was fascinated by an enormous desk that took up the entire length of one wall. The desk-top, which rested on a steel base, was made up of smallish square wooden blocks. 'That,' she said, indicating the desk-top, 'was once a floor in an old villa. They were going to lay linoleum on top of it, the philistines, so I bought it from them. They have linoleum on concrete and I have a splendid desk that even has a patina.'

The room also contained a divan and an armchair, by which stood a steel standard lamp whose base, I noticed, was formed from the three spikes of a garden fork. You see, she said, a lamp like that has to be in here, Samuel can't abide anything that's slightly off-beat. She lay down, groaned and asked me to cover her with the rug that was lying on the armchair. I asked her if there was anything I could do for her, whether she was thirsty or hungry. She told me I wasn't here to wait on her; no one had ever waited on her. All she wanted was for me to sit down and be with her now. If you hadn't come, she said, I would be brooding on my powerlessness and death.

We chatted for a while like close friends who don't see each other often enough. I told her about Eva's drug-taking. She reassured me that it was commonplace nowadays and didn't mean anything. When she was eighteen she must have tried everything they forbade her, and in fact there was very little they did forbid her. She had felt such a need to set herself apart from the world she was forced to live in that in the end she had slashed her wrists.

The telephone on her bedside table rang several times and she talked to people I didn't know.

At one moment she asked me to pass her a large black folder from the desk. It contained her latest set designs and several interiors. It was her first chance to display her work to me. She showed me her design for the interior of a country manse – a Catholic one, naturally. She explained that she had tried to make use of the old furniture that remained in the house, simply adding a number of small armchairs that could be built according to photographs of Schinkel's armchairs from the beginning of the last century. I hadn't a clue who Schinkel was, but I didn't ask. I don't understand furniture, and the furniture we have at home simply assembled over the years as we acquired it. Some things we bought, some we inherited, some were given to us. I was always of the view that the objects didn't matter. They serve a purpose and they should not attract attention either by being in bad taste or enticingly unusual. But I realized she was waiting to hear what I'd say about her work, so I said I liked it, and also that I liked her desk and her idea for the lamp.

Then the phone rang once more and she suddenly changed and became wary. 'Is that you, my love? It's nice of you to call.' And she glanced at me in mute appeal.

I realized it was her husband calling and I crept out of the room. I drifted around the spacious house until I ended up in the kitchen. I located a saucepan and found ketchup and milk in the fridge. Salt, sugar, rice and flour were in containers on the shelves. It was gone noon and it occurred to me that I might make some soup while she was on the phone.

'Why are you so kind to me?' she asked when I brought the bowls. 'You are putting me to shame, for heaven's sake. We could have easily had a sandwich.' Then she said that her husband had called to say he'd finished his work and would be returning that same afternoon.

I was about to get up and leave.

'But it'll take Musil at least two hours to get here.' Then she asked reproachfully, 'You would actually leave without making love to me?'

I had a dream. Two men were leading me down a long passage. At the end of the passage was a hole, so narrow that a cat could scarcely have squeezed through it. Nevertheless the men stopped in front of the hole: this way!

I stood nonplussed in front of the opening, until one of the men made it bigger with his heel while the other pushed me forward. I was falling through the opening. I don't know how long I was falling but at last I found myself in a dismal office where no one was sitting; there was just an enormous mastiff lying in front of the door.

'Take a seat,' I was instructed by a voice from some unknown source. 'You realize why you're here?'

I sat down in the seat opposite the desk and said I didn't know. The mastiff raised its head and snarled.

'A lying pastor.'

'I don't know why I'm here,' I repeated.

'What about the scandal then?'

'I don't know what you're talking about.'

'You preach scandal. And in addition you went into the pulpit naked.'

'That's not true.'

'But you had yourself photographed doing it.'

I banged my fist on the desk. 'That's not true.'

'And what about the little girls in Sunday school? What do you teach them?'

'I teach them the word of God.'

'No, you tell dirty stories. I have a pile of complaints here. In children's handwriting.'

All of a sudden a pile of envelopes appeared on the desk in front of me. 'Read that one there, for instance.'

I found in my hand a piece of paper that was indeed covered in children's handwriting but I couldn't decipher a single letter. But I knew that there could be nothing against me in the letters so long as they were genuine. Except that these were definitely not genuine.

'So what do you say to that? Great, isn't it? What do you think your missus will say when it's published?'

'What missus?'

'You've got more than one?'

I became uneasy. There was something out of order here, something bad had happened. After all, my wife was ill and dying. 'You can't do that,' I shouted.

'That depends on you.'

'What do you want of me?'

'You know full well! Take a leaf out of your father's book. He understood the right way to behave.'

All of a sudden the room was full of big fellows in grey clothes, each one identical, the same unfamiliar faces, but they seemed to be smiling in a friendly way and actually offering me a glass of wine. 'We'll reach a deal, though,' said the one offering me the wine.

'You scratch our backs, and we'll scratch yours,' said a fat, grey-haired man as he entered the room. He seemed to be their leader – I recognized him in fact. It was Berger, my old Secretary for Church Affairs.

But there aren't any Secretaries for Church Affairs any more, I remembered to my relief. We're free again, it's just that these chaps don't know it and are threatening me and trying to bribe me with a glass of wine.

I took the glass and smashed it on the ground. The wine spread all over the floor, blood red. And at that moment I realized that Jitka, my good, gentle wife, had died long ago, and I had been left alone, and it made me sad.

Daniel generally took a holiday in the second half of August. Sometimes he would stay in Prague but usually he would set off with Hana and the children for a manse in the country run by one of his friends or a former fellow student.

This year, for the first time, they could afford a holiday that would depart from the normal routine.

When he suggested to Hana that they might go abroad it occurred to him that it wasn't so much foreign travel that appealed to him as the possibility of escaping somewhere a long way away. Escaping from the other woman? No, from himself, more likely. Except that there is no escaping oneself.

Hana agreed that he should take a rest. It was necessary to renew one's strength or one day it would run out. But why go on a foreign holiday and leave the children here? What if something happened to them?

The children would be at Grandma's and we don't need to travel far. Just to the Alps, say.

The Alps held no appeal for Hana. The Šumava Mountains seemed more feasible to her, besides which she could make herself understood there.

Fine, we can drive to somewhere in Western Bohemia and maybe go on an excursion to Germany from there.

While Hana was doing the packing he quickly sorted out his correspondence. When the phone rang, he felt a strange agitation and hesitated before picking up the receiver.

'It's me, Dan,' said a familiar voice. 'I'm calling from our castle in the country. Samuel has gone fishing and I thought I might still catch you.'

'Your instinct was sound. We are about to leave any moment.'

'And you don't mind me calling?'

'No, I'm pleased to hear you.'

'And are you on your own there?'

'My wife is packing.'

'So go and give her a hand! I just wanted to tell you I'm thinking of you and that I'm missing you, that I wish I could be with you.'

'I'm thinking of you too.'

'Nice things or nasty?'

'That's not a proper thing to ask.'

'I wanted to ask whether you'd forget me.'

'It's almost impossible to erase anything from my memory.'

'And you'd be so vile as to want to erase me?'

'I didn't say anything of the sort. I only said I have a good memory. And I'll never erase you from it.'

'That's good. I wish you lots of sunshine. And I don't only mean the sort that comes from the sky. I mean the sunshine you have within you.'

'I don't know whether I ever had it within me, and even if I did, I fear it's hidden behind the clouds now.'

'Do you feel that I'm the clouds?'

'No, if it's possible to have sunshine within oneself then the clouds must also come from within.'

'That's true. And you have love within you and that sunshine. I'll hang up now, you have to go and pack. And forgive me if I've hurt you.'

'How could you have?'

'It's possible to hurt someone without wanting to, even someone you love.'

'The person you can hurt most is yourself. And then those you love, of course.'

'I know that. So I'll say cheerio. And don't forsake me.'

He and Hana were staying in a new hotel near Domažlice. Their room had a bathroom and a colour television, and there was a telephone on each of the bedside tables.

'Do you like it?' he asked his wife.

'It's unnecessarily luxurious.'

'We could make a trip over the border to Regensburg tomorrow.'

'Why Regensburg?'

'It's only a short drive from here and it's a beautiful city. With an old cathedral.'

'If you like.'

'I thought you'd like it too.'

'I'm happy wherever we are together.'

'Do you fancy a little walk before dinner?'

'That's a good idea. I'll just have to change my shoes.'

'It's ages since we've been for a walk together, isn't it?' he said as they left the hotel.

'It's because we've had so little time. Whenever you had a spare moment you had to visit your mum. And apart from that, you've had so much on your plate.'

He had the feeling they hadn't done much walking even when his mother was still well. Sometimes he got the impression that his wife was afraid of being left alone with him. Maybe it was more shyness than fear. And now it was he who avoided talking to her.

They set off along a path that led between meadows. The edge of the path was yellow with hawkweed and cat's ear and a kestrel circled above the meadow.

'I wonder what the children are doing,' Hana said.

'They're rejoicing at having got rid of us for a while.'

His conversation with Hana tended to be mostly about the children. And sometimes she would tell him about goings-on in the hospital and he would share with her his parish concerns. They almost never talked about books. Hana had no time to read, even if she had the inclination. They only rarely went to the theatre and he didn't watch television. Whenever they had guests, which was at least once a week, she would worry about what they would eat or drink and see to it they had fresh bed linen, but she seldom took part in the conversation, which generally dealt with theological issues or the situation in the church.

Also he did not talk to her about things that happened to be on his mind, and he would prepare his sermons without discussing them with her.

She differed from his first wife in almost every way, both in character and appearance, and maybe that was the very reason why he had never managed to be completely intimate with her, even though, until just recently, he had had nothing to conceal from her.

They reached a bush that was covered in blackberries. He bent down and picked a handful of them to offer his wife.

'You're so kind to me, Dan.'

'But it's nothing at all.'

'It's lovely here. A pity Magda isn't here, at least.'

'Magda's fine at your parents.'

'I know. It just struck me that it would be nice if we were all together.'

He stroked her hair and then took her by the hand and they continued along the footpath towards a village some distance away. He couldn't remember the last time they had walked along like that, holding hands. But that time it must have been from a sincere feeling, whereas now he was trying to atone for his offence in some way. That was why he had booked an expensive hotel room and thought up the trip to Regensburg. He would buy her some clothes there, anything she fancied – as if that would in any way change what had happened or make up for anything. At most it would delay the moment when he would find sufficient courage – or hard-heartedness maybe – to tell her at least something of what he was perpetrating.

'And I'm a bit worried about Eva too,' Hana said a moment later. 'Once someone starts to experiment with drugs, there is always the temptation to return to them. We oughtn't to leave her for a long time at home on her own.'

'We wouldn't be able to keep an eye on her all the time anyway. If someone really has a mind to do something, there's no way you can watch them continuously. They don't even manage to keep the inmates in prison under permanent surveillance. All you can do is explain, entreat, ask and trust.'

'When someone's eighteen and on their own it's a temptation for them. Besides which, she's attracted to Petr.'

'You've noticed that too?'

'It's not good. Not for her, anyway.'

'Don't worry. When she gets to the Conservatoire and into a different environment, she'll find other friends.'

They had dinner together in the hotel dining room and he prevailed on his wife not to look at the prices and just have what she liked.

That night they lay down beside each other as always. The blue reflections of the neon signs shone into the room. He got up and drew the curtains.

Then Hana said, 'It's been a lovely day, Dan. Did you enjoy it too?'

His wife quickly fell asleep. It had been a long time since he made love to her. He knew it gave her no pleasure, so he had the feeling he was molesting her or taking physical advantage of her.

He could not get to sleep. It was his custom to meditate last thing at night, turning over in his mind everything that had happened or pondering on what he had to do in the coming days. Now it was as if everything, both the past and the future, fixed him with a reproachful look. He tried to pray. To think about a sermon. On what text? *Put off your old nature which belongs to your former manner of life and is corrupt through deceitful lusts, and be renewed in the spirit of your minds, and put on the new nature, created after the likeness of God in true righteousness and holiness. Therefore, putting away falsehood, let everyone speak the truth with his neighbour, for we are members one of another.* (Ephesians 4: 22–25)

For a moment he tried to summon up the image of his first wife and recall the words he used to lavish on her. The tender words returned but not the image of his first wife, instead the image of the new one – the one who had come on the day of his mother's death – forced itself upon his consciousness. What had brought her to him? What was she intended to recall? His mother's love or her death? Why had she appeared that particular day? Who had sent her – what force?

He strove to dispel the picture of her face, but instead her voice imposed itself on him: Don't forsake me!

How was it possible not to forsake a person one wasn't with and oughtn't to be with? Or was it the despairing cry of someone who feels forsaken? Forsaken by whom?

My God, my God, why hast thou forsaken me?

Suddenly the telephone rang on his bedside table. He snatched up the receiver and in spite of the absurdity expected to hear the voice of the woman he had been thinking about.

'Reception here,' said the voice on the telephone. 'I'm sorry to disturb you, but I noticed the stamp of a Protestant church in your identity card and thought you might be a pastor.'

'I am, yes.'

'I thought I'd just ask you: one of our guests, an old gentleman, has had a bad turn. We've already called the doctor but the gentleman also asked for a priest.'

'But I don't give extreme unction.'

'If it wasn't too much trouble to you, I don't understand these things, but seeing that he did ask . . .'

'Yes, of course,' he said, and started to get dressed.

206

4

Matouš

Matouš is seized by the demon of activity. He scarcely sleeps and he wrote sixteen articles during the month of September. In fact, though, it was not he who wrote them, but some essentially alien and rather unpleasant being that occasionally worms its way into his mind and, before he can expel it, commits all sorts of indiscretions. He knows by now that when it whispers something into his pen he mustn't sign it with his own name, and so for at least a year now he has been delivering these inventions under the name of Lukáš Slabý.

Matouš brings a feature about schoolchildren smoking pot to one of the tabloids, and pretends he wrote the article himself. He tells the editor that in these times the only successful stories are about drugs, prostitution, contract killings, and billion-crown scams, or so it seems to him. But he has an advantage over the others who write about the same things: he can enrich his stories with his experiences of the hashish dens in Hong Kong or Singapore, although – to be honest – he felt safer there than here. His colleague nods, Matouš's articles read well. Then he goes off with Matouš to a cheap wine bar for a drink. After the fourth glass he mentions that Matouš's ex-wife Klára spends her time sitting around with foreigners at the Hotel Evropa. Sitting around and lying around, most likely.

Matouš, who makes a practice of referring to Klára as his ex-wife although he is not yet divorced, gives no indication, even now, that this news affects him in any way and simply says, 'She always was a tart.' And he concurs with his colleague that women are tarts by nature, although some lack the courage to be so brazenly open about it.

However, when he gets home he feels to his surprise something akin to grief, disappointment or bitterness. That woman still continues to use his name and can even keep it should she cease to be his wife. When he first met her she had seemed to him innocently girlish and he loved her, trusted her and brought her into his home, from which she soon drove out all peace and tranquillity.

He sits down in the armchair placed in front of the television set. As the news is about to start, he switches on and watches the reports with the professional eye of Lukáš Slabý to whom he owes his living. On the screen, they are just carrying away the corpse of a woman covered in blood, another woman tears her hair – a Bosnian or a Serb. It doesn't register with him anyway. Countless unknown corpses affect one less than one single betrayal close to home.

Matouš watches the flickering colours impassively and he is suddenly seized by torpor. He stares for a moment at the stuffed canary sitting motionless on its perch in the cage. He recalls a park not far from Peking University where the old men would bring their caged birds to give them an airing. Birds flying out of their cages. The scent of jasmine. Bright-coloured kites. Nostalgia. He won't find the energy or resolve to make any more journeys, he is gradually losing the will to live.

Then he makes up a not particularly successful haiku in his head about his not particularly convincing notion about his own death:

Just dream a sweet dream
Be awoken by no one
Turn into a shade.

He won't even write it down, but with his last ounce of strength he forces himself to get up from the armchair, puts on a white shirt and the silk tie he brought all the way back from Shanghai years ago, and sets out for the Hotel Evropa.

Klára is indeed sitting there. It is still early, so she is sitting on her own, slowly sipping from a glass containing wine or something purporting to be wine. Her long red nails glitter, her blouse pretends to be embroidered with gold, while from her ears dangle rings that are genuinely gold, like the rings he had given her.

He approaches her and asks if the other chair is free.

Only now does she notice him and gives him a startled look. Then she says, 'Yeah, for the time being. What are you doing here, for heaven's sake?'

'I'm the one who should be asking you that!' Matouš comments.

'You've no right to ask me anything!'

'You're still my wife.'

'That doesn't mean I can't sit where I like. I'm a free person, aren't I?'

'I hope you make a decent living, at least.'

'Don't be disgusting, Volek!'

'You've not shown up in a long while,' he says. 'You've still got

208

some things at my place and it's about time we went to court at last, so you can feel truly free.'

They argue for a while about their mutual relationship, each blaming the other for breach of faith. Klára maintains that the only reason she is sitting here is because he drove her to it, because of his lack of interest in her, his insensitivity and his meanness. 'Don't you understand you are impossible to live with?' she asks.

He asks her why, and *she*, whose brain was never disturbed by the slightest interesting or original thought, *she*, who was capable of listening to inane pop music from morning to night or gawping at even more inane television shows, *she* who has never once in her whole life read one decent book (and probably not even an indecent one either), says to Matouš, who has always prided himself on the breadth of his knowledge and his ability to entertain people: 'Because you're insufferably boring!'

'Does that mean you have no intention of ever coming back?' he asks pointlessly.

'I couldn't give a toss about you.'

'Or my money?'

'With the money I get from you, I could hardly afford widow's weeds.'

Then a group of foreigners arrives in the dining room and Klára tells Matouš he had better clear off.

Matouš instantly suppresses a fit of helpless rage. Most of all he would like to hit her but it goes against the grain to hit a woman. Besides, here in the restaurant it would probably cause a scandal. So he gets up and whispers, 'Have a good time then, you dirty slut!' And he knocks over her wine glass with his elbow. Klára leaps up out of her chair just in time to stop the wine running into her lap and kicks Matouš in the shin with the imprecation, 'Fuck off, you impotent old bastard!' Matouš does not stop to hear the remaining curses. He limps away across the square as evening falls. He feels dreadful, and is aware of a great number of bizarre-looking individuals and dark faces that look even darker in the night. Whores, pimps, drug dealers and addicts stand around. One of the youngsters loitering in front of the arcade looks familiar, he has the impression that he noticed him at that church he visited not long ago to hear the husband of the motherly looking matron from the hospital. But he was probably mistaken, these people don't look much like churchgoers – unless they were making a night-time foray. Matouš turns away in disgust. He no longer has the feeling of treading the familiar pavement of pink and slate-blue paving blocks, but is instead groping along a narrow jungle path and has even left his machete behind; maybe the fellow in front will hack a way through, but the fellow suddenly disappears underground and Matouš becomes entangled in some sort of creeper from which he can't extricate himself. He sits down on the ground to take a little rest, but then he is horrified to see, dropping down from the branch above him, a gold-coloured snake. The boiga drops on to his chest and strikes. The searing pain forces him to rise from the ground. He shakes off the snake; he ought to run away and get first aid or, instead, just lie down here on the ground and wait for death. To be born is to begin to die! Why resist?

Nevertheless he raises himself up and drags himself through the jungle burdened with pain and the weight of his own body.

Back home he takes a few tablets to ease the pain. The tablets make him drowsy but the pain remains and sleep refuses to come, even though the exhaustion which now seizes him is almost too much to bear.

The solitude in which he spends his life and the purposelessness of everything weigh on his chest and burn more than the snakebite. When he wakes up the next morning after a brief sleep he doesn't get up but goes on lying there in his bed, with linen that has not been changed in weeks. He stares up at the ceiling, listening to the din of the cars and trams outside the window, and it occurs to him that he will never again get up, never again write a single line. Besides, everything has already been written and everything wise has been said long ago, and anyone left striving for wisdom prefers to remain silent.

At midday he eats a piece of stale bread and goes back to bed. At last he falls asleep for a while and when he awakes he remembers his mother who has been dead for eight years and he bursts into tears and cannot tell whether from pain or hopelessness.

He writes:

Autumn approaches
The softness of the snow attends
missing tenderness.

It then occurs to him that in fact he should be feeling liberated: that frightful woman with whom he rashly encumbered his life, that creature who hadn't the first idea about anything that enlivened the spirit, and was solely interested in the pleasures of the flesh, had finally disappeared from his life.

He brews himself a pot of very strong Malabar from Java, takes out the seven tangram dice of yellowing ivory and makes them into a figure carrying a cup of tea. Is it the figure of a man or a woman?

It is a woman, and her features come into focus before his eyes. Dark hair and dark eyes: that matron has something exotic about her, something brought from far, far away. He recalls the kindly smiles of the Chinese women who welcomed him into the humblest of shacks.

Matouš is already drinking his fourth cup; his stomach pain is still there, but instead of dwelling on it he thinks that fate may have sent that foreign-looking yet motherly nurse his way. Alternatively, fate has sent him her way because her husband was coming to the end of his life's journey and the matron would be left on her own.

Matouš once more dons the white shirt that he wore so briefly yesterday that he didn't have time to dirty it, then puts on a tie, and sets off for the hospital.

At the hospital, they examine him and give him a prescription for some new medicines, reassuring him that the findings are negative and it is just the scar that is hurting. They advise him not to overdo it and to avoid everything that might over-excite him.

Matouš then glances into the room where the nursing officer sits. The pastor's wife is there, tidying something in the medicine cupboard. When she sees him she smiles and invites him in.

The surroundings are far from intimate. Moreover, the door is open and he hasn't the courage to close it behind him. Still, he sits down opposite her and when she asks him the reason for his visit, he tells her how yesterday he was overcome by pain and today by despair, but since then his hope has been renewed. 'Good fortune follows upon disaster, disaster lurks within good fortune,' he says, without betraying the source of his wisdom.

'You certainly do look a bit poorly,' Hana comments and she too advises him to take care of himself. Then she adds, 'Whenever you're feeling downhearted like that you're welcome to call us or just drop by. My husband might help raise your spirits.'

'I'd sooner come to visit you, Matron. And talking about visits, it's your turn to visit me, isn't it?'

'Take a seat then.' It looks as if both his attempt at flattery and his

211

invitation have passed unheeded. She asks him if he'd like a cup of tea and when he accepts her offer, Hana takes two cups from the metal cupboard, and after apologizing that she only has ordinary teabags she goes off somewhere. For a moment, Matouš looks around the room in which everything is coldly white; the refrigerator hums quietly and specks of dust swirl in the rays of sunlight. He then takes out his notebook and spends a moment composing a three-liner.

The pastor's wife returns with the small teapot from which steam now rises and asks him if he is already back at work.

He explains to her that his work consists of writing something and taking it to an editor. He also tells her that he doesn't really enjoy journalism and has never particularly enjoyed it.

'What would you enjoy doing, then?'

He says he once spent a lot of time studying Chinese philosophy. He found it a source of reassurance when the Communists were in power. Things were bad in China too during the rule of the first emperor of the Ching dynasty. For the first time in history they burned books and ownership of them was actually punishable by death. But the emperor died and ying – the spirit of conciliation and love – was restored. He has also translated and written verse, he tells her. He would like to publish his poems, but whereas in the past it wasn't possible because his poetry was not sufficiently optimistic or politically committed, nowadays no one's interested in publishing poems, unless he pays them to. He opens his notebook and reads out his newly written tercet:

Even the river
will melt when over the waves
flash flocks of black coots.

Matron Hana nods. She is unlikely to see anything poetical in the statement, let alone realize he wrote the lines to impress her. She used to read poetry, she says, but it was a long time ago, these days she doesn't have the time.

'These days nobody has the time,' Matouš says. 'Either for poetry or for living. Life rushes on and from the emptiness one knows one falls into the emptiness one doesn't. And what will one leave behind here? You will leave behind children. But what will remain after me? A bed, a couple of dictionaries and books and a few tattered clothes.'

'Everyone leaves something behind,' Hana disagrees, 'providing they've lived decently. And those poems of yours,' she recalls, 'I'd like to read them now I know you.'

'I'll bring them to you, or I'll show them to you when you visit me.'

At that moment, some nurses burst into the office and Hana no longer has any time for him, nor, clearly, can she pay him attention.

So Matouš gets up and as he is leaving suggests that he might wait for Hana at the gate.

'But I won't be finished for nearly an hour,' Hana objects. But that is not the sort of objection that would put him off.

'But just for a moment,' Hana says when they meet. 'You know they're waiting for me at home.'

He escorts her to the same bistro as last time and on this occasion he offers her a glass of wine. Hana declines and just has a coffee.

They chat for a while about Matouš's health and the tablets that don't relieve his condition.

'Once when I was travelling westwards from Peking,' Matouš recalls, 'I got a swelling of the knee. There was no doctor in the vicinity so they brought me to the local soothsayer who was also a healer. She tried to find the cause of the illness. Your grandfather on your father's side, she said to me, suffered from leg trouble, until in the end he was unable to walk. And when he was dying he didn't have his walking stick with him.'

'Was it true?'

'I don't know whether he had his stick with him or not, I wasn't born then. But apparently he suffered with his legs and before he died he was unable to walk. So that old woman advised me to cut a walking stick out of paper and burn it at the crossroads at full moon in order to appease the suffering of my grandfather's spirit, and then I would find relief.'

'And did you do it?'

'What harm was there in trying? It happened to be the day before the full moon.'

'But the spirit of your grandfather . . . After all, your grandfather didn't live in China.'

'I have no particular belief in ghosts, Matron, or in the survival of the spirit, but if ghosts did indeed survive somewhere, then I expect they could accompany us on our travels.'

'And did it help you?'

'I don't know. The swelling went down and the knee hasn't hurt me since. Now it's my stomach that hurts me and I don't know which of my forebears I'm supposed to appease.'

Then he tells Hana about his troubles with Klára, from whom he is getting a divorce. Hana is sure this is the real cause of his pain.

'Do you know I never used to have any fear of solitude,' Matouš confides to her, 'nor of death, for that matter. I didn't think about it. While you're still young, you have the feeling that everything is opening up before you, and in fact you shun any commitments that might bind you. But then the dread of solitude descends upon you. On that point I differ from the sages I have read about. The wisest of them, once they had fulfilled their obligations towards their family and brought up their children, went away to a monastery or to some isolated hermitage and there they devoted themselves to contemplation and to understanding the Order. I haven't managed the first and I'm not even prepared to do the other. What else can I expect from life now? At best a nursing home.'

'But you're not going to stay on your own, are you?' Hana says. 'An interesting person like you.'

Matouš objects that no one is interested in what he has experienced or seen, nor the things he knows. Particularly not women.

'You're wrong there. Almost all women yearn for something different, for some change.' She stops short, and then says, 'I know this from our congregation and from the hospital; I know what the women talk about.'

Maybe she is only consoling him. Maybe she is only passing on the experiences of others. But most likely she is speaking about herself. Matouš would like to stroke her hand, at least, but he is shy to do so here in a bar where there are lots of people. Besides, he is afraid it might startle the pastor's wife and frighten her away.

It occurs to Hana to ask whether it really costs so much money to get a poetry collection published.

Matouš explains that it depends what one means by a lot of money, but in any event it would have to be at least enough for a publisher, if there was one, not to suffer a loss.

'I'll ask my husband,' Hana promises. 'Perhaps we could give you something towards it.'

'I couldn't possibly ask you to do such a thing.'

'Why not? People should help each other.'

'You're an angel, Matron.'

Hana waves her hand as if to ward off his words.

'No,' Matouš says, 'you're completely different from other women.'

'Different?'

'Better.'

Hana blushes, then says it is time she was going. So Matouš pays the bill and then before they part he repeats his invitation. Hana should come and see his collections. She says she's not sure that her husband will have the time, but Matouš may visit them whenever he likes. She will be pleased to see him and looks forward to the poems. The manse is there for people to come to whenever they feel low in spirits.

When Matouš gets home, he realizes that his stomach pain has gone. He makes himself another pot of tea and lies down fully dressed on the unmade bed. He makes up his mind to get rid of Klára once and for all, and when the pastor dies, he'll marry his widow.

5

Daniel was to write an article on the theme of Advent. The Bethlehem story had excited him ever since his youth: the Son of God appearing as a needy, even persecuted, human being; God arriving from somewhere other than people expected and not arriving as a bolt of thunder, not descending from the heavens, but being born of a woman – helpless and defenceless, just as we all arrive in the world. By accepting our fate from beginning to end, God made known that He accepted us and loved us, receiving us exactly as He made us, i.e. as His children whose death would grieve him.

Now Daniel sits at his computer and is incapable of finding within himself the requisite certainty of faith in God's birth.

Years ago, he had known a country doctor who had converted from Judaism to Catholicism. He was an outstanding doctor, a man who made a genuine effort to believe. The greatest problem for him was accepting the virgin birth. Perhaps his medical training proved an obstacle. One day he had come running to Daniel with an epic piece of news. He had just read in a specialized American journal that something of the sort was possible, that in one in a trillion cases self-induced conception could occur and a sort of human clone was produced. That would explain Mary's immaculate conception. Except that, as he himself pointed out, it would entirely eliminate Jesus's divine origin and His identity as the Son of God would only be symbolic, as would His resurrection from the dead in that case. 'Or am I mistaken, Reverend?'

At the time, Daniel had told him that God's actions were one single mystery and it made no sense to try to explain them by some scientific hypothesis or other. That was what he himself believed or strove to believe then. For him, faith had represented a path that led from inhuman conditions towards humanity: Jesus embodied the spirit at a time when matter was invoked on every hand and science was proclaimed as the all-powerful conqueror of truth. Jesus represented love that had to be defended, when hatred was proclaimed as the driving force of history. The language of Scripture had sounded like music amidst the cacophonous caterwauling of the political leaders' speeches from every radio and television set. The hatred showered on Jesus's teaching by those who embodied violence, hypocrisy and treason, and who despised the free or independent spirit, had seemed to confirm the truth of those who then stood by Him – persecuted and mocked as in the early days of Christianity. The world seemed divided between good and evil by a clear and straight boundary.

The boundaries were now crumbling, both within people and outside them. The doubts that Daniel had thrust deep into his subconscious suddenly surfaced. The words that until recently he had solemnly proclaimed – aware of the greatness of the message they carried – now stuck in his throat.

The event at Bethlehem had probably occurred quite differently from the way he had so far expounded it, and therefore its significance was also different. It was mankind who, in their age-old longing to escape the inevitability with which life always ended in death, and in the spirit of the ancient myths and archetypes, had thought up both a royal and a divine origin for the crucified Christ, and devised His birth and hence His divine nature which they then proceeded to debate in subsequent centuries.

In the area in which Jesus lived, worked and was crucified, people had been sacrificing their king for thousands of years in the conviction that he would be resurrected. Before killing him, they used to hang him between heaven and earth. They then ate his body and drank his blood in order to achieve their own rebirth through his resurrection.

Jesus, above whose cross was said to have been fixed the mocking label 'King of the Jews', died hanging between heaven and earth. His death was to open the gates to the Kingdom of Heaven, which he entered, reborn – or as we say, resurrected. To this very day we symbolically consume his body and blood in order to share in his resurrection.

But anyone who lets such comparisons enter his thoughts risks being accused of one of the age-old or more recent heresies.

How could God create the universe and time and transform Himself into a baby who then grew up and aged until one day, in totally human time, He allowed Himself to be executed by some imperial bureaucrat?

On that occasion, he had not replied to Bára that God is capable of everything. Had he declined to give her that answer because he himself was in doubt, or because it was an answer that could be used to dispose of any question? Or was it perhaps because the order which had governed his life was beginning to crumble?

As usual in the past weeks, his mind somehow strayed to that other woman, the woman who had appeared because the order in his life was beginning to crumble. Or had it started to crumble because she had appeared in his life?

He got up and switched off the computer. He couldn't concentrate anyway. From inside the flat came the strains of the piano. Eva was playing Bach's *Prelude and Fugue in G major*.

The idea that God who created the universe and time probably did not take upon Himself the form of a Jewish infant was an idea, Bára, defended from the very beginning of the church by the proponents of poor Christology. For them, Christ was simply a prophet, a mere human. And some of the first bishops were excommunicated from the church for those very same doubts about Jesus's divinity. They were outvoted at the councils and thereby became eternal heretics. There were countless heretics: some did not accept Jesus's divinity, others did not recognize the Holy Spirit, the immaculate conception or the assumption of the mother of Jesus. Later there were those who rejected the sale of indulgences and demanded communion of both kinds at the Lord's Supper. At first, the church used to excommunicate them, later it tortured them and turned them over to the secular authorities to be burned alive.

Perhaps it would have taken very little for the dogmas to be completely different, or for the Gospels to be different, for that matter. But the person who defended the present version happened to be more eloquent or had more supporters, and everything turned out the way it is accepted today. Even such transcendental issues as the essence of God or the resurrection were decided by vote.

I have never voiced this opinion to anyone before, Bára. It would be difficult to hold it and go on working as a preacher. And it's going to be difficult if I go on thinking the way I do and living the way I am now.

So I don't know how I'm going to live. No, I'm not thinking about supporting the family; in fact, I wouldn't have to work at all any more, I could simply live from what I made on the sale of the house. It's the meaning of my life that concerns me. What meaning will I give to my last few years on earth? Will I bring some work or project to completion or, on the contrary, abandon everything, cancel it, and stand in no man's land; in other words, at the end of my days will I find myself back at the beginning? And with whom, my love? With you? With my family? Alone? At the end you always stand alone.

That's what Dad always used to say to me: Dan, in death you're always left on your own, whether you believe or not. And he saw lots of people die: during the war in that concentration camp and after the war in prison, and in fact for the entire remainder of his life – being present at death is part of a doctor's job.

Daniel flinched at the memory of his father. He had not finished the job of clearing his name. He had not found out anything; in fact he had stopped searching.

He entered the room without Eva noticing him. He observed her mutely for a moment. His daughter, Jitka's only child. She played faultlessly, her head slightly inclined, her thoughts in heaven.

She called Hana 'Mummy', but she knew from her childhood that her real mother was not on earth but in heaven. When she started to learn the piano, she asked him if Mummy could hear her up there. 'Of course she can hear you,' he had assured her. Since then she had played to her. Once she said to him, 'Mummy told me I played well.' He had thought she was referring to Hana, but when he asked Hana she told him she hadn't praised her. The praise had come from her mother in heaven.

'How about us playing a duet?' he now suggested.

Eva gave a start. 'That would be lovely. It's ages since we played together.'

He brought another stool and Eva made room for him.

Music had always brought him relief. The awareness that whatever happened in life, there existed something that was so elevated and elevating above the mundane filled him with calm and gave him hope.

He had still not been to a concert with Bára nor had the opportunity to play anything to her; he had only heard her sing, and could only sing with her during the service.

'Did you know they called Bach the fifth evangelist?'

'You told me that before, some time!'

'Really? I'm starting to get old and repeat myself.'

'Maybe you're just absent-minded. You've got too many worries.'

'What do you think I'm worried about?'

'Me, for instance,' said Eva. 'But my piano teacher complimented me yesterday,' she added quickly, 'on my technique.'

'I'm glad she complimented you.' He suspected that he worried more about the fate of his eldest child than about the fate of her brother and sister. As if he felt accountable for her to her late mother. Or maybe he wanted Eva to achieve what her mother had not had time to achieve.

'She wants me to practise at least three hours each day,' Eva went on to inform him. 'At least. Four hours would be better and five hours best of all. That's pretty tough, don't you think?'

'It requires effort to learn anything. And to learn anything well requires even more effort. It's just that in some fields it's possible to cheat a bit. That's not possible in music because it's immediately noticeable.'

When they finished playing he went downstairs to his workshop. He had a new carving half-completed there. He ought to finish it. And prepare that exhibition the gallery owner had asked him for.

The wood was fragrant in spite of being dried out, just as it was in his grandfather's long-defunct workshop. From the dead material familiar features emerged. Instead of a violin shape a woman's face.

Most of the time he managed to concentrate on this work, but otherwise he really was absent-minded and worried. About himself.

In the corner of the room, there still lay the boxes of correspondence, just as he had brought them from his mother's flat. He ought at least to take a look at them, sort out what he would keep and take the rest to the recycling depot. Maybe he would find among the correspondence some clue as to whether his father had really committed something dishonourable. He had probably not looked in the boxes out of a subconscious fear of what he might find there.

He hesitated a moment and then brought out a box of his father's letters. It was stuffed with large envelopes on each of which his mother had written a description: *Pre-wedding. Letters from prison. From the camp. From the tart.* He stared in amazement at the last inscription. He took the envelope and opened it. There were only a few sheets of paper inside and a card on which his mother had written: *I found these letters in Richard's desk at the hospital after his death.*

On the first sheet, written in large, neat – apparently female – handwriting, he read:

Dear Ritchie,
I couldn't phone you my love so this is just a note to say that I'll be all on my own for the next three days. Do you think you'll be able to find some way of slipping away from your Mumsie? I know you can do it. You can do anything. At least for me who loves you the most. Looking forward to you, my little doenut. A lot . . .

He skipped the remaining few lines; he oughtn't even to have read the previous ones. You shouldn't read what isn't intended for you. Or rummage in letters full of bygone feelings, spelling mistakes and betrayals that we leave behind.

He recalled his father's funeral. Hundreds of people came to it; the room at the crematorium had been full. Most of them were women, some of whom were weeping. His father had been a gynaecologist and had no doubt saved the lives of many of them or restored them to health. Maybe they included his mistresses too. By now they would probably be old ladies, if they were still alive. Sixteen years had passed since that day.

Even the serious crimes and real betrayals of the living were no longer prosecuted after that length of time.

Even the lists had almost been forgotten now, although it was only three years since they had been published. Everything slipped into the past. More quickly nowadays than before, because the times were fast-moving and forgetting was one of the ways to escape going mad.

My children don't remember Dad any more, they know their grandad only from stories and nobody is likely to tell their children about him.

So what is the point of investigating and trying to seek some sort of judgement?

Judgement, he had always believed, was the Lord's when He came again in glory – the Lord who taught love and forgiveness.

But it was unlikely there would ever be any Last Judgement. It was just a fiction, just a longing for a higher justice which would redress all the wrongs and injustices committed on this earth; a fiction from the days of the first church when they were still awaiting Christ's return in their lifetime. Christ had not returned; how many wrongs would have to be judged since those days?

There was nothing more to be done with his father's life. On the other hand, he ought to do something with his own.

6

Hana

The hospital director summons all the senior nursing staff and announces to them that he already owes three months' laundry payments. In all, it come to three-quarters of a million. Unless he is able to obtain credit from somewhere or to persuade the laundry to wait another month, they will be obliged to close down the hospital or do the laundry themselves. For the time being, he asks them to go easy on the linen and try to wash any slightly soiled items on site. He realizes this will mean extra work but he won't be able to pay them for it; he'll be happy if he can find the money to pay their salaries at the end of the month. 'The insurance companies owe me over a million crowns,' he says finally. Then he dismisses them and Hana returns to her ward where she reluctantly conveys the director's request. Recently the worries at work have grown while her sense of satisfaction has waned.

She makes herself a coffee, sits down at her small desk and tries to think of something pleasant.

A few days ago she got a call from that journalist who had showered her with kind words. He complained a bit about his health; he had run out of tablets and he didn't feel like going to the doctor for more. He didn't feel like going out at all, in fact. He didn't feel up to it even though at home his only companions were gawping Buddhas and a stuffed canary. Then he renewed his invitation to her to come and see his collection. She told him that it would not be proper for her to visit him – unless she were to bring him his medication, it occurred to her.

Then she did pay him a visit. She was unsure why she decided to, and persuaded herself that she was only doing it in order to deliver his medicine to him.

And of course when he opened the door she told him that she wouldn't be coming in, but then let herself be persuaded to sit down for a few moments.

He made her tea – a truly fragrant and interesting tea. They drank it from almost translucent little cups and he talked non-stop the whole time. Hana realized, incredulously, that this fellow, who must have travelled the whole world over and had no doubt met distinguished personalities on many occasions, felt even shyer than she did just then.

They drank tea and she was thinking that she ought to get up and go. At one moment, when he was showing her some Japanese engraving and moved up close to her, she was scared. What would she do if he tried to cuddle her, for instance?

But he didn't.

He read her a few poems which didn't mean a great deal to her. She merely sensed in them a sadness and a yearning to escape the daily routine into a better, unreal world, where love, purity of heart, friendship, calm and order reigned. But he didn't lend her the book he had told her about. He had to read the poems through once more himself, he explained, before daring to lend them to her.

Anyway, she stayed there longer than she ought to have done. But what was the harm in it? Daniel was often away from home until late at night. And she told him about her visit that very evening. Only she did not divulge to him that when the journalist looked at her she had felt an odd excitement, or more accurately a kind of satisfaction that the man felt disconcerted by her presence. Nor did she mention that he had asked her to address him informally, and she had not refused. She was used to informality with the members of the congregation. When at last she was leaving, she shook hands with him. His handshake was, as she had expected, soft and boyishly reticent. He asked her if she would come again some time and she replied: 'Should you ever need tablets and were unable to come for them . . .'

He would definitely be needing them, he had assured her, but she had made no response.

During her visit he had tried to persuade her once more that she ought to be doing something other than her present job.

Hana now writes out who did how many hours overtime on the ward. She had never before entertained the thought that there was no longer any need for her to stay here obliging nurses to wash out soiled linen as quickly as they could. Daniel had inherited a house and sold it for a lot of money. He had told her for how much, but she had preferred not to take it in. They definitely no longer depended on her earnings.

Maybe she could do social work within the church or even establish a Diakonia centre in their own building. There were guest rooms there; one was empty and Alois was still using the other, but it was high time that he found somewhere else to live.

Not long ago, when she and Daniel were on a trip to Northern Bohemia, she had seen a centre where the handicapped were producing pottery and had even built themselves a kiln. They could try a different activity, such as weaving, painting on glass – flowers on glass – that was something she could learn to do herself and then teach it to the handicapped.

As she contemplates her potential new vocation, it occurs to her that it could open up some new avenues for her, and that she should definitely talk to Daniel about it. It's unlikely he'd reject her idea. She actually picks up the phone and tries to call him, but Daniel is neither in his office nor the flat. Eva answers and tells her that Daniel has some meeting with the moderator, but she is glad Hana has called because Daddy had left her a message to say he wouldn't be coming to the concert at the Rudolfinum this evening as they had planned. If Hana wanted, Eva could go with her instead of Daniel – 'but only if you really want me to, Mummy'. Hana says she'll be pleased for her to come, of course, and then asks if Marek and Magda are home from school yet.

Magda is already home, Marek has a practical class in the afternoon. Suddenly Magda's voice comes down the line: 'Mummy, I've got some great news for you. I got an A for my essay on Hus.'

'That's good.'

'I knew what he said about truth. Seek the truth, listen to the truth, learn the truth, cleave to the truth, defend the truth and that.'

'I'm pleased to hear it.'

'But there's something you won't be pleased to hear.'

'What did you do?'

'I wrote "I done". I knew the right answer, but I just goofed because I was nervous.'

'OK, Magda. But I have to hang up now. The doctor's waiting for me.'

'Bye then, Mum. And come home soon.'

Hana goes about her work with a vague sense of disappointment and dejection that no longer has anything to do with what the director told them that morning. Something unpleasant has happened that she can't exactly put her finger on, or she is reluctant to contemplate. It clearly has something to do with her home and with Daniel. When did it last happen that Daniel gave anything precedence over a concert? Besides which, they were supposed to be playing Bach. And why hadn't he phoned her – why had he only left her a message? After all, he knows she is at the hospital all day.

It strikes her that there is something wrong with almost everyone these days – people are changing. She notices it all around her, at the hospital and in the congregation. Maybe Daniel is changing too. Now he has more work, more money and more freedom. After years of crouching in the shadows, he has come out into the light and it has blinded him.

Perhaps she's doing him an injustice. Maybe he simply had to rush off somewhere and couldn't get through to her on the phone. The hospital line is often engaged. Or maybe there was no one at the nurses' station.

Hana checks the medicines that a young lad on civilian military service has brought up from the pharmacy, but she ponders on the fact that Daniel has changed: he is less affable and definitely does not behave like someone who longs for her company. Sometimes she even gets the impression he's avoiding her and evading conversation about anything but the most mundane matters.

It occurs to Hana that every love tires in time. Perhaps their love has grown tired too, and the two of them remain together only for the children, and because it is right that people should stay together when they have promised to.

The medicines are in order. The young lad on civilian military service asks her if she has any jobs for him and she tells him she has nothing for the moment and that he may take a rest.

That evening Hana sits with Eva at the concert. They are playing Bach's violin concertos. On their way there Eva seemed to her pale and out of sorts and said virtually nothing. And now she is sitting here all slumped and Hana wonders if she has been taking drugs again, although it is possible she is just not feeling well.

Then she stops thinking about Eva and pays attention to the music. Hana doesn't have perfect pitch like Daniel or her step-daughter but when she listens to powerful music she falls into a strange trance in which pictures and live scenes pass in front of her eyes. She closes her eyes, so that Daniel often thinks she has gone to sleep, while on the contrary she is experiencing something so powerful that she is suffused with an ecstasy that she has never experienced even during love-making.

The dejection of the morning quickly leaves her and she screws up her eyes. While she is still aware of the violinist's face, it is gradually transformed into the pimply face of the journalist who invited her to his home and served her tea and talked to her about a river that melts. He had said: You're an angel. You're completely different from other women. You're better. Those words now blend with the music and together they caress and fondle her until she quivers beneath their touch. Then she notices that the journalist's face is growing handsome; he is now wearing a Geneva gown with a white band, and the other members of the orchestra have donned gowns too and are no longer playing on the concert platform but on a beach by a pond. A big pond with lots of water – it may be the sea. Hana suddenly realizes that the conductor is now looking straight at her and giving her a sort of sign with his baton, inviting her to join him. At that moment she becomes aware of her heart thumping, like in the old days, like the time when Daniel first invited her for a date and she realized that she could love him. Something she thought would never happen to her again could actually happen. Maybe if she accepted that invitation . . . But at that moment something starts to surface from the water: a long, dark object – it's a coffin – and it rises higher and higher. Alongside it, four pale girlish faces also emerge, they are bridesmaids in dazzling white dresses from which the water gushes in streams; they are bearing the coffin. They pass in front of the orchestra and come to a

225

halt in the open space just in front of Hana. They carefully put the box down on the sand.

The music is still playing. The violinist, whose face is no longer visible, steps over to the coffin and leans towards it, as if playing solely for the one who is inside. And the one inside can hear because the lid slowly rises and Hana beholds a female figure. Oh, how well she knows that face from the photographs as well as from Daniel's carvings, even though he imagines she has never noticed: it is his first wife. The face is as white as the bridesmaids' dresses, the wax-like ghastly face of the dead. But she is alive and approaching Hana with her hands stretched in front of her. Get back, you accursed creature, Hana whispers, you're the one who still steals his love from me, you always stole his love from me, and yet there's nothing for you here among the living. The white, accursed thing starts to stagger and then collapses lifelessly on the ground. At that moment Hana becomes aware of a painful sympathy for the poor creature; after all Jitka has a daughter here, whom she hasn't seen for eighteen years. It must be awful for a mother not to see her own daughter for eighteen years and not to be able to hold her even once. People are sorry for the orphan but don't spare a thought for the mother. Tears of pity gush from Hana's eyes over that wasted, unfulfilled maternal love.

The orchestra are coming to the end of the finale. The violinist has his own face back again and he and the conductor are bowing and shaking hands.

Hana glances at Eva; the girl is as white as that apparition a moment ago.

'Is there something wrong with you? They didn't play badly, surely?'

'It's nothing, Mummy.'

'Would you like to go home?'

'No, Mummy. It's just . . . I just need to pop out for a moment.'

After the concert Daniel is waiting for them on the steps. He wants to know how the concert was. Eva says it was lovely. It occurs to Hana that she ought to tell him about her vision, but suddenly it strikes her that it had been not just unreal, but also ungracious: it had been nasty to Daniel, in that she had thought tenderly about another man; nasty towards Jitka who is long dead and it is therefore unbecoming to be jealous of her. It shows Daniel in a good light that he didn't completely forget Jitka, that he tried to capture in his carvings the memory of that face which, after all, will never come alive again on this earth. In the afterlife only God knows what face we will be endowed with, if any at all.

They walk side by side across the bridge, ahead of them the illuminated castle buildings, below them the water whose odour is indiscernible, smothered by the smell of the city. Hana notices that Daniel stoops slightly as he walks, as if sagging beneath some load. She also notices that his shirt collar is badly turned down and the striped shirt he is wearing doesn't go with his checked jacket.

They are now walking along in silence. Hana realizes she could never leave Daniel, not so much on her own account as on his; Daniel is probably unaware of it, but without her he would be left like a child abandoned somewhere on an empty shore.

7

Three days before Bára's birthday, Daniel invited her to a restaurant for dinner. He brought her a letter he had written to her in a sort of trance, and also a gold ring with a small diamond. (He had never given a woman a ring before, not counting the wedding ring he had given Jitka.)

'You wrote me a letter?' she said. 'Should I read it? No, not now. When I'm with you I have to make the most of you and not be reading.' Then she opened the little box and for a moment she gazed at the ring. 'You're crazy, Dan, a thing like that. How am I to explain it at home?'

'Perhaps you could say it was a gift from your first husband.'

'From him of all people!'

'From your mother, then?'

'How could Mum afford it on her pension? You're crazy, I don't need a ring, do I, when I have your love?'

'Don't speak about it any more.'

She slipped the gold band on her finger and for a few seconds looked at it with delight. 'It's a perfect fit, it's obvious you know my hand off by heart.' She kissed him and then she recalled: 'I've invited my son Saša to come too, I hope you don't mind?'

Daniel was astounded. 'What did you tell him?'

'He knows about you anyway.'

227

'You told him about me?'

'Ages ago. Mum too. They are my folks. And I don't want to keep anything from my folks. He likes you, even though he's never set eyes on you, because he knows you love me and you don't boss me about like his stepfather. I also thought you might put him straight about some things.'

'I'm supposed to start putting him straight about things, at our very first meeting?'

'No, I don't mean it like that. It will be enough for him to meet someone who knows what he lives for. While being a good person.'

'I'm not sure if I fulfil those requirements.'

'He'd so much like to have a father, because there has been no decent man in his life. I deprived him of his own father. Or his father deprived himself of me and the boy. It makes no difference, but he gave the boy nothing. And his stepfather never accepted him. He simply provided for him and let him know it. As far as he is concerned, Saša is a good-for-nothing wastrel. And it's possible that he, my little boy, is indeed growing up wild. Nothing appeals to him, work least of all. All he does is play basketball and tennis, or watch people shooting each other on television. He also enjoys fiddling around with all sorts of little mechanical gadgets and getting music out of them. You're not cross with me for inviting him without asking you first?'

'No, you did right.' It was the right thing to do in a wrong situation. If you loved someone you had to take them lock, stock and barrel, which meant their folks above all. 'I've not been faring too well with young people just lately.'

'In what respect?'

'In trying to persuade them about anything that I believe in. Not even my own children. Sometimes I get the impression that they're persuading me.'

'One's own children are the hardest to persuade. One's own husband and one's own children,' she added.

The lad was slim and almost as tall as Daniel. He seemed to have inherited his high forehead and hair colour from his mother, but otherwise he was quite unlike her. His eyes were light blue. 'They gave me a really silly name,' he said, introducing himself, 'after some Russian tsar or Pushkin. Mum adored Pushkin when she was young. Mind you, she still is young, but she was eighteen years younger then and identified with Tatyana. She's still got the one about her on her bookshelf and she makes me read it:

> *'Such a heavenly gift,*
> *To be strongwilled and wild,*
> *Of mind so swift,*
> *Passionate – but tender as a child.'*

'Saša,' Bára cut him short, 'don't you think you've said quite enough to be going on with?'

'It's only because I'm shy,' the boy said and blushed. 'Thank you for the invitation. Mummy says such nice things about you that I wanted a chance to meet you. But I don't need to stay to dinner, I'm sure you have things to talk about.'

'We can all talk together,' Daniel suggested.

'Thank you. Musil doesn't talk to me; I get on his nerves the moment he claps eyes on me. And my dad only asks me how are things in school because he hasn't got any idea what to talk to me about when we see each other twice a month.'

The waiter brought them menus. 'I really am afraid I'm going to be in your way,' the boy apologized, 'and anyway I'm not used to going to such posh places.'

'Neither am I,' Daniel said quickly, 'and I don't intend to become used to it either.'

'Do you think I could have the lamb stuffed with chicken livers?'

'Have what you feel like.'

'Maybe it's a daft idea; I've never eaten anything like that before. The Big Boss doesn't take us out for meals and Dad only takes me to a sweet shop sometimes or to some buffet where he has a beer and orders me some sickly muck.'

'Saša won't drink alcohol,' Bára explained.

'And what would you like to talk to your father about, for example?' Daniel asked him after ordering the food.

The lad shrugged. 'I don't know. With the lads and the girls we just talk drivel. You know what I mean.'

'Are you going out with someone?'

'Of course, but I can't talk about it. Not here, at least.'

'I didn't mean to pry. It's just that I have a daughter of your age and a lad just a bit younger.'

'I know. Mum told me. She knows them from the church where she used to go to see you.'

'Saša,' Bára interrupted, 'you're talking too much. The reason I went to church was to hear something to raise my spirits.'

'That's true, that is the reason she went,' the lad chimed in. 'She often got the blues. We all suffer from depression, in fact. It's a kind of virus we have: we are all frightened of the Boss and of death. The Boss – Musil I mean, the architect, the Doctor of Science and laureate is only afraid of death, of course, but quite a lot because he's old and has high blood pressure. He's always swallowing pills. We used to call him the Builder of the Tower of Babel because he had a hang-up about grandiose projects, but now we just call him the Pill Popper. And we also call him Vampire Bat. Whenever he gets a downer he starts to wail. He climbs up on to Mum's shoulder and starts to suck her strength. Then Mum has to comfort him. But there's no one to comfort Mum: I can't, and anyway when the catkins arrive on the trees I start to whine too because I can hardly breathe. Aleš is healthy but he's still small and silly. And then you came along. But Mum deserves you, she's a lovely person.'

The waiter interrupted his monologue and started to serve their meals from large metal bowls.

'Wow,' the lad commented, 'I feel like the Little Prince. We'll have to persuade Pill Popper to bring us here too some time.'

'Saša's putting it on a bit,' Bára said. 'He's acting as if he grew up on bread and water.'

'Come off it, Mum! When did we last go out for a meal?'

'Last spring at the seaside,' Bára said. 'Were you living in a cave, or what? And we went there on your account, because the doctor recommended sea air for your allergy.'

'And it did me good too!'

He observed the two of them. It seemed to him that they were merely continuing a long-established game in his presence: the fellow-conspirator son taken by his mother into another home in search of true love, and now brought here because she was still searching, while the son was seeking a father. The question was whether it wasn't already too late for both of them. Even though the expression 'too late' was one he always challenged – at least as far as faith was concerned.

'I used to go to Divinity classes,' the lad said. 'Mum wanted me to and Musil let me. But it meant nothing to me – no, nothing's too strong – very little. It was all too otherworldly. All those miracles and angels and fallen angels and hell and damnation. Anyway, I immediately forgot it all.'

'I used to send him to the Catholic class,' Bára explained. 'I could have sent him to a Jewish class on account of Mum, but there wasn't one. I wanted him to hear something about God at least, so that he could make up his own mind. The trouble was their teacher wasn't like you. He hadn't the slightest bit of enthusiasm, he was just bitter somehow, and he talked to them more about hell than about the need for people to love one another.'

'Anyway, I could have got more out of it,' the lad admitted, 'but I found it impossible to concentrate. It's the same with all subjects, apart from geography. I enjoy geography because it's about real things.'

'Would you like to travel?'

'Everyone would. But I'll have to wait for the time being because the Big Boss won't let me: I don't behave well enough at school or at home. But anyway I wouldn't like to travel to big cities and go sightseeing around monuments. I prefer it where there are fewer people, such as in the forests or mountains. People in cities are like ants. Thousands of ants all over the place, in cars and walking down the street. I'm not just getting at the rest. I'm an ant too, and a lazy one at that.'

Bára said, 'It's not surprising he has an aversion to monuments and buildings in general, seeing his stepfather and mother are architects. I haven't a clue how he's going to make a living.'

'So what that you haven't a clue,' the boy commented. 'What's more disturbing is that I haven't got one. But if the worst comes to the worst I'll be a hunter.'

'What would you hunt?'

'That's the problem: I wouldn't kill a frog, or even a butterfly.'

'Castles in the air are the most he'd ever hunt!' Bára said.

'I'm no worse than you, Mummy!'

When dinner was over, the lad got up, and after rather profuse thanks – he was his mother's son, after all – he left.

'You have a splendid son,' Daniel told her.

'Did you like him? He made a real effort. He's not usually that talkative. Most times he's a fairly quiet boy. He's a bit lazy but his heart's in the right place.'

'Definitely.' He recalled the lad's remark about the lazy ant. Once, when he himself was still a boy, he had observed an ant that had fallen into the cleverly constructed pit of an ant-lion. He had watched its

231

vain efforts to free itself. He had watched it fulfil its destiny. He could picture it so clearly that he shuddered involuntarily.

She noticed and asked, 'What's the matter? Is something wrong?'

8

Letters

Dear Bára,

This is a letter for your birthday. Although I know but a modest six months out of your forty-one years I feel as if I've known you longer than people I've known for many years.

I think I knew true love with my first wife – and I love Hana. I never thought I'd be able to love another woman. I genuinely had no wish to. I don't know whether I secretly yearned to in some corner of my soul, but if I did it was so secret I didn't even discover it. And then you appeared. For me, every moment with you is special and beautiful (even though it also fills me with a sense of guilt – guilt towards Hana, towards you, guilt towards God who, while I believe He is merciful, could hardly approve of deceit).

Birthdays are times for wishes. So I wish you first of all, that wherever you go, you should dwell in mercy, understanding, freedom and kindliness. I wish you moments of peace and a faith that will overcome your anxieties. I wish you the love of your sons. I wish that everything of importance that happens in your life will be better than what went before. I wish (and pray) that death, of which you so often speak, should stay away from your door. I wish that your eyes should see what the eyes of others cannot, that your fingers should work wonders, that your plans should find fulfilment and that your words should be heard, that your heart should find love and your dreams peace.

> I ask God to forgive us for yielding to love.
> My sweet dove in the cleft of the rock
> concealed above the ravine
> grant that I see my own face
> allow me to hear your voice.

Thinking of you,

Love, Daniel

My love,

I still feel you to be a miracle. (How long can one live with a miracle?) It's as if you were wanting to demonstrate to me everything that is unbelievable. You surprise me again and again, either with something new or with something that endures.

I read your birthday wishes over and over again and each time they thrill me and move me. No one has ever said so many beautiful things to me. What I find most fascinating of all is that I believe every word, that I trust you, that I believe things can last. The possibility of things lasting dumbfounds me because it is something so rare, so difficult and even unseemly. That love could last – I don't mean the everyday kind, but the love that is a celebration – is something I had ceased to believe in when I realized the weakness and weariness of the poor little human creature and its inability to stick at anything.

I think of that first day I entered the church where you were preaching and it was the day when your mum died, which was something I didn't suspect and in fact at that moment you didn't yet know about it. Such fateful coincidences have been written about. Who arranges them? But in order for one to obey that mysterious command it is necessary to have a very special sort of perceptiveness. You summoned me to you and I know of no boundary I wouldn't want to cross with you. I'm not afraid of you. I trust you. When I'm with you the only feeling I have is one of security. I'm not afraid of you and I'm not afraid of myself with you. I'm happy, I'm unhappy that one day I'll discover it's the last day. I feel I'm morbid the way I'm often thinking about death, but most of all about the end. One day it will be adieu instead of au revoir. At every beginning I've always sensed the end and known that life only has meaning because it has an end. Like every embrace, every day, every joy, every pain.

I'd like to be with you now and instead I'm going away. With a husband who isn't nice to me, and with my children. They need me. I am their mother after all and I want to be a good one. At least that. I'll try and write you a letter if they leave me a few moments to myself.

I'll be back in Prague on Monday. Will you phone? Or write?

I'm thinking of you. I love you. Don't leave!

Love, Bára

Dearest,

Again I haven't seen you for several days. You're not sitting opposite me.
You're not asking me questions. You're silent. But I know that for most of
the time you'll be with me only in spirit. I can't tear myself away from you.
It looks as if I – or we – might have crossed some inner barrier beyond
which it is impossible to tear oneself away. Is that good? I don't know, but it
is only beyond that barrier that real intimacy begins.

People oughtn't to lie to each other, they shouldn't lie about their
feelings. One often forces oneself to have certain feelings on account of
the children, or out of cowardice, or from a sense of duty, or out of
sympathy (that's a feeling too), or from inertia, or anxiety, or from fear of
being left on one's own or even of losing property. The two of us share
neither children nor property, nor any duty to each other. All we have is
love and I will never lie to you about it, I promise you, so you will be able
to say: 'I believe everything you say'. Loveless love-making is humiliating
and soul-destroying. Sometimes when I realize that's the way it is with
most people (or so I believe and I have some knowledge from my
experience as a clergyman), I say to myself: What hells people create
instead of homes.

I read your letters and I'm almost afraid to believe them: they contain so
much tenderness, anxiety, pain, longing, determination and despair. We
have so little time and yet it flies at its age-old speed and we don't even
manage to tell each other what has happened over the past hours let alone
what has happened in the course of our lives. But love is not measured in
minutes. What is it measured in? Completeness? Or devotion? Or the
extent of longing? Or intimacy? What is completeness? How far does
devotion extend? Giving one's life for another. Being frank with them.
Standing by them in suffering. Not abandoning them even at moments
when they seem quite distant. Thinking about them every moment. Saying
not a single word to hurt them. Having patience. Knowing how to listen.
Knowing how to understand what seems incomprehensible. Knowing how
to wait. How to forgive. What is intimacy? There must be several degrees of
intimacy and which of them is the highest degree, the most special, I am
not able to say.

Something else occurs to me: the fact that you yearn to live in love means you are closer to Jesus than those who pray every day yet call for revenge or harbour hatred in their hearts.

I'm talking like a preacher again. But I love you so much that I lose for a few seconds at least the feeling of guilt that pursues me almost unceasingly.

What will become of us?

Love, Dan

———

Dear Dannie,

We're having an Indian summer out here in Oregon and it's our second year fighting for the survival of the salmon. I've had loads of work as we've been repairing the house and changing the heating system, apart from which we've taken in my mother-in-law. She is eighty-five (see, there are even older grannies than me) and a bit confused. The other day she took the old pendulum clock off the wall, weights and all, and started to fiddle about with it. When I asked her what she was doing, she told me she was changing the batteries. I told her that that was something we all needed – to have our batteries changed – but unfortunately (for the time being anyway) it's not possible. So I have to shoulder everything here. My Bob can just about manage to trim branches and mow the lawn, but he's helpless in the house, even though it's his mother and he loves her.

Re. what you told me about Dad: I don't know what to think, I've been away for twenty-five years (a quarter of a century, brrr!). As far as his moral conduct is concerned I don't think he had too many scruples. He two-timed our mother. He thought Mum didn't know, but she did and she let me in on it (though probably not you), and she actually used to write to me about those women. She used to call them 'Daddy's tarts'. But I don't condemn Dad. In fact, I might have a teeny bit of understanding for him. He was a good-looking guy and women were crazy about him. I noticed it in the hospital. Mum was from another world, he must have had to live like a hermit with her. I don't think he and she hit it off too well, but since he was basically a nice guy, he never abandoned her. On the other hand, he lost a lot of years of his life. Maybe you don't know, but when they arrested him they held him for eight months in solitary. Can you imagine how horrific that was? And they beat him up. But seemingly they didn't manage to beat anything out of him, which is why they jailed him afterwards. What happened after I've no idea, but I can understand that when he got back from there he wanted to make up for everything he'd missed. Or to experience something really powerful that would exorcize the horror of it. I expect I'm talking about something other than what you wanted to know, but then again, maybe not entirely. I don't know what's worse: to betray people you don't know, or betray your own folks. I understand your desire to clear Dad's name insofar as it's in jeopardy. I've always been pragmatic to a fault and it seems to me that when someone is that long dead, it's best to let him rest in peace. Those who loved him will go on loving him as long as they live. Those who didn't are not going to be swayed by you anyway. And in the end we'll all be forgotten, along with all the good and the bad things we did on earth.

I wrote that Dad was a good guy and like you I don't believe he wanted to hurt anyone, or ever did.

Do you remember how they stopped you from attending grammar school when the poor guy was in jail? And how they admitted you when he was released. Maybe the two things were connected. The best thing is to say: it's a closed book.

There goes the mother-in-law ringing for me again. She rings for me at least twice a day, but at least it's cheaper than when she calls her friends on the East Coast or in London. She does that all the time, unless she happens to be eating, sleeping or ringing for me.

We're planning a trip to Europe next year so maybe we'll see each other. What's new in my dear homeland? Have our films, hamburgers, chewing gum and tourists reached you yet? Poor country!

Give my love to Hana and the kids.

And a big kiss for you, saintly man!

Love, Rút

———— • ————

Dear Dan,

It's Sunday morning, the sun is not yet fully awake and the rest are still asleep so I'm actually all alone. The garden is beneath my window. The grass is full of leaves that give off a scent of mould. There is music playing. Heaven must be something like this. Forgive me for such a banal image of heaven in which I rejoice in the song of the birds instead of the nearness of God.

I started to write to you because I need to be with you, yet I don't know when I'll see you again in the flesh. On the radio they were just reciting some poem by a Lebanese poet. Among other things it said: if love gives you the signal, obey it; also, love not only crowns you but also nails you to the cross. So I ask myself: is there within me a love that crowns and also crucifies? Do I have the self-discipline and patience to accept from it both the exaltation and the torment?

I had a bad day yesterday and the cross was almost unbearable again. My dear spouse had a headache and declared that it was because of me, that all his ailments were because of me. I wanted to know why. He said he was tired of explaining it to me all the time. I apparently lack any sense of order. I was playing music when he was trying to concentrate. I slammed the door and disturbed him. I splashed the water in the bathroom too loudly (!!). When he needed me to do a transfer of a plan I wasn't home (I'd gone shopping). So many crimes in one day.

I told him that none of it was important. What was important was that I was with him. He started to shout that I didn't understand a thing and one day I'd kill him, unless he killed me – or himself – first.

That's how things have been with us for years now, but every time I shiver like a cur. All it takes is for him to give me a little smile and a look (not a kind one, just a look) and straight away I suck up to him again.

Am I really so terrible? Do I really ruin my husband's life? What am I like, tell me? I have the feeling that you can judge, that you can be a judge of people because you have it all within you: patience, humility, kindness, a yearning for freedom and a sense of duty.

You write about a sense of guilt that pursues you. You ask what will become of us? It will come to an end, because everything on earth comes to an end. But just this once I'm not thinking about the end, I'm not thinking about the consequences of our actions, I don't want to think about what will be, I want to feel what is now. I think about you with tenderness and only wish that you'll be all right, and that I can help you to be, even from a distance.

I also want to tell you something I've never told you. My husband was never concerned about what I felt when we made love, in those far-off days when

237

we still made love. He was only interested in his own body. With you it's different. With you I've discovered that a man's love doesn't have to be selfish.

Life close to you has meaning because you are able to think about the other person. I'm not just an object for you. You are able to love and listen and also seek an answer. You answer questions like no other man I've ever known. All men are scared of answering questions, committing themselves, stepping out of themselves and their selfishness. They live in fear. Of themselves, of solitude, of death. What kind of man are you? Is it because you were born that way, or because you recognize someone higher than you, the Lord who commanded you to love people? You treat me in a way no one has treated me before and in so doing you give my life another dimension. I want you to be with me always. I know that it won't happen, either today, tomorrow or in the future. If we were both single I would want you as my husband. The tarot card reader predicted that I will be hanging around till I'm eighty-two, which means I've still got half my life ahead of me. And you won't be my husband in the second half either. You're not going to be with me, but perhaps you'll be with me for a little while longer, as long as I deserve – as we deserve. I'm sure you see things differently and when I talk of deserving something you hear in it pride or sacrilege, just as you do in the fact I believe some fortune-teller. I don't really believe her, it's just a game, and I know that I might not be here tomorrow and that I might never see you again.

We're only here for a short moment, the length of a dream, you once wrote to me. And life is a dream, I feel like saying, because from the point of view of an eternal universe and time it lasts less than a millionth of a second. But I want a life in which I've consciously lived millions of seconds, so I don't want life to be just a dream. I want a conscious life, not one that is just dreamily unconscious. Since I've known you I've had dreams every day. I try to decipher them but I just can't. Every morning I'm glad it was just a dream. I don't have beautiful dreams. They must be the outcome of some conflict between my conscious and my unconscious. Or my conscience perhaps? Perhaps they're the outcome of my conflict with God. Or the fact I bring you into conflict with your faith, that I'm harming you, that I'm harming the best person I ever met.

I was writing about heaven. I'm in heaven with you, another heaven than the one you believe in, but a heaven like the way I used to imagine it when

I was a little girl, when I looked forward to my dad coming home and saying: Hello sweetheart, I couldn't wait to see you again. But he never did. That's why I'm so receptive when someone's kind to me like you are. I sense that you wouldn't let me fall. That you would appear wherever I might be in danger of dying. I'm miserable when I think I must live this gift of my life without you. I'm happy that I can live at least a moment of this gift with you. Don't forsake me yet a while. Because when at last you do forsake me I will have an empty space inside me and I don't know what I'll fill it with. Work? Faith? An empty space left by love can't be filled with anything but love and most likely it will remain an empty space till the end.

I haven't started to pray yet. But I know that in every prayer one says: Don't forsake me, Lord! I don't pray, but every evening when I'm falling asleep I repeat in the quiet void: Don't forsake me yet a while, my darling.

Love, Bára

P.S. Now that I've written a litany about myself and my woes I expect you think I don't see anything else and that nothing else interests me. But actually the whole world and its future interests me. In fact, that's one of the few things I can talk to Sam about without fear: how everything around us will collapse one day, leaving only ruins behind!

———

Dear Reverend,

I was sorry your visit did not prove as successful as you'd hoped. After you had gone I tried to check my memory, particularly regarding the members of the service your father might have been seeing. Some of them came to mind. Even though some of them have gone where I won't meet them again, should I happen to see any of them I'll mention your problem to them. Maybe they'll have a better memory.

Seeing I wrote: I won't meet them again, I'd like to trouble you with a few questions, Reverend. As you maybe know I was dismissed from the service during the screenings back in sixty-nine and did various jobs afterwards to earn a living. I don't deny that in my youth I was a red-hot fighter for the socialist cause and against its enemies. In accordance with my training I regarded them as the enemies of everything progressive and therefore of the working people. For the same reason I regarded religion as opium to turn

239

the working man away from the just struggle. For me God was something invented by people and particularly the priests.

But now I read lots of other things in the press and I even watch religious broadcasts on the television on the odd occasion. Not that I've entirely changed, though! But it occurs to me that if I could have been misled about the rest I could have been misled about this too. Apart from which I'll be seventy-four this autumn and I have to admit that it's not easy to come to terms with the thought that you've not long to go and that's that.

So my question is this. Do you really believe people have souls and that the soul can live after death, and that it will even be rewarded or punished for what it did, that it will be sent somewhere? There's supposed to be hell, purgatory and heaven. Could you explain to me where they are all supposed to be? On earth or in outer space? Also, you declare that the soul is not a material substance. But can something that's not a material substance exist in the world? God is supposed to be something similar. I just can't imagine it. And also souls are supposed to pass from the dead into the living. But who can testify to it? After all, every baby is born without intelligence.

Reverend, if I'd written you a letter like this twenty years ago you might have taken it as a provocation, but not now, surely?

Looking forward to your reply,

Alois Bubník

——— ——

Dear Bára,

From our first or maybe our second conversation, I was taken aback by your gratitude for every sign of interest and for every answer to a question. Then I realized that you were someone thirsting for love (since childhood?) and that was why you were so grateful and humbly thankful.

I can imagine the gratitude you heaped on your husband, particularly since he was a professional whom you respected, when he left his wife and daughter on your account (or so you thought, although he no doubt did it on his own account as well, because he wanted you).

Gratitude, humility and praise are the way to kindle love in a good heart, that is what you believed and you behaved accordingly, as you still do. But when gratitude and admiration are expressed constantly they can have the opposite effect. They become a kind of drug for the one who is on the receiving end, who then starts to demand admiration and gratitude at all costs, by means of violence, blackmail or threats.

In so doing you can cause the person on whom you shower gratitude and admiration to believe in his superiority and above all his superiority over you. In place of a companion from whom you expect love you create yourself a master who regards himself as a god, who gives orders, takes decisions and issues pardons and rewards where appropriate. But all those functions belong to another Lord altogether. The human reward for gratitude and recognition tends to be ingratitude. The person who has tried to obtain love by means of gratitude and service tends to receive the opposite. In the words of the apostle: love is the fulfilling of the law. Everything in life that is given apart from it is of less account. Therefore, he who gives thanks for love without accepting thanks for the love he himself gives, helps to enfeeble or even destroy it.

You heap gratitude on me but forget about yourself. You're very special. And don't thank me for every caress – after all, you do your share of caressing.

I'd like to caress you now, for a long time without stopping. I'd caress you like that until the world outside the window disappeared along with my 'mission', our obligations and commitments and we'd remain all alone in the world (for a moment, at least).

All alone – does that mean without God too? I expect so. He might be able to accept our love but not our deception.

I'm sorry for also mentioning the thing I fear, but perhaps it only shows how much I love you that I act the way I do.

Love, D.

P.S. Re. the future of the world and humanity. I think it all depends on whether we manage to feel another's pain as our own.

———

Dear Rút,

I've hesitated a long time, wondering whether I ought to write to you about something I've not talked to anyone else about, or whether I was able to. But even though you're so far away, you are still the only really close relative I have and the only one who might possibly have some understanding for me.

I've committed something I never thought I'd be capable of doing. No, of course I've not killed anyone, or stolen the Sunday collection. Maybe you can guess. Yes, I've been unfaithful to Hana and still am and I've not had the courage to tell her yet.

I'm not able to explain my behaviour let alone excuse it. I still love Hana. But it's sort of a calm and unexciting relationship. The other woman excites me. She is passionate by nature and she lures me the way one is lured to an abyss. I've made up my mind a hundred times to put an end to it but then she phones me or I catch sight of her and I realize that I haven't the strength to break it off with her. Besides which, she begs me over and over again not to forsake her. I have the feeling she needs me in order to live. Maybe I'm deceiving myself as I have on so many occasions when I have trusted my conviction that people mean what they say. I know you can't advise me and it's not advice that I want, nor understanding for that matter. I simply needed someone to confide in and don't really have anyone but you. What a pity you're so far away.

Best wishes.

Love, Dan

Chapter Six

1

Old Mrs Houdková is on the point of death. She wants to stay home, she has no wish to die in hospital. Daniel therefore calls on her at least once a week, usually on a Thursday. He doesn't even need to say anything or comfort her, just his presence reassures the old lady.

A bunch of asters is wilting slightly in a vase. Daniel makes the old lady some tea and puts the piece of tart that Hana has sent her on a plate, which the grandmother hardly touches. 'How is it out?' she wants to know.

Outside it is fine and unusually mild for the third week in October.

'But the birds haven't flown away yet,' the old lady says, 'and the roses are almost finished.' Then she asks Daniel to say the Lord's Prayer with her and she adds the Apostles' Creed of her own accord. She believes that Christ will come to judge the living and the dead and also in the resurrection of the dead. 'Verily, verily, I say unto you He that heareth my word, and believeth in him that sent me, hath everlasting life, and shall not come into condemnation; but is passed from death unto life.'

The old lady glances up and says without warning, 'I'm anxious, Reverend.'

'About what, Sister Houdková?'

'About what's to come.'

He ought to reassure her and tell her that she can expect bliss in the presence of the Lord, eternal love, in other words, but he remains silent, and suddenly feels as if he is on the edge of a dark pit into which every living thing falls, in which nothing lasts, neither hours, nor days, nor years, nor centuries, nor millennia. Nothing will escape it.

Make haste to answer me, O Lord!
My spirit fails!

Hide not thy face from me,
lest I be like those who go down to the Pit.
(Psalm 143)

He merely takes the old lady's veiny, wizened hand in his and says what anyone might say: 'Have no fear, Sister Houdková!' That's all. He doesn't even add: The Lord is with you and will not forsake you. Not even what he had once said to his father: that his soul would not die but would live for ever. He just holds her hand in silence. Then he gets up, promises he will be back soon, and leaves her.

When he leaves the house he realizes he is still standing on the edge of a dark pit, with emptiness below him and before him, and he is overcome by dizziness.

It is just midday and suddenly he is at a loss what to do with his time. Hana is at work and the children aren't back till the evening. He can go and sit in his office and wait in case someone comes requiring help, which he won't give anyway. Also he could prepare his sermon but he has the feeling he will never again be able to mount the pulpit to say a single word. He could go to his workshop and do some carving, wrest from the formless wood all the shapes it contains. He could sit and play the piano. Or write a letter to Bára. Instead he stops in front of a telephone booth and hesitates for a moment. He knows Bára doesn't like him calling her at home or at the office where her husband might be present, and even when he is not there, his and her colleagues are, and are always watching her.

Nevertheless, he dials the office number and an unfamiliar female voice announces it to be the design studio. He asks for Mrs Musilová, the architect.

A moment later Bára takes the phone. 'How do you do,' she says in a formal tone. 'One moment, please,' she says then, 'I'll take the call next door.'

He waits in the booth, aware of a strange agitation; another step and he'll fall.

'Dan, is something up?' her voice says at last.

'No, or rather yes. Something has come over me. It's strange, on such a lovely day. I need to see you.'

'Right now?'

'If possible. The days are getting short.'

'But I'm at work.'

244

'Maybe they could spare you for once.'

'But what would I say? Sam will be back and he'll come looking for me.'

He waits for her a few blocks from her office.

'For your information, I'm on my way to the land registry office,' she announces on her arrival. 'I can get held up there for once. Where do you want to go?' He doesn't want to go anywhere; he wants to be with her because he is frightened of being on his own. He is frightened of his own teeming thoughts, which threaten to engulf and drown him unless he manages to divert them from their present course.

'I thought we might go for a drive somewhere, to a park, maybe,' he says, because she always expects some suggestion.

'Out of town? You're crazy. But I've got to be at home this afternoon when the children come home from school.'

'We'll be in the country in ten minutes.'

'There are no parks in this direction, apart from Šarka. Or Veltrusy. Now that's a park I like, because it was my favourite when I was a child and also because it's romantic. But it's a long way out.'

Some destination at last. He drives across the narrow bridge over the dark pit and sets off for Veltrusy.

On the hillsides, he notices, the larches are yellowing while the guelder roses and dogwood are turning red; the fields have been ploughed and above the horizon there hangs the grey haze of the autumn mists. She is sitting next to him, he feels her closeness, her scent, her breath. That narrow bridge is love; when it ends the bridge will collapse noiselessly. But now it is here with him and he starts to feel ashamed for having succumbed to anxiety, that he who should console needed comfort, or more likely a companion to escape with. He asks her if she's cross with him for dragging her away from work.

'I've dragged you away more than once. Besides, the work I do is slave labour anyway.' The architect, she explains, bringing him back down to earth, spends nine-tenths of his time on organization and the remainder on creative activity, at least that is how it works out with Musil. She doesn't even get that tenth, and spends her entire time dealing with phone calls, running between official departments and keeping an eye on construction firms to make sure they're not cheating too much. Formerly people stole from the State and thought there was nothing wrong with it. Now they steal from the State and have the feeling they are acting according to market principles. She leans over and kisses him: 'You're trying to escape my chatter and you're driving like a lunatic.'

'I thought you were in a hurry.'

'We don't have much time, darling, but if we get killed, we won't have any. Not here on earth, at least. And up there, as you believe,' she says, pointing to the roof and on the source of his anguish, 'people don't meet again, do they? And certainly not sinners like the two of us.' Then she remembers something: 'Saša liked you, he said you're a man, which in his book means a real man.'

'But he hardly knows me.'

'Well, the most important things you don't learn anyway, you have to sense them. I also sensed it about you the first time I met you.'

'I liked him too.'

'My little lad has a high forehead and a good heart. Takes after me. I expect he likes the fact you believe in God. I like it too. Maybe that's why I love you so much, the fact you can believe in something that is mysterious and beyond us and that I still can't bring myself to believe in.'

They drive through shabby villages. He is still aware of Bára's closeness and realizes that something has radically changed in his life.

At a moment of anguish he had not run to the Lord, he had not battled for his faith, but had given up and run to this woman who did not belong to him, nor he to her. To the woman who likes the fact he believes. Or it excites her. And meanwhile his soul is filled with doubts. Formerly he would strive to act well according to his conscience, so that one day he could look back without shame, so that he should not do anyone any harm or lead others to sin by setting a bad example. *And if your hand or your foot causes you to sin, cut it off and throw it away; it is better for you to enter life maimed or lame than with two hands or two feet to be thrown into the eternal fire.* (Matthew 18:8)

The pit terrifies him, whether it is full of fire or empty, but he is not only abandoning what he has believed his whole life – or has striven to believe in – he is also forsaking everything he has lived for so far: his family, his vocation, his future. A man without a future. That's the title of a novel. No, the title is: *A Man Without Qualities. Der Mann ohne Eigenshaften.*

One such method, that admittedly kills the soul, but then preserves it,

as it were, in little jars for general use, is to link it with reason, con-
viction and practical dealings, as has been practised with success by
all moral codes, philosophies and religions.

'Darling,' Bára breaks the silence, 'you're sitting beside me but in fact you're not here at all. You're not taking the slightest bit of notice of me. What's up?' He blames all the bends in the road.

Half an hour later they pull up in Veltrusy Park. A chemical stench hangs in the air, mingling with the scent of mouldering leaves.

'Do you know it here?'

'No, I've never been here before.'

'I haven't been here for ages either. At least ten years. But when I was small, my parents used to bring us here. My grandad who died before the war used to be the superintendent here, so in a way it was our park. There wasn't a stinking chemical works here then, although the little bridge with the sphinx and all those crazy neo-classical pavilions and artificial ruins were here, of course. And a flaming horse's head used to haunt the park not far from here, though I never saw it. I didn't believe in ghosts. I didn't believe in anything that wasn't real. I couldn't manage to even when I was small.'

She leads him to a spot from where it was possible to see an Egyptian chamber and tells him that water still flowed through it in those days. She shows him a rare, enormous tulip-tree, a gingko pine and a true chestnut tree.

They sit down on a bench opposite the Temple of the Friends of the Countryside and Gardens. She unbuttons her yellow and blue coat and rests her head on his chest, her face turned to the sun. 'I once saw a gnome here,' she says. 'He had a big head, short crooked legs and red trousers, and he had a pannier on his back.'

'How old were you?'

'I don't remember. Four or five maybe. I called to my dad to come quickly and see, but he was reading the paper, the stupid paper – there wasn't any other kind then – and before he put it down the gnome had run off. What's wrong with me today? First I waffle on about being cheated, now I'm going on about gnomes. Haven't I managed to put you off me yet?'

'No, you mean more to me than you can ever imagine.'

'You don't just want me for my body, do you?'

'Whatever makes you ask?'

'I just wanted to hear what you'd say. That you're also interested in my soul.'

'Love is a coming together, isn't it? And most of all a coming together of souls.'

'You think so too? And what form does it take?'

'Words, for instance. Words are the seeds of the soul. Even a dog or a crocodile has seeds of the body.'

'What made you think of a crocodile of all creatures?'

'Actually it was a dragon that I first thought of. In the legends, dragons used to have maidens thrown to them.'

'Yes, I know. I wouldn't want you if you made love to me like a crocodile! Tell me, are you happy to be with me?'

'I couldn't be happier with anyone else.'

'So why aren't you with me always?'

'You said yourself . . .'

'No, you don't have to explain anything. I have a husband who is my son's dad. It would be hard for him to lose him and me. And you have a wife and children, apart from which you are a pastor who is required to set an example to others.'

'Do you really think I lead an exemplary life?'

'You lead your life as best you can. That's why you're with me now. I also think I lead my life the best way I can. That's why I'm here with you now, and why I will never be with you for ever. When I was getting divorced I thought that it was all or nothing in this life. Either fidelity or infidelity. Love or indifference. Truth or lie. Either I'm with someone one hundred per cent or not at all. But in reality nothing is either or. With one exception.'

'Are you thinking about death again?'

'Yes. I can see you really don't like what I say.'

'I have so often preached and defended the text that our yes should be yes and our no be no. Anything beyond that comes from evil.'

'And do you think that always applies in life?'

'I definitely thought so when I preached it.'

'You'll leave me anyway,' she says, 'as soon as you grow weary of me. Or until it occurs to you that there are better ways for you to spend your time. In order to save your soul. In order for you to be sure once more what is good and what is evil. Because I come from evil. I have no written permission to have you!'

'I won't leave you.'

'Until when?'

'Until death.'

'Whose?'

'I'm speaking of my own.'

'I'd like you to be with me when I'm dying.'

'I won't be alive by then.'

'I would like you to be with me and hold my hand. Because I'll be frightened. But when you're with me, nothing frightens me. Even death wouldn't frighten me. Tell me you'll come.'

'I'd come if I were still alive.'

'Do you promise?'

'I promise.'

'I believe you. I believe everything you say.'

'What shall we do?'

'How do you mean?'

'In order to be together.'

'Nothing,' she replies quickly. 'We can't do anything except what we're doing. We can go and make love now, and know that we're as together as it's possible to be.'

'Here?'

'Here. Have you never made love in a park?'

'What if someone sees us?'

'Who would see us? There's no one here, is there?'

They find a spot that is separated from the path by a none too thick bush.

They lie half-undressed in the autumnally withered grass with scattered dry leaves and a smell of sulphur dioxide. The branches of the trees now shield the sun, so they feel the cool of the shade on their naked legs. 'My love,' he whispers to her, 'my dear little girl, you came to find me and now you're with me.'

'Danny, you're making love to me in my own park. I bet you've never made love in the woods before. You're a servant of God, but now you're mine. You are the Lord's compensation for all my suffering. You're my divine compensation, my boy.'

All of a sudden they catch the sound of children's voices apparently just nearby.

'Oh, God,' Bára whispers, 'he begrudges me it.' For a moment she grips him even more firmly before suddenly releasing him. 'Fear not, my darling, they're only gnomes!'

They manage to get dressed and return to the footpath before the first childish figures emerge from behind the trees. Her mother's dark hair and Eva's old skirt. It's Magda! What is she doing here?

His immediate instinct is to dash back into the bushes, but at that moment several other little red figures hobble into the open on short legs.

His sight really must be failing, or perhaps his bad conscience is beginning to distort the world and people.

A young nun approaches, pushing a wheelchair containing a handicapped child. 'Children,' she calls, 'let's not forget our manners!'

'Lord Jesus Christ be praised!' the handicapped children chorus somewhat erratically.

'It turned out fine,' the nun says, 'so we decided to take a trip and let our darlings have a chance to enjoy the last of the sun.'

'Yes,' says Bára, 'we enjoyed it too.'

I am filled with disgrace and look upon my affliction . . . (Job 10:15), comes to mind but he remains silent. It's too late for him to save his soul anyway.

2

Diary excerpts

Invisible chimneys spew smoke and sulphur
on to the neo-classical summer-houses.
The brook no longer flows through the Egyptian pavilion
Leaves fall in drops from the trees
never to grow again maybe.
From the bushes squint the eyes of twofold death.

Gazing with love on a noble lady
as she walks through her allotted park
I am suffused with the fateful tenderness of her eyes
and the anguish falls in drops from my soul.
Upon the lovers blinded by their love
from the bushes squint the eyes of crooked gnomes.

I gave Bára these few lines to read when we met in Mum's flat. 'You're crazy,' was her appraisal. 'You're a lovely lunatic. You see what others can't see and hear things that are beyond the hearing of others.'

Afterwards, when she was lying beside me, she asked me whether I still loved her and I said yes, as she expected. I was suddenly overcome with the falseness of the situation. The strangeness of the body that I was touching. It occurred to me at that moment that Bára had come to me to take revenge on her husband. But she was not vengeful. No, she had come to obtain something she felt cheated of. Maybe it was belief in some higher power, maybe just kindliness or words of love. She had come on her own account, of course, not mine. And one day she'll leave the same way.

How did I come to be lying alongside a woman who didn't belong to me, telling her that I love her and having congress with her as with my wife?

'Dan, my love,' she said to me at that moment, 'why are you looking at me like that from so far away?'

'I'm looking at you from right close up.'

'Don't make excuses. And don't pretend you don't know what I mean!' She put her arms around me and hugged me to her. 'Yes, it's me. I'm here with you.'

When we were saying goodbye she told me that for All Souls she usually went all the way to Boskovice in Moravia to lay flowers on the grave of her maternal grandparents, even though they were Jews and hadn't, of course, observed All Souls' Day or laid flowers on graves. Her husband, for his part, travelled to South Bohemia to lay flowers on the grave of his forebears. She generally stayed in Moravia overnight at an old aunt's. Were I to go with her we could stay that night together somewhere.

Magda came down with tonsillitis. She tends to exaggerate her feelings. When she is happy she is wildly joyful, when she is sad, one would think she was the most miserable person on earth, when she has a pain, it always hurts terribly. Perhaps she really was feeling very bad – the antibiotic hadn't had time to take effect yet and she would groan and be wanting something at every moment: tea, or a book, or another blanket because she was shivering with the fever. Then she wanted me to sit and talk to her about something.

I asked her what she wanted me to talk about. She said, 'About Jitka, for instance.'

For a moment I wasn't sure who she meant, and I asked her why she wanted to hear about her.

'Because she had a pain too. And because you've never talked to me about her.'

I told her instead about how I had been ill when I was a little boy, and then about how I trained to be a bookseller. Then I recalled the beginning of the revolution and how I had gone to meetings at the theatre and taken part in demonstrations. 'Do you remember I took you with me to the one on Letná Plain?' For a moment, I relived my feelings of that day: the enthusiasm, the expectation, and the hope for a life of greater truth and freedom.

'Yeah, I know,' she said, 'but it was no fun for me. It was awfully cold and the people just stood there and there were terribly long speeches that were no fun at all.'

'And there were all the flags.'

'Flags are no fun either.'

'What's your idea of fun, then?'

She pondered for a moment and then asked, 'That time, or in general?'

'That time or in general.'

'My idea of fun would be to fly. Not in a plane, but to actually have wings. To be a flamingus, say.'

'A what?' I said, baffled.

'You know, a bird of some kind,' she explained. 'A beautiful bird that flies where it likes. And I shouldn't think it suffers from sore throats and it doesn't have to go to a stupid school,' she added prosaically.

I gave her another cold compress and spread her some bread and butter. Then I told her I had to pop out for a while, but that her mother would be back in an hour.

She asked me where I was going.

I told her I had a meeting with the moderator but actually I had a date with Bára. We had arranged it when Magda was still well and I hadn't had a chance to call her and cancel it.

I knew that Magda would survive on her own for an hour; most fathers are out at work during the day and are therefore unable to sit with their sick children, but I also knew that if I left her I would be taking one more step towards the destruction of myself and my family. 'A home that is divided inside cannot survive.' I went anyway.

———◦◦◦———

There was an autumnal storm in the night. The sky lit up and went dark and the thunder gradually got louder. I love storms. Maybe because they signify change, or more precisely a change that does not disturb order but on the contrary happens in harmony with it. Suddenly I recalled a storm in the distant past: the centre of it seemed to come to rest right over where we were living at the time. The lightning flashed again and again and the thunder roared without stopping. Mum was visibly scared, though she scarcely ever showed her feelings and certainly never fear. She was so scared that she made Rút and me move into the middle of the room and say a prayer with her.

So I relived the moment when my mother, still young at the time, stood next to me asking Almighty God for protection. I could still hear her voice that was lovelier and more powerful than any other sound and truly drowned the thunder.

I was overcome with nostalgia. How cruel is the law that God has imposed on all life. Death takes one's dearest and there is no appeal.

———◦◦◦———

'Remember,' John Hus writes in The Daughter, 'that God created thee eternal and wants to dwell in thee for ever: eternal, to wit, immortal, for thou wilt never die. And in order that, immortal, thou shouldst be in eternal joy, God the Father gave His only begotten Son, true God, His own equal, and for you the Son submitted himself to a most loathsome and most cruel death, so that thou shouldst never die, He the best, the most beautiful, the most wise, the most rich and the most honoured!'

Half a millennium later, the Czech – or more accurately, Moravian – philosopher Šafařík wrote: 'We can thank Darwin for having brought nature into history and thereby thrown light on the nature of "success" as a historical phenomenon: in "survival of the fittest" he distinguished success as an animal category and demonstrated that a live dog is more successful than a dead saviour . . . In this respect, Jesus's life was a total failure. In historical terms, Golgotha is a place of execution and Jesus is *dead. The gallows are history, the cross mythology. Science and technology represent the hangover of a Christian world woken and sobered up after a mythical dream about the magical giver of cheap immortality . . . It is an irony of the "history of salvation" that whereas salvation was supposed to put paid to history, history, on the contrary, has put paid to salvation.'*

—◦◦◦—

In Prague almost every second marriage ends in divorce. That doesn't apply to our church and even less so to married clergy. I know only a few divorced clergymen. They are condemned by their congregations and in most cases the pastor is obliged to leave. Does a man have a right to fall in love once he is married? Has he the right to look for intimacy with another person when he is unable to find it with those nearest to him?

The trouble is it is hard to recognize rights in love. It happens when one doesn't want it and even when one resists it. One tries to suppress that illegitimate feeling, but the more one suppresses it, the more it grows.

I don't want to excuse myself or find excuses. I have acted irresponsibly. Certainly I acted irresponsibly that time, at the very beginning. When I held the hand of a woman who was still a stranger at the time. When I invited her into a house where I was alone and asked her not to leave yet. When I first embraced her. And I've only myself to blame that I wasn't able to confide in my wife.

The last time we met I put the following suggestion to her: What if I told my wife about you and you told your husband about me?

How old is your little girl? she asked.

I told her she was just twelve.

And you want to abandon her?

I said nothing.

Do you want to leave your wife?

I said nothing.

So why do you want to hurt them?

But it's just not possible to go on deceiving forever the people you live with.

Nothing lasts forever, she said.

I wanted to know what she meant.

Everything comes to an end one day. Even the tallest skyscraper has a roof. Life isn't a television serial.

You mean our love will end?

I mean everything will end. Life too.

I tried to persuade her that lying corrodes the soul. By doing things in secret we did more harm than if we acted openly.

No, she stuck to her guns: it wouldn't change anything, people would only suffer more. Then she added: Maybe it would change something, after all.

For a moment I fell for the hope that she knew of some solution, but she said: We'd stop seeing each other, because they would give us an ultimatum.

Then she burst into tears. You want to leave me. You're only thinking about it because you want to leave me! Then she said: There's nothing to stop you leaving me and no reason not to hurt me because I contravene the Ten Commandments!

I don't want to hurt her or Hana, but there's nothing for it but to hurt someone now. Either that or live a lie and destroy my soul. Can someone preach the Gospel to others, knowing that he is going to hurt another, or when he is living a lie?

Oh, Lord . . . you are not a God who takes pleasure in evil;
with you the wicked cannot dwell.
The arrogant cannot stand in your presence;
you hate all who do wrong.
You destroy those who tell lies.

(Psalm 5)

On the way home I decided I would make a clean breast of it to Hana. The moment I decided, I felt a sense of relief. I also considered each of the sentences I would say and their possible consequences.

When Hana came home from the hospital in the evening, she sat down as usual and made herself a coffee. I went to her but instead of asking her what was new at work I told her there was something I would like to speak to her about.

She glanced in my direction. Has something happened? she asked.

Her face, so familiar to me, reflected her tiredness, but in her look I saw total unsuspecting trust and I suddenly felt like a criminal lying in wait for his victim and raping her, thereby depriving her of any belief

*she had in love, in people, in God, in life in general. Oh my God, I
realized, she's been through that once already!*

*She waited expectantly for what I would say, but I could not bring
myself to say any of the things I had prepared. So I told her I had been
thinking about the Soukups, and beginning to wonder whether divorce
might not be better than living together when there is no love.*

*But it's up to individuals, she answered, whether they were capable of
keeping their love.*

*I nodded and left quickly, because I was ashamed. Ashamed of my
cowardice, my dishonesty and my faithlessness. Unless I find the courage
to tell Hana everything, there is nothing for it but to break it off with
the other one. To put an end to our relationship. Or to myself?*

---

*We had a seminar up in Hejnice. It was also attended by several
professors who were at the faculty in my time. The theme was
predestination and the meaning of good works. It's an eternal theme
about which, as with most themes, everything has been said that could
be said. In the evening I went for a walk with Martin and his wife
Marie, and we were joined by a few other friends. Martin spoke on his
favourite topic, saying we oughtn't to lay such stress on the supernatural
passages of the scriptures. I pointed out that the moment we abandoned
them, we abandoned the divinity of Christ, and all that we would be
left with would be the original Judaism or some mishmash of
philosophical opinions several thousand years old.*

*Martin said: 'But he wasn't God, though. He wasn't even the Son of
God in the sense we preach it. His mother and father were ordinary
people. We all know that, don't we?' We all glanced at him in surprise,
but amazingly enough nobody voiced any objection.*

---

*At the end of the youth meeting, Marika talked about the mysterious
forces that inexplicably manifest themselves in her surroundings.*

*She was on her own at home one day, for instance, and all of a
sudden the doorbell rang, not just a little ring, but ringing like mad. She
rushed to the door and when she opened it there was no one there. And
there wasn't even any movement on the staircase.*

'Or I'm lying in bed,' Marika went on, 'on my own at home again and all of a sudden the light comes on in my bedroom and when I go to switch it off I notice that the lights are on all over the flat. And yet they were all off when I went to bed. So I call out: Is anyone there? I switch them all off one by one and when I go back to bed they all come on again.'

'You're having us on,' Alois declared. 'Someone was home and you didn't know.'

'Do you mind?' Marika said, taking umbrage. 'Who could have been there? Mum had gone out, one of my brother's inside and the other one's in Ostrava. I was there all on my own, I can swear it on my mother's death!'

'No, don't do that,' I said to her, 'save your oath for something really important.'

'And what is really important?' someone asked.

Only six months ago I would have replied: fidelity, for instance. Or honesty. Or decency. I didn't reply.

'Forgive me, I didn't intend to criticize you,' I said to Marika. 'I wanted to say that I believe you. There are things that happen that one just can't explain and they remain a mystery forever. The entire Bible message is one great big mystery, although I wouldn't want to compare it.'

When the young people were gone, I wondered whether I really did believe Marika, or whether I had said it because I wanted to defend her dignity in front of the others. I wasn't able to make up my mind, all I knew was that I would like to have believed her.

I dreamed that I was still quite young and attending the booksellers' training school, apparently quite unaware that I would one day become a preacher and on the contrary being interested most of all in the girls. I made a date with one of them who had just quarrelled with her boyfriend. When I arrived to meet her at her house I discovered I was wearing odd shoes. I tried to conceal the fact by hiding my right foot behind the left one. She invited me upstairs and I was relieved that I could change out of my shoes into the slippers that she had prepared for me. We did some petting and then went out again. We were already outside when I realized I was still wearing the slippers. She told me to

257

wait downstairs: she would bring me my shoes and we could leave the
slippers in the letter box. Then I realized that she would now discover I
was wearing odd shoes. I dashed up the stairs after her in order to
explain somehow. But she only laughed and praised me for having each
shoe a different colour. She told me it had cheered her up.

Each shoe different. The left foot from a different home than the right
one. Making love in a strange flat and praise for something I'm trying to
conceal.

3

Máša Soukupová was sitting opposite him and making an effort to
speak coherently. Her husband had moved out and he wanted to
take the children. He had hired a good lawyer and they were planning to prove in court that she was incapable of bringing up the
children. And she had actually signed some paper when she was in a
state of shock at learning that her husband wanted to leave her. It
was possible that the paper said she agreed that he should take the
children.

The sound of the piano could be heard from downstairs. In recent
times, Eva really had played at least four hours a day, sometimes just
improvising in a mournful and laboured fashion. Something was still
bothering her. On a few occasions her eyes looked as if she had been
crying. Whenever he asked her something he would get fragmentary
replies, mostly just a single word.

'How do you like school?'

'OK.'

'Is there anything the matter?'

'No, I'm all right.'

He ought to have a proper talk with her, find half a day to talk to his
own daughter before something irreparable happens. Instead he was
sitting here with Mrs Soukupová, and even if this poor woman wasn't
here, he would most likely be using any spare time to meet the woman
he oughtn't to be seeing.

'But I took good care of them, Reverend. I didn't leave them for a
moment. It must be two years since I last went to the cinema or the
theatre, apart from the puppet theatre. And they depend on me. I'm

their mother after all! Surely they can't take them from me! Surely God couldn't allow it!'

God had already allowed other things. Sometimes when Daniel considered all the things He had allowed, he doubted whether He would display the slightest interest in what was happening to mankind and the world, let alone to any one individual. But he didn't say so. Nor did he say what not so long ago he would have said: that it was only a test, that the Lord had tested even Job, and when he stood the test, He blessed him more than ever before.

'You must fight to keep your children, Máša. And I'll ask Dr Wagner to represent you.'

'But how will we live?'

'You have to tell yourself that there are lots of people worse off than you, Máša. There are mothers whose children die. Others give birth to blind or crippled babies. And you've not been left entirely on your own. You have the Lord Jesus and all of us, your brothers and sisters, who support you.' He stopped short, sickened by his own words, his hypocrisy. It was as if he wasn't talking to her but to his own wife. Even though he had not abandoned Hana, had not moved away, not taken the children; instead he always returned to them and behaved affably as if he still dwelled with them in love and peace. Who was behaving worse, in fact, he or Máša's husband, who had made his choice? Let what you say be simply 'Yes' or 'No'; anything more than this comes from evil.

'Life is like that, Máša,' he added. 'There are also moments when we are put to the test and we have to come to terms with that. Maybe it's better to separate than to live without love. Now your heart is too full of pain, but it will pass and you'll start to see that life's worth living.'

The piano fell silent.

Máša thanked him tearfully for his words of comfort, though he knew he had been no consolation. However, he shook her by the hand and stroked her hair as she was leaving.

Then he went down to the chapel, but his elder daughter was gone and he did not even find her in her room. She must have left a few moments before Máša.

He went all the way up to the attic and found his son with Alois as he expected, making improvements to their home-made telescope. 'Have you discovered anything yet?' he asked.

'You couldn't discover anything with this telescope,' Marek

explained. 'It's impossible to see anything that isn't in the Milky Way.'

'We're sort of learning to observe, that's all,' Alois added.

'What I'd be really interested to know,' said Marek, 'when I see all those stars – what I can see of them anyway – is how it was all created. The stars, the sun and the earth.'

'You don't think God created it?'

Marek shrugged. 'Our Principal says: Reason was more likely the outcome than the origin.'

'That's why everything is so rationally organized, I suppose?'

'I don't know, Dad. But it couldn't have been as simple as it's described in the Bible.'

He noticed that Alois was listening with expectant interest.

Of course the world we all live in is moving faster and faster away from the one inhabited by those who wrote down the Bible message, and the interest that people have in it will continue to wane. How much easier it was for preachers in the days when the earth was the centre of the universe and the moon and stars were there to rule the night, and the lamps of heaven had simply been kindly lit by God so that the night should not be so hopelessly dark.

'I understand what you're saying,' he said to Marek. 'The universe arose fifteen or maybe eighteen billion years ago. A billion either way doesn't matter, it's beyond our imagination anyway. It is expanding. The earth and the sun are somewhat younger. Stars are born and die. There are more stars in the universe than we can count. The Lord told Abraham: Look toward heaven, and number the stars, if you are able to number them. There are black holes and white dwarves. All those things can be determined. But what was at the beginning, whether it was divine intention or a big bang when all of that came into existence from a speck of matter, is purely a matter of belief.'

Unlike his companion, Marek continued to look sceptical. And Daniel wasn't pleased with his own speech either. In such a universe, a God who created it and at the same time assumed the form of a Jewish infant, who grew up, was baptized by John, preached, was arrested, condemned and shamefully executed, seems less and less likely, less and less possible, harder and harder to defend.

'Listen,' he said to Marek to cover up his uncertainty, 'you didn't deign to come to the service last Sunday? Or did I miss you?'

'No, I wasn't there,' his son reluctantly admitted.

'It's no fun listening to your dad on Sunday as well?'

'It's not that,' his son replied. 'I just didn't feel like it. If it wasn't you preaching I'd feel like it even less.'

'And what did you feel like doing?'

'I did some reading.'

'About black holes?'

'Why about them in particular? I read a novel.'

'About what?'

'It's hard to explain, Dad. Science fiction.'

'A journey into space?'

'No. It was about another civilization. But they were ants, not humans.'

'You found that interesting?'

'Fairly. But it's made up, a civilization like that doesn't really exist. And even if it did, we'd never find out about it.'

'Are you sorry?'

'About what?'

'That you'll never find out about the ant civilization?'

'If it existed, yes. It would be a pity if we never found out.'

'Fine, Marek, I'm glad you have an interest in those things, but perhaps you could spare me that hour on a Sunday?'

'The hour's not the point, Dad!'

'What is the point, then?'

'I just believe that everything was completely different from the way the Bible says and the way you preach it.'

'It's certain that nothing was literally the way it is written in the Bible.'

'Well, there you are.'

'But nor was it exactly the way it is described in scientific texts either.'

'That's possible, Dad. But what those books say is more likely.'

'Marek, it's not a question of what is more likely. The essence of the Bible message is not about how life developed, but how we ought to live it.'

'People don't live by it anyway,' Marek commented stubbornly, and suddenly Daniel had nothing to refute him with.

'So you won't be going to church on Sundays any more, then?'

'It's not that, I'll be coming all right,' Marek said, suddenly startled at his own defiance.

He had not managed to persuade Marek. Likewise, he was incapable of talking to his daughter or finding out what was troubling her. He had failed to comfort Máša or advise her how she ought to live. He had not managed to stay faithful to his wife. He wrote letters to Bára that were possibly tender and in which he spoke of his great love for her, but he couldn't bring himself to yield to her entirely.

He had been incapable of bringing anything to a satisfactory conclusion recently. His life was definitely out of kilter with the Bible message and even with ordinary human decency.

As he was coming downstairs, he caught sight of his wife who had just rushed out into the passage. 'Dan, where have you been? I've been looking for you everywhere. There's just been a call from the police in Plzeň. They've arrested Petr.'

4

Samuel

Samuel returns from a two-day business trip to Ostrava several hours earlier than he told Bára he would. Bára isn't home, of course. The flat is tidied and empty, and it doesn't appear to have been heated. There is just the musty smell of stale tobacco smoke in the air. Aleš must be at his grandmother's and Bára will be somewhere with some chap. He still suspects young Vondra, he's good-looking and he definitely has a better way with women than Samuel had at his age, not to mention now. When it was Bára's birthday he brought her a rose. And he's always looking in on her whenever he gets a chance. Not long ago, he offered to accompany her to Příbram on business. Bára refused, but that might only prove she's more cautious than he is. He calls his mother-in-law. Yes, Aleš is with her; Bára said she had something to attend to. No she didn't say what or with whom; she never gives her details. His mother-in-law wants to know whether she is to bring Aleš, or whether he is to sleep at her place.

That depends on when Bára will come home.

She's bound to be home soon, it's not six o'clock yet.

Sam tells his mother-in-law he'll call her later. He could have spoken to his son, but he didn't think about it in the surge of rage. He walks nervously around the empty flat; he dislikes emptiness, it unnerves him. He tries phoning the office but there's no one there any more. What sort of business could Bára have to attend to?

She could have all sorts of business. Bára is almost unbearably active. She manages to do the housekeeping, work in the office, deal with clients and also act on television from time to time. When he comes home dog-tired in the evening, Bára is there teaching Aleš something, chatting to Saša, making phone calls, singing and she's even willing to talk to him until midnight about his ailments, his work or the political situation, and after all that she expects him to make love to her.

There was a time when he regarded her activity as a positive attribute, but now that he is continually tired, he finds Bára's craving for life, activity and constant change infuriating. What infuriates him, he realizes, is her youthfulness. She does not yet feel death at her back or understand how futile is the longing to touch everything, try everything and be part of everything.

He should have realized it when he married a woman so much younger than himself. Except that at the time he was still full of energy and Bára's submissiveness concealed her craving for life.

Of course she has no business to attend to. Why should she tell her mother? Anyway, the two of them stick together against him; all women stick together against the common enemy – men.

He then dials the number of Vondra's flat. Vondra is home and immediately wants to know how he fared in his negotiations in Ostrava. 'Very well, excellent, in fact,' Samuel says, even though things didn't go at all well, but he isn't in the mood to talk about business matters.

Vondra says he is pleased to learn of Samuel's success and they say goodbye. For a moment Samuel has a feeling akin to relief. Then he realizes that Bára could have been lying there all the time in the arms of that playboy. What's more, she could be lying in the arms of thousands of other men he knows nothing about.

He switches on the television where they are just giving the weather forecast. He listens to it: a fine autumn day is expected, but it won't be fine for him. He doesn't feel like watching the news, but the room feels so inert and empty that he turns down the sound and just watches the pictures move.

Bára is still not home. There is nothing for it but to wait; time that drags on interminably because there's nothing else to do, nothing sensible to concentrate on. Occasionally, when he gets held up somewhere in the evening, he tries at least to call her, but the phone always tends to be engaged and he can only conjecture who she might be talking to. Whenever he finally gets through and asks her, she says it was to a girl-friend or her mother, or that Saša was gossiping.

He knows that it could well be true, but is not necessarily so: Bára is deceitful. She manages to smile at him even when he can feel her iciness. The smile merely conceals her real intentions. But she's quite adroit and alert and never lets the cat out of the bag, never leaves any real clues. Her countless phone calls are innocence itself and she never leaves any love messages in her handbag.

And when he asks her to be home on time, Bára explains to him all the commitments she has and tells him he sometimes comes home late too. He ought to put a stop to her television appearances, at least. Those rehearsals or performances are just a pretext for her to go and see her cronies.

But if he tried to talk her out of anything Bára would start to wave her rights in front of his nose. He has noticed she has been reading feminist pamphlets lately. Although there was hardly any need for her to read them, she could write her own.

Some sort of actors' dressing-room appears on the screen. Samuel can imagine his own wife in it, and she's not alone, of course.

For God's sake, it's only too obvious to him that there is no keeping an eye on a woman: she can make love anywhere – on the floor, on a table, in an armchair, on a heap of straw, in a wood, in a meadow, standing up in a gateway, on a car seat or in some shed where building materials are stored.

When they were at that reception given by the English last week, he noticed that she was approached by men he didn't know at all. Where did they know her from? He registered the note of pleasure in her voice that they were interested in her. They addressed him with respect too. Indeed, many of the guests would have been honoured for him to spare them a moment, but his mind was elsewhere: he was watching Bára and feeling so hopelessly deserted and betrayed, that in the end he dragged her off home on the pretext that he wasn't feeling well. So she steered him to the car and insisted on driving even though she had drunk at least four glasses of wine. And when they got home she made him take some tablets as if she didn't know full well that his illness was simply caused by her.

At half-past eight Bára arrives at last. 'You're home already?' she says, and in her voice feigned satisfaction is mixed with fear and dis-appointment. She comes to embrace him, but as she brings her face close to his, he detects the odour of wine and refuses to kiss her. 'Where have you been so long?'

Bára has a perfect alibi ready, of course. In the afternoon at the building department and in the evening she dropped by Ivana's because she had promised her some drops to prevent migraine. And she actu-ally takes a brown medicine bottle out of her handbag: ten drops in a small bottle of water. Water to be added as the contents are used up.

Samuel doesn't listen to her. 'What about Aleš?'

'I'll phone Mum to bring him. Or should I go and pick him up in the car?'

'Why didn't you pick him up on the way?'

'I wanted to get home as soon as possible. In case you came in early and had to wait here on your own.'

'I did come in early and I did wait here on my own.'

'I'm sorry about that, I really am,' and she adopts an expression as if she really was sorry. 'How did you make out?'

For the second time he says it went well, excellently, in fact.

'I'm pleased. And most of all I'm pleased you're home.' She acts as if she really was pleased and waits for him to kiss her after all, but he would sooner give her a thrashing and get out of her where she really has been and how long she's been carrying that bottle around in her handbag as an excuse and what those drops are really to prevent, that's if the bottle contains drops for preventing anything. He turns on his heel and goes to his room.

'Aren't you going to eat?' Bára calls after him.

'There isn't anything yet.'

'I'll make something straight away. But I'll just call Mum first and ask her to bring Aleš.'

'It's too late,' he says. 'Surely you don't want your mother dragging him home through the city in the dark?'

In his room he sits down at his enormous desk and switches on his computer, but he doesn't feel like working. It occurs to him that he will never again create anything decent or original anyway. He's getting on for sixty and there are other, younger and more ambitious fellows with much better opportunities than he ever had, with different back-grounds and happier homes, maybe. What he hasn't managed to achieve so far, he never will.

He can feel the despondency growing in him, as well as anger with Bára. He had asked her where she had been for so long and he had accepted her excuse, not letting on that he totally disapproves of her dumping their son on his grandmother instead of taking care of him, and there is no way he can agree to her wandering off God knows where, with God knows who the moment his back is turned.

At that moment, the door of the flat bangs: it is his stepson coming in. As usual, he mistakes the front hall for some woods and is whistling some mind-numbing pop song.

Samuel rushes out of his den and gives Saša a ticking-off.

Saša looks offended and says he has hardly done anything terrible. He didn't know his dear daddy was home, he was supposed to be away.

Samuel explains to him that one acts civilly at home even if one is on one's own.

His stepson asks him what is so uncivil about someone whistling to himself at home when he is on his own.

Samuel starts to yell that he's had enough of such rudeness and impertinence.

Bára peeps into the front hall and asks what he's annoyed about.

Samuel, his voice faltering with annoyance, informs her that he has reason enough to be annoyed. He has come home to an empty flat. One of the children has been dumped on his grandmother and the other is out mooching around somewhere, and it's no surprise seeing that his mother sets such a splendid example.

'What's that supposed to mean?' Bára asks.

'That no home would be better than such a home as this.'

'Nobody's forcing you to stay here,' Bára says.

'Stop fighting,' Saša begs them, afraid that a row is brewing between them. 'After all, nothing so terrible has happened.'

'Does that mean you want a divorce?' Samuel asks.

'You're the one who doesn't feel at home here.'

'And are you trying to say this is a home?'

'Jesus Christ,' Bára shouts, 'what's a home supposed to be then? Am I supposed to sit at home like a slave even when my lord and master isn't meant to be here?'

'And what about the children?'

'Children, children. The boy's not even allowed to whistle in the front hall.'

'Your son does too much whistling.'

'My son is not allowed to whistle because he's my son,' Bára shouts. 'If you loved me just a little bit you'd love him too.'

'If you loved me just a little bit, you'd behave differently.'

'If *I* behaved differently – it's always me. I spend my time running around you like a maidservant and when did you last even say a kind word to me?'

'If you were to behave differently I might say kind words to you.'

'What is behaving differently supposed to mean?'

'Not behaving like a tart!'

'What did you say?'

Samuel can feel the blood rushing to his head and at the same time he feels a sharp pain in the region of his heart: she'll actually cause him to have a heart attack.

Bára sobs and her son comforts her. Samuel turns on his heel and without a word locks himself in his room.

He feels like breaking something. He picks up the newspaper, crumples it up and throws it in the basket; then he kicks the basket, which overturns and scatters papers all around the room.

Coloured stars move around on the computer screen. He stares at them for a moment; he could throw the computer on the ground, but he knows that he won't, he'll just switch it off to stop it irritating him.

His anger gradually gives way to despair.

He opens the top drawer of his desk in which all his various medicines are neatly arranged and he takes two diazepam tablets to calm his nerves, although he knows that no tablets will help him. She's the only one who can help him, that damned woman. If only she were to come and say: I love you, I don't want to be with anyone, anyone, anyone but you because you're the best man in the world. The best man of all – the way she used to repeat it when they first met, when she was fighting to win him and to get him to marry her.

Then he remembers how they spent a holiday in the firm's chalet in the Western Tatras three years after their marriage. She was already expecting Aleš and couldn't go on hikes. So he and two of his colleagues set off on a long hike to Ostrý Roháč via Baníkov. When they set out in the morning it looked like the start of a sunny summer day, but on the return journey the weather changed completely and a storm arrived with hail, fog and cold. They were obliged to shelter for some time beneath a rocky cliff, and instead of returning at dusk they didn't get back until late at night.

When at last they arrived totally exhausted, she threw herself on him, hugging him and kissing him and helping him out of his wet clothes and rubbing his frozen feet, all the while repeating over and over again how she had been afraid for him, and had actually prayed for him to return safe and sound, and how happy she now was that he was back with her again. Then all of a sudden she burst into tears. He asked her why she was crying and she said, 'because I love you so much and couldn't live without you'.

It occurs to Samuel that if he had died that night he would have died happy, because he was loved. Still young and loved. He won't ever manage that now, he has lost his chance to die young and loved. His chest tightens more and more with self-pity and he notices that his face is wet. Now it is he who is crying; he is crying because if he were to die now Bára would not even shed a tear, instead she would probably heave a sigh of relief.

If only he had the strength to leave this hell, this insecurity. If only he had sufficient determination to be alone. If only he had just one pillar to lean on. Samuel sits crumpled up in his armchair. He listens to the movements in the flat. But his stepson isn't whistling any more and Bára has most likely locked herself in her bedroom. He would wait in vain for her to come and ask him to forgive her.

It strikes Samuel that he should buy himself a dog to share his dog's life with him.

5

First thing in the morning, Dr Wagner rushed into the parish office and informed Daniel that he had some important news for him about his father. He had managed to find a man in the ministry who had access to the secret police files and he was willing to let him have a look at them. 'I needed it in connection with something else but as I was there I asked him whether I might not take a look at your father's file too, if it existed. He brought it to me and I discovered that it contained no agreement signed by your father.'

Wagner then started to explain that State Security classified their collaborators into several categories. At the lowest level were the 'confidants' who were often unaware what they were being used for. For instance, it was enough to persuade a doctor to send someone for spa treatment or clinical examination and that would allow their agents to enter his flat undisturbed in order to install a bugging device or photograph something.

'The doctor would have to have been willing to do what they wanted,' Daniel commented.

'But they wouldn't introduce themselves as secret policemen, would they? They would pretend to be someone who was concerned about the health of one of his subordinates. Or as the chairman of the trade union branch. On other occasions, they would pretend to be investigating some crime or other.'

'Do you think they merely took advantage of my father, then?'

'Definitely.'

'For how long?'

'That's the second piece of good news. Less than two years. Then your father, as is clear from the report of his controlling officer, started to suspect they were playing some game with him and began talking to his friends about it, and that fact was reported by one of the secret police agents working in the hospital. So they terminated the connection.'

'When did all this happen?'

'Shortly after your father's release from prison. *Inter alia* they classified him as a 'has-been', on account of that house of your grandfather's.'

'Poor old Dad. They would stick a label on people and shove them into a category from which there was no escape.'

'But your father did escape, as you can see.'

Yes, the best way of escaping them was by departing from this world. Dad managed that seventeen years ago.

'Thank you very much, I'm extremely grateful.' He ought to make a greater show of gratitude and pleasure, even though, as he noted to his surprise, he felt nothing of the kind. He was too aware of his own burden to feel any real sense of relief at that moment. None the less he said, 'I am in your debt, very much so.' Then the thought struck him: 'Figuratively and literally. I expect that information must have cost you something, not to mention the time that you have spent on obtaining it.'

'But Reverend, I did it on account of your father's good name. Moreover, as I explained to you, I got in contact with that fellow in connection with another matter.'

Dr Wagner took his leave and it struck Daniel that it was possible that the file the lawyer had seen had also contained details about his father's private life. The thought that a member of his congregation might know about his father's peccadilloes, and perhaps even the names of his mistresses, did not cheer him.

Fortunately no one was keeping a file on him any more, or so Daniel hoped.

However, if *they* weren't keeping a file on him, he was keeping one himself by storing Bára's letters. It would be more sensible to get rid of them, but they seemed to him so special, so full of love, that he could not bring himself to destroy a single one. But he ought to do something with them, all the same. Take them to his mother's flat and transcribe them in a secret code, or translate them into a little-known language like Hebrew and then discard the originals.

When, after supper, he shared Wagner's news about his father with Hana, she said, 'There you are. And all the torment you had.'

'Only for a while. Then I said to myself that it was already outside the statute of limitations whether it happened or not. Still, I'm glad that Dad didn't lead some secret life,' he quickly added.

'There's something I was wanting to tell you too,' his wife said in such a serious tone that it made him jump.

However, what she was wanting to tell him had nothing to do with the concealed part of his life, but concerned her work. She had more and more worries in the hospital; sometimes she came home completely exhausted. And now that her salary was no longed needed, it had been occurring to her that she could find some other work for which she could be her own boss, to a small degree at least. What if she were to try and set up a diaconal centre here in the house? She would enjoy being involved in its work. But she immediately added, as if she was suddenly startled at daring to make such a radical proposal, that she didn't want to add to Daniel's worries, and she realized how much effort it would require.

But her idea appealed to Daniel. If he could get fully involved in that kind of work, he could excuse himself from his other duties, for a time at least. Caring for the handicapped was not the same as preaching about the Son of God or officiating at the Lord's Supper while entertaining doubts about himself and the institution.

Furthermore, in establishing a diaconal centre he could find a use for the money that he still felt ashamed of possessing, or rather he was ashamed of the way he had used it so far.

He promised that he would speak with the moderator of presbytery and the director of Diakonia. Hana could definitely quit the hospital as soon as it was possible.

As he was passing the children's room, he overheard Magda screeching. He went in and discovered Marek fighting over some object with his sister.

'Tell him to leave me alone, Daddy,' Magda begged, 'he's taking my things!'

'Look, Dad,' Marek said accusingly, 'she buys these stupid sprays that are full of CFCs.' He manages to wrest two metal containers from Magda's hands and displays them to Daniel triumphantly.

'Why are you taking them from her?'

'But that's what I'm telling you: they're full of CFCs.'

'What do you need them for, Magda?'

'Nothing. But they're mine. I bought them.'

'What does she need them for? To spray stupid signs on walls.'

'Is that true, Magda?'

'It's none of his business.' Magda had tears in her eyes. 'He's got no right to boss me about.'

'And what do you write?'

'Nothing.'

'Magda!'

'Love, for instance,' Magda said.

'And what else?'

'Nothing else. Just that. And once I sprayed a bird. A flamingo.'

'I think Marek's right. There's nothing nice about spraying things on walls.'

'Love is nice, and so are flamingos.'

'That's precisely why you shouldn't spray them on walls.'

'The others do it.'

'That doesn't make it any cleverer.'

'So make him give me back the sprays.'

'Give them back to her, Marek. And don't you spray anywhere with them.'

Marek stood the tins up on the top of her wardrobe, out of Magda's reach, and left without a word.

'First you tip things on passers-by from the window and throw spiders at them, and now you're writing nonsense on walls.'

'What am I supposed to do then, Daddy?'

'What do you mean?'

'To have a bit of fun.'

He was about to tell her that having fun wasn't the only purpose of living, but at that moment the phone rang in the next room.

'Daniel, I'm sorry to be calling like this but something terrible has happened. Sam has gone and swallowed a whole lot of his pills.'

Something like this had to happen, naturally. What they had done could not go unpunished. He feared the answer when he asked, 'Is he alive?'

'Yes.' Bára hurriedly explained how she had woken up in the night and heard strange noises. She had found Samuel in his room. The noise had been his choking. On the bedside table, he had left two empty tubes of his anti-depressant tablets. And a farewell note. The first thing she did was call an ambulance. She had been in the hospital until Sam revived a short while ago.

'What did the note say?'

'What notes like that usually say. That he's old and has nothing to look forward to, that he's just a burden on everyone and on me in particular. That he feels I yearn for freedom and so he is giving it to me.'

'I'll come and see you.'

'No, not now. I have to go back to the hospital, he needs me there. I just had to tell you, that's all.'

'I'd like to help you somehow.'

'I don't know what you could do to help. There is one thing, though. Tell me you're not cross with me for always adding to your worries, and tell me you won't forsake me!'

6

Bára

Bára now divides her time between visits to the psychiatric hospital where they continue to hold her husband and work in the office where she is obliged to stand in for Samuel. She feels sorry for Samuel's suffering. At the same time, however, she feels a long-forgotten sense of freedom, with no one to watch over her, no one to tell her off for coming in late, no one demanding that she create the semblance of a home by her constant presence, care and tenderness. Daniel calls her each morning and sometimes in the evening and they usually talk about Samuel and how his action will affect her life. Daniel is a good listener who isn't trying to catch her out all the time and tell her off in order to demonstrate his male superiority. Bára has the feeling that Daniel shares all her worries, anxieties and doubts, so it is easy to talk to him.

She can't make the trip to lay a wreath on the grave of her grandparents since she has to visit Samuel every day in hospital, but she is loath to lose the opportunity of spending at least one night with Daniel. She suggests that they could spend it in her flat. There's no chance of Samuel being discharged at night and she won't be visiting him then either. She'll send Aleš to his grandmother's for the night and Saša can sleep at a friend's place.

Daniel says nothing for a moment as is his wont, but she already knows that his silence does not simply mean silence. Daniel says nothing because he is in a quandary or is suffering a feeling of anxiety that he is departing more and more from his idea of how he ought to live. He is scared of the sin he is committing.

'Will you come?'

Daniel promises he will.

All Souls' Day is the following Wednesday. Immediately after lunch, Bára dashes to the hospital, stopping to buy Samuel not only fruit, but also a big bunch of asters. She brings with her a candlestick and a candle for her husband to light in memory of his dead, seeing that he is unable to visit their grave.

Outside, the day is misty and damp, and the heavy sky oppresses even those who are in good health.

Samuel is alone in a three-bed ward and doesn't feel at all ill. He considers psychotherapy to be nonsense, and can see no good reason why he should talk about his relationship with his mother or about his first and second wives when his greatest pain – the wound from which his life has been draining away for years – is Bára. And he can't understand why she has to visit him every day, when she only goes away again, leaving him at the mercy of loneliness and his doubts. Why isn't

273

she persuading him to come home straight away? Why isn't she telling him that if he came home she would stay by him and take care of him and never wander off again? Why, instead of that, is she traipsing into the hospital with flowers and a candlestick as if the place wasn't cluttered enough as it is? He scolds her for needlessly throwing money away on flowers.

'I thought you'd be pleased,' Bára says, stroking his forehead and telling him he looks really well today.

Samuel can walk, of course, but now he deliberately lies on the bed and does not look in her direction. So Bára takes the vase and goes into the ugly bathroom to fetch some water in a battered bowl. As the water runs from the tap, Bára weeps. Then she puts the flowers in the vase, wipes her eyes and actually manages to force her mouth into something resembling a smile – since she is here to comfort, not to grieve. She returns to her husband and asks him if she should light the candle.

Samuel says nothing. His silence does not mean mere silence or anxiety, instead it is the attempt of a powerless person to prove his superiority and his power. That power is now expressed solely in the ability to hurt – himself and her. So Bára lights the candle and gives him the news from the office. She also tells him she has bought Aleš some new shoes and helped him with his history homework and civic education. These future citizens are told about the unity of body and soul. Aleš had asked her what the soul was.

Samuel stares at the ceiling. Maybe he isn't listening, although it is quite likely he is but wants to demonstrate his lack of interest.

'What is the soul?' Bára asks him.

And without looking in her direction, he says, 'It's what you lack.' Eventually he looks towards her in order to see her reaction, so Bára says, 'Thank you for the explanation, I'll pass it on to Aleš.' And she thinks of Daniel: Daniel wouldn't have fobbed her off, he'd have tried to explain the soul, which he says is eternal. Daniel believes in something, something noble, unfathomable and mysterious, whereas her husband simply believes in his own strength and power, which is now gradually waning,

She peels Samuel an orange, separating the segments and arranging them neatly on a saucer. Samuel displays no interest in the orange, because that would entail him showing interest in her, the source of everything bad in his life, including the fact he is lying here on a hospital bed and everyone stares at him as if he were a suicidal maniac. 'Wouldn't you like a bit of a walk?' Bára suggests.

To her astonishment, Samuel raises himself without a word and puts on his slippers. Then he walks out into the corridor at her side, shuffling his feet slightly. And Bára realizes that she is walking alongside an old man and she feels sorry for the man who is the father of her younger son, for the man she once loved more than anyone else, the man she once admired and revered, and whom, at the same time, she feared and whose love she longed most humbly to earn. She feels sorrow that Samuel never understood that love has to be gained through goodness of heart not through orders, that in spite of his horror of solitude he is driving himself into it because his harshness repels even his nearest and dearest.

The hospital corridor is not a long one; men in blue-and-white striped dressing-gowns sit here and there on benches and in the autumn gloom they seem to her like figures from a prison drama.

Samuel is now holding forth to her about himself and his prospects, and the unlikelihood of his ever returning to work. He feels he has lost not just interest in life, but also his powers of imagination; maybe the pills he swallowed have affected his mind. An architect without imagination is like a woodcarver without arms, she surely must appreciate that.

It's odd that he should say woodcarver. After all, Daniel does woodcarving. Sam might equally have said that an architect without imagination is like a pastor without faith. At that moment, she would have been worried that Samuel suspected something. But he suspects nothing, he simply has one of his depressions that can't be checked even by chemicals or psychotherapy; Samuel is too strong a personality for that: stubborn and unbending, even though his strength is already on the wane. So Bára comforts him: everything will sort itself out again and he will be home in a few days; he'll be properly rested and as soon as he gets back to the office he'll see that his head will be teeming with ideas.

'I'm too old,' Samuel says, 'I can't cope with it all any more. If you want to leave you're welcome.'

'What do you mean?'

'Just what I said. Leave for good.'

Bára is weeping again. She'd no intention of ever leaving him, had she? Not unless she died first.

When they say goodbye she kisses Samuel on the mouth and notices that his lips are dry and he himself is cold: he doesn't put his arms around her or hug her. Samuel's body may still be alive, but his soul is already dead.

Bára promises that she will come tomorrow morning and she rushes away because she must drive Aleš to her mother's. On her way out, the senior consultant stops her in the corridor and invites her into his consulting room to ask her a few questions about Samuel's past, and how often he used to have depressions. He wants to know whether any of his forebears had suffered from mental illness. Bára recalls Samuel's mother who refused to associate with her on the grounds that Bára had been invaded by some dark and destructive forces. At the time, Bára used to put those irrational theories down to her age. Samuel himself always said as little as possible about his mother, and when, shortly after their marriage, she died, he never spoke about her again. So Bára tells the psychiatrist that she knows of no mental illness in Samuel's family. None the less, the consultant is of the view that Samuel is not entirely fit and may never be again. His mind is hampered by delusions that are clearly paranoid in character. It will require extraordinary patience from her because Samuel's delusions centre on her; she is their focal point. And the psychiatrist goes on to say that people are reluctant to recognize mental illness as an illness, even though it is a disease like any other: the patient requires love and understanding. While he is speaking to her the consultant gazes fixedly at Bára as if wanting to discover whether Samuel is indeed suffering from delusions or whether his beautiful wife isn't in fact a beauty with the soul of a monster. And Bára bursts into tears for the third time that day.

Finally, the consultant promises her that he will release Samuel next week, even though, in his view, he should be under permanent psychiatric supervision in future.

Afterwards Bára drives Aleš to her mother's. They are scarcely on the road when the boy asks her what she'll be doing in the evening. She fobs him off with a story about tickets for the theatre.

Being not just her son but also his father's, Aleš is naturally curious to know who she's going with, seeing that Dad's in hospital. Bára snaps at him not to be so nosy. Then, suddenly ashamed of her evasiveness, she tells him she's going with a friend. Aleš offers to stay at home with his brother, or even on his own, but Bára gives him a hug and tells him it would spoil her evening because she'd have him on her mind.

Bára has to spend a few moments with her mother and then do some shopping for her as she now finds it hard to use the stairs. She does her own shopping at the same time. She ought to cook something, a celebratory dinner, but she feels too tired all of a sudden. It's late already and she wouldn't have time to prepare things in advance. Besides, she's hardly going to waste the precious time she could be with Daniel on cooking. So she just buys the necessary ingredients for a cold supper. She drops off her mother's shopping and takes leave of her and of Aleš, who is scarcely aware of her any more, since he is gawping at a television programme which is demonstrating a new car. Oh God, she really is a terrible mother to leave him at the mercy of these pictures of dead objects.

Daniel is waiting for her in front of the telephone booth where they met the time when she called him out at night. He has brought her roses: white roses with a red border. 'You're crazy,' she tells him and gets him to sit in the back seat. Luckily it's autumn and already dark, so no one will notice there's someone in the car. She drives him in the luxury jalopy right up to her house and asks him to stay in the car while she opens the entrance to the garage. She then drives him right into the garage where he is again told not to get out until she has closed all the doors: they can gain entry into the house direct from the garage. Only when they are inside at last does she kiss him. His lips are hot and moist.

Daniel puts his arms around her and hugs her to him. His body is alive and so is his soul: she must ask him what the soul is.

'Welcome,' Bára says when they enter the lounge, where one of the lemon trees is in blossom and filling the place with an overpowering scent. Oddly enough she feels it somewhat inappropriate that Daniel should spend the night with her; it is her and Samuel's home, after all.

It's sad, everything is so sad. All her life she has longed for love and whenever she thinks she has found it, she turns out to be mistaken. Is she mistaken now?

There are four enormous black armchairs in the lounge. She sits him in one of these and switches on just the small light above the drinks cabinet. She brings a bottle of wine and glasses and, for the second time today, goes to fill a vase with water. The bathroom is tiled with Italian tiles that fit together to form flower shapes. Samuel's dressing-gown is hanging from a hook. In the corner, Samuel's slippers await his return. Especially warm slippers, because Samuel usually suffers from the cold. People with cold hearts tend to have cold feet too. Samuel's toothbrush is missing from its glass.

And Samuel is missing from the flat. For a split second she is gripped with anxiety that he will turn up out of the blue, see the roses, see Daniel and hurl himself at her and kill her – kill them both.

The water is already pouring over the edge of the vase and Bára thinks about how she used to love Samuel. All of a sudden, she conjures up past embraces, secret rendezvous, making love in borrowed flats, declarations of love and mutual reassurance. Will you ever leave me? Never. We'll never leave each other! He hasn't left her. Samuel has never gone back on his word.

Before going to join Daniel, Bára glimpses herself in the mirror. She looks tired. She can't ignore the wrinkles on her face. She is weary: she's old and worn out. A vampire has been sitting on her back for years: not a real vampire, they kill you, just a little vampire bat that has slowly sucked her blood and drained her strength. Bára unties the ribbon holding back her hair and lets it fall about her face, concealing it slightly. It's something she knows men like.

She arranges the roses and returns to Daniel. 'You're always bringing me flowers,' she says, 'I bet you could never be nasty to me.'

'Nobody could be nasty to you, could they?'

They drink to each other. Then Daniel asks how her husband is. Bára answers that he is better and says he'll be coming home next week.

Daniel says it's good news.

'You were afraid he'd die and you'd be lumbered with me?'

The question leaves Daniel flabbergasted, but before he has time to utter any rash assurances, Bára sidetracks her own question by saying she too is glad that Sam is better. It's just that it's impossible to envisage what their life will be like from now on. Samuel says he intends to stay at home, which means he'll want her to spend all her free time with him and she won't even have the tiny bit of freedom she managed to wrest for herself lately.

'The amount of freedom one has depends on how much one wants it.'

'I know but I'm not self-assertive enough,' Bára admits. 'I completely lack the will when it comes to my own needs.' Then she mentions what the consultant told her today. Maybe he really does think that Bára has driven her husband to despair.

She observes Daniel and notices that he has become a trifle uneasy. His clerical conscience has no doubt taken fright at that prospect and his own involvement. 'Do you also believe I drove him to it?' She doesn't give him time to answer but shouts at him, 'You're like all the rest, you think it's the woman's place to put up with it all. And your commandments even give you a rod for her back.'

'But I broke them with you, just as you did with me.'

'Why do you think such vile things about me, then?'

'I don't!'

'Fifteen years I was faithful to him and scarcely glanced at any other men, but he used to bully me long before I knew you existed, before I knew that someone like you could actually exist.'

'I believe that you loved him.'

'First he courted me, then he started to educate me. After that he started to regard me as his servant, then as his enemy and now as some kind of monster that deceives him every moment of the day and night. He's got hold of a revolver – as protection against criminals, he says. But I'm the greatest criminal of all, aren't I! How am I supposed to put up with this to the end of my days?'

'I don't accuse you of anything.'

'But you do think I've hurt him.'

'People hurt each other when they live together without love.'

'I looked after him the whole of that time. You know yourself. I almost never had a moment left for you.'

'I know you to be someone who wouldn't want to hurt anyone else.'

'If you thought I would, I wouldn't be sitting here with you.' She stretches out her hand to him and he kisses it. Then Bára gets up to go and fix them something to eat, but first she takes a video-cassette out of a cupboard, puts it in the video-player and suggests that in the meantime he should watch a film in which she played one of her bit parts. She abandons him to coloured shadows of herself.

No sooner does she get to the kitchen than the phone rings. It is Vondra, her office colleague, asking her to have a look with him at a project from the National Savings Bank for the reconstruction of a building. It's a splendid contract worth several million. She tells him she'll take a look at it tomorrow.

And how's Samuel making out? What is she doing with herself? Isn't she feeling lonely all on her own with the nights closing in?

As if she were necessarily on her own just because her husband has swallowed some pills. Or because that young Casanova hasn't yet invited her for a glass of wine. She peeps into the lounge, where Daniel is dutifully watching the screen, but even though he has his back to her, Bára senses that he is not taking in anything that is happening on the screen. Daniel is still unsettled by her presence, he is still burdened by the awareness of committing something that conflicts with his faith and the commands he accepted long ago. Daniel is a big, superannuated child. He had definitely not had many women – probably only the two he had lawfully married – and had not been unfaithful to either of them.

Nevertheless he comes to her and is here now, which means that he loves her more than his principles and his vocation, more than peace of mind and a clear conscience. He loves her more than his wife, but he would still never leave his wife. He wouldn't even do it on her account. He is more likely to leave Bára. He'll leave her as soon as his infatuation passes and she will remain alone once more with a half-crazed Samuel who hates her and sucks her strength.

The phone rings once more. This time it is Samuel himself asking her if she is saving all the bills, as they will be needed for claiming tax relief. Bára reassures him that she is, even though she knows full well that at this moment Samuel has not the slightest interest in the bills. He merely wants to find out whether she's home. She asks Sam how he is and he snaps back, 'What makes you so interested all of a sudden?'

'I'll come and see you again in the morning,' Bára promises. 'Now go and get some rest. Don't think about the bills any more, think of something pleasant.'

'Like what, for instance?' and this time there is a note of genuine, unfeigned despair in Samuel's voice. And she realizes that this man, her husband, truly doesn't know of anything pleasant to think about, and she has no advice to give him, nor has she the strength, at this moment, to reassure him of her love. She brings the call to an end, then quickly slices some bread and prepares a cold supper. There is the sound of the piano from the lounge; the video must have finished. Those phone calls have taken up too much of Bára's time. For a moment she remains in the doorway listening to Daniel's playing.

Then she enters the lounge and starts to set out the plates and cutlery. 'What was that you were playing?' she asks.

'Nothing much, just some tunes that come to me when I'm thinking about you.'

'You think about me when you're at home?'

'Almost all the time.'

'In what way do you think about me?'

'With love and anxiety.'

Bára doesn't ask him the source of his anxiety, but as he is sitting opposite her at the table she enquires: 'Do you really love me enough to compose tunes for me?'

'They're only improvisations.'

'And do you love your wife?'

Daniel doesn't know how to reply, and that's all right, it's better than overwhelming her with a lot of big words that would not be true.

'Don't worry,' she says, 'I do know you have a wife and children and a congregation. I don't want to take you away from your family, I just want you to be with me for as long as you feel you love me.'

They eat.

'I'm sorry I shouted at you earlier on,' she says. 'I couldn't take any more at that moment. Maybe I really have hurt Sam. He must sense how I've gone cold inside, that my smiles are forced, that I speak to him out of duty and that I caress him out of sympathy not desire. He must sense it, but he'll never realize that he was the one who destroyed everything that was alive in me.' And there is nothing forced about the smile she gives him; it comes from her eyes and her entire being.

'So long as I lived according to his way of thinking,' she adds, 'he was satisfied. But one doesn't live to fulfil someone else's notions. You only have one life and that's your own, and you have to live according to your own way of thinking, at least partly.'

'So long as you can manage to.'

'You say that as one who can?'

'I can't manage to at all.'

'Are you trying to say that I've wrecked your notions?'

'What I feel for you is more powerful than my ideas about how one should live.'

'You forgot to say: so far.'

Daniel says nothing.

When they finish their meal, Bára gets up and brings a box full of

281

photographs. She puts it on the table and starts to pull out pictures. This is her at the age of seven, and in this one she is sixteen. Her father. He's quite a snappy dresser – the photo is from the war years. 'That's Mum during the war too, a six-pointed star on her coat; it was yellow. Seemingly Jews were always marked out with the colour yellow; in the Middle Ages they made them wear yellow caps. Why yellow, when it's such a warm, sunny colour? Mum was always sunny, and still is.' The very young, beautiful woman is Bára's sister; this is the last photo of her, taken just a few weeks before she had the accident.

She takes out some old yellowing photographs showing her mother's parents before they were taken to Auschwitz. They are all here: her mother's two brothers and her sister some time at the beginning of the war.

'You never told me about them,' Daniel says.

'I never knew them. They were all killed before I was born. Only Mum survived and she doesn't like talking about them, because it's so terrible. But she still has their photographs on the wall at home. Grandad was a court clerk, Grandma had a tiny little grocery shop, but she gave too much credit and went bankrupt. I find it strange to talk about them as Grandad and Grandma, or about my uncles and aunt, as I never saw them alive. One of my uncles studied to be a doctor and married some girl from an awfully rich banking family. But the other one and his sister were still children and they were gassed straight away.'

'It was appalling.'

'For a long time Mum told me nothing about it and I had no inkling that anything of the kind had happened. When I was small I was more afraid of an atom bomb falling on us. Whenever I asked Mum about Grandma or her brothers, she would just say they'd died. Only later did she tell me about them. For me it was like hearing a horror story dreamt up by some totally demented Edgar Allan Poe – I hadn't heard of Hitchcock then. Only when the truth finally came home to me did I start to cry. I also started to feel really afraid that something similar could happen again.'

'It was appalling,' Daniel repeats. 'I was never able to come to terms with the thought that God could permit such a thing.'

Bára is suddenly filled with accumulated anger. Her husband told her that a soul is something she doesn't have and poured contempt on her, and now here is Daniel trying to persuade her that everything she has been through, even what preceded it, all happened because of some higher will.

'What God? What are you talking about?'

Daniel seems to grow uneasy. 'God. There's only one God.'

'God, God,' Bára says, raising her voice, 'do you really think some-one all-powerful and benevolent still rules over this world and looks on while people massacre each other and the brunt is borne by poor people who can't defend themselves? If there was any God he'd have to be a real bloody sadist!'

Daniel remains silent and she goes on to ask him if he really can't grasp that they were simply a triviality that just happened to appear in the universe for a split second.

'I wasn't intending to offend you,' Daniel says. 'I really wasn't.'

'I know you weren't. You just think that it's better to have a love that is certain when there is so little of it in the world.'

'Nothing is certain, either here or there,' he says.

'But there can be love here. Here it is in our power. Whereas there, there will most likely be nothing at all.' She gazes at him and stretches out her arms to him and he hugs her to him.

She leads him into the bedroom, sits him down in one of the small armchairs there, and orders him to wait a moment. In the chest of drawers she finds a night-dress with the inscription 'Love Me' in English (love gets written about on walls and on night-shirts) and goes to take a shower. When she returns she is a trifle nervous: although she has made love to Daniel so many times already, it has never been here in the room where for years she used to make love to her husband. So she quickly lights a cigarette and sits down on the edge of the divan opposite Daniel. Daniel gets up with the intention of going to the bathroom too, but she stops him. 'Don't go yet, please. Wait with me until I finish my cigarette.'

Daniel looks at her. She seems to sense devotion in his gaze. When was the last time someone looked at her like that?

A large oil painting of her husband hangs on the bedroom wall alongside photos of his buildings. Samuel is omnipresent here but Bára isn't thinking about that now. 'Do you really love me?'

'Yes.'

'Enough for you never to leave me?'

'Yes.'

'You'll leave me anyway. Everything comes to an end one day, doesn't it!' She finishes her cigarette and when Daniel goes off to the bathroom she dims the light enough for the shadow to conceal all her wrinkles.

'I'm glad we're going to spend a whole night together,' she says when they are lying down together. 'Spending the night together is perhaps more than making love.'

7

Next morning, Daniel had to go to Plzeň to visit Petr.

He found an empty compartment on the train and sat down, full of Bára's kisses and caresses and the scent of her body.

They had slept for only a short while when he was awoken by her crying. He had asked her what was wrong.

She had had a terrible dream and now she was afraid. Afraid that her husband would die. Afraid that he, Daniel, would die and that she would die too. Life was senseless. It was badly devised. You were either unhappy and suffered or you were happy and afraid that everything would come to an end.

He had taken her in his arms and she had begged him: Stay with me. Hold me tight. Don't forsake me! Then she had fallen asleep. He had felt an oppressive tiredness. The bridge that led across the dark pit ended on the brink of another dark pit. What was the point of seeking bridges that led nowhere anyway? Was life really just the outcome of a lottery run by nature? Just a cluster of incredibly complex proteins? Would everything come to an end? Our soul, this earth, the entire universe? And he, for most of his life, had merely cherished false hopes, and consoled himself and others with the news of the great, miraculous event of resurrection, an occurrence that overturned all the natural laws that had applied up till then?

> *Death is swallowed up in victory.*
> *O death, where is thy victory?*
> *O death, where is thy sting?*

A lamp had been shining weakly in the corner of the bedroom so he had been able to make out that the room he was lying in was not his home and the woman lying at his side was not his wife. He had been gripped by a strange feeling of uncertainty or even angst. As if someone had thrust him into an alien world, a tree in a foreign garden, a landlubber in a wobbly coracle or a sailor in the desert. He had got up and tiptoed out of the room, finding the toilet in the dark. Then he had drifted around the strange house for a while. The emptiness of the universe had stared out at him from the abstract paintings that covered the walls. One of the house's inhabitants had placed a model of some lofty and extremely concrete hangar in a glass case. A desk was strewn with rough drafts of plans, as well as several journals. He had picked up the topmost one. *Discovering Modernist Art in Catalonia.*

He had leafed through it nervously, registering in passing the bizarre shapes of buildings in coloured photographs: Casa Vicens, Casa Battló, Palau Güell, Casa Lleó Morera . . . He had put the journal down again and closed his eyes for a moment.

It was an alien world. Six billion people. Six billion separate worlds. What were the chances that the one he had entered into a relationship with, maybe by accident, maybe by divine guidance, would turn out to be friendly? What if the woman on whose account he was staking everything he had lived by so far had really driven her husband to that desperate action? How could he have agreed to make love to her in a suicide's bed? How could he believe in the totality of her love, knowing that she was deceiving another man?

Because he is a foolish clergyman, who has more experience of Scripture than of women and childishly believes that his vocation is to believe!

From somewhere a carillon could be heard, no doubt sounding the hour. It was six in the morning.

When had he returned, Bára had been sitting on the bed. 'Something up?'

'No, nothing.' What did it mean that this woman had first appeared at the very moment his mother was leaving the world?

'Don't you like being with me any more?'

'What makes you ask?'

'You're looking at me so strangely.'

'It's the unfamiliarity, that's all. I'm not accustomed to seeing you the moment I wake up.'

'Do you find me frightful in the morning?'

'I never find you frightful.'

'I hope not.' She had let him embrace her but then had pushed him away. 'You've got your prisoner to go and see and I must go to the hospital.'

'First thing this morning?'

'I must go to the hospital,' she had repeated, 'and sort out lots of other things. You forget I also have a job, and I'm a mother and a wife.'

He couldn't understand her. She cared for her husband with the selfsame devotion with which she had made love to him a few hours ago. It didn't perturb her to make love to him while her husband was lying in a mental hospital. Was she callous or just desperate? Perhaps her husband had hurt her so much that she felt free to heed the promptings of her heart. Or perhaps this was natural behaviour, the way that most men and women behave, and it was only that he had never suspected it till now, because he had lived in the artificial, long-abandoned world of biblical commandments?

'Do you love your husband?' he had asked, when they were sitting at breakfast.

'Don't parrot my questions!'

'Sorry.'

'I'll tell you the dream I had last night.' She had briskly cut and buttered some bread. 'Do you like honey?'

'I'll have what you have. Are you going to tell me that dream?'

'Dream? Oh, yes, the one that gave me a fright. Wait a mo, I must try and remember the beginning. Oh, yes. I was walking along a road; it was in the country, where we have our country seat, and all of a sudden I saw an overturned motorcycle at the side of the road and alongside it a headless human body – the head was lying on the ground a little way off. But living eyes were staring at me from that head and when they caught sight of me, the head started to speak, begging me to save it. And I dashed back like a wild thing to the village post office and shouted at them to call for an ambulance, that there was a man lying there in need of help. In the dream I believed that the head could be joined back on to the body, but the women sitting there gossiping weren't perturbed in the least, they just pushed a telephone in my direction and told me to call whoever I liked. When I managed to get through to the hospital and tell them I'd found a head without a body and a body without a head and they had to come and help quickly, the doctor said to me – and I remember it word for

286

word – "I fear, madam, that it will be too late, we don't resuscitate the dead." '

'A strange dream.'

'Why strange? All I've got left of Sam is his head which has achieved things I have great regard for. And I don't want to accept that a head without a body is dead and can't be saved. That's the way it is with my love for him, seeing that you asked.'

She had accompanied him all the way to the station and on to the platform. 'So we won't see each other again today?' she had asked, as if she had only just realized that he was leaving. They had kissed, but she had stayed waiting on the platform until the train had pulled away.

He opened the window, letting in a gust of cold air full of smoke, soot and poisonous fumes, and leaned out to cool his forehead.

Then he sat back in the corner and closed his eyes. I ought to focus my thoughts on the prison visit: what am I going to tell that lad? Am I to cheer him up or reprimand him for letting me down and tell him he can no longer count on my help? His thoughts didn't obey him. He was unable to tear himself away from the previous night, from his own promises, from the caresses that his body could still feel.

How long ago was it since he first set eyes on that lad among the inmates? Petr had aroused his interest because of the rapt attention with which he followed his message about a forgiving Lord who calls to Himself all those who are pure in heart.

That time, two years ago, he still had some enthusiasm and strength and could impart it to others. Or perhaps he thought he had some, and thought he could impart it. When he baptized Petr, he believed he had managed to wrest one victim from the clutches of Satan. And he had said as much to the lad, even though for Daniel, Satan was just a pictorial expression of the fall into the void, into the dark pit, where nothingness reigns. When he formally pronounced the words: Petr Koubek, I baptize you in the name of the Father, the Son and the Holy Spirit, he noticed the lad starting to shake with emotion and saw a tear roll down his cheek.

But apparently he had been wrong about him and about himself.

Perhaps he had only imagined his strength. Perhaps he had only imagined his faith – he had simply needed it to give his actions a goal and lend meaning to his life, to cover up the emptiness that terrified him.

Faith could offer an escape from reality, from the cold indifference of the universe, from the cruelty of the world and from life's sufferings, in the same way that drugs or love could.

'He wants to help people,' his daughter had said about Petr. Help people find an escape from reality. From the cold indifference of the universe. Etcetera.

If I accept that, in what way do I differ from that lad, whom I should console and try to wrest once more from Satan's grasp? What kind of moral relativism will I end up in?

Less than two hours later he was sitting opposite Petr in the visiting room, where cheap curtains sought to conceal the bars. Daniel passed him a parcel of food and a few books that Eva had chosen for him. But he did not let on who had wrapped the parcel or chosen the books.

Petr was pallid but didn't seem to be low in spirits. Everything he had done, he now asserted, he had done in a good cause. Nothing in the world could be achieved without money, not even spreading the faith in the saving power of the Holy Spirit. He had already come to an agreement with some of his new friends – he'd better not mention their names here – that they would start to publish a magazine and he had promised to get them a few thousand at least to get it off the ground, for paper and printing. Once they had started selling the magazine, everything would have been different. He had tried to explain that to the people who interrogated him, but there were so many ex-Communists among them and they hated any mention of God's work. In fact they enjoyed obstructing it.

'If you think,' Daniel interrupted him, 'that you were doing God's work, then you're very much mistaken.'

Petr was ready for that reproach. 'So what about those who were doing God's work and were tortured or burnt at the stake as heretics?'

'You're not being prosecuted because of your beliefs but because you sold drugs.'

'That was only a beginning, Reverend. It was necessary if I was to show people they had to believe. Mankind is on the wrong path and Satan is leading it to destruction.'

Daniel said nothing. Petr's words echoed around the room: as empty, wretched and hollow as this place with its curtain-covered bars.

It was strange how for years he had striven to spread belief in a Saviour who rose from the dead and could resurrect others, and had never before doubted that the belief was good and that therefore he was doing good, and rejoiced over every single person he managed to persuade to listen and reflect. But what if he had been wrong throughout his life and the belief was neither positive nor negative? What if it was conducive to good and evil alike, in the same way that, as so often in the past, what was said in its name could be life-giving or deadly, hollow or meaningful, helpful or despicable. Was it possible to murder in its name and help the sick?

'But Reverend, you know me, don't you? You know I've taken the path to a new life, and what I did I did to guide to that path everyone who is looking for it.'

He felt like shouting at him to hold his tongue, and stop yelling about his great plans, that they were simply a means of trying to cover up his contemptible behaviour. But he wasn't here to accuse Petr. He had lost the need to reproach him for letting him down, and could not find in himself sufficient conviction to trust him again, or convince him of anything.

When they were saying goodbye, Petr asked him to take his best wishes to Eva, but he pretended not to hear the request. Anyway, there was nothing to stop him writing her letters should he wish.

He left the prison. Large snowflakes were flying through the air. It seemed to him that they were a dirty grey colour even before they reached the ground. Maybe they only looked that way to him. It occurred to him that his decision, after the revolution, to visit the prisons and try to save prisoners' souls, was maybe just a sign of overweening pride.

8

Letters

Dearest Dan,

I am so filled with you, and so desperate to talk to you (and when we're together there's never time for anything – why must one eat and sleep?)

that I will pour my heart out to you through the computer at least. But fear not, there'll be no blood on the paper, just ink (my printer runs on ink).

It's odd how in spite of having death so near to me I am unable to perceive it as something real. I perceive it with my intellect, but not with my entire being. As if I was most aware of death at moments that seem unconnected with it. Such as when love or enthusiasm die, or if I say to myself: that's nothing new. Maybe it's because I was in a kind of shock and didn't have time to take in what had happened as something real. Now that I'm gradually getting over it, I feel an intense sorrow. I can't help thinking that life is so fragile, and the boundary between when someone is alive and when they turn into a corpse destined for nothing but decay is such a fine line and so hard to be aware of, that we can cross it at any moment, without warning and without a farewell.

We will all die. We are no more than flowers that wilt, for instance, or animals that die.

Perhaps I'm sad because people are being nice to me, while the man that I devoted most of my care, my time, my energy and my life to wants to hurt me, wants to bring me to my knees even if he has to die in the attempt. Now I've realized how cunningly he dreamed up his revenge (for what, dear God, for what?). Either he'd survive – which he definitely hoped he would – and I'd have to live with the permanent threat that he would do it again, or he wouldn't survive and he would burden me for ever with guilt by making a murderess of me. It was his intention to bring me to my knees, not to kill himself. If he had really wanted to kill himself, he has a revolver at home. All he had to do was take it out, place it to his head and press the trigger. Except that that would ... I won't talk about it any more.

Darling, I'm so miserable that when I wake up in the morning I wonder whether I ought to get up at all, whether there is any sense in living. But then I remember the children, my mother and you, and think to myself that you might be sorry if I wasn't around, so I get up and keep going.

I thought about you today, how I woke up yesterday to find you there. I ask myself whether I really deserve you and persuade myself that I do, but the very next moment I am unable to figure out why you love me. I think about the worth of a person and what is important in life. I think about the fact that no one has ever been so kind to me as you. I'll never get used to it, I'll never take it for granted. It will always remain a miracle and an honour, a favour, a whim of fate, maybe an accident, but in that case the accident is God or his mercy (see how you've already trapped me in your web?), in other words, something I didn't dare believe in, but must have been heading towards, after all. He made me a gift of you even though it went against his own Commandments, and his gift will last as long as I deserve it. I don't mean as a reward for anything specific, I mean a reward that won't ever be assessed, let alone enumerated or named. Maybe it will be for as long as I remain pure, hopeful, undemanding, unselfish, and believing that only pure love gives life meaning. Our love cannot be impure, even though, in the eyes of the holy joes and all the rest who aren't capable of it, all love-making is impure. You're incomparable and I thank the Lord God that he led me to you. If ever again I had the right to choose the man I'd like to live with, you would be the one.

Love, Bára

———

Dear Bára,

Last night, the moon was shining a day after full moon, and it was strangely veiled as if behind a luminous, translucent curtain. (The Manicheans apparently believed that the sun and moon go dark because they use a special veil in order not to see the cosmic battle.) Yesterday Magda said to me: It's amazing how fast the moon moves. It's moved a whole chunk in just a little while. I said: But it has to circle the earth in a single day. And her comment was: It moves terribly slowly then. I said: It's because it's a long way away. Things that are a long way away appear to move slowly even when they are flying at the speed of light.

You're a long way away. To be in the same town and yet so far from each other. When you're close, when we are together, time flies at the speed of light, because the distance is in fact still there and the imminence of parting weighs on the short moment of togetherness. When I can't see you, time drags by like a night on the rack. I wanted to tell you not to become downhearted. I can understand that you have death on your mind, but death is part of life. 'Though I walk through the valley of death I will fear no evil,' for He is with me. I share your suffering and think of you constantly.

You write that sometimes you wake up in the morning and wonder whether there is any sense in living and that it helps you to think of those who would be sad at losing you. It is undoubtedly important to know that there are people who love you so much that it would be extremely hard for them to live without you, but all the same, you ought to live because you yourself need to live, because you rejoice in the gift of life. And a woman like you certainly has no need to justify her existence in terms of how many people would miss her.

I'm not sure whether our love can be completely pure, but I do know that I love you.

Love, D.

P.S. You write that I am incomparable. I'm not. But you are! You're amazing. I've never known and couldn't even imagine a woman like you. It's as if you were a distillation of all creatures, as if you were a composition by Bach and Beethoven together.

Dearest love,

I'm sad again today. Why? Because I don't lead a virtuous life? Because you don't think I have a pure heart? Because there is always some new source of worry? After all, I could just as easily shout from the rooftops that I am happy because I've found you.

Or can I be happily sad?

I was with Sam today, as I am every day. At least they have managed to dispel some of his low spirits and he is in his usual form again, so that he is able – and eager – to domineer me. And in two days' time he'll be back home already, and that means he can domineer over me day and night. I drove home from the hospital in the dark with a whole line of cars coming in the opposite direction. It was Sunday evening and I said to myself the main thing is to get there and not think about what is going to happen.

I heard again for the umpteenth time that I am the cause of everything bad in his life. What he did was on account of me; apparently he was toying with the idea for at least a year. Twelve months ago I hadn't even met you, twelve months ago I was running around after him and trying to get at least a smile out of him, seeing that he no longer wanted the slightest physical contact with me. By then I simply served as a lightning conductor for him, always to hand, a dustbin to take all the refuse, a sewer for all the slops.

That's what it had been like for all the previous years, as a WOMAN, that was all I was good for and nothing else.

The trouble was that I started to find it too little, I emancipated myself, and that hadn't been agreed on. I liberated myself and there was nothing about it in the marriage contract. I'm a different person from the one he first knew, and that's not on, really. So either I have to be the way he wants me to be or it is necessary for one of us to disappear from the other's life. He wanted to leave for good but I stopped him. So today he offered me a divorce. Or was it separation? Since I already know something about the scenes from my own married life, and therefore know that I am required to serve as the one on whom all the depression, the anxiety and fear are poured out, I don't take it seriously. Were I to take it seriously, he really would try to take his own life. At the same time I'm happy to be of service if it lets him get it off his chest, but sometimes I give into the feeling that I'm human too. That I too have anxieties, I too would like to be weak and not have to play the strong man. I know that's how I can be when I'm with you. But you're a long way away. No, I'm not complaining. I even believe that your loving ubiquity will last precisely because I'm actually of no use to you, because I am not at home with you – by which I mean we don't have a home together. At home I was always there to be used, always ready and waiting, arranging everything and doing the necessary. I was as useful as the sewer that takes in everything.

There used to be a saying that a woman's skirts hide all sins. Except that instead of a skirt I am strapped into a bottomless dustbin. But the rubbish and the muck doesn't come out, it sticks to my body. Can't you smell it when I'm in your arms? Are you willing to hug me in spite of it?

I don't even know how many of the tablets he took. In fact, he could have put those bottles on the table empty. And the farewell note could have been part of the game, part of the blackmail he thought up in order to drag me to him and bind me hand and foot, because that's what he was after, not to give me my freedom.

I'm gradually coming to the realization that it was all dreamed up to ensnare me. Now I'll be systematically blackmailable, which means he'll blackmail me. I know I don't accept it, but I also know that I mustn't upset him, I mustn't say what I think or feel, seeing that I'm almost a murderer, even though I spent fifteen years believing that my life's number one task was to care for him at home and ensure a sense of security, sharing and happiness. I don't understand why I let myself be manipulated, blackmailed and driven to tears. After all, I know I can take care of myself, that I don't have to ask anyone for anything. Inside me there are some toxins from my past that I can't remove. I used to be bewitched, spellbound. I wanted to serve body and soul, soul and body. I knew I was demeaning myself, trampling on my own dignity, so why has it lasted? I know that Sam is dependent on my love and care, and for my part I'm dependent on his whip.

So there I was driving along in the car and suddenly I felt like stepping on the accelerator and driving straight into a wall or a street lamp and putting an end to it all, but then I remembered you. You've told me so many times that you love me and have provided practical proof of it. That means that I am possibly a lovable person. And so I drove on with the thought that I must go on living. I would simply like to know: Why is it men are so weak? You aren't. Maybe it's because you have your faith, or quite simply you were born that way. So I can rely on you for a little while. Or on myself perhaps. Or on God, who you're persuading me exists and never forsakes one. Or maybe on some vital force that I can feel within me, which does not allow me to perish, but enables me to love. I'd also like to love the one who destroys me, who brings me down, takes my self-esteem and does not value me. I love him as a human being who is suffering, who will die and won't be here any more. But how am I to love him as a man, when he is so weak and dependent that he uses it to blackmail me, when he is so grudging and unloving? But loving someone as a human being is not the same as loving someone as a man. And I'm nothing when I don't have a man to love. When I love a man I know I'm alive. I love you and I'm not sure if I'll be good enough for you: not now when I'm getting over the shock, but in general. Sometimes I feel that I'm worn out and no one could want me any more and I don't deserve anyone. My darling, don't be cross with me for pouring out my sad heart to you and writing to you at sixes and sevens. Before I finish I want to tell you how I've taken you into my life as someone who is mine – who belongs to me more than one could expect after just six months. You are mine because I feel that you love me. Like my mother. For myself alone. I'm cuddling you, missing you, crying over you, loving you, believing you. You're the best man of my life. Really.

Love, Bára

P.S. Monday a.m. Last night I wailed about myself, but I don't like feeble self-pity. I want to tell you that I am happy on account of my love for you.

Now the sun has come out again, a spider has crocheted me a lovely web in the lounge that is a real architectural achievement. (What will the poor thing eat now there are no more flies around?) The day is beautiful. And so is life.

— —

Don't cry, little girl, don't cry,

And don't despair. Your husband is more despairing because he feels that the order he was accustomed to is crumbling (it is something that is happening to all of us but we have to find the strength to endure it) and in addition, he has heard death knocking on the front door. He felt lonely and still does. And he blames that loneliness on you. It would require great wisdom for him not to try using force to extort what he wants. You say yourself that men tend to be weaker and neither weakness nor despair are conducive to wisdom. A person in despair makes fatal mistakes and acts foolishly and self-destructively. Don't ascribe evil intentions when someone is shaking with despair. Despair has no logic or rational cause, in this it is akin to love or hate or any other emotion.

You haven't told me much about your life but one thing I've understood is that you wanted an outstanding man at your side. What you failed to realize is that men who have achieved something tend to be engrossed with themselves; they follow their own goal and don't look around themselves much. They want to be cosseted and praised, they require obedience and service. I expect that was and is your experience, which is why you praise me so much and apologize for not being of service to me. Why ever should you be? One can't serve another's interest and will and live and create at the same time. If two people want to live together they must give up at least some of their selfishness, in fact it is a major opportunity for people to prove their ability to love selflessly. If they're not capable of it, or if one of them isn't, it is generally bad for both. Those that felt themselves the centre of the universe suddenly discover that they have been left all on their own, but they rarely admit their fault. Instead they start to lament or blame their companions. But there's no reason for you to be depressed. You're not alone, it's just that your cross sometimes weighs you down. Nobody's going to forsake you. Even your husband got into such a panic at the thought of losing you that he made up his mind to do what he did.

It's late now. Outside it's a starry night even here in Prague and I'm still

295

affected by your letter. I'm thinking of you and am beginning to understand that the praise that you heap on me so often and which seems to me unmerited I am actually hearing on behalf of someone else. It is someone else that you're constantly apologizing to, someone else you're trying to explain to that he is marvellous, whereas you are no rose of Sharon, no lily of the valley, no turtle dove in the cleft of the rock, but nothing, the dust of the earth to be walked on. You do it in the hope of receiving mercy at last. Dearest, you are the cause of your own suffering, you give rise to a situation in which the one who should be thanking you is angry instead, and the one who does the giving also does the thanking. And I have the feeling that the scar on your wrist is not your only one, nor the most important one for that matter: the main one is inside, in your heart, in your mind, in your soul. Somewhere in that scar, in that wound, is the root of why so often you feel you would like to end your existence, end your life, to escape. Those who are denied the right to an equal share of love (as they see it) are affected in the very ground of their being.

For me you remain a rare treasure, a rose of Sharon, a lily of the valley, a dove in a cleft of the rock, where I would always come to find you and hold you in the palm of my hand, so that you should know you are worthy of love.

Love, D.

——— —

Dear Reverend,

I am sending you these two roses which have miraculously flowered with many thanks for the words you said at my dear Betty's grave. If she could have heard them and still been able to understand them, she would have wept with emotion the way I did. Even though I'm a pagan, Reverend, and the only thing I believe is that we are dust and to dust we will return, I'm grateful to you that you bring some dignity to that departure from this world. There is nothing worse than an assembly line ceremony and I am sure that you would render me the same service.

When I entered the greenhouse this morning for the first time since the day she died, I came and gave the sad news to all the flowers. You might not even be aware that my late wife had a very special relationship with them and she was endowed with a great power. Whenever the roses started to wilt or when they didn't come into flower, she would come and talk to them or sing them a song and the roses would perk up and a few days later would blossom abundantly, and the same applied to other flowers too.

Now we've been left on our own, motherless orphans, but I can look after myself. In the final months I had to take care of Betty too when she was unable to look after herself any longer.

When she was still alive, you mentioned that you were looking for a room for that lad who's staying with you. I've got plenty of room here and he wouldn't even have to pay anything. What need have I for money? I only hope there won't be any problems with him like with that Petr Koubek, although even he parted company with us peacefully. On the other hand, at least I wouldn't be alone in the flat and I don't want to think about a woman in place of my Betty. I'm too old to change my ways now.

The roses are a hybrid tea called Bettina. I grew them on account of their name and they used to love her. Whenever she walked among them they would bow their heads to her. Once more, please accept my thanks.

Respectfully yours,

Břetislav Houdek

———

Dear Dan

The first thing Samuel did when he came back from the mental hospital was to lay into me verbally: I didn't have enough fresh bread at home and water had been splashed in the bathroom (Saša had taken a shower in the morning). I was told that life with me is quite simply unbearable because I constantly force him to concern himself with crap. I'm not sure whether the crap is supposed to be me or whether he meant it figuratively, but quite simply I drag him down with banalities. I had, of course, scrubbed the place from top to bottom and done the shopping as if expecting a visit from the President himself. This was his response to my efforts, and at moments like that something inside me rebels and I cease wanting to live.

I have to admit that after Samuel's scene I took myself off and visited my tarot reader. And she read it all: suffering and illness in the family, but what was most important of all was the location of the king of hearts which led my card reader to utter: You have a big love on the way. Not on the way, I said, it's here already!

I'm happy. I've met you. You are the most beautiful thing that has ever happened to me. In a lasting sense too, I believe. And that's coming from someone who every minute of her life thinks about finite things. The joy you bring me is pure; it is unsullied by doubt, lack of trust or fear – or, you may be surprised to hear, by pangs of conscience.

When I fell in love with my husband, I believed there would never again be anyone who would mean more to me. I valued the fact that something like that had happened to me. In the end it all came to naught. How naive it is to think that something is going to last, that it will be the same at the end as at the beginning. Is it a failure? Is it a defeat? I still believe that love outlives everything and it can last. I know that as long as I live I shall love, as long as I breathe my heart will yearn for deep, complete feeling.

I write about my heart – what sort of an animal is it?

My love, I want to deserve you and I don't know how. I have the feeling I do nothing for you. I just am, and in addition, I complain all the time. I serve a husband who destroys me and whom I fear, and do nothing for you whom I love and who are kind to me. I'm afraid of losing you if I do nothing for you. I just keep asking you all the time: Keep me for a little while longer, for as long as destiny or your God allows, for as long as we're happy that we have each other, for as long as the miracle lasts. We won't be hurting anyone that way, will we? We'll just have a little extra . . .

(A day later. I had to stop writing yesterday. Sam wanted me to discuss his state of health with him.)

I have something to boast to you about. Now that I myself decide what I do, I took the opportunity to design an interior for a rich Czech American who has come back here to do business. Complete décor for seven rooms. I asked him today whether he liked real wood and he said: Sure! I sometimes work with a little firm in a village that is not very far from Prague, and they are capable of making furniture according to my design from any wood that is available. A miracle! So I thought about you, and the fact you like wood too and that your grandfather worked with it. You carve it and I venerate it at least. I love wood, in fact: its smell, its colour, its grain. I just don't understand how anyone can put a piece of plastic, tubing or chipwood in their home. For that American's living room I designed some bird-armchairs, a bit like herons standing on one leg with their long necks. I like storks, herons and flamingos (I'll show you the designs when I see you). I was so het up about doing

298

something decent that I enjoy doing, that I couldn't get to sleep. Now it's two in the morning and I'm thinking about you. You're the most loving person on earth, someone from another – a better – world. (Maybe it's because in your world Jesus reigns instead of male selfishness.) You even managed to write an understanding letter about my husband. It is against your nature, as it is against mine, to harm somebody, to do anything artful or malevolent.

But I still think I deserve you and at this moment it is the peak of my self-confidence, because to deserve it is necessary to be pure, kind and good-hearted.

When we were sitting in Veltrusy Park recently I was calmly and serenely happy in a trusting and devoted way. The heavens opened up for me. There was only now. There was only you. The poisons that contaminate my soul had drifted away. And the poisons that you smelt in the air are nothing compared to the poisons that infest the soul.

What I feel for you is a trust that is so complete that it might be something like faith. It seems to me that someone who believes in God feels something akin to what I feel for you. So through you I have come to understand what is felt by someone who believes intrinsically, i.e. something I have never really experienced. Don't protest! I'm not comparing you to God Almighty, it's just that human beings, including Jesus Christ, were always closer to me than some abstract God. I believe you. You are my security. With you I don't even fear death. You've turned me into a queen, i.e. a relatively self-aware person, who would otherwise have a tendency to fall into the depths of doubt about herself. Forgive me all my weaknesses and inadequacies, all my omissions, and ascribe them not to the selfishness of my soul but to the extreme weight of the burden I have rashly accepted as my fate. I don't want one day to regret not having done everything I could for you. Oh, God! What am I to do? I love you. I love you.

Bára

———

Dear Dan, my unholy brother,

Well, your recent letter about you falling in love knocked me sideways, I must say. As your sister I ought to have understanding for you, but as a married woman I ought, on the contrary, to be cross. Since I am both, I understand you, but I don't share your enthusiasm for your new feelings.

Not at all because it is inappropriate for a man of your calling – to hell with the calling and the good Lord has better things to do than worry about your philandering. But to two-time your wife, who trusts you and stood by you even in the bad times, giving you two children and also caring for Eva, is simply disgusting. I'm surprised at you and I don't know this person you describe.

No doubt like all unfaithful husbands you have plenty of good excuses for your behaviour: the other woman is more interesting, younger, she understands you better and is on the same wavelength, she attracts you and adores you (that's something you men are suckers for). You experience something unique and incomparable with her and moreover she needs you because, like you, she fails to find understanding at home. But surely you're not too infatuated to see that it's a bit hackneyed.

You say you don't expect any advice, so I'll refrain from telling you off like an older sister – it would make no sense anyway. Perhaps you're not entirely to blame. You've inherited Dad's inconstancy and even though you tried to escape it through your vocation, it caught up with you anyway.

Of course I wish for you to enjoy the few years remaining to you on this earthly roundabout as much as you can. It's up to you to decide what is best for your happiness or for you to feel good, and I just hope that your God preserves your mental balance.

With kisses and a tweak of the ear,

Love, Rút

——— —

Dear Bára,

You write that you're afraid of losing me because you do nothing for me. But I expect no service from you. After all, the only way you can bind another person to you is by love. All other bonds can be broken, and most of all they feel like chains. In most cases, people want everything from their partners, but as the proverb wisely puts it: He who wants everything usually has nothing. People have only the right to want things from themselves. Except that people expect things anyway. They expect caresses, kind words, understanding and companionship. They even hope that they won't be forsaken.

People read about the history of the universe over billions of years and most of the time they can't even cope with their own allotted span. I look forward to time with you: it is a time of fullness. I love you and trust you.

Love, Dan

Chapter Seven

1

The candles are burning on the Christmas Tree. Under the pine-tree, as each year, there stands a crib that Daniel started to carve when Eva was still small and he only completed a few years ago. When dinner is over Daniel fetches his guitar, Marek brings his violin, Magda plays the flute and they sing a carol:

> *The Son of God to us is born*
> *To sinners all upon this morn*
> *Welcome, Lord, Welcome!*

By now Magda can't wait for the presents, of which there are more than usual beneath the tree, and she starts to raise the tempo so much that Daniel suggests she put down her flute.

Being country born and bred, Hana adores Christmas customs: so they pour molten lead and float little boats made out of walnut shells with candles inside. In the past the table would be laden down with cookies and fruit, but there would be few presents: there was little money left over to buy them. But even if they could have afforded more, Daniel took pains to ensure that the joy of the gifts did not over-shadow the joy of the message: that by divine dispensation, the curse of sin had been abolished, along with punishment for it. But now he needed to do something to make up for distancing himself from his family, besides which they suddenly had money to spare.

'Daddy, I'd like to unwrap the presents now!'

'Hang on for a little while longer, Magda!'

Hana was in the middle of making cookies when, a few days earlier, he went to ask her what she would like for Christmas, and she replied that she didn't need anything but they could give something to Máša.

What a suggestion!

'But she's abandoned,' his wife explained, 'she has nobody. Last week she called in to see me and wept. She's lost her husband and her children. Do you realize how awful that must be for her?'

'Nothing we can give her is going to cure her loneliness.'

'But she'll feel that we are fond of her and thinking about her.'

'Fine.'

'She goes around in such a threadbare coat.'

'If you think so, then you – we – can buy her a coat. But I want to buy you something too.'

'But I don't need anything. I've got you.'

To conceal his embarrassment, he picked up a tray of filled cookie-moulds and carried it over to the oven. On the way, he skidded on some spilt oil that had been badly wiped up and just managed to catch the edge of the cooker to prevent himself from falling, but all the metal moulds in the shape of stars, pine-cones and hearts tipped on to the floor with a crash.

Everything was falling to pieces, and even the things that still held together, only held together illusorily.

He didn't buy Máša a coat but took her some money. He noticed that she had a bruise under her eye. Her ex-husband had punched her when she came to collect the children for the weekend. At least that is something Daniel would never do. A reassuring thought that all around him there were people harming each other who had fallen even lower than he.

'Money won't help me, Reverend, I have lost the will to live,' she said.

'Whatever are you saying, Máša?'

'Every night I think of jumping off somewhere, from a rock or some bridge, and never waking up again.'

'Stop tormenting yourself over someone who did not deserve your love.'

'And what about the children?'

'You have to get the children back. You've lodged an appeal, haven't you?'

'I won't get them back. I know he won't give in. He has money and knows people, and he wants to destroy me! What have I got?'

'You have truth on your side.'

'No one gives a damn about that, Reverend. Money is the most important thing, not truth.' Máša spoke in a tearful whine, which aroused his aversion rather than his sympathy. As if she were blaming not only her ex-husband but him too.

'You see?' he said. 'You could have a use for the money. You mustn't give up. We will all be on your side and help you.' He left the money in an envelope on the little table in the hall and fled.

> *A time of joy and mirth*
> *has now come to the Earth*
> *for God eternal,*
> *is born of a virgin.*
> *There in Bethlehem town*
> *upon the straw she laid him down . . .*

He lays aside the guitar. Magda can at last distribute the presents.

Daniel looks on in silence. He has been striving the whole evening, since morning, in fact, to revive within himself a festive spirit. But it is beyond him. Instead, he feels a growing sense of uncertainty and shame. He preached about the birth of the Saviour even though he has growing doubts whether the birth occurred in the manner described. And now he is sitting here pretending to be in the same loving relationship with them all as at any other Christmas.

In previous years his mother would still have been here with them at Christmas. The sudden feeling of loss grips his throat. He has lost his mother, as well as the purity of a life unfolding in truth. His mother departed and a woman arrived offering him love or passion or maybe passionate love. He received her and gave up truthfulness and honesty.

Magda revels in her new skates and Marek can hardly believe that they have bought him a real astronomical telescope. (Dad, it must have cost a packet!) Hana went to try on her new skirt. He fobbed Eva off with a CD-player. He should have given her his mother's old flat, of course, but he needed it for himself.

He had met Bára there the previous week. He had thought long and hard about what might give her pleasure. Their lives tended to impinge on each other outside the world of material things so he didn't know what she needed, had never looked in her wardrobe, and he had spent such a short time in her flat and in such a state of mind that he had scarcely taken in the individual items. Then he remembered that she had once daydreamed about Barcelona and its warm, bright winters, and about Gaudí. He went to a travel agency and paid for two excursions to Catalonia, leaving the departure date open for the time being. It crossed his mind that it would be wonderful if he could accompany Bára on such a trip, if it were actually to take place, but then he shrank back from his own idea: he would offer the second place to Bára's older son, of course.

Magda hands her father her own gift: she has knitted him a stripy winter hat. (Do you like it, Dad? It's fantastic – I didn't know you were so handy.) From Hana a shirt and a set of gouges, from Eva a book about Plato and Augustine, and from Marek a photo album.

When they were still in the highlands they used to receive gifts from every member of the congregation. The older members brought them food, the younger ones drew them pictures or made little figures out of dough, or plasticine, or even conkers.

A gift may be an expression of love, respect or sympathy, or a ransom for insufficient love, respect or sympathy.

Hana reappears in her new skirt, he pours everyone a glass of wine – even Magda gets a few drops – and they all drink a toast: To love, as is appropriate on a day recalling the Saviour's birth.

When Bára opened the envelope with the tickets for her forthcoming trip, she looked puzzled, and then she said: 'You're out of your mind! Do you really suppose that Musil will let me go to Spain just like that?'

'Why wouldn't he?'

'On my own?'

'With Saša.'

'He can't stand my son.'

'Maybe he's open to persuasion.'

'And how am I to explain to him that I want to travel with Saša and not with him?'

'He says he's ill, anyway.'

'No, he'd never let me go anywhere that was nice, with Saša and without him.'

Marek opens the window slightly and gazes up at the sky, which, as usual at this time of year, is starless. Eva says: 'What do you think people in prison are doing now?'

*

'And anyway I can't accept it from you,' Bára said. 'What possessed you to send Saša to the seaside when his own father never sent him there? At least if you were going with me.' She thrust the envelope back at him, but he refused to take it. Then they made love and Bára suddenly burst into tears: 'Nobody was ever kind to me the way you are. Why are you always leaving me? Why do you leave me at the mercy of a guy who tortures me?'

Hana sits down next to him. 'I really like it when we're all together like this at home and we're all in a festive mood.' Quite exceptionally, she kisses him in front of the children.

This is his home: a good home. Why is he leaving it?

When he prays that evening, Daniel asks God for strength and help. He wants to step out of the circle in which he now moves. He wants to put an end to the deception and live in the truth. He has prayed for this on several occasions in the past, but today he feels a vague kind of hope that he'll really manage to step out of the circle without harming anyone in the process.

When one prays one becomes a believer. One expects neither reward nor profit, nor even an answer; simply a sign that one has been heard. A sign which, even if it came, one could never be entirely sure of.

It is gone midnight when they go to bed. Hana snuggles up to him as usual. Then she asks him if he still loves her and Daniel says yes. Exhausted by the Christmas celebration, Hana quickly falls asleep, while Daniel stares into the darkness and silently asks her for forgiveness and also for help: stay with me and don't let me fall. Then he can hear Bára's voice begging him: Don't forsake me! and he feels a heart pang. Anxiety and love and despair.

2

Diary excerpts

Marek is happy. He has his cloudless sky at last and he and Alois were gazing at the stars until midnight, until I drove them out of the attic. Marek enlightened me about galaxies. There are infra-red galaxies and

X-ray galaxies. Moreover, galaxies cluster. Our galaxy belongs to a group
of over twenty such clusters and those clusters measure three million light
years. The clusters then form nests, and these can contain several
thousand galaxies, which span as much as fifteen million light years.
Supergalaxies, however, contain millions of galaxies and apparently light
takes half a billion years to get from one to the other. The universe is
composed of supergalaxies, but between them stretches empty space
measuring hundreds of millions of light years.

It's true that I hesitated before I bought Marek the telescope. Not
because it was expensive, but because it was a virtual endorsement of the
doubts and comments that he tries to provoke me with. Then I said to
myself that I would buy it for that very reason. We all live in doubt
about the beginning and the end, and when he realizes this he won't
need to test the firmness of my faith any more.

When I was carrying the telescope out of the shop I remembered Dad
taking me to the planetarium. It was after his return from prison, and
he talked to me about the boundlessness of the universe and how time
defied the imagination. I wasn't particularly impressed by the
planetarium, though; everything there was artificial. But that evening
the sky happened to be clear and I went out and spent a long time,
possibly an hour, gazing up at the stars. First of all I tried to identify the
main constellations at least, but then I gradually became dizzy as I
imagined the distances and the enormous quantity of burning matter.
The idea of infinity excited me but also unsettled me. In fact I started to
flee from it as I did from the gloomy notion of death which equally
defied the imagination. Faith was a good way of escaping it, and still is.
Except that there is no way one can entirely evade a reality that impinges
all the time. After all, God is just as unimaginable as infinity.

For the first time in years I am reading Augustine, whom I used to
revere for his intuition when I was a student and also because he
considered love to be the basis of Christ's teaching. Now I find that, like
Plato, he lacks sufficient knowledge of the world and nature to
substantiate his views. Thus he reached most of his conclusions by
deduction on the basis of assumptions which, without any evidence, he
proclaimed to be beyond doubt. His explanation for God's existence
outside of time and space was that in time and space one could not

discover supreme bliss and perfection. It is possible to displace everything great and beautiful from time and space, but not oneself or one's imagination.

These days we don't even have to worry about such justifications of God. I noticed the following sign on a wall not far from Tyl Square.

Posthumous experiences – The A.D.E.

I felt like adding: God on display 3 p.m.–5 p.m., Wednesdays and Fridays.

Hana no longer goes to the hospital and has started to take charge of all the necessary arrangements for setting up a centre in our manse. There is a great deal to see to. It crossed my mind to commission Bára to design the structural alterations to the house. I like the idea of our undertaking a joint project. But she refused, saying we shouldn't tempt fate.

Hana is happy. She wants to install a potter's wheel and build a ceramics kiln, and also fit out a tailoring workshop. The board of Diakonia promised me they would get someone to undertake the structural plan gratis or at a very low cost. We have also given thought to people in the neighbourhood that we might employ at the centre. I thought of Máša: she could care for handicapped children; the work could give her some satisfaction seeing that her husband has deprived her of her own children – for the time being, at least. For her part, Hana suggested Marika. She sings beautifully and plays the guitar. I wasn't too sure whether Marika would be a suitable person to work with children. She struck me as being too much of a daydreamer. (Alois likes Marika, although 'likes' is probably an inadequate description of their relationship.) However I said we could give her a try. Talking about the Diakonia fills me with an almost unexpected sense of relief. It's a bit like a shipwrecked sailor watching the arrival of a ship that might rescue him.

What's far more important though – to continue with my banal simile – is whether the people on the ship catch sight of the shipwrecked sailor.

I see Bára very seldom now. Her husband doesn't feel fit and assigns her most of his office duties. And he demands that she devote her remaining time to him. She says he often speaks about life losing meaning for him. He also offers her a divorce or his own death, both of which would save her work, he maintains.

Whenever Bára and I meet, she seems to be in a hurry. At the same time she looks at me with love and I have the feeling that her every movement is a plea for me to help her. Help her in what way? To find meaning in our life here on earth. She came full of doubt and misgivings about Jesus's divinity. She came to me to dispel her misgivings. But I failed. Instead of leading her towards the love of Jesus, I started to embrace her. I started to talk to her about my own love, which even lacks the fullness and purity that can be achieved by imperfect human love.

Except it is more likely that Bára came because she was seeking human love, not on account of her doubts about God. That was just a pretext.

You prove your love by your deeds. By being helpful and self-sacrificing, by standing by your loved ones when they need you. Love can also be defined negatively: not harming, not abandoning, not lying and not betraying.

But how can that be applied in the case of two women who both regard you as their own? What then remains but a desperate effort to fulfil at least a few promises and resolutions; you then pay for it with further betrayals, lies and deceptions. It occurred to me that if I took a decision, irrespective of what it was, I would find relief. I could continue with my work without feeling that I've lost the right to proclaim the Bible's message. But then I realized that I couldn't continue anyway, as I lack sufficient faith!

Regarding the trip to Spain, Bára says her husband told her she could go to hell as far as he was concerned, but that Saša didn't deserve anything of the sort and he therefore opposed it. So they won't go anywhere.

I found it odd that she should accept someone else's decision like that without demur.

'And what if he did something to himself while I'm there?' she asked. Then, apropos of nothing, she said: 'OK, I'll start to learn Spanish.'

I'd like in some way to define my state of mind, or more accurately, the state of my feelings.

Formerly I lived more calmly. I was not particularly happy but I definitely wasn't unhappy. I experienced neither moments of ecstasy nor of hopelessness. I did lots of useful and beneficial things and even had time for my hobbies.

Now there are times when I seem incapable of doing anything at all, unable to complete anything. And then all of a sudden I fall into some kind of trance and I sit down at the piano and improvise tunes that seem to me worth noting down, but mostly I don't bother because it seems to me more important to create them than to preserve them. Likewise, the carvings I do are different: more complex and dynamic. These days I usually portray a couple: a woman and child – as if previously I tried to capture a state whereas now it is a relationship, the tension between two human beings, whether mutual longing, alienation or passing each other by.

If I were to try and generalize, I would say that love awakens within my soul an unusual power, but the circumstances of that love crush my soul. Often I feel an unbearable longing for the other woman but the moment she suggests to me that we might stay together a little longer or even go away somewhere for a day and a night, I become frightened that it might threaten my home even more. My heart is staggering, in the words of the prophet. But what is a home? Can it still be a place where we sleep but at the same time yearn for someone who is not allowed to cross its threshold? Then I thought to myself how many spouses lie alongside each other in their homes and think about another. Is it perverted? It isn't natural, that's for sure. Except that man is losing touch with nature and therefore also with natural behaviour; therein lies his exclusiveness. His exclusiveness can be seen in his recognition of God above him, in having eaten from the tree of knowledge of good and evil and being aware of his end here on earth, as well as in the way he destroys nature, exterminates other creatures, deceives his nearest and dearest, and kills his brothers. In addition he prays and is always ready to converse with someone who never replies.

———— ❦ ————

Two days ago Martin and I were returning from a ministers' course where we talked about absolution, among other things. Some were of the

310

view that it is actually a duty specifically rooted in Scripture to rid the believer of his feelings of guilt. (Paul to the Galatians: 'Bear one another's burdens.') Others pointed out that the priesthood has usurped this right for themselves, thereby improperly lording it over others.

'In my opinion,' Martin said to me, 'those are all artificial quarrels. If one wants to lord it over others, there are plenty of other opportunities to do so. But people will always look for somebody who will tell them that even though aspects of their lives have gone wrong, they still have the hope of leading a decent life. If you don't tell them that, then someone else will, but they won't say the most important thing: Go and sin no more!'

I realized that my life was also going wrong and I too needed to hear that I have the hope of leading a decent life. Martin would undoubtedly give me absolution, maybe he'd even understand me, but I haven't yet made up my mind to talk about it. There is one thing that I have to talk to him about, though: I feel I can no longer go on preaching and I want to ask him or maybe Marie to take over my congregation for a while.

We said goodbye in front of the metro station and then the following happened to me: I took the train to Hradčanské and in the subway I came upon a group of obviously drunken skinheads surrounding a dark-skinned lad. I'd say he wasn't a gypsy, more likely an Indian. They weren't beating him, only yelling and jostling him. The people leaving the metro walked past them, giving them a wide berth, and the police as usual were nowhere to be seen. I came right up to them and saw the fear in the eyes of the encircled youngster.

Although I too felt some fear I addressed them: 'Why don't you leave him alone, lads?' I couldn't think of anything cleverer to say at the time.

One of them turned to me. 'What's it to do with you, you old git? Want your face smashed too?' And he shoved me with such force that I staggered sideways.

So now the others turned to me too. They seemed to be hesitating over which of us would make the more suitable victim. That momentary hesitation was enough for the dark-skinned youngster to take to his heels and for me to mingle with the people leaving the metro station. Martin's right; they're all artificial, the things we debate on those courses, and they have precious little to do with modern-day life.

Mention of the police and the subway brings to mind something else that I noticed yesterday. I was walking along our street when suddenly a police car overtook me and stopped at the corner. Four policemen got out. I observed them from a distance. They drew their pistols and looked as if they were releasing the safety catches too. They then lifted a manhole cover and started to descend into the sewer. I looked on in amazement at this film sequence but there was no camera or producer to be seen. I'd have loved to know if they were going underground in pursuit of mafiosi or skinheads, or to shoot at sewer-rats or to visit a ceremony by some particularly extreme underground sect. I reached the open manhole and stood there listening for several moments, wondering whether I would hear pistol shots, a shout or music. But there was deadly silence. It occurred to me that those four men would never emerge again. 'So they and all that belonged to them went down alive into Sheol; and the earth closed over them, and they perished from the midst of the assembly.'

The remaining policeman sat in the car observing me with indifference.

Bára's Saša has his spring allergy and Bára decided she would take him to the seaside whether her husband liked it or not. She asked me if I would mind her taking the trip to Barcelona.

I expressed surprise at the question.

'But I'll be away from you for a week,' she explained. 'You'll have sent me out into the world and left yourself behind here.'

I told her I often went a whole week without seeing her even when she didn't go away anywhere.

That's different. She asked me whether I wouldn't come after all. I replied — as she had recently — that we oughtn't to tempt fate. When I got home the thought occurred to me: Why shouldn't I go over and see her, if only for a day? I can afford it. It was a tempting thought although I knew I would never actually do it.

A dream: I was on my way to a final-year class in my secondary school, bringing with me from home a drawing board, a blanket and a pillow. Then I realized I had taken my school-leaving exams long ago and there was no reason for me to go to school at all, so I decided to go home again. I didn't have a coat or a bag, so I put my purse and my wallet in the *back pocket of my trousers, aware that it was not a wise thing to do. But what else could I do, seeing that my hands were full? I kept checking every few moments in case my belongings had been stolen. They were, of course. And by ill chance it was the wallet, which was worse than losing money. Luckily I caught sight of a boy running away from me; I ran and caught hold of him and started to search him. His pockets were full of wallets, including mine. Once I had retrieved my wallet I walked to the tram stop. The tram didn't arrive, but instead a green bus with strangely high wheels appeared. A ladder was lowered down from the door and I was going to climb up it when I realized I had lost my blanket and pillow. I didn't know what to do, whether to get on the bus or to look for my lost things. I let the bus leave without me but I didn't go anywhere. I just stood there.*

That is my (our) situation: we are each losing our home but lack the courage to go and meet the other. She because she's afraid of her husband, and I because I'm afraid of God and the thought that I would be deceiving those who trust me. And we are both afraid of destroying our children's homes. But where are our homes? Not in the bedclothes or the identity cards, certainly. Either we carry them around within ourselves, or they are lost for good.

3

Daniel travelled to Zlín for a two-day pastoral conference. He had never been a particularly sociable person, which might have been one of the reasons why he had chosen such a solitary profession. Admittedly it involved one speaking to people and even experiencing mystic unity with them at the Lord's Supper, but at the same time one was separated from them by the pulpit, the gown and the exclusiveness of one's vocation. However, until recently he had always looked forward to these meetings with his colleagues: the more isolated he felt in his day-to-day activity, the greater the comfort he derived from being among those who shared the same fate and had to cope with similar problems and ask themselves similar questions.

At that very moment, one of his younger colleagues was at the rostrum dealing with the question whether it was possible to accept that Jesus was born of an immaculate virgin, or whether those few verses about Mary's virginity were merely a reflection of early biblical tradition. What lent credence to the opposite view was not only the fact that two of the gospel writers did not hesitate to prove Jesus's kingly origins by giving Joseph's family tree (each of them different, moreover) but also that the other two did not even mention Mary's virginity, so they either didn't know about it or did not accept it.

Even though the gospel account of Mary's virginity had always raised doubts in Daniel's mind and he had tended to see in it the influence of ancient pagan cults rather than a report of an inexplicable divine act, Daniel was unable to give the speaker his full attention. He had become increasingly absent-minded recently and he found it impossible to concentrate on anything that was at all abstract. On the other hand, his thoughts repeatedly wandered back to the problems of his private life.

During the lunch break, the conference broke up into groups. Daniel went for a walk with Martin.

They spent a few moments talking about what they had just heard. It seemed to Martin that the only thing that remained unshaken or beyond doubt in the New Testament message was the ethical message of the Sermon on the Mount. The virgin birth, along with the expulsion of evil spirits, miracles with bread and the calming of the sea, even the miraculous resurrection of the body, were all simply the products of the mythologizing talents of the early Christians.

Daniel would normally argue with him, refuting his heretical ideas, not because he regarded them as unacceptably wayward, but because they were too much in tune with his own doubts. When he used to assert that it was not possible to take one part of Christ's message and consign the rest to the realm of mythological notions, it was himself he was trying to convince rather than his friend.

On this occasion he remained silent, however. What point was there in talking to his friend about theological issues when he remained silent about what was preying on his mind most of all? His very mode of life called into question even the Sermon on the Mount. He didn't hunger and thirst after righteousness, he didn't commit adultery solely in his heart, and he was guilty of falsehoods.

Perhaps he had overestimated his failings. The modern world takes failings into account; it frees people from the burden of the soul and sin.

What sort of category is it, the modern world? Is it an awareness

314

that everything is permitted so long as it isn't an obvious and demonstrable crime?

'On the other hand, by casting doubt on what our forebears believed,' Martin added, 'we cast doubt on the tradition as a whole. And when people get rid of tradition, it's like someone losing their memory.'

'Except that what constitutes tradition,' he added in the next breath, 'we ourselves determine according to our taste and convictions. Because tradition can include all superstitions, prejudices and customs, such as knocking on wood in order not to speak too soon, or guardian angels. Not to mention the death penalty, faith in astrological predictions or the Christmas carp. Eat raw cabbage on an empty stomach on Wednesdays in Lent and you won't go astray the whole year. Swallows' droppings from a church tower will cure the fever. Eating an odd number of young mice will cure a fever . . .'

They turned into a field and the path continued uphill. The day was unusually mild for January, only the tops of the distant hills were covered in snow.

A horse and cart suddenly appeared on the low ridge which they were approaching. It stopped. The person driving it was not to be seen and the motionless horse looked like a statue at that distance.

'When I was still in the highlands,' Martin recalled, 'there was only one private farmer left in Herálec. He had a horse – it must have been over twenty years old, but it still outlived his master. That man, before he died, asked to be drawn to the cemetery by his horse, not taken in some car belonging to the undertaker. The trouble was it turned out there was no funeral vehicle to be found anywhere that a horse could be hitched up to. So in the end we covered a dray in black muslin, decorated it with flowers and loaded the coffin on to it.'

'What brought that to mind now?'

'Maybe it was because of that horse standing in front of us. Or perhaps because we happened to be talking about tradition. That fellow wanted to preserve a tradition.'

'Well, people like that are a dwindling band.'

They walked on in silence for a while and then Daniel made up his mind to ask the favour he had been planning to ask for a long time: he needed someone to stand in for him for a while at work.

'And what would you be doing? Are you going off somewhere?'

'I've been offered an exhibition of my carvings,' he explained. 'I'd like to rid myself of all duties for a while at least.'

'You could ask Marie, she might be only too happy to do it!' Then the thought struck him: 'Those carvings aren't the main reason, though, are they?'

'No,' Daniel conceded.

'Something personal?'

He hesitated a moment. Martin was his best friend, the only real friend he had, in fact. They had never had any reason to conceal anything that went on in their lives. But now he remained silent about something that had transformed him more than anything else in the past. He felt an almost compelling urge to confide in him.

When Bára first came into his life, the only thing he had been conscious of was deceiving his wife, but as time went by he had become increasingly aware that the deception had spread to everyone he associated with. What is left for someone who conceals the most important thing in his life? Just words, empty words, a smokescreen that he erects around his own deeds. Martin might conceivably understand his feelings, but he could not condone his behaviour, his deception. He would tell him what he knew already: Go and do not sin again! But he knew he did not have the strength to do it. No one would help him out of the trap he was in. Besides he felt ashamed in front of his friend, and the shame was stronger than the need to confide in him. 'What isn't personal?' he said.

'Sorry, I didn't mean to pry.'

'We're also preparing to build a diaconal centre in the manse,' he said as an excuse. 'It's Hana's idea, she's had enough of working at the hospital.'

When they got back, there was a message at reception for Daniel to call home. He became alarmed. Hana usually didn't phone. Anything could have happened: to her, to the children; she could even have found out about Bára. He ought to be prepared with some explanation if that was the case.

Even over the phone he could tell Hana was upset.

'Sorry I'm disturbing you.'

'There's no reason to be sorry.' If she was apologizing, then he wasn't the reason for the call. 'Has something happened?'

'Yes, it's Eva. I thought you ought to hear about it as soon as possible.'

'Has something happened to her?'

'No, nothing that you might think. Dan, I've had a long talk with her and she knows I'm calling you. She herself told me to call you.'

'All right. So what's happened then?'

'She's expecting a baby!'

'She can't be . . . Who with?'

'Petr, of course.'

'No . . .' Then he said, 'I'll come home as soon as I possibly can.'

'You don't really have to, if you still have things to do there. We just wanted you to know. And don't be cross with her. There'd be no point now.'

4

Bára

The plane lands at Barcelona airport shortly after midday. Bára is somewhat ill at ease because it is years since she has travelled on her own, whereas Saša is a pilot's son and acts as if it was the most normal thing in the world for him to move about an unknown airport. Admittedly, his eyes are red and he sneezes from time to time, but he manages to retrieve his own and Bára's luggage and to find the stop for the airport bus that is to take them to Catalan Square. From there, according to the map, it is only a short walk to the hotel booked for them by the travel agency.

The hotel is luxurious. A doorman in purple livery and a red top-hat stands in front of the glass-panelled doors. The front hall is all marble. They smile at Bára from the reception; all they want is her signature and then they issue her with a key. Saša rebuffs the porter who is making for their luggage and he takes his mother up in the lift to the sixth floor.

'Here we are, dear Bára,' he says to her when he has opened the door, 'I know I'm not the one you'd prefer to be here with.'

'Now, now, darling,' Bára says, stopping his mouth, 'I may have taken you away from your father, but I've never rejected you.'

'That's true,' her son admits. 'Shall we unpack?'

'No,' Bára decides. 'We've come to see Gaudí, haven't we, not to hang up our clothes.' And she remembers how at home about a month earlier she first cautiously mentioned the possibility of their all going together to see Gaudí's buildings. Samuel snapped back that he hadn't the slightest desire to travel anywhere; as far as he was concerned, Gaudí's work was more a farewell to the old era than the starting-point of the new one. Then he made a scene about Bára wanting to run away from the jobs she had in hand and enticing her son to idleness, as if he wasn't indolent enough already and good for nothing. She pointed out that she also had the right to a few days' leave and it would do Saša good to get away before his allergy came on.

Samuel generously conceded that he couldn't stop her from going but he wasn't going to pay her son's fare (he always referred to Saša as 'your son').

She felt like saying that he wasn't going to pay her fare either, but simply commented that she earned enough money to afford to treat her son to a seaside holiday, particularly since it was what the doctors had recommended for him. Samuel did not agree, of course, and it sickened her to argue about money. But Samuel was outraged at the very fact that it had crossed her mind and launched into a monologue about a spoilt mother spoiling her son too. He concluded by offering her a divorce or his own death. He wouldn't be in her way any more and she wouldn't have to put up with sickening rows over money.

Bára said no more, but when she went to bed that evening she wept over the hopelessness of their marriage and her entire future.

She can feel the tears coming to her eyes once again, but they are not tears of despair. Instead, she feels like weeping because for the first time in many months, or years even, she feels free from the husband who has become her torment. For the first time in her life she is alone like this for a whole week with her son to whom she so often feared showing affection in front of his stepfather.

They leave the hotel. There is a clear blue sky and a tepid wind is blowing in from the sea. Gone is the suffocating blanket of cloud that hangs over Prague in February. Even Saša is able to breathe without difficulty. A short way from the hotel, as she discovers from the town plan, stands Gaudí's Casa Mila, nicknamed the stone quarry on account of its colour, asymmetry and massiveness.

Bára knows the building from photographs, of course, and knows almost everything that has been written about it, but now, standing in front of it, she is overwhelmed by the unfettered genius while feeling somehow overcome by her own ordinariness and insignificance.

They are fortunate to find that a group of tourists, or rather interested professionals, is just making its way into the building and they manage to tag along behind and see the round courtyard and climb the staircase between the countless pillars. Everything here is unusual, from the lattice work to the windows, not to mention the enormous lamps, and when they climb right up to the roof, they find themselves in a bizarre realm of chimneys, each one of which could be a sculpture by Henry Moore or Miró. Between the chimneys she can see the sky and the towering mountains in the distance. As always when she finds herself somewhere high up, Bára gets an attack of dizziness, but on this occasion it is caused not by the height but by the beauty of the scene. She finds it stunning. She puts her arm around her son's shoulders and kisses him, before thrusting the camera into his hands and requesting him to take a photo of her beneath a chimney resembling a giant in armour.

When they leave the roof Saša praises it as 'really something' and Bára bursts into tears for the second time today. She weeps because she is happy and also because it never occurred to her husband, whom she has loyally served for fifteen years, that he might grant any of her wishes or do something to please her, which would earn him no more than her love and gratitude. It had taken that pastor for whom she was able to do nothing but show love and gratitude. But what is showing him love when she scarcely has any time left for him? What sort of nonsense is it that she spends her time with someone who torments her and doesn't have time for someone who is kind and considerate to her?

They leave Gaudí's building on their own, but Bára's impatient thirst is not yet slaked. She is anxious that what she doesn't manage to see today she never will. After all, she might not live to see tomorrow or some bad news might arrive from home and she'll be obliged to return immediately.

So they take a taxi, and since Saša prefers the countryside to the city, they drive to the Parque Güell. They walk past the fairy-tale porter's lodge and then go up the steps guarded by the terrifying Python, before hurrying through the avenue of palm trees and sitting down on a stone seat covered in crazy ornaments.

Bára asks her son whether he isn't bored and promises him she'll take him to a disco tomorrow and also to a football or tennis match, or a bullfight, if anything of the kind is held at this time of year. Or they can go on an excursion somewhere, maybe to the mountains, that seem so close from here. Saša tells her he is totally happy here and then he remembers his stepfather who is sitting home swallowing tablets instead of sitting here and having a good time. But it's just as well, because if he were here, they wouldn't be having a good time.

We have to call him anyway, Bára realizes, and feels a cold blast of air from her distant home; in a few days' time she will return to her trap and Samuel will never forget that she opposed him and left without him, and actually took her son with her, even though he had expressly forbidden it. She knows that she has rebelled and will have to pay for it, though it is not yet clear to her in what manner.

They drive down to the sea and watch the cargo ships in the distance and the enormous cranes. Green buoys rock back and forth beyond the harbour. Bára makes out two seagulls sitting on one of them. Their positions are so perfectly symmetrical and they are so still that Bára is no longer sure whether they are real or carved. She gazes at them steadily while Saša inhales the sea air which is free of the swirling pollen that suffocates him at home. At least a quarter of an hour passes and the gulls are still motionless. Perfect symmetry, Bára realizes, and in her mind she confides it to Daniel. Like the perfect order that Samuel dreams of, it means the end of life and it's even the death of art since it precludes shifts or movement and rules out surprise. And yet art has always sought symmetry: in drawing, in verse, in music, in building, in ornament. It seeks paradise but falls prey to the urge for death. Wasn't that like religion? It seeks to confine life and love within an order, by means of regulations and proscriptions. It makes it a sin to break them and therefore banishes any freedom and movement from life. Happily, from time to time, some wayward soul is born, some Gaudí, who questions the prevailing order and symmetry, in order to rescue life.

Finally, in obedience to the same law of life, the gulls move and both fly off together and soar above the waves.

As Bára and her son make their way back, their route takes them through a market where exotic birds are being sold. Saša enthuses over the rich colours of the Amazonian parrots, as well as the toucan and the cockatoo's golden coronet. They could buy one of them and take it home. His stepfather could get himself a coronet too, so everyone could see he's the chief. And Aleš would be sure to love a parrot.

'You're crazy,' Bára tells him. 'We'll bring home a parrot and it'll split on me when it overhears me telling someone on the phone that I love him.'

Before they go for their dinner, Bára calls Sam from the hotel. As soon as she picks up the receiver it emits a long and, to her ears, plaintive tone, but she finds precise instructions alongside the telephone and she manages to dial the Prague number.

Samuel answers, which means he's alive and has survived her rebellion. Bára informs him that they have arrived safely and that it is lovely there. It's a pity he didn't come, she tells him, the Gaudí is unforgettable and Saša feels better.

Samuel remains silent, so she asks him how he is, but he continues to say nothing. The telephone is dead, maybe they have been cut off or Samuel has hung up.

So Bára calls again, but this time nobody answers the phone at the other end. Samuel refuses to talk to a wife who has disobeyed him.

It is humiliating. Bára feels as if she has proffered her hand to someone who has refused to shake it and she is aware of her blind submissiveness. She called Samuel instead of calling Daniel and telling him she loves him. So she dials another number. The telephone rings for a long time and then at last a girl's voice answers at the other end. Bára asks Magda if her daddy is at home.

'He's leading a Bible study class,' and Magda wants to know if she is to give Daddy a message.

It is evening and they go out once more into the street. They find a restaurant offering Catalan food and wines at reasonable prices. The waiter chooses them a table by the window. It is a table for five but there are no places taken so far. In her newly learnt Spanish, Bára orders three kinds of fish for herself and rabbit in an olive sauce with rice for Saša. She orders herself some red wine and orange juice for Saša who refuses wine.

Saša tries to entertain his mother by reading out suggestions for excursions to her from the guidebook: gothic bridges and castles, a Roman fortress, poetically foreign-sounding names like Sant Pol de Mar, Castelló d'Empúries, Torroela de Montgrí, Vendrell – Casals' birthplace. And the Pyrenees are not far away either.

'Listen, darling,' Bára interrupts him, 'we're only here for six days

and we can't see everything, and I'm not going mountain-climbing –
you know I've ruined my lungs with smoking.'

Saša leafs through the phrase book for a moment and then
announces *'Pues yo me he quedado con algo de hambre. Pediré algo más.'*
Bára asks him if an ice-cream sundae would suffice and she realizes
with emotion that this is the first time she has been with her son
acting as a chaperone and companion, that for the first and maybe last
time she is sharing something special with him alone. She would like
to hug him, her little boy, and say: Forgive me, I've bungled so many
things in my life, but she simply says: 'Have a giant sundae or whatever
you fancy.'

Before bringing the ice-cream and another glass of wine for Bára,
the waiter grumbles that the place is very full this evening and asks
politely if he may sit a customer at their table.

Bára agrees – they'll be leaving shortly anyway – so the waiter brings
the customer over. It's a man, although he looks more like a black-
haired demon, if one accepts that demons can be as handsome in their
fallen state as the angels they once were. The man has a large devilish
nose, long, dark Arabic hair, a high forehead like Bára's, eyes even
darker than hers and broad kissable lips. He is dressed entirely in black
apart from his snow-white shirt. He bows and excuses himself in
Spanish, telling her his name, the only bit of which Bára manages to
understand is the Christian name, which she takes to be Anselmo,
although she can't be sure. So Bára introduces herself too and she
admits that Saša is her son.

Saša eyes the fellow with distrust and obvious displeasure. He wants
to be alone with his mother and so he tells her he needn't wait for the
ice-cream. But Bára has already ordered it and she doesn't feel they
need to rush off anywhere. It's nice here, after all.

On hearing this strange tongue, the demon Anselmo asks in English
where they are from and Bára tells him, 'From Prague.'

'Oh, Praga, Praga,' the man says. He was in Prague five years ago
and saw the paintings from Picasso's classical period in the gallery
there. Does she like Picasso?

Bára says she has had little opportunity to see the originals of his
pictures.

So she must not miss the opportunity to see a collection of paintings
by the young Picasso, because without that it is impossible to understand his genius. A man who at the age of fourteen had mastered

technique to the extent of painting like Leonardo or Van Dyck could not help overthrowing the old forms and conventions and going on looking for newer and newer forms of expression.

Bára replies that they would be sure to visit the museum as they were here for another six days.

If she permitted he would be happy to act as her guide, the man offers. It would be a pleasure to guide a beautiful woman from Prague and her son.

Bára smiles at him and leaves his offer unanswered, while Saša scowls. He bolts his ice-cream, but the demon has already ordered Bára another glass of wine.

Don Anselmo slowly eats his scampi while talking softly in an alluring voice. He talks about Picasso and Dalí, whom he loves and admires as a unique giant among artists and the most remarkable, albeit extreme, genius. He had spoken to him on several occasions, as he had once written a major study of him. He regrets that the lady from Prague does not have enough Spanish, but will gladly make her a gift of a copy. Art history is the demon's field of study and Dalí is his speciality. If Bára is staying longer he will gladly drive her to Figueras and show her the master's birthplace.

'Bára dear,' her son rebukes her, 'we ought to go.'

But Bára has no wish to. She is sipping heavy wine that has the scent of muscatel and Catalan sunshine, and watching the man opposite, no longer particularly aware of what he is saying, but being conscious only of the melody of his voice and the message of his gaze, which unlike his mouth professes admiration, requests an assignation, demands her embrace, and in fact slowly undresses her and fondles her breasts. And she realizes that she is free, totally free. No one is watching over her, she can do just what she likes; she can delight in the fact that she is attractive to a man she finds so alluring that merely looking at him gives her physical pleasure.

Then she listens to a story about how Dalí kissed the teeth of a dying horse when he was small and then when he was five he hurled an even smaller boy from a bridge. She doesn't know whether it actually happened, or whether they are only empty words to fill the time that must elapse between first acquaintance and making love.

Saša once more presses her to leave with him, and she suggests that he should go on ahead to the hotel if he is tired, that she'll join him shortly. But this her son refuses.

She realizes that Saša has decided to keep an eye on her, but she does not feel it as a curb on her freedom; she is grateful to him, to her little boy, for not abandoning her and not leaving her to the mercy of the demon and her own urges.

'Just one more glass,' she tells her son and allows herself to be soothed once again by the sweetly insistent voice that now speaks of love, Dalí's of course – for his Gala, who was matchless, loyal and inspirational.

Bára's speech is already becoming slurred and she is unable to find the English words, but she asks nevertheless whether it was the love that was matchless, loyal and inspirational, or Gala. Anselmo replies that it was both the love and that remarkable woman who, he now realizes, was Russian too.

The words 'Russian too' cut Bára to the quick. The demon had been in Prague which lay in Russia. But it's all right, at least she now has an excuse to accede to her son's wishes and walk out of this place. So she says that she must take her leave. She feels a touch of regret that she will never see this man again. The time between first acquaintance and love-making has lapsed and there is no returning, and it's all to the good, it has been a pleasantly exciting moment of freedom. She calls the waiter but the demon Anselmo will not hear of her paying. He thanks her for her pleasant company and a delightful evening which he hopes will not be the last. He will now drive Bára back to the hotel and tomorrow to the museum, and should she wish he will drive her and her son to Figueras or anywhere they fancy. He then presses his visiting card on Bára. Bára thanks him as warmly as she is able and allows him to kiss her hand. However, she refuses a lift back to the hotel, as she and her son want to walk a little more, but she gives Anselmo a hotel name, even though it is only the name of a hotel she happened to notice on the way to the Parque Güell. She invents a room number and the poor demon carefully notes it down. In the doorway, Bára stops once more and turns to wave to the enthusiastic admirer of Dalí.

'Don't be cross with me,' she says to Saša, when they emerge into the warm Barcelona night. 'Don't blame your old mother for flirting on her first evening in Gaudí's city.'

It is half-past one in the morning when they reach the hotel.

While Saša is having a wash, it crosses her mind that she could and should call Daniel. She'll tell him she met with Gaudí's ghost and a handsome, real live Catalan, who loves Dalí and would no doubt have loved her because he thinks she's a Russian like Gala. But Dan, she will say, I love you, only you, even here so far from you, and wherever I'll be, because you are the best person I have ever met. I've met so many people and there were many that I thought I loved, even though I didn't know what love meant until I met you. And she lifts the receiver which emits the long mournful tone. She forgets which is the number she is supposed to dial to get an outside line, and she has also forgotten the code for calling home. She'll have to ask Saša, he's bound to know, because he's young and only drinks orange juice last thing at night.

When Saša emerges from the bathroom, his mother is already asleep, holding in her hand the telephone receiver which emits a long, mournful tone.

5

It was night when Daniel reached home. Marek and Magda were already asleep and Hana was watching television. The surface of life seemed unruffled here. Hana hugged him. 'I'm glad you're back.'

'Where's Eva?'

'Upstairs in her room.'

'Have you talked about what she's going to do?'

'Naturally, but it'll be better if you talk to her yourself.'

He went upstairs and knocked on his daughter's bedroom door.

She was seated at her desk over an open book. Now she quickly pushed back her chair and got up. 'Hi, Dad. I didn't think you'd be back till tomorrow.'

'That was what I originally planned. But it didn't work out.'

'Are you cross with me?'

'I'm cross with myself, more than anything, for having brought him into the house.'

'But I love him.'

She was standing facing him and suddenly he had the feeling it was his first wife standing there. She used to speak to him in the same tone of voice: I love you. That was how old she was then. But hadn't he deserved her love? He had not been a blackguard. Not in those days, anyway.

'Are you sure, Eva?'

'About what?'

'That you're expecting his baby?'

'Yes.'

'And that you love him?'

'I'm sure of that too.'

'Why?'

Silence.

There's no answer to that question. Whatever she said, it wouldn't explain anything anyway. If only he had that blackguard here right now!

'How did it happen?'

'The way things like this happen.'

'Thank you for your explanation. It isn't what I expected. It's not what I expected of you. How long is it now?'

'Three months almost. I was afraid to tell you. Besides which I was hoping it . . . that it would go away.'

'Even if you loved him, what made you do that?'

'I was afraid he wouldn't love me any more if I didn't want to have anything to do with him.'

'A fine sort of love if you have to fear for it like that.'

'When you love someone you want to be with them totally.'

'But he'll be found guilty and sent to prison. You won't be with him totally or even partly. You won't be together at all!'

'Maybe they won't find him guilty.'

'You know full well they will.'

'Maybe something could be done . . .'

'Eva . . .'

'Yes, Daddy?'

'I thought and I believed that you'd finish at the Conservatoire. That you would play, and play really well, seeing that your mum didn't manage to.'

'I know, Daddy.'

'What do you want to do?'

'About study?'

'About study and life.'

'I don't intend to run away from my studies. They'll let me interrupt the course. For the birth.'

'And what about Petr?'

'I'll wait for him,' she said, exactly as he expected. 'If Petr wants to, we'll get married. We can do that there, can't we?'

'If he wants to! I would have thought it was what you wanted that counts! You don't have to marry him. You don't have to marry him just because you're expecting his baby.'

'I want to marry him because I love him.'

'You can stay here with us,' he said, ignoring her answer, 'with the child too. You don't have to marry someone you know precious little about. Precious little good, at any rate.'

'He is good. He's just unfortunate, that's all.'

'Eva, you know very well how hard I try. I almost feel duty bound to believe that everyone is good and everyone can be reformed. But that man is so unfortunate, since you choose that expression, that he will bring misfortune to everyone around him.'

'No, he just needs to know that someone loves him.'

'But you loved him and look what happened.'

'He needed to earn some money.'

'He could have worked.'

'But he did.'

'For how long?'

'He had a debt to pay and apart from that – he needed money to get hold of . . .'

'What?'

'You know, Dad. Speed.'

'No, I didn't know. You knew but you didn't tell me. And in spite of that you wanted to have his baby and marry him?'

'I didn't want to have a baby. It just happened.'

'You must have been doing something that made it likely.'

'But I'm not trying to excuse myself.'

'Don't you realize the baby could be damaged?'

'It won't be, Dad. I don't take anything any more. Not since the time I told you.'

'But he was taking it. You say so yourself. And have you any idea at all what life with a drug addict would be like?'

'No,' she said stubbornly. 'I've no idea what sort of life to expect. No one knows what to expect. Nor what is good or bad for them.'

'This won't be good anyway.'

'And do you think someone else would be better? People do far worse things than injecting themselves now and then.'

327

'Such as?'

'Stealing, lying, being cruel to each other.'

'Not everyone is like that.'

'Daddy, you know so very little about life.'

'Petr told me the same.'

'Not long ago a boy told me that they should exterminate everyone who is defective. And also old people who are unable to work any longer.'

'Who was telling you that?'

'It was at a disco.'

'That's just talk.'

'It isn't.'

'There's no point in our talking about people at discos. I'd prefer to talk about you and Petr.'

'Well, *he* isn't wicked and he loves me.'

'Eva, now you're not talking sensibly. You're just being obstinate.'

'Why do you think he was having shots? It was because he couldn't stand all those things.'

'That's simply an excuse.'

'It's not. I found out for myself. When you give yourself a shot or just smoke marijuana, the world looks better. And you don't even feel like coming back.'

'Babies are born into the real world.'

'I know, Dad. I know I've been a disappointment to you.'

'That's not the point. It's not me that matters, but you and the baby that will be born. How will it live?'

'I'll take care of it!'

'How do you think you'll take care of it, when you can't even take care of yourself? Seeing that you think the world is such a horrible place.'

'It's not that I think it – it *is*. But he'll help me!'

'Who? Petr?'

Silence.

'So God will, then,' she said in the end.

'Let's hope so.' Then he said, 'We'll help you too, but no one will be able to help you if you don't know what to do about yourself.'

She turned her back on him and he could see her shoulders start to quiver.

He would like to have cried too, but he had forgotten how to, long ago.

'Don't condemn me, Daddy,' she said in the midst of her tears. 'I'll cope, you'll see.'

He had no right to condemn her. She would have more right to condemn him if she knew everything about him.

6

Samuel

Ever since Bára returned from Spain with her son, Samuel has refused to speak to her about anything but those things strictly connected with the running of the household. Instructions related to the office he gives her in writing. On the occasions when Bára tries to tell him something, Samuel either hears her out in silence or turns and walks away while she is still speaking. Bára gives him a hurt look and begs him to make it up with her, because she loves him, because he is her home and because it is impossible to live together all the time in silence. When he still remains silent, her eyes fill with tears and she goes off to find the children or to her own room and locks herself in. He can't deny that she makes efforts to discharge all her obligations and tries not to do anything that might arouse his anger further. So perhaps she really is suffering, but what is her suffering compared to his?

He has to live with a woman who constantly flouts order of every kind. She thereby destroys not only him but also the order on which life is built. For years he has tried to explain it to her but to no effect, or rather with the opposite effect. Bára is more recalcitrant than ever: right in the middle of March when the work load is greatest, she takes herself off with her son, who is only just managing to scrape through school. They go off on an excursion, but not to the Giant Mountains, for instance, but right to the other end of Europe instead. Why? Bára used Saša's allergy as an excuse, but in reality her intention was quite simply to let him know how much she disdained everything that mattered to him, as well as all his wishes. She wanted to demonstrate to him that it was her sacred right to do just what she felt like. And obviously she didn't give the slightest thought to the fact that her bit of fun cost a lot of money that should have been invested in developing the practice. Then she pretends to be surprised that he has lost all interest in work at the office. What reason could there be to continue with work which his wife so obviously holds in contempt, to build up something that she will destroy with a mere wave of the hand the moment he leaves the world?

He barely goes in twice a week to check on the work and assign jobs, but he cannot summon up the least desire to design anything himself, let alone come up with ideas or create anything. One of his reasons for stopping work is to demonstrate to Bára how deeply she has wounded him in the very essence of his personality, and the suffering she is causing him.

And he is suffering terribly. The days loom emptily ahead of him, and he just gazes at them impassively, wondering to himself which of them will be his last. In desperation he wonders how he might still change his life. What if he were to return to his second wife? It is years since he last spoke to her, but she has not found another partner as far as he knows. Maybe she'd take him back. He'd be better off with her; at least she wouldn't try to destroy him. But if he were to do that he would deprive his only son of his father, as he had already done to his two daughters. Besides, everyone he possibly still cared about would consider his return to the old woman that he left fifteen years ago to be an acknowledgement of total failure. No one would ever believe he had done it of his own accord, that he had left a woman whom everyone regarded as beautiful, interesting and attractive, who treated every man apart from her own husband considerately or even seductively, simply because life with her was no longer bearable. He could, of course, find a new wife entirely, one who was young and maybe interesting but definitely less extreme; or at least a mistress. But he didn't have the stomach to go behind his own wife's back, besides which he didn't feel he had the strength any longer to start a new life for the fourth time.

For a while he toyed with the idea of buying a dog, but in the end he realized that a dog was more likely to disturb him. It would require care, time and attention, and until it had learnt to understand the order demanded of it, it would actually worsen the muddle sown by Bára and her son – both her sons.

In her monologues Bára asks him, begs him not to upset himself, but to see a doctor, a psychologist or a psychiatrist who would prescribe for him an anti-depressant or send him for psychotherapy, or at least advise him how to overcome his depression. So she says, but in fact she's hatching a plan to get rid of him from the house, have him locked up among lunatics, have him declared insane and then take away his son, his property and eventually his life.

His life is drawing to a close anyway. If Bára doesn't manage to take it from him, or if he doesn't take it himself, how many years might he have left? A life devoid of hope, meaning and peace of mind can't have much staying power. Depression destroys the heart and encourages malignant tumours.

For some time now he has found the thought of death attractive, though at the same time he is terrified by the void that yawns behind it. For years he has tended to give greater thought to his body. There was a time long ago when he would take plenty of exercise, but just recently he hasn't done more than just keep it ticking over. Now it occurs to him that he should pay more attention to his soul. It is no accident, after all, that he has turned out this way. Could one state with certainty that someone whose plans had been used for the construction of at least a hundred buildings in this country would one day simply disappear into the void, that his consciousness would die and his spirit simply vanish? That the only things that would remain for some time would be those very buildings. The master of ceremonies or whatever devil would preside at his funeral would be right in declaring: And he will live on in his work – thereby elegantly implying that nothing else of him would survive.

For the first time in his life, he starts to feel disgusted with his parents for having failed ever to speak to him about the soul and for leaving the world themselves with bitter resignation; disgusted with himself in his younger years when he didn't find the time to worry about anything else but work, materials and numbers, when his head was soaking up countless figures, definitions, building plans, the characteristics of dozens of architectural schools, charts, ground plans, elevations, but not a single thing about the meaning of his own existence, not a single thought about who he actually was, or how it was that he of all people had come to be washed up in this cosmic sea of possibilities.

It is interesting that even Bára has been to church from time to time over this past year. When she first ventured there, he suspected that it was simply a cover for some other tricks, but when he cautiously asked her how it had been at church, she recounted to him almost the entire sermon with such fervour that he had joked at the time about her joining a convent in her old age. She had replied that after her marriages and her experiences with men in general it would come as a relief, but that she had been at a Protestant service and Protestants don't have convents.

Maybe she too was seeking a way out of emptiness. Maybe everything we do is only a search for a path that will lead us from emptiness and allow us to forget the nothingness we came from and to which we must return.

Had he not found it humiliating to show interest in something that interested her, he would have asked Bára then to take him with her to church some time.

While Bára and her son were away in Spain against his wishes, Samuel went to a church in the Old Town for the first time in many years, but he did not feel at ease in the midst of all that marble, all that baroque ostentation and the crowds of tourists. The preaching did not catch his imagination and the Mass seemed to him like a long-drawn-out production of a play that had long since ceased to mean anything to anybody.

And then, for some unknown reason, he remembered an experience he once had in Amsterdam when he had found his way unerringly to a hidden market, even though he had never heard of it before, at least not in this life. And then there was that odd feeling when he first set eyes on Bára. She seemed familiar to him, as if he had met her a long time ago. What if, in both cases, it was the projection of some experience from a life long past? What had he been? Why was he born on the first day of September, the very same day as one of the most famous baroque architects? He recalled how, during the trip to Brno, that young colleague of his had referred to some Indian sect that believes in reincarnation. Apparently death takes one of your bodies, but God or fate offers you a new one. The sect has members over here too, according to Vondra.

Why shouldn't he visit them, seeing that Bára can swan off around the world with her son?

He found the name of a sect that ran a vegetarian restaurant in the directory, and he also discovered where to go if he wanted to find out more.

On the Sunday before Bára's return, he set off to the far side of town where, amidst factory buildings and grey blocks of flats, there huddled

332

several small villas, one of which apparently housed the temple.

He hesitated for a moment outside the front entrance but then a young woman appeared wrapped in a pink sari and asked him if he was coming to visit them before inviting him in straight away.

He had to take off his shoes and then mount several steps to a prayer room of modest dimensions, at the far end of which stood a small altar with rather tacky and cheap-looking statues of some deity with several pairs of arms, as well as a whole lot of even more tasteless artificial flowers. The room was full of people, most of them young, who were sitting on the floor or on small cushions with their legs crossed beneath them. Most of the men had shaven heads and were dressed in white or pink flowing robes.

By one of the walls, hung with cheap garish prints, a priest or a guru or whatever he was sat enthroned behind a microphone, playing an exotic keyboard instrument and intoning a monotonous chant.

Samuel sat down on a small cushion at the very back of the room, and it took several moments for him to realize that this section was apparently reserved for women, but he didn't dare stand up and move forward for fear of disturbing the ceremony.

The priest/guru was still singing the selfsame melody and words, invoking Krishna over and over again, and the people in the room joined in his chant, some of them clapping their hands in rhythm, others beating on small drums or jingling cymbals.

The melody had an insidious effect and he had the feeling that some of the women around him were falling into a trance.

He would have happily surrendered to the melody and that invocation of an unknown force but his mind was not relaxed enough, and as the chanting of the monotonous melody continued he felt himself becoming increasingly alienated from the ceremony and this gathering, and his thoughts started to wander: from the arguably successful buildings of his early days to his unsuccessful marriages, *Hare Krishna, Hare Krishna, Krishna, Krishna, Hare, Hare, Hare Rama, Hare Rama, Rama, Rama, Hare, Hare*, to the daughters whom he had abandoned, who called him Daddy but didn't love him; to the people he had helped by finding them jobs or passing on to them his knowledge free of charge – the only thing he had asked in return was a little professional integrity, without which buildings collapse and walls cave in, but even that had not gained him friends; there was no one on earth, not one single person, that he could say loved him. One travels through life, up hill and down dale, and with the passing of the years one becomes more and more aware of the futility of all effort, self-deception and loving words.

Samuel thinks about his wife, the last one, who feigns love even though she feels nothing towards him any more, except hatred maybe, or fear of his anger. And suddenly it emerges, goodness knows from what depths: a name – Mary Ann. In his mind he calls his wife, Mary Ann, and it occurs to him that he has just found her real name. Admit that you hate me, that you want to destroy me!

At that moment, one of the shaven-headed youths steps up to the altar and draws the curtain; the guru finishes his chanting and starts his address with the assuring words that people are good and innocent, but they are misled, they are impatient, the *dharma* is in decline, the present age is *Kali-yuga* and gives rise to conflict, intolerance, rebellion and a longing for material happiness. People want to consume everything immediately and in this respect they resemble animals, and like them they easily fall into the trap set for them by *Maya*, the ruler of the material world. She leads people to neglect the Lord *Krishna*. It is necessary to raise the self above the body while focusing on the supreme personality, who is *Krishna*. He does not require us to give up everything, but simply wishes us to do everything we do with our minds on him. We can't help eating, sleeping or conceiving children: after all, we are a combination of body and spirit. But it is necessary for us to satisfy our needs like people, not animals. One has to be *gosvami*, in other words, someone in perfect control of one's senses and mind.

When the guru finishes they start to distribute metal plates of food smelling of exotic spices. Samuel is also served.

They all now eat their food in silence and what seems to him humility, and it strikes him that the place is run according to an order which they all observe. He doesn't yet understand its rules or its source, but is aware of its presence and imagines that if Mary Ann, his latest wife, were to find herself here she would flee the place like an evil spirit exorcized by bell, book and candle.

When he has finished eating, one of the young men comes and sits with him and starts to talk to him: he welcomes him and wishes to tell him something about Krishna, who is the Supreme Personality of Godhead, and about *atma* or the soul, the spark of life in the body, which goes on migrating from one body to the next until it achieves such a state of perfection that it may escape from the cycle of life and death. Then it fuses with the cosmic soul and thereby attains its pure, true identity. If people live badly, serving only things and harming other people, their souls migrate into worse bodies, and can even enter the body of a dog, a cat or an ape.

Samuel nods, even though it all sounds alien to him, being so very different from anything he has lived by so far. He makes an effort to listen attentively and when at last the young man invites him to come again some time, he thanks him for the invitation.

And indeed, three weeks later, by which time Bára and her son are back and he is treating her with silence, he sets out once again for the same assembly and listens once more to the same chanted invocation of the god about whom he knows nothing (but what can one know about God?), listens to the homily which confirms the order which he still knows nothing about either, hears that he, like every man, is fundamentally good, just corrupted, but there is hope for him to overcome that corruption and strengthen his true self. He eats the fragrant vegetarian food and on his way home it comes to him in a flash that Mary Ann was a mass murderer who poisoned several men and eventually her own children too. In fact, she got rid of her last husband when she was the same age as Bára is now. She was executed over a hundred years ago.

Is it possible that he had been one of her victims in some earlier existence and had only now recalled it? Is it possible for the souls of two people to meet again in this world and link their fates again by some tragic error? It seems unlikely to him; after all, nothing of their life together has ever come into his mind, only the features and that name, so it could be that *at that time* he had simply caught sight of the likeness, the name and a brief account of the case.

When he gets home, Bára is ironing in the lounge while listening to some piano concerto on the radio. Mary Ann glances at Samuel and even smiles at him, asking how it was and whether he wants dinner, but he declines, saying he has already eaten.

Bára asks how the food was and he tells her it was good.

He doesn't go off to his room as has been his wont in recent days, but instead sits down in one of the armchairs and says nothing. He reflects on the possibility of a soul being reincarnated in another body. It sounds odd but the fact is there must be about a billion people who believe it. And how else could one explain all the *déjà vus* he has read about, and also experienced himself?

But even if such things could happen, is it possible that the soul of a murderess could return to a human body and continue her poisoning? How many bodies would she have had to pass through since the time she was hanged?

It all seems strange and improbable to him, but how then is he to explain the fact that as every day passes, the sense of imperilment grows within him and he is constantly aware of Bára's perfidy, in her every word and every movement?

A thought suddenly occurs to him and he says: 'Wouldn't you like some tea, Mary?'

Bára stiffens, then turns round and says, 'Are you asking me?'

Samuel stares at her fixedly and says nothing. He has the feeling that Bára has blushed.

Mary Ann returns to her ironing. Samuel gets up and turns the music down.

Bára asks: 'Why did you call me Mary?'

'Why did you react?'

'There's no one else here!'

Samuel says nothing.

'Sam, you're off your head!' Bára says in shock.

'I'd like some tea,' Samuel requests.

Bára switches off the iron and goes to the kitchen. She doesn't close the door behind her so she disappears from his view for a moment before reappearing once more. He can see her run water into the kettle and then push the switch down. The water boils in the invisible kettle. Bára takes a cup and puts a teabag into it before going to fetch the kettle and something else. Once more he can see her: she pours water into the cup and then, from a little packet, she adds some sort of powder, and finally stirs it all with a spoon. The poisoned tea is ready. He has unmasked Bára's true identity and in so doing brought nearer what was intended to happen anyway.

She wordlessly hands him the tea and switches the iron back on.

'Don't you want any?' he asks.

'No thanks. I had some tea a moment ago.'

'You can have some of mine!'

'No, thank you.'

He rises, picks up the cup and hands it to her. 'Take a drink!'

'Don't force me. I don't want any!'

'What did you add to this tea?'

'What do you mean?'

'You added something from a sachet to it.'

'Do you mean the sugar?'

'I mean, what was in the sachet.'

'Sugar.'

'That's if it was sugar.'

'And what else was there supposed to be in it?' Bára goes into the kitchen and returns with the sachet: *Sugar granulated. Weight 5 gm. Hygienically wrapped.*

The sachet has had its corner ripped off and is empty. It is impossible to tell when it was torn and its contents replaced.

'That's if there was still sugar in it.'

'No, it was full of poison, you madman!'

'Drink it then!'

'I won't. And leave me alone. You really are insane.'

He feels the impotent rage rising up inside him. He should grab her and force the liquid down her throat.

'So take a drink if it's only sugar.'

'Leave me alone.' She picks the iron up again and runs it over his shirt.

Samuel stands up and goes to his bedroom. He opens the bottom drawer of his desk, where his pistol is hidden beneath a pile of old plans. He takes it out and loads it. He returns to the lounge. 'Look at me, Mary!' he orders Bára and takes aim at her.

'Are you crazy?'

'Take that cup and drink it.'

'Is it loaded?'

Samuel says nothing.

'You really have gone off your head!'

'Drink that tea, you bitch!'

'No,' she says, 'I won't. I don't feel like it.'

'Are you afraid of what you prepared for me?'

'I don't fancy any tea, that's all! And you can go ahead and shoot me!' Bára yells hysterically. 'Go on, shoot the mother of your own son. I won't have to put up with you any more, at least. Or with anything else. What sort of life is this, anyway?' Bára takes the cup and comes up so close to Samuel that he prefers to move away. 'I'd sooner chuck it in your ugly face,' Bára yells, 'but I'll leave it for you. You can take it down to the police station and let them analyse it!' and she turns and runs out of the room. Samuel hears her lock her bedroom door. That is followed by several hysterical sobs and silence.

The very thought. Taking the cup of tea to the police. He'd done all sorts of things in his life, but he had never denounced anyone.

Samuel lays the pistol down next to the cup of tea and hesitates for a moment. But if it's to happen, then let it happen. He picks up the tea cup and drains it to the bottom.

7

The trial was held in a small court room. There were only three benches for visitors but two remained empty.

The State Prosecutor's Office was represented by a woman, perhaps slightly younger than Hana, and there was nothing strict about her rather maternal appearance. If he were to meet her without her gown Daniel would never guess her profession. But then, if anyone were to meet him without his gown, they would hardly guess he was a pastor either. The chairman of the court was an older man. Petr's lawyer, Dr Kacíř, maintained that he had been a judge under the Communists, but had apparently behaved decently.

The prosecuting counsel accused Petr of obtaining and selling the drug pervitin, chiefly to minors. He had admitted the offence but refused to say who had supplied him with the drug, saying that he used to meet the person regularly on Republic Square in Prague but did not know their identity. Likewise, he didn't know the people he sold the drug to. The accused maintained that he sold only very small quantities of the drug, but no credit could be given to this assertion, as he had already had a previous conviction for the same offence. The prosecutor then went on to talk less about Petr than about the danger of drugs, how young people's lives were damaged or even destroyed; according to certain estimates, as many as 300,000 young people had tried drugs and about 13 per cent of young people were addicts. In such circumstances the behaviour of the accused represented a particular danger to society and the motives for his actions were entirely despicable. The profit motive had dominated his behaviour to such an extent that he had not been deterred from his activity either by the previous punishment or the care of those who had acted as his social guarantors. Although the accused denied it, it was obvious that he acted as part of an organized gang involved in the manufacture and sale of drugs. Society and particularly minors had to be protected from these people. The prosecutor asked for a sentence at the upper end of the scale.

Daniel felt as though he was in the dock. His throat was dry and his forehead burned as if he had a fever. Eva sat next to him motionless, her gaze fixed on the prosecuting counsel. What was she going through as she heard such negative judgements about the father of her baby?

Daniel was unable to come to terms with the fact that his daughter was expecting a baby out of wedlock, let alone the fact that the father was a criminal who had betrayed her trust and his. He had tried to persuade her that it was better to live as a single parent than to bind herself to someone who repeatedly demonstrated that he was incapable of leading a decent life. But Eva stuck to her guns. Petr wasn't bad, he had just had a hard childhood and suffered from insufficient love. 'Haven't you always preached the importance of love for people's lives, Daddy?'

'Yes, real love.'

'What is real love? How do you recognize it?' And she answered herself: 'Real love never abandons others even when they fall short.'

At least he had persuaded Dr Wagner to undertake Petr's defence. He based his case on the fact that Petr was not a normal dealer who sells for personal gain but was a dreamer who was incapable of distinguishing between reality and his own fantasy. He assured Daniel that he would manage to get Petr a 'first paragraph', in other words, a fairly short sentence, although probation would be out of the question because of the previous offence.

Petr's examination began. Petr admitted that he felt guilty about selling drugs on several occasions to random customers, but he had never sold them to 'beginners'.

How could he tell, maintaining as he did that he did not know the people who bought from him?

'You can just tell, can't you?'

'So you have plenty of experience in this field!'

'Even if I have, I didn't get it through dealing.'

'So how did you get it?'

'On my own or from friends.'

'Have you been using drugs for a long time?'

Dr Wagner objected that drugs use wasn't part of the charge.

The judge considered that it helped none the less to give a fuller picture of the defendant's character.

Petr declared that he could not remember. He just knew that when he was in a bad way, drugs helped him to survive.

'Why were you in a bad way?'

'I didn't have a dad and my stepfather hated my guts. He used to beat me and Mum. So I ran away and lived as best I could.'

'In a gang?'

'I had pals who would let me sleep in their pads.'

'What did you live on?'

Petr could not recall. Then he said: 'But I never stole.'

'Or you didn't happen to get caught,' the judge commented. 'Did you know how to make the drug yourself?'

'Manufacture it, you mean?'

Dr Wagner objected once more.

'I never tried,' Petr said.

'How old were you at the time?'

'It depends. When I first ran away I was thirteen.'

'Did you first use a drug at that time?'

Petr could not remember.

'Surely you can recall something as important as that in your life?'

'I don't know whether it was then, but it was fairly early on. Everyone was popping it then.'

'Who was everyone?'

'My pals.'

'The members of your gang! Do you still mix with them?'

'No.'

'So who were you mixing with when they arrested you?'

'I'd found new friends and acquaintances.'

'Where?'

'At the place I was working, and in the church.'

'I assume that they didn't incite you to crime.'

'No, on the contrary.'

'Did they know about it?'

'No, definitely not!'

'And what would they say about it?'

Petr said they would definitely try to talk him out of it.

'So you deny selling drugs to minors?'

Petr said he had never sold anything to beginners.

'We'll see what the witnesses have to say. You have testified that you did not know the person who supplied you with the drug, is that not so?'

Petr repeated that he did not know the person.

'Doesn't that strike you as rather implausible?'

'In that trade it's best not to know anyone by name,' Petr explained.

'You weren't interested where he got it from or when you were to come for a new supply?'

'We'd reach an agreement.'

'What did you call him?'

'We didn't use names.'

'Did he know yours?'

'No.'

'And you'd never met him before – on some trip, I mean?'

'No.'

'Did you know any other dealers who got supplies from him?'

'No.'

'When you were interviewed,' the judge said, 'you stated that you wanted to get money to publish a magazine. What kind of magazine was it supposed to be?'

'I wanted people to understand the importance of the Holy Spirit for their lives.'

The judge was taken aback by the answer and said nothing for some moments. Daniel was gripped by an almost suffocating sense of shame. That lad was misusing terms that would be better left unsaid. People should avoid words whose meaning was still a mystery to them. But who respected that principle? We live in a world of empty words. He glanced at Eva once more. She had reacted differently to Petr's statement: there were tears in her eyes.

Then the judge dictated Petr's reply word for word. The sound of the clattering of a typewriter and Eva's sobbing.

At last the judge asked: 'And didn't it seem odd to you to obtain money for that purpose by means that were diametrically opposed to your objectives?'

'I didn't know of any other way.'

'But you had a job of work, hadn't you? Except that you left it.'

'Because you can't make money by working.'

'That's rather a bold statement.'

'I couldn't have saved a single crown from my pay.'

'And didn't it occur to you that there were other ways of obtaining money?'

'What other ways, your Honour?'

'Some church or other might have given you a contribution for such a purpose.'

'No, your Honour. They wouldn't have given it to me.'

'Did you publish at least one issue of the magazine?'

'No.'

'In other words, the magazine existed only in your imagination.'

'I really wanted to do it. I wanted people to lead better lives. I wanted them to know that only through the Holy Spirit, not through any of our deeds, can we be saved.'

The judge said that Petr wasn't here on account of his magazine, and never would be. He was here for quite a different offence. If he had genuinely wanted to obtain funds for a useful purpose, then in his view it was most regrettable as he had only harmed the thing he sought to benefit. Finally, he asked if he was sorry for his actions.

Petr said he was sorry he had been unable to start doing what he had wanted to do.

'I am asking you,' the judge said, 'whether you are sorry for the crime you have committed?'

Petr said nothing. Then he glanced quickly at the place where Eva was sitting.

'I'm sorry,' he said quietly. 'I'm sorry most of all that I deceived the people who believed in me.'

8

Letters

Dear Reverend Vedra,

I ought to have written to you ages ago, but I was shy and I didn't want to take up your time either. Most of all I want to thank you for Barcelona. I think it has to be the most wonderful experience of my life, not just because we saw so many wonderful things such as paintings, houses, parks and even that old Roman fort, for instance, but most of all because I was there with Mum. We'd never been on our own like that before, except for when I was in first class at the primary school. And thanks to you my allergy has disappeared. The sunshine and the sea air sent it packing.

I thought to myself that you really must be very fond of Mum to have done something for her and for me that neither my Dad nor my stepfather would do. I'd like to repay you in some way but I don't know how or what I could do for you. Some time in the future perhaps. One possibility is that I enjoy fiddling around with tape recorders and suchlike machines. If anything went wrong with something of yours, even the computer, I could have a go at repairing it (no guarantee though).

There was something else I wanted to tell you. Ever since Mum first met you she's been totally different. She doesn't get the blues any more and she is actually glad to be alive. So I'd like to thank you for that too and hope that you are happier, because Mum is the best thing alive. I know it sounds daft coming from her son, but it's a fact.

Best wishes and thanks again,

Saša

———

Dear Bára,

I hoped we'd see each other as soon as you got back, but something happened that has taken maybe not all my time but certainly all my energy. Or rather, it rudely awoke me from the state of rapture I had been in. I told myself I wasn't going to burden you with my troubles, you have enough of your own. But I can't keep to myself something that has deeply affected my life. So: Eva's expecting a baby. And what's more, with Petr, one of those two lads I'd promised to take care of when they were still in prison. Petr is back inside again (he's just been given another two years) for drug dealing.

I always regarded myself as liberal-minded. Far more so than my vocation permitted, in fact. I understand young people making love before they get married, but her choice frightens me because it will probably burden her for the rest of her life, and I feel guilty for having influenced that choice, by my exaggerated belief in people's capacity to reform themselves and by the sympathy I've shown, both of which have influenced Eva. I also feel guilty about neglecting her over these recent years. First of all because I became so enthused about the freedom I now had to pursue my vocation. I gave generously of my time and energy wherever I went, but left almost nothing for my home. And then, as you know yourself, my life became centred on my love for you and I let Eva out of my thoughts just at the moment when she needed me, just when I could and should have been at hand. And she had no one else but me.

I don't know whether it is still possible for me to make amends in some way. I feel as if I have betrayed everything and everyone, that I have hurt the people I loved and still love. You too, in other words. No harm was intended, it was more a matter of weakness. The trouble is it is deeds not intentions that count in life. The same applies to love which I've preached about so often and which I declared to you.

Love Dan

———

My dearest, my one and only love,

It's ages since you last got in touch with me. I called you twice, but your wife always picked up the phone. Yesterday I wanted to run to you, to find you and place myself under the protection of your love and your strength. It wasn't from some whim but from desperation. Sam has gone mad and I mean that seriously: he has gone mad and wanted to kill me, to shoot me like quail, like a little Bosnian girl caught in a sniper's sights. I don't know why he didn't in the end, the pistol was loaded. He has gone mad and he is crazy enough to do anything.

My darling, you of all people know that even though I found you and love you, I haven't abandoned him. I've taken care of him a thousand times more than I have you, I've respected his sense of order. I wanted to preserve the home on account of Aleš, but for Sam too, because I once loved him. I was sorry for him when I saw how his powers were declining and his manliness was going. Yes, I was sorry for him and not for myself and I tried hard to satisfy his whims, all his selfish requests, anything to stop him lapsing into those depressions of his.

But now he's gone completely round the bend. He thinks I'm the reincarnation of some murderess that murdered her husbands and children in England about a hundred and fifty years ago. It looks as if he really believes that I want to poison him too – he can think that about me, who has sat by his bedside when he was ill and held his hand so he shouldn't feel alone in his illness.

Darling, I don't know what I'm supposed to do, what I'm to do with him and with myself, what I'm to do with his life and mine. If I didn't have you, I wouldn't want to live any more, I might even have begged him to pull the trigger when he had me in his sights. You are my salvation, the only person I have left, not counting my mother who is already old and my children who are in no position to help, apart from giving me another reason to live.

Can it be possible that I really am so terrible and that my husband is so desperate on account of me that it has unhinged his mind? Tell me truthfully, do you really think I'm impossible to live with?

I feel sad because I miss you. I feel sad because of me, and life and my husband who sits locked in his room and is probably even more desolate than me, because he doesn't have you, he just has his ailments and a pistol, that he can use to shoot himself or me, depending on his mood.

I know that everything has to end one day, but don't forsake me yet, don't forsake me now, my darling.

Your sad and loving Bára

Prague, 20 March 1995

Dear Brother Vedra,

The board of Diakonia has discussed your proposal for setting up a centre connected to your congregation.

The Diakonia organization is a great gift from Our Lord and gives us an opportunity to make our church, our principles and our work more visible.

Even though the work of the Diakonia receives a partial subsidy from the state we are always fighting to make ends meet, among other reasons because the wealthier churches in the democratic countries which generously supported our activity after the revolution have now found recipients in other parts of the world, those who have greater need of their gifts than we do. The board therefore particularly values your commitment to finance part of the costs of converting rooms for diaconal activity and for the purchase of necessary equipment from your own private funds. This is a further reason why we chiefly leave it up to you whom you wish to employ in the centre and what area of handicap you wish to focus on. For your information, however, we would like to tell you that the greatest need at the moment is for the care of young paraplegics and people with a hearing disability.

We all have a high regard for your work and regard your decision as further evidence of the goodness of your heart and the intensity of your faith, that you so readily confirm in your actions.

May the Lord assist you in your work.

On behalf of the Board.

Bárta

Dear Daddy,

I've decided to write to you, because when I speak, the right words never come to me quickly enough and I am no match for your eloquence.

I know you wanted me to become a pianist and perform for people because you consider music to be the first step towards a better and more spiritual life. And apart from that you hoped I'd continue what Mum scarcely had time to begin.

Dad, there have been times when I also wished very much for all that on account of you, on account of Mum's memory, and also on account of myself. The trouble is that I, unlike you, lack the will. I'm unable to do the real groundwork in order to achieve what I want. Or I only manage it sometimes. Then there are other moments when everything seems pointless to me. I just feel like lying about, looking up at the sky, or not looking anywhere at all. But I did show a bit of willpower though: when I gave up speed in time. You won't want to believe this, but it was Petr who helped me with that most of all. He explained to me the horrible situation I would be rushing into. He also helped me with his love. Or rather it was not so much his love as my love for him. And that's something you taught me, after all, that love is the most important thing in life. That to believe in Jesus means taking the path of love, compassion and sacrifice. That's the way you have lived, after all, and so has Mum – by whom I mean Hana.

346

I know you're cross with me, as if I've betrayed something, and you refuse to accept that Petr and I could live in love. But I can't abandon him just because he's slipped up.

I thought you might have understanding for me in this, or that at least you wouldn't condemn me.

Something else I wanted to write to you about is the feeling I have that things have changed at home somehow. It started some time ago when we had so little time for each other, but now it's as if we're almost strangers. Since when? Could it be since the time you sold that house? We live differently. You'd say we think less about the spirit and more about material things.

But maybe it's not to do with that house, or any of you. Maybe it's just me. Maybe the fact I'm dissatisfied with myself gets projected on to you.

Daddy, the only thing I feel I could be a little bit pleased with myself over is precisely the fact that I didn't abandon Petr when he needed me. And after all I haven't abandoned the piano either. As soon as the baby is born and gets a bit bigger, I'll go back to playing again, God willing.

Please understand me and don't condemn me. I believe that Our Lord won't condemn me for the decision I've taken.

Forgive me for this letter too.

Love, Eva

———

Dear Dan,

I've received your letter about Eva. I can understand you're unhappy about what has happened, but now that something like that has happened, perhaps some good can come of it. That would be my view, anyway, because you can't see inside other people and what looks like a misfortune to one person can look like good fortune to another. Don't think these are just empty words, in my own experience that's the way things are generally.

I also read into your letter that you blame yourself for neglecting your daughter because of me as well, and that you're wondering whether you oughtn't to expel me from your life as soon as possible.

My darling, I can assure you that I will never be a burden for you. You're important to me only as a loving person not as a self-constraining one.

If you feel that our love is in some way an obstacle in your life and prevents you from fulfilling what you see as your duties, you just need to say: go away! And I'll disappear from your life and you won't hear of me again.

Your loving and understanding Bára

——— —

Dear Dan,

Marie and I have discussed what we spoke about in Zlín. If you really need someone to stand in for you, and providing you obtain the agreement of the Elders, Marie could take it on. (Our children are already big enough to do without her fussing over them.) So come to some agreement with Marie about how long you'd need her assistance, and whether it's only to be assistance or if you want to divest yourself of all responsibilities. I think that Marie would prefer the former. After all, it's ten years since she worked with a congregation and she is afraid that by now she might not cope with it all.

The way I understood it, what led you to request help were various matters connected with 'work'. None of us can avoid crises in our lives, nor moments when we are at a loss as to where to turn, when we question everything we do and the way we live. Dan, I've always been fond of you and respected you precisely because you never made any secret of your anxieties and misgivings, and yet you managed to live the way you have lived. I believe you'll manage to cope with things the way you have coped with them in the past. And may the Lord help you in this.

Yours, Martin

——— —

Dear Bára,

Don't go away, don't go away, don't go away!

Dan

Chapter Eight

1

Spring is only just beginning. It is raining and a cold wind is blowing; and there are reports of snow in the mountains.

An ex-minister and his daughter have been killed in an avalanche in the Tatras. The billboards display an advertisement of a crucified naked woman. A poll has shown that four-fifths of the country's citizens want euthanasia, and skinheads have been demonstrating for the return of capital punishment. Is a new multi-storey hotel to be built on the embankment and transform the panorama of Old Prague?

Daniel and Bára are sitting together in the bedsitter at Červený vrch and discussing events that are extraneous or at least have no direct bearing on themselves. Until very recently, their favourite topic of conversation was love, but now they each have their own worries and they try to mask them with talk. In a few days' time it will be a year since Daniel's mother died, a year since the day he first set eyes on the woman now sitting opposite him.

They both try not to think about the bad things or about the difficulties that they face in the world outside this incubator they have created for their meetings.

Daniel has brought Bára a bunch of roses and an art nouveau glass from which she is now sipping wine.

'Why this goblet?'

'Because you came to see me that time.'

'I came on my own account.'

'But you helped me.'

'How?'

Yes, how? 'To think more about life and stop being miserable and brooding on death!' he says.

'I came because I was miserable and was brooding on death. I found you attractive – ' she then says, ' – you preached about love and I felt you were searching for it like me.'

He kisses her for those words but finds himself unable to rejoice in her love as he did only a few weeks ago. Too much has collapsed around them. To get closer to her he has to struggle through the ruins.

Bára mentions that her friend Helena is getting a divorce.

'Why?'

'Her engineer is a drunkard and she couldn't stand being with him any more. And she has fallen in love.'

'Who with?'

'It's immaterial,' Bára says. 'She simply wishes to be with the one she loves.'

Her announcement contains an implicit reproach. 'Everyone's divorcing,' Bára adds.

'Do you think we should too?'

'Maybe we should, but we won't.'

They quickly finish off the bottle of wine – they have little time. Then they make love. Making love at least distances them for a moment from the world in which they move for the remainder of the day, for the remaining days, and they may quietly speak words of love.

Afterwards Bára bursts into tears.

'What's up, my love?'

But Bára shakes her head. She doesn't want to burden him with her concerns, she knows he has enough worries of his own.

'I don't have any worries when I'm with you.'

'I'm happy too when I'm with you. These are my only moments of happiness.'

'But you're crying.'

'I'm crying because I have so little time with you. Because I don't know what to do now . . . Sweetheart, I'm so disheartened, so miserable and you won't protect me, all you do is lure me to you, and then you turn me out into the cold wind.'

Daniel says nothing. Then he asks if there has been any change at home.

Bára tells him that Sam mostly says nothing. He takes tablets and that calms him slightly. It looks as if he might have got over his insane notion about the reincarnated murderess; Bára has locked the pistol in her own desk and he has not come looking for the weapon, even though he's sure to have noticed its disappearance. He hasn't apologized but behaves as if he could remember nothing of that mad scene when he wanted to shoot her. Perhaps he really can't. But he constantly makes it plain that Bára is his misfortune. She disrupts the order of his life, creates commotion and neglects her duties.

'He's sick,' Daniel says.

'Don't I know it. And he always will be.'

'Shouldn't he be in an institution?'

'I'm hardly going to send my husband to a loony bin, am I? I've seen the inside of one myself and I know what it means. Death would be better than that.'

'Do you want to leave him?'

'Are you, a pastor, advising me to walk out on a sick man?'

'I'm not giving you any advice. I simply asked what you intend to do.'

'You ask me things instead of being with me and saving me. Tell me, why aren't you with me?'

Daniel remains silent. He knows that either he ought not to be lying at her side or he ought to be with her completely. He has gone too far in adopting her comforting, and seemingly comfortable, assertion that there is no such thing as either/or in life. In reality there are situations in which people simply find excuses because they can't make up their minds and such indecision destroys both them and those around them. He has known that since the outset, but he accepted this offer of escape from responsibility because it let him put off the decision, because it allowed him to rejoice in his new love without having to draw the conclusions which he feared.

'I know,' Bára says as usual, 'you can't be with me when I'm with Sam. And I can't abandon him because he's mentally ill. And it'll be like that till the end. Tell me, don't you think it's terrible that I'll have to put up with this torture for the rest of my life? Do you think it can be endured?'

Daniel says nothing.

'I always thought I could put up with anything because I'm strong, but these days it sometimes occurs to me that it will drive me round the bend. Tell me, will God take into account the fact that I stayed with a tormenting husband solely to nurse him?'

'No,' he says.

'Why?' she asks in surprise.

'God has other worries. And anyway you don't stay with your husband.'

Bára almost leaps up. 'That's rich coming from you! Why don't you tell me like he does that I torment him and am driving him into his grave!'

Daniel says nothing.

'You're like all the rest,' Bára yells at him. 'You teach and preach and prattle about love instead of doing something about it. For you, a woman is good for only one thing. Go away, go away, go away, I don't want you any more.' And she starts to sob.

Daniel puts his arms around her and holds her head in his hands, kissing her and telling her he loves her.

At that moment it strikes him that he has already overstepped the limit anyway. He has been treading a completely different path to those in his entire previous life. It's simply a matter of acknowledging it and stopping pretending to himself and to his nearest and dearest. Who is the pretence intended for most of all, who does he lie to most of all? He is too attached to this woman, he has steered his course by her for almost a year now and there is no turning back. He says, 'If you like, I'll stay with you.'

'How do you mean?'

'Exactly what I say.'

'You'll abandon your wife and children?'

He says nothing, but doesn't deny it.

'You're crazy,' she says. 'And what will I do with Sam? Am I supposed to kill him, or what? I told you I can't walk out on a sick man.'

'I'm not asking you to.' And he realizes that Bára will never leave her husband. She will stay with Samuel not because he is sick nor because she has a son by him, she'll stay with him because in a strange way she is bound to him: because of her long years of devotion, because of her fear of him and for him, and because of an unquenchable longing to win back his favour and his love. None of that will change, not even when she's in the arms of Daniel. It wouldn't even change if Samuel were to beat her or shoot at her.

'My poor dear love,' Bára says. 'I know I'm awful. I don't know what I want. No – I know I'd like to be with you, but I know it's impossible. In the end I'll ruin everyone's lives, including yours. You were better off a year ago. You had no need to add my worries to your own.'

'That year of my life has meant more to me than you can ever imagine,' he says. 'In spite of all the worries.'

'So don't forsake me yet. Bear with me for a little while longer.'

She pulls him down into her abyss, into her dark pit, where the only light comes from her dark eyes. She hugs him, they hug each other and he promises her he'll never leave her.

Before they part they make a date for the following Monday as usual.

Everything is as it was, except that he has the added burden of a promise.

2

Diary excerpts

The house is full of workmen. They are knocking down partition walls, pulling up floors, replacing window frames, making conduits for new wiring. In one of the rooms I pulled up the floor myself and cut out a hole for the cables.

'You don't want to be doing that, Reverend,' the foreman told me. 'That's our job and they'll put it on your bill anyway.'

I told him I was doing it for enjoyment's sake not to save money.

In fact I was doing it to take my mind off things and to tire out my body. It's a relief just to have to think about keeping strictly to the plan when cutting a hole in a wall. And it's easier to get to sleep at night when your body's weary.

I observe Hana who is full of vitality and looking forward to her new work. I realize that I love her. I'm capable of leaving her for a while, but I couldn't abandon her. I think about the other woman and realize that I am capable of being without her most of the time, but I couldn't abandon her either.

The awareness of my duplicity is a constant torment to me, but what if it is simply the human lot? Maybe we have confined our nature with

more commandments than we are able to fulfil and then we torment
ourselves with feelings of guilt.

———⦿———

I was surprised to find Eva singing a lot just lately and playing happy
tunes on the piano, such as Janáček's Nursery Rhymes. *'I'm playing to*
him, of course,' she told me, indicating her tummy that is already
swelling slightly.

We have the same conversation over and over again. She believes that
as soon as Petr returns from prison he will begin a new life. Petr has
promised her. He writes her long letters every week, she even reads out
some sentences from them: a whole lot of beautiful phrases, promises and
resolutions. Eva thinks Petr will feel responsibility for the child. After all,
he suffered so much himself from not having a father and growing up
without love.

Perhaps. What is more likely is that he will take fright at the
responsibility and flee from it, either literally or metaphorically. She
oughtn't to forget that drugs weren't his only escape, he also made several
attempts at suicide.

She explains to me that he was unhappy. Nobody loved him.

We end up with me trying to persuade her not to marry him, but to
wait and see how he'll behave after his release, when action will be
needed, not words. Talking is easy, I told her, it's living that is terribly
difficult sometimes.

But that goes for everyone, she objected.

I said nothing. It goes for me too, of course.

And this is the condemnation, that light is come into the world,
and men loved darkness rather than light, because their deeds were
evil.

———⦿———

Alois announced to me that he would like to marry Marika. 'What
would you say to it, Reverend?'

I told him it mainly depended on the two of them and I asked him
whether they were having to get married. Alois assured me this was not
the case, but that they loved each other.

If you love each other and think you're old enough, why not?

He told me the main reason he was asking me was whether it mattered . . . for a moment he was lost for words, but then remembered what some of his mates from the building site had told him. He said they laughed at him for going with a gypsy girl and prophesied that they would have thieves for children.

I convinced him that was nonsense. That cheered him up.

Then I asked him about the date, and he replied: some time next month, but we haven't agreed on an actual day yet.

I almost envied him his easy-going, irreproachable love.

Nietzsche in chapter 42 of Antichrist: 'The type of the redeemer, the doctrine, the practice, the death, the meaning of the death, even the sequel to the death – nothing was left untouched, nothing was left bearing even the remotest resemblance to reality. Paul simply shifted the centre of gravity of that entire existence beyond this existence – in the lie of the "resurrected" Jesus. In fact he could make no use at all of the Redeemer's life – he needed the death on the Cross . . .' And in chapter 43: 'If one shifts the centre of gravity of life out of life into the 'Beyond' – into nothingness – one has deprived life as such of its centre of gravity. The great lie of personal immortality destroys all rationality, all naturalness of instinct – all that is salutary, all that is life-furthering, all that holds a guarantee of the future of the instincts henceforth excites mistrust.'

Every lie destroys one's soul. If everything we believe in is a lie what happens to our soul then?

My father would have said: The soul? No such thing. All we have is a brain – a higher nervous system. And the brain is the first thing to rot after death.

Martin called me to ask if I'd heard about the death of Jaroslav Berger, the Secretary for Church Affairs in the district we were both exiled to for a time. I hadn't heard about his death. From time to time he would call me in for a ticking-off. 'Reverend Vedra, you are in breach of our laws. You're welcome to preach the Bible, but don't go addling people's brains, and particularly not our youngsters'. Do you think we don't know how

many of them come to your meetings on the first Monday of the month?'
On occasions he was tipsy and once he was totally drunk. 'Reverend,' he
said to me on that occasion, 'you're a fortunate man, you don't have to be
afraid of death. When you die you'll go somewhere, to heaven or
whatever. I, on the other hand, will die just like a dog.' If I'd heard
about his death in time, I would have gone to his funeral, in the same
way he came to Jitka's.

Magda has reached a beautiful age. She still retains her girlish directness
and likes to giggle and play childish tricks, but at the same time she is
beginning to assert her individuality. She draws well and writes wittily,
and apart from that she seems to have obvious acting talent. Sometimes
I catch her standing in front of the mirror making faces.

The other day I came into her bedroom and noticed a diary lying
open on her bedside table.

'You're not to read it, Daddy!'

'I'm not.'

She consulted the diary herself. 'Here's a bit you can read. There's
nothing in it.'

On one page there was quite a good caricature of one of her teachers,
on the other, a text of some kind.

The writing was childishly uneven and didn't manage to stay on the
line. Maybe her longsightedness has something to do with it.

I've just hoovered the front hall and the washing-up, Mum tidied
the living room. The Partridge is completely loopy, today she wrote
in Zuzana's record book: You daughter was lacqering her nails and
was determined to continue with this activity even in my presence.
Then I did an imitation of her and made the class laugh. What
makes me laugh are words like maggot or worm . . .

I said: 'How many is a maggot to the fifth minus a worm to the two
and a halfth?'

And she burst into merry laughter and for a moment I was happy too.
Irreproachably happy, I'd even say.

An extremely odd thing happened to me. I was sitting in my office writing something. Suddenly there was a loud bang on the window and I just managed to catch sight of a bird's body dropping to the ground beyond the window pane.

I ran out in front of the house and saw a blackbird lying paralysed, as I thought, in the grass. I leaned over to pick it up and see what had happened to it, but to my surprise it revived and with some difficulty flew across the lawn and hid behind the blackcurrant bush.

The following day, almost at the same hour, there came the same bang, even louder than on the previous day.

This time it wasn't a blackbird I found in the grass, but a white dove. When I picked it up, it turned out to be dead. I've always tried not to fall prey to superstitions, but what explanation can there be for two birds of different kinds colliding with the same pane of glass on two subsequent days, when no bird had even brushed against it before that?

Various myths and fables featuring birds, and specifically doves, came to mind. Birds have always symbolized messengers between the cosmos and mankind and the souls of saints assumed the form of a white dove. And indeed wasn't the Holy Ghost portrayed as a white dove? What sort of sign was this and where precisely did it come to me from?

The damaged blackbird that flew lurchingly away and hid itself in the bushes, that's me, while the white dove that will never fly away again, that could be my soul.

⊶◦⊷

A dream: I found myself before some tribunal made up entirely of Catholic dignitaries. Lots of cardinals and bishops. I was to defend myself against the charge of heresy, that I had propagated Archimedes' Principle and violated the vow of celibacy, and actually ravished women. The entire indictment was brought by one of the cardinals, a small, fat and choleric old man, who demanded that the church excommunicate me and hand me over to secular justice. I answered the charge by stating that I was not a Catholic priest and therefore could not violate the celibacy vow, but the only response to that was surly laughter.

Then some kind of bailiff came over and manacled me before

leading me from the court. I was expecting to be led to a stake where I would be burnt, but that before then I would be given the opportunity to recant, even though I was no longer sure what I was to recant and what to proclaim. The fellow didn't lead me to the stake but to some open space where two immense brewers' dray horses stood. I was ordered to lie down between them so that my head was at the hindquarters of the one and my feet at the hindquarters of the other. Then they attached some kind of straps to me and harnessed them to the horses. I heard a shout and then the crack of a whip. The horses took the strain each in opposite directions – I was to be torn asunder. I could feel my muscles tautening, the tension was gradually transformed into unbearable pain.

When I awoke, I realized that I really could feel a pain somewhere between my stomach and my heart. I wasn't sure whether I was to attribute the pain to the dream or vice versa.

I raised myself slightly. My wife was sleeping peacefully at my side. Her presence calmed me and the pain seemed to recede.

It suddenly struck me: Is this still my wife?

3

Daniel announced to the elders his intention to relinquish his pastoral duties for a period of several months. The building of the diaconal centre was taking up too much of his time, in addition to which he would like to concentrate on preparing the exhibition of his carvings that was due to open at the end of spring. Neither of those reasons was the real one, but the elders received his request with understanding and accepted his proposal that Reverend Marie Hajková should stand in for him while he was on special leave.

For his farewell sermon he chose his text from Paul's letter to the Philippians:

> *Therefore, my beloved, as you have always obeyed, so now, not only as in my presence but much more in my absence, work out your own salvation with fear and trembling; for God is at work in you, both to will and to work for his good pleasure. Do all things without*

grumbling or questioning, that you may be blameless and innocent, children of God without blemish in the midst of a crooked and perverse generation, among whom you shine as lights in the world . . .

Thus he took leave of them as a good and conscientious shepherd who leaves the flock entrusted to him, in the knowledge that it stands aside from the crooked and perverse world just as he himself does.

Was such an exhortation, such a challenge, a sign of pride or simply of a yearning for a fairer world? Could anyone be denied that yearning?

Those who yearned to become the children of God, he declared, often looked upon those around them as pitiable wretches, who regarded their stomachs as their god, whose thoughts were earthbound, who took pride in things they should be ashamed of. In other words, they regarded the rest as a crooked and perverse generation. And when we also look at the world around us, it appears to be going to ruin, and that the whole of life is being increasingly transformed into a dance around the golden calf. But let us not be haughty or proud, let our hearts not be hardened by our severe assessment of our neighbours. It is not our task to condemn them, it is our task to do our best with our lives and realize that each of us will go astray. Our lives cannot be without blemish, but there is hope for us in that the Lord Jesus Christ will not forsake us, that in Him we have a light that will shine in the darkness and lead us back out of it.

Daniel spoke and as in a mist he could make out familiar faces; he knew everyone gathered here, knew them by name, knew their life stories, their cares, their jobs, the names of their children.

Large flakes of spring snow swirled outside the window. Like that time a year ago. All of a sudden that critical day came back to him: that is if it were possible to designate a particular day as a turning point. His mother was dying and he was endeavouring to rekindle his faith, to rekindle it or to beg for its return, for the return of his belief in the immortality of the human spirit. And at the very moment, when his thoughts were taking a completely different direction, into these confines stepped a woman who was destined and willing to transform his life utterly.

His thoughts wandered to the past while his lips spoke of the importance of bringing light into the lives of others. Nothing in your life is more important than that. To be a light in the life of your neighbour means more than any wealth, more than any power.

He didn't say that for years he had striven for it, had tried to live that way, and perhaps he had indeed lived that way in spite of all his mistakes. Daniel felt a sudden pang of regret that something of importance in his life was coming to an end, something so important that it was as if his very life was ending. He struggled to control his voice, while at the same time he became aware of a real pain gripping his chest.

He had survived the time of oppression but not the time of freedom.

When the sermon ended, silence descended on the chapel. Had he announced that he was leaving his post for good, someone would most likely be rushing up with a bouquet and a speech of thanks, but he had kept his defection secret, so they all simply waited for him to introduce his replacement. He led her to his place and allowed her to say a prayer and the blessing.

He did not go out into the street; the weather outside was too inclement. So he and Marie said goodbye to the congregation in the passage. People shook him by the hand and wished him all the best, voicing the hope that the building work would soon be successfully completed and that he would also enjoy success with his carvings. Everyone wanted to know the date of the exhibition and he promised to let them know in good time.

He still had to go to his office where he and Marie received the money from today's collection from Brother Kodet. Here he handed over to Marie various keys, promising that he would, of course, still attend the next elders' meetings and the Bible study class. Then he went downstairs to his workshop.

A half-finished carving sat on the small workbench: a man astride a small donkey. Jesus entering Jerusalem. How many artists, both renowned and unknown, had portrayed that event, which may never have happened?

He took the gouges from their case and started to hone them on a small oilstone before sitting down to carve.

A few days earlier the gallery owner who had promised him the exhibition had visited him to ask how the preparations were coming along. He had also taken a look at the latest carvings and seemed to be delighted with them. He maintained that they were not just better from a technical point of view, they were also better in terms of expression, in the way that his figures, through each of their details, expressed a turmoil of mind and emotion that was almost tumultuous.

The gallery owner's praise had gratified him although he ought to have told him that the mental and emotional turmoil in the wood reflected a far more passionate and tumultuous agitation in his soul.

He had preached today for the last time. He had told no one, not even himself, but he knew that he would never again return to the pulpit. Was it because of the woman who had entered the chapel unexpectedly and uninvited?

No, he had brought it on himself; the woman simply stood at the end of a path he had embarked on a long time before she appeared. He had been guilty of deception before then, when he had concealed his doubts about the fundamentals, about the message he brought and about the Christ he proclaimed.

His only excuse was that he had deceived himself too. He wanted so much to believe in everything he preached, to believe that God assumed human form, that He suffered, that He died on the cross, that He descended into a vague and unimaginable hell and on the third day rose again from the dead. That He ascended into a heaven that was situated in a vague and unimaginable space, and there sat down at the right hand of His Father, God Almighty, where He will remain until the day He returns to earth to judge the living and the dead. He wished to believe it and so he used to convince himself that everything was just the way he preached it, precisely because it was unbelievable and inconceivable. He wanted to believe it because if nothing he preached was true, then life would be no more than a meaningless cluster of days between the beginning and the end, between the eternity that preceded it and the eternity that would come after.

Previously he had trodden paths that people had followed for centuries and now all of a sudden he found himself in the middle of an immense plain devoid of paths. He could set off in any direction. Admittedly he could not see the end of the plain but he knew that whichever direction he took he would eventually confront an insurmountable, bottomless abyss.

He had done what he could to dispel that image of an open space leading to an abyss that engulfed everything and everyone, but he had not succeeded.

He was conscious of a cold panic, dizziness and gripping heart pain.

He ought to get up and leave this tiny room, go and find his children, his wife, go and make love to Bára. He ought to kneel down here before this unfinished carving of Jesus on a donkey and beg for the gift of faith that alone could dispel the anxiety, bridge the abyss and offer the grace that is denied to all other life.

He didn't kneel down.

The pain in his chest grew.

He got up and walked over to the window. There was a sudden break in the clouds and the heavens were revealed. Beyond them an endless universe. Billions and billions of stars. An infinity of time and space. And astonishingly, there was no place in it any longer – no fitting place in it – for a God who had become man and watched over events on this insignificant planet.

Beads of sweat stood out on his forehead and turned cold; Daniel realized he was beginning to fall. Everything started to rush away from him. And tomorrow he had a date with Bára; how would he get there? He groped around him for something to hold on to.

4

Hana

This is Daniel's fourth day in intensive care, so Hana returns to the hospital, this time as a volunteer nurse. The heart attack was fairly extensive, affecting almost a quarter of the cardiac muscle, but the doctors are satisfied with the progress of his recovery so far.

Hana sits by Daniel's bed holding his hand and trying to appear calm to boost his confidence and strength. Each day she tells him again how everyone is praying for him, at home and in the congregation, how people call the manse asking how he is. Hana smiles at Daniel, strokes his hand and tells him for what must be the hundredth time already that everything will be fine, his heart will have a little scar, but otherwise it will be back to normal and serve him for a long time to come, except that he'll have to take care not to overdo things, and when he comes home he'll have to have a proper rest. After all, he has scarcely had a holiday in recent years.

Daniel gazes at her in silence. It's as if old age has crept into his blue-grey eyes, or rather, as Hana has come to know so well during her thirty years in the hospital, it's as if an intense weariness stared out of them.

Hana then reports on how the rebuilding work at the manse is progressing; the potter's wheel is already installed and the joiner is putting up shelving. Máša comes to the manse every other day; she has been looking out books and already has several boxes full, most of them for children.

Daniel asks after Máša's children.

There will be a new court hearing next week and Dr Wagner believes Máša will get the children back. She will have to declare that the paper in which she relinquished the children was signed under pressure from her husband. Even a few weeks ago she would have been incapable of declaring anything of the sort, but at least now she has recovered somewhat from the shock of her husband's abandoning her. Hana always makes a point of talking to her about it in order to give her encouragement.

Finally, Hana tells him about Magda and Marek who can't wait for Daniel to be moved on to the general ward where they will be able to visit him. Then she dries up. She is not sure what interests Daniel at this moment. She fears that her concerns may seem remote to him, that other people's worries must seem preposterous, seeing that his body and particularly his soul are contending with the weariness that Hana can detect in his eyes. She ought to do something to cheer him up but she doesn't know what. So she tells him how much she misses him. She says, 'I love you, Dan. You're the person I'm fondest of. When you come home I'll take care of you and make sure everything's all right. We'll take a trip down to my folks perhaps, or anywhere you like.'

Tears suddenly appear in Daniel's eyes and his lips move silently.

'Were you wanting to say something?' Hana asks. She wipes away the tears and hands him a glass of tea to moisten his lips.

Daniel asks, for the first time, 'How did it happen?'

And Hana tells him how he was a long time coming to lunch and how she went down to the workshop and found him lying by the window, groaning.

'I got an awful fright,' Hana says. Her immediate thought was that it might be his heart so she called the emergency services. 'They brought you here and you've been here ever since.'

'That's what I thought,' Daniel says and closes his eyes.

'I was at your side all the first night, but you didn't know anything about it.'

Before going, Hana pours fresh tea into his glass and changes the water in the vase containing roses that Daniel probably doesn't even notice.

Then she gives Daniel a kiss and promises to come again in the afternoon.

'What's the time now?' Daniel asks her.

Hana says it is nearly noon. She just wants to check that Magda is safely home from school and give the workmen something to eat.

'You don't have to come,' Daniel says. 'They are taking good care of me here and I'm getting better, aren't I? You said so yourself.'

'No, I want to be with you!'

At home she finds everything as it should be. Magda is chatting with the joiner, who is having a beer. Magda is scarcely aware of her mother as she tells the joiner how two boys in her class lay down in the middle of the street and were almost run over by a lorry. 'The driver leapt out of the cab . . .'

'Aren't you even going to ask how Dad is?'

'I can tell he's better,' Magda says.

'How can you tell?'

'You'd be crying otherwise. And what did Dad say?'

'He said he was looking forward to seeing you all.'

'So are we,' she says and gets ready to finish her story.

The joiner is looking for some drawings that he was talking to Daniel about, but Daniel hadn't had a chance to give them to him.

Hana promises to try and find them. She goes to Daniel's office; the desk is locked and there is nothing resembling drawings or plans lying on it or on the shelves. Then it dawns on her that Daniel would probably have taken all his things home, since he had handed the office over to Marie on the very Sunday that it happened.

So Hana goes up to Daniel's room. Here too the desk is locked, but a bunch of his keys remains in the flat. One by one Hana unlocks the drawers in which there are stacked dozens of labelled files. Hana has no idea what the drawings are supposed to look like so she looks for a file with a label saying something like DIACONAL CENTRE, but finds nothing of the sort. The best thing will be to ask Daniel in the afternoon.

In the very bottom drawer, beneath all the files, lies a black note-book without a label. Hana opens it almost involuntarily and recognizes Daniel's handwriting, and her eye just happens to fall on her own name. She cannot resist the temptation even though she's in a hurry, and she reads how Daniel could not relate his dreams to her. Then she turns over several pages at random and discovers an unfamiliar woman's name.

Hana sits down at the desk and reads Daniel's diary, all about her husband making love to some unknown female. Hana's heart thumps so hard that she feels she is about to suffocate. She tries to persuade herself that Daniel was writing some sort of story, that he had dreamt up a fictional account to use in some article or other, or in a sermon, but as she reads on there can be no doubt that this is Daniel's record of his own life: an incredible double life led behind her back, behind the backs of their children and everyone who trusted him. Hana closes the notebook and puts it back where she found it. She is at a loss as to what to do next. How is she to go to the hospital, how is she to speak to Daniel knowing something that she obviously wasn't supposed to know: that he lied, even to the children, that he had concealed a whole part of his life, possibly the most important part?

Somehow she couldn't grasp the extent of what had happened, as if what she had seen on paper hadn't yet become reality.

Could it really have happened? Could the man she trusted most of all have deceived her? How could he have done it while preaching to others how they should live? If it really had happened, what or whom would she ever dare believe again? Perhaps it was all just a terrible mis-understanding. She needed to talk to Daniel about it.

Tears run down Hana's face. She feels defiled, the way she did the time when that unknown man raped her not far from Písek.

It occurs to her that she should have heeded her conscience and gone off to Bosnia to help the wounded, perhaps a bullet would have found her and she wouldn't have had to live through this moment.

And she was such a fool that she had actually had qualms of con-science on the few occasions she had nostalgically recalled the lonely journalist who liked telling stories about China.

How is she now to behave towards a man who has deceived her, with whom she has children and who at this moment is balancing between life and death?

And suddenly it strikes her that Daniel's heart gave way precisely because he was not equipped for a life of duplicity. After all, Daniel was almost childlike – neither disloyal, nor deceitful. He was defenceless, more than anything else, in a world in which everyone was out for himself. Anyone could pull the wool over his eyes with fine words. He had believed Petr and apparently he believed some unscrupulous tart who had muddled his head and then latched on to him the way such women know how, and Daniel was unable to shake her off; he wasn't able to abandon his home or abandon the other one and in his desperation he let himself be dragged along almost to his death.

A feeling of regret and sympathy for Daniel starts to grow in Hana and she might even be ready to forgive him. God forgives our sins, so we humans should be ready all the more to forgive others. But at the same time she can feel a growing anger towards the other woman who wanted to usurp Daniel for herself, ignoring the fact he had a wife and children, heedless of the fact that he was actually suffering, not caring that she was driving him to despair and hounding him to his death.

Hana feels a need to do something, to change something straight away, to find the other woman and tell her what she thinks of her, tell her she's a murderer, a mean, selfish and self-seeking murderess.

Only she doesn't know who the woman is or where to look for her. She had only managed to make out that her mother lives somewhere in the Small Quarter and that she herself lives in some sumptuous villa, apparently in Hanspaulka. Women like that tend to be spoilt, and think they have to possess everything they take a fancy to, from clothes and perfumes to a man they find attractive.

Daniel knows her name, of course, and knows where to find her, except that she can't ask Daniel anything, not now at least. It would agitate him so much, he might die. Although it might be a relief for him to rid himself of the burden of deception.

I have to think of a way, it strikes Hana, to indicate to him that the worst thing for him in his situation is to suffer mentally, to torment himself over the things he has done and the way he has lived.

Hana cannot stay any longer in this confined space with this black notebook, tempting her to open it once more and read it through properly, except that she is terrified to open it again and read the terrible testimony that Daniel has penned in the confusion of his heart.

If only she had someone she could confide in, but she knows that she has no one like that in the world; the only person she was close to has let her down.

Hana wipes her eyes and goes to the bathroom where she rinses her face with cold water. Then she tells the joiner that she couldn't find the plans but will ask her husband about them at the hospital.

Then she hugs Magda and says, 'Oh, my poor little girl!' And before Magda has a chance to ask why she is supposed to be poor, she leaves the flat and rushes back to the hospital.

5

Daniel had been moved on to the general ward.

He was no longer tormented by physical pain, but only aware of the void into which he would sink again and again. On several occasions, mostly at night, he wept for pity.

Everyone here was kind to him and called him Reverend. 'Should you need anything, Reverend,' the fellow in the next bed offered almost as soon as they had brought him in, 'you have only to say. I can already walk about normally.' He had obviously been informed in advance.

Daniel needed nothing. He wanted to call Bára and tell her what had happened to him; explain why he hadn't kept their date and why it was unlikely he would ever keep a date again. But nobody could make that call for him. He actually had a telephone at his bedside and all he needed to do was lift the receiver, but the mere thought of doing so set his heart thumping so rapidly that he felt a pain in his chest.

After lunch, Marek and Magda visited him. Magda had cut some daffodils from the garden for him. While she was sticking them in a vase she asked how he was and whether he still had a pain. She made do with a single-word reply and without prompting announced that she had got three As, although, because of a fatal oversight, she got an E for maths. 'I'm going to be an actress, anyway,' she consoled herself and him.

'What will you act in?'

'I don't know – something to make people laugh. And to become famous.'

'Magda,' Marek rebuked her, 'Dad's feeling rotten and you just talk drivel.'

Apparently they had said nothing to Magda about his actual condition, so she had no inhibitions about gossiping like that, whereas Marek wore a serious expression. 'I really regret not going to church for your sermons a few times, but now I've been praying for you and I'll start going to church again,' he declared in a previously prepared apology and statement of intent.

He was touched by his children. He felt regret, even shame. 'That's nice of you. But only do what you are convinced is right.' He stopped short and then he added, 'If you have sufficient strength and determination.'

'Exactly,' said Marek, 'that's my concern.' He also brought an important message from Alois: they were postponing the wedding until Daniel returned. 'Because he wants you to marry them, and nobody else.'

'That's nice to hear, but tell him I don't know when I'll be coming back. Tell him it doesn't matter who blesses them, it means the same thing. And it's chiefly up to them if they are to be happy together.'

'They will be,' Marek promised on their behalf. Not a word was uttered about stars or the universe. What do his children believe in, in fact? What will become of them, how will they live? Would he ever find out, even if his heart did get better? One never finds out the important things.

'We'll help you,' Marek said finally, as he was saying goodbye.

'What with?'

'Everything, of course.'

When it came to the fundamental issue one had to help oneself. What was the fundamental issue? How one lived, of course.

'You have nice children, Reverend,' his neighbour said after Marek and Magda had left. 'And well-behaved too, I expect.'

'Yes.' And once more he was seized with regret.

'You'll have to get back to them soon. But what is one supposed to do for one's health? I thought to myself that as soon as I'm able to get about a bit I'll make a trip to Częstochowa or Medjugorie, or even to Lourdes. What do you say, Reverend? Do you think Our Lady will help with heart trouble too?'

'No,' said Daniel. 'You'd do just as well to visit some healer in Smíchov or Košíře.'

'Don't you believe in her miraculous power, then?'

'No one will save us from death here on earth. Even Lazarus, who Jesus might actually have raised from the dead, died once more. Maybe the very next day. Or the year after.'

'I heard one priest saying how some famous scientists in America had measured the power hidden in the human brain when it's dying,' his neighbour said. 'In the case of a believer, that power is five hundred degrees positive and twenty-five times stronger than one of the most powerful radio stations in America.'

Daniel turned his back on the man. What made everyone want to talk to a clergyman about metaphysical problems? Why did they have to reel off to him all the obscurantist nonsense they'd ever heard? Would they even come and bother him when he was on his deathbed?

'In the case of an unbeliever,' his neighbour went on to say, 'the power was five hundred degrees negative.'

'Please don't tell me any more,' Daniel requested him. 'I'm a Protestant minister and my father was a doctor. I don't believe in such nonsense.'

The man relapsed into an aggrieved silence.

When Daniel first came round in the intensive care unit a week earlier, his wife was sitting facing him and stroking his hand. At the time, the pain permeated his entire body. Then it gradually receded and he could distinctly hear a familiar melody and a huge mixed choir singing faultlessly the old Calvinist hymn:

> *How beauteous is the blue sky,*
> *It wondrously doth bless.*
> *This gift to man from God on high*
> *Is so hard to express.*

> *How often, though, the light of dawn*
> *Is hid by evening's fear.*
> *Man wakes perplex'd and all forlorn*
> *And trust doth disappear.*

Tears started to flow from him and fear concealed the light. He didn't know what he feared more, death or life. He closed his eyes and whispered to Hana, 'Am I dying?'

'Don't worry, everything will be all right.'

After that he no longer heard a coherent melody, just a weary, monotonous drumming.

Ever since then, Daniel had pondered on his life. The drugs that they introduced into his bloodstream filled his mind with disconnected images. They were mostly images from his own life: long-forgotten fragmentary memories and phrases were washed up and then dissolved. Faces the way they looked long ago. His mother lighting a candle before a storm, her face still unwrinkled; the high forehead, the Byzantine nose, and the halo of hair around her head. Father returning from prison emaciated, his eyes lost in the depths of their sockets. Who is this man picking him up? I'm frightened of him, he's a stranger. His sister, whose pigtail always tempted him to pull it, waits for him at some station, or maybe it isn't his sister; can it be Jitka? Jitka laid out in the closet. Jitka-no-longer, just her body. May I lift the sheet? No, don't, Reverend, the image will only haunt you afterwards. I want to see her once more. It would be better to remember her alive. The cold touch of her cheek on his lips. Hana in a long white dress with a posy of white roses. Dan, I trust you, you'll never let me down. Nor you me, I'm sure. Children running in the garden of the country manse. A dog barking: come to think of it, what was its name? Daniel just cannot remember, as if it mattered at all that the bitch was called Diana. Don't cry, my little Eva. But my ear aches. Mum will give you something warm to put around it. It's a boy. Reverend, if you'll wait there we'll bring him to show you. Marek Vedra, I baptize you in the name of the Father, the Son and the Holy Spirit. Magda, whatever possessed you to throw spiders at people? And suddenly that unexpected woman: Don't forsake me! Darling, don't be cross with me for pouring out my unhappy soul to you in such a miserable way. I miss you. I just want to tell you that I'm happy that you're alive and thinking about me.

The pain near his heart again. Maybe he should call the nurse.

Don't think about anything that might upset you!

Augustine was the first one to talk about the heart as the site of love. A father of the church, Bishop of Hippo. During his life he had several quite worldly loves and he wasn't too worried about being unfaithful to his betrothed. For him love was the highest attribute, the true form of God. Love of God is simply a reflection of our capacity to love man.

Mount Durmitor. Dannie, would you dare tackle that chimney?

If you'll anchor me!

Lord Jesus, be with all those who are suffering and ill, and also with all those who in these moments are dying. Be with my wife and don't forsake her; look down on her in your love. Do not forsake me! I am sated with you. You fill me with love. You are the most beautiful thing that ever happened to me in my life. I share everything with you, Dan. Sorrow, pain and even this anxiety. I've fallen in love lots of times, Daddy. I wish you a life of love, and that you should dwell in mercy, understanding, freedom and kindness.

Daniel lifted the receiver and started to dial Bára's number. If her husband answers, he'll replace the receiver. If she takes the phone, he'll simply tell her he's in hospital and still alive.

For a moment, he had the impression he had stopped breathing.

There was a ringing tone. He waited. The ringing tone continued; he realized his hand was shaking.

Apparently there was no one at the other end. Should he take it as an omen?

'I wouldn't bother,' his neighbour chips in. 'The telephone costs you three times as much these days and you don't get through anyway.'

Daniel hung up.

'Even if you are a Protestant,' his neighbour returned to his favourite topic, 'I don't see how you can reject the Virgin Mary. We should all work with her for the salvation of the world.'

We can't work for the salvation of the world unless we work first of all for the salvation of ourselves. Who will help us, seeing that the mother of Christ and her son have long ago rotted in their graves? Will we manage it without the help of someone above us? The starry heaven above us and the moral law within us.

Fortunately, the door opened with a creak. It wasn't Hana but quite a young nurse. 'How are you feeling, Reverend?'

'Not too bad, thanks!'

'In a few more days you'll be out running . . .' She stopped short; she was probably about to say: running after the girls, but such encouragement seemed out of place for a clergyman. Clergymen don't run after girls. They try to live according to God's commandments as best they can. And they pray to Almighty God, as long as their faith remains. And when they don't live according to the commandments and their faith dwindles, so that all that remains are empty words? Then they can run after the girls, but they try to conceal them from the rest of the world. When they succeed, they don't conceal them from their consciences, or their hearts. Then their hearts fail.

Daniel pondered on what had happened to his life. The other woman was now very remote and seemed to him like a dream, as if from another life. It was odd, almost incredible, that just a few days ago they had lain in each others' arms and made love. Had it been bad or just human, the way he had behaved?

One succumbs to a longing for love, for new companionship, for feelings that seem stronger than all other feelings. These then overwhelm the sense of duty and promise of fidelity, putting at risk everything: family, reputation, honour, and in the end, one's life too. But now, as he lay here with only a remote possibility of seeing the other woman, and the illness widening the gulf between them, not only in space but also in time, Daniel was overcome with shame and regret for what he had dissipated, and above all that he had deceived his nearest and dearest. Hana showed him love even though he had betrayed her and that made him feel ashamed. He didn't know whether he would live or how he would live, he only knew that he oughtn't to go on living the way he had been: in deceit and duplicity.

6

Matouš

Matouš leaves the courthouse. Even though he feels that the woman judge who has just released him fairly willingly from the shackles of marriage has removed his life's heaviest burden from him, he is overcome by nostalgia. He stops outside the front entrance. Although he won't admit it, he is waiting for Klára.

Finally Klára appears and notices him. She seems to hesitate for a moment, wondering whether to walk past him disdainfully as if he was of less interest than the window display of some boutique, but then she stops and says: 'Ciao then, you poor old devil. Enjoy yourself!'

She then permits Matouš to light her cigarette before walking away on high heels towards a Honda car in which some foreign devil is waiting for her. She climbs into the seat next to him and then drives out of Matouš's life, probably for good.

Matouš should feel relieved and light-headed at the prospect of a future of calm stretching out before him as well as the fulfilment of his destiny, but instead his legs become heavy.

He walks home, takes off his coat and stretches out on the bed. He lies there for a long time, several hours, gazing up at the ceiling and slowly drags himself through the thicket of hopeless contemplations. On the bedside table there is a jug of wine from the previous day, along with a loaf of bread going stale and a bowl of boiled rice with peanuts. There is no knife to hand so he simply breaks off lumps of bread and slowly chews them. There is also a pile of books by the bed. From time to time he picks up the topmost one and leafs through it for a while before tossing it to one side.

The ceiling is covered in cracks and the dirty threads of cobwebs which flutter in the draught that wafts into the room along with the screech of tram wheels and the din of lorries.

Faces flicker across the greyish surface of the ceiling. Some of them are savage and long forgotten, others are familiar: they are alive, more alive than all the faces of actors and non-actors that move across the television or cinema screens. Women whom he trusted or on whom he even showered love, while knowing they would leave him in the end, scowl and leer at him. He tries to ignore them and to ignore Klára who wantonly tumbles into bed with unknown men.

His thoughts turn to the nurse whom he now takes the liberty of calling Hana. He has already been twice to the church and listened to the confused litanies of her husband, whose aura has already totally disappeared, or possibly Matouš has not been able to concentrate enough to make it out. The time that Matouš was invited to lunch by the minister's wife, he actually had a conversation with the minister. He had felt an unconscious need to take issue with that follower of the resurrected Christ. Did the minister know that the Chinese, the world's most populated nation, had managed to get by without believing in a god and yet the people did not live any less morally than in those places where they acknowledged a god or gods? The minister was aware of this. In the East, he said, there was less individualism and people were more obedient to an order that had been established over centuries.

Did that mean that concepts of a god or gods and an immortal soul

373

were simply products of our individualism, of our reluctance to countenance the extinction of our own selves?

The minister said that was not what he had in mind, although anxiety about the extinction of the self certainly played a role in our notions of God.

The minister was either incredibly conciliatory or was consumed with doubts of some kind. Either about himself or about God.

Matouš has only spoken to the minister's wife a couple of times since he promised her his poems, and he still hasn't taken them to her. He has been waiting for some more suitable moment: he has the feeling that his poems ought to crown his acquaintance with that woman, rather than be an opening gambit.

But on one occasion, when he was feeling particularly bad and Hana brought him his medicine for the second time, he had recited to her some of his poems and told her that she had been the inspiration for them.

Surely not – she replied in astonishment – how could I have?

Just by being you, he told her. There is something mysterious about you, something oriental and mystical.

That's all in your imagination, she commented.

No. My whole life was meaningless until I met you.

You sound delirious, she laughed in embarrassment, and even touched his forehead to see if he had a fever, but she took her hand away before he had time to press it to his forehead.

Now Matouš thinks about that good woman with particular intensity. He thinks about her not only because his solitariness was officially confirmed today, but also because he has an odd premonition that something bad has befallen Hana and that she might perhaps welcome Matouš's attention.

He ought to phone her and offer his help should she require it, but at this moment he lacks the will to do anything.

He who does, loses. All we hold we lose in the end.

Matouš falls asleep.

When he wakes up he can hear the boom of the ocean waves and the murmur of the crowd as they watch condemned prisoners being driven away to execution. Curiosity and indifference in the ant heap. Blazing fires.

Then his mother's voice intrudes upon him: Mattie, why aren't you eating? Stop complaining, Mattie, and pull yourself together, everything's going to be all right again. The touch of his mother's hand stroking his hair.

Matouš realizes that it is a long time since he visited either his mother's or his father's grave. That's bad. It is one's duty to pay respect to those who gave one life, and his mother was the only good woman he had met in his life. Then Matouš's thoughts stray once more to another woman, to Nurse Hana, and he realizes that he misses her; he misses her voice and her smile, he misses a mother's love.

At last he gets up, opens the refrigerator and finds in it a piece of dry salami and gobbles it down. Then he opens a can of goulash and with his fingers he fishes out pieces of meat from the unpleasantly smelling sauce before throwing the can into the pedal bin which emits a swarm of flies the moment he opens the lid.

He takes a shower and puts on a clean shirt.

For weeks now his poems have lain waiting on the table in a black binder. He has chosen almost two hundred of them, precisely one hundred and eighty-seven of them, in fact: the ones he feels sure are successful. He resists the temptation to open the binder and read at least the best ones once more – he knows them by heart anyway.

He lifts the receiver and hesitates for a moment before dialling the number of the manse. Luckily enough, the minister's wife answers the telephone.

He announces himself, but apparently she cannot recall his name, as she says: 'I expect you want to speak to my husband. I'm afraid he's in hospital.'

The nurse's voice is unusually sad.

'Anything serious?' he asks.

'A heart attack.'

'I hadn't heard. I'm sorry to hear it, Hana. And how is he?'

'Thank you. I think he has got over the worst of it.'

'I'm glad to hear it.' Nurse Hana is wrong, because she believes in some medical gadgetry and doesn't realize that her husband's life force is fading. She doesn't realize she will come into his wealth. It is unlikely she gives it a thought. He therefore says once more, 'I really am glad to hear it, you must have been very worried.'

'I expect you're calling about your poems,' the minister's wife recalls. 'You promised me them ages ago.'

'Only partly. I just had the feeling all of a sudden that something had happened to you, that something was troubling you and I ought to give you a ring.'

'Troubling me? Oh, yes, there's always something troubling one.' The minister's wife remains silent for a moment and he says: 'Everything will be all right again, you'll see.'

'Nothing will ever be the way it used to be,' says the minister's wife and Matouš makes out a quiet sob. Then that good woman forces herself to turn her thoughts from her own distress and ask him what his poems are about.

He says that it is impossible to say in a few words. They are attempts at capturing his moods, but he wouldn't like to bother her with them now, not unless his poems might bring her a little comfort.

Yes, that's something she would need at this moment. From the tone of her voice Matouš recognizes that Hana's thoughts are divorced from her words. None the less he tells her that poetry is there to console. Like music. Or meditation. Or prayer.

'If you like, and if you happen to be passing, you're welcome to drop by with them,' the minister's wife decides all of a sudden.

'Right away?'

'If you like. I have to visit my husband this afternoon.'

'Thank you, matron. I'll come in time to spend a little while with you. After all, you visited me when I was feeling low.'

Matouš is suddenly full of energy. He puts on his most expensive, pure silk tie – a golden Chinese dragon against a blue background – and carefully combs his thinning and already grizzled hair. Then he puts into his briefcase the black binder containing the one hundred and eighty-seven poems that will perhaps, be published after all, just as he might eventually hope to receive some love or at least understanding. At the kiosk by the tram stop he buys three white carnations.

The minister's wife opens the door and thanks him for the flowers before inviting him in. She is pale and her eyes are red, either from lack of sleep or crying. If Matouš were to be taken to the hospital, or if he actually died there, who would weep for him?

Matouš asks after her husband's health once again. Hana is making coffee and in the process she gives him some of the details in a succinct and matter-of-fact way. Her husband is getting better; if things continue the way they have gone so far, he could be home in two weeks.

He is being well looked after in the hospital and he is even in a side ward now, with a bedside telephone.

Matouš has the impression that her description of her husband is all a bit too professional, as if the sorrow in her face was related to something other than her husband's illness.

'So there's no point in upsetting yourself, Hana,' he says. 'In any case, you won't change fate by upsetting yourself.'

'Don't you think so? There are things I can't tell you, anyway.' The minister's wife pours the coffee into pink cups.

'All the more reason not to upset yourself,' Matouš repeats. 'We have to take life as it comes and realize that everything will pass away one day: pain and joy, and in the end ourselves too. Because what are we compared to the sky and the stars? Or even to a tree? At least within trees there is peace, whereas we just wriggle around in the throes of passion, rage, longing and betrayal.'

The matron sips her coffee. She looks away from him. Then she says: 'You're not like I thought you were.'

'In what way?'

'You're more serious.'

'We all have several faces. And we generally conceal the real one from other people.'

'I always thought there were people who didn't conceal anything.'

'And don't you think so any more?'

'I've never concealed anything,' she says, avoiding an answer.

'Everyone conceals something,' Matouš objects, 'we all have some secret or other.'

'All right. I've never done anything I would have to conceal.'

Matouš is now convinced that the source of her distress is not merely her husband's illness. Some duplicity or other has shaken her faith in human goodness. 'I'm sure that you would be incapable of harming anyone,' he says. 'I have never deceived anyone either.'

He looks at the woman opposite; there is still sorrow in her face, but also kindness. All of a sudden it is as if he was transported back whole decades: his mother is waiting for him with his lunch and asking how things were in school and he is starting to speak, complaining about his fellow pupils for mocking him or even beating him up. Matouš starts to take the minister's wife into his confidence. He doesn't speak about his travels, or about his real or imagined experiences in foreign parts, he speaks about himself, how he was deceived by women he loved, and most of all by the latest one, whom he took into his home and whom he divorced only yesterday.

Matouš starts to lament over his own goodness of heart and the ingratitude that has been his reward. He also talks about everything he had wanted to achieve in his life, but how he had managed almost none of it, because the world is not well disposed towards people like him, people who don't elbow their way through life, who lack both influence and property. The world is not wise – it respects strength, not decency and honesty. It's not interested in real values. People want to have a good time and live it up, regardless of what they destroy in the process.

The matron listens to him, the same way his mother used to. He has the feeling she agrees with him; subconsciously, Matouš is expecting this nice little lady, this good woman, to rise and come over to him, stroke his hair and say: Stop complaining, Mattie, and pull yourself together, everything's going to be all right again!

'You're not part of that world either,' Matouš goes on to say. 'That's why you are in low spirits. People like us ought to get together and live in mutual trust, so as to bear our burden more easily.'

Hana makes no response to his challenge, to his declaration. She looks at her watch and says, 'I'm sorry, but I have to dash to the hospital to see my husband.'

Matouš is taken aback. He starts to apologize for holding her up and heaping his own troubles on her when she has plenty of her own.

'Don't worry, I'm used to it. People often used to come to me like this; I am a minister's wife after all.'

Matouš suddenly collapses inside and can scarcely find the strength to get up. He doesn't even offer to accompany Hana to the hospital or take her there by taxi, seeing that he has delayed her.

No sooner does he reach the street than he realizes he has forgotten to give Hana his poems. Now he is unlikely ever to show them to her. In fact he is unlikely to show them to anyone at all. His poems will remain hidden like many other people's verses and, like many other people, he will end his days in loneliness.

7

Two days after Daniel was first permitted visitors, Eva appeared in his ward. The dress she was wearing was new to Daniel; it was loose fitting to conceal her condition. 'Hi, Dad, how are you?'

'It's getting better every day, thanks. And how about you?'

'There's nothing wrong with me, is there?' She leans over to kiss him. 'Well, maybe there is, but at least my life's not at stake.'

'Life is always at stake.'

'I've brought you some peaches.' She took out a large paper bag. 'I know what you mean.' She drags one of the free chairs over to his bedside. 'I wanted to come yesterday with Marek, but I had two full days at college. And I couldn't manage it before.'

'Don't apologize, I'm glad you're here now.'

'Daddy, I've been thinking about you all that time. An awful lot. And apart from that, I was wanting to tell you something. I haven't told you. Shall I wash you a peach?'

'No thanks. I'd sooner hear what you were wanting to tell me.'

'Right away?'

'It's best not to put things off.'

'OK. I didn't tell you that when I discovered what had happened to me with Petr, I felt I just couldn't leave it like that and I went to the doctor to see about a termination. The waiting-room was full of women and they were almost all talking about the same thing. It made me feel dreadful. I recalled a Scottish ballad about a mother who stabs her baby through the heart and then she meets it and it blames her for laying it in the grave instead of in its cradle. And I also realized that the doctor had known Grandad and most likely knows you too, and that as soon as he saw me he'd say to himself: a fat lot she's achieved. Or he'll ask: What does your dad have to say about it?'

'What I'd have to say is hardly the most important thing.'

'I know. I'm just telling you what I felt. I knew you'd be terribly disappointed in me when you discovered what had happened, but there in that waiting-room it occurred to me that you'd have been even sorrier to hear that I had had it killed, that you'd tell me my mother would never have done such a thing. So I got up and left.'

'You did the right thing, Eva. But why do you keep talking about what I'd think or say? It was a question of you and your child!'

'I simply wanted to tell you that I was thinking about you even at that moment. Because I blame myself, Daddy, that I might have been the cause of what went wrong with your heart!'

'I could just as easily blame myself for being the cause of you and Petr going out together.'

'Exactly. I know you expected something else from me. That I disappointed you.'

'No. If anyone disappointed me, it was myself. Remember, you must live in such a way so as not to disappoint yourself.'

'I know, Daddy. But you always wanted me not to be like me but like Mummy.'

'I don't know what you mean.'

'You saw her in me, Daddy. But I couldn't be her because I was me.'

'That's perfectly in order. I'm fully aware of that.'

'But you used to compare me with her more and more. And I couldn't help but lose every time, because no one can be as good as someone who is already dead, that you only remember the beautiful things about.'

'I must say that never occurred to me. I didn't realize. If that's the way you felt, I'm really sorry.'

'I've been thinking a lot about everything. Ever since they brought you here and we've been worrying about you so much. Daddy, when I told you and also wrote to you that I might marry Petr straight away, that was the reason. I wanted to demonstrate that I was someone else. That I wasn't like Mum, that I was me. But at the same time I knew you were right, and that I ought to wait, that there was a chance I would be making up for a stupidity by committing an even worse one.'

'It's good you realized.'

'I'm not going to marry Petr. Not for the time being anyway. Not until I can be sure he'll change.'

'And you're doing it on your own account, not mine?'

'On my own account.'

'I'm glad. I wouldn't want you to be blackmailed by my illness.' He reached out to his daughter and squeezed her hand. 'I'm glad. Glad that you've taken that decision and glad you told me those things.'

'I'd like to help you get better.'

There was a knock at the door. Then Bára entered with a big bunch of roses. 'I've just brought you a few roses, Reverend. I don't want to disturb you.'

His heart gave a painful jolt.

'You can stay if you like,' Eva said. 'Dad will be glad of a visit, and I was going anyway.'

'Your daughter looks very well on it,' Bára said when they were on their own. 'You're not cross with me for coming?'

He took the bunch of roses from her and placed them in the vase on his bedside table.

'I just wanted to come and say hello. To see you and ask how you were. Please don't be cross with me, I couldn't bear not being able to see you.'

'For the last time?'

'For the last time, if that's what you want.'

'I didn't mean it that way.'

'I wanted to see for myself that you were getting better.'

'I'm feeling better. I am already up on my feet and I took a walk in the corridor yesterday. Today I'm allowed out into the garden. We could go out there together if you like. Thanks for the beautiful roses and for coming.' He took an envelope out of his bedside table and put it in his dressing-gown pocket. Even though they were now alone, it was better not to stay here.

'I'm not going to take up your time, Dan,' she said when they came out into the corridor. 'I really did just want to see you.'

'How did you find out?'

'At church, of course. From Ivana.'

They walked down the steps. Behind the building there were a number of benches on which the sun was now shining. They sat down. 'What have you gone and done to me, Dan?' she asked.

'I don't know. I once read that shortly before his death Kafka wrote: My brain and my lungs have ganged up on me behind my back. It looks as if my heart and brain have ganged up behind my back.'

'On me?'

'No, on me.'

'The sun doesn't bother you?'

'No, it doesn't.'

'Does it bother you that we can be seen here?'

'I didn't say anything was bothering me.'

'I've been missing you, Dan. Awfully. And I was so afraid for you, from the moment you didn't come that Monday.'

'It's the first time I didn't turn up when I promised. I thought about it when I came round, how you must have waited in vain.'

'Dan, that wasn't important, was it? Nothing was important but your life and ever since Ivana gave me the news I've thought about nothing else.'

He had the impression Bára was holding back tears. 'I didn't want to burden you with extra worries on top of all the ones you had already. I never wanted that.'

'You're hardly going to apologize, are you?'

'Any change at home?' he asked.

'None. Saša sends his regards. He says he's thinking about you and hoping you get better. Apart from that, the place is as cold and silent as a freezer. The only warmth I ever got was with you. And when you didn't turn up I knew something had happened. Something really bad, otherwise you wouldn't have abandoned me without saying a word.'

'I called you from here. Several times, but there was never any reply. I took it to be an omen.'

'Of what?'

'I don't know. That I'd never get through to you.'

'I know what you mean. An omen that I don't belong to you. No, it wasn't an omen, we were just away for a few days. I couldn't stand being in a city where you were lying ill and I wasn't allowed to visit you.'

He felt her closeness. Here she was sitting next to him again, drawing him to her again.

'Do you realize it's already over a year since I first came to hear you preach?'

'Of course. I could hardly forget that day, could I?'

'And we once sat together on a bench in Veltrusy Park, remember?'

'My heart may be in a mess, but there's nothing wrong with my head.'

'There are some things you remember more with your heart than your head.'

'And my heart's alive too for the time being.'

'Does your wife visit you here?'

'Yes. She takes care of me.'

'That's good. Even though I envy her. I'd like to visit you and take care of you.'

'Thank you. Thank you for coming now.'

'Dan, don't worry about anything,' she said. 'I unloaded so many of my woes on you and now I feel guilty that they were only the woes of a spoilt brat. You're not to worry about anything. You must give your heart a rest.'

'I'm trying to.'

'I wrote you a letter, but don't read it now.' She took an envelope from her handbag. 'Though I'd better not give it to you now either. Another time.'

'It's not entirely certain I'll have another time.'

'No, you're going to live. I wanted to tell you that I will love you to the end of my days. You were a revelation to me and will remain so even if we never see each other again.'

'Thank you. I wrote you a letter too.' He pulled the envelope from his pocket.

'All right, I'll give you mine too. It's like an exchange of diplomatic notes,' she said. 'The meeting took place in an atmosphere of mutual friendship. Shall I walk you back?'

'Perhaps not.'

'I'd like to stay with you. We never had much time to stay together, especially me. Now I regret it. I blame myself. Maybe I'll still make up for it.'

'Don't blame yourself for anything. It's not the amount of time that matters. Most of the time quantity doesn't matter, even though everything tends to be measured by quantity.'

'I know. I'm grateful to you for everything. I know it's something you're not supposed to measure, but it was more than I had ever received and more than I deserved. I'd better go now before your wife comes. Get well. Get well as quickly as you can, and don't worry about anything.'

He went to put his arm around her but stopped short. They were too much on display. But what did that matter seeing he might not be alive tomorrow?

She noticed the unfinished movement and kissed him on the lips. 'Thank you for everything, Dan!'

'I thank you too.'

'And don't forsake those of us who need you!'

He watched her as she walked quickly away; as his love retreated from him.

His legs were a trifle shaky and he was obliged to sit down twice before reaching his ward. His legs weren't important; the main thing was that his heart had survived the encounter.

When he got back to the ward Hana was already waiting for him.

'I took a little walk,' he said.

'You oughtn't to go out on your own.'

'I feel fine.'

'I'm glad to hear it.' She took some fruit out of her bag.

'How are the children?' he asked.

'They're coming too. As soon as they're out of school.'

'And how's the building work?'

'All right. I think we could enrol our first children next month. You'll be back by then. I had to pay some bills too, but I don't want to bother you with them now.'

'I'm looking forward to it. A lot.'

'To being home?'

'And to the work.'

'So long as it won't be too much for you! You realize you're going to have to take it easy for some time!'

'People aren't born to take it easy. And besides, I won't be preaching any more.'

'Not preaching any more? Why not?'

'I don't think it would be honest.'

'Maybe you only think that way on account of your heart. But it'll be all right again.'

'My heart maybe.'

'Well, what won't be?' Hana is staring at him. Then, out of the blue, she asks, 'Are the roses from her?'

'From whom?'

'Bára, I think you call her.'

How did she find out? It's immaterial. She knows and that's good. Now if he dies, he won't die and leave behind only a lie. 'Yes, she brought them for me.'

'They're nice.'

'I wanted to tell you about her, but I didn't want to hurt you. Never in my life have I wanted to hurt you. I loved you. I still love you,' he corrected himself.

'Dan, it was awful. I couldn't believe you could lie to me, and for so long.'

'Do you think you'll be able to forgive me?'

'I've already forgiven you, haven't I? Haven't you noticed?' And his wife takes a handkerchief from her handbag and weeps. She weeps because he deceived her and because she doesn't know whether she'll ever believe him again.

8

Letters

Dear Bára,

Today I walked a bit for the first time, freed from the tubes. Walking is a sign of life and so I'm still alive, even though I don't know how many steps I am destined to take. But I am alive and that means I can still talk to you, in spirit at least. Or take leave of you, so that should I depart I won't do so without saying farewell. Taking leave doesn't mean saying goodbye but instead saying the most important thing, the thing that I didn't have the time or the determination to say before . . .

An hour later (I came over faint).

My whole life I have yearned for the closeness of a loved one, for intimacy, in other words. Is it at all possible between two people? There are many degrees of intimacy: people are close to each other when they are able to converse without fear, when they embrace, when they make love. Is love-making the ultimate, the supreme degree of intimacy? One can make love to all sorts of people (although it has never been the case with me), but is that the ultimate intimacy?

The ultimate degree of intimacy – surely that is the capacity to trust utterly and therefore to confide everything, even one's deepest secrets, even the things one conceals from oneself. Not concealing even the things one deceives oneself about . . .

Night time: Where did I break off? You came to me, like many others, because you were afraid of death. I told you, as I'd told so many other people, that death had been overcome by that one single sacrifice, by that one single death on the cross. It's what I told myself too. I wanted so dreadfully much to believe it and I confided to no one, not even my first or my second wife, that I doubted it. That I was proclaiming as the highest truth what was my own wish, yearning and hope. Now at this time, when I don't know if it will be my last message, I admit it to you at least. You will not condemn me, I'm sure. You won't be scandalized, but will have understanding for me.

I told you and others that God's love will redeem us, but I think I was wrong. I don't think there is anyone who would one day judge our faults, forgive us and give us absolution. There is no higher justice than our own. Nothing lasts for ever, except forgetting, maybe.

What is left of all the things in my life that I proclaimed and worked for? Maybe just the conviction that love is the greatest thing we can encounter in life and the most important thing we may strive for. I'm talking about human love; if God's love doesn't exist then only the human sort remains: fleeting and imperfect. But Christ talked about that sort too, and thousands of others after him. And we are still incapable of appreciating it and living by it.

Maybe it's a bad message, but accept it from me as something that is more than a declaration of love, something that is the ultimate degree of intimacy . . .

Love, Dan

———

Dearest, dearest, dearest,

I want to let you know I'm thinking about you all the time. I wanted to tell you that thanks to you I have discovered what love is. I'm not referring now to anything physical. I have in mind what you sometimes talked to me about. I was selfish, I wanted you for myself. I am ashamed of it and I apologize to you for it.

When I learned what had happened to you I was in despair and didn't know what to do. I dashed around the city like a mad thing to all the places where we had been together. And I was afraid for you and I wanted to cry and then rush to the hospital to find you and be with you and hold your hand and beg you not to forsake me. Not to forsake us. To stay here. Here! And then it suddenly struck me: I knelt on the floor and I asked Him to forgive both of us for all the bad things we had done and begged Him that you should live. I told Him that I did not want it for myself, that I no longer want you for myself, I just want you to live, because it is only right, because the world without you would be worse than it is.

And all of a sudden I felt something extraordinary, something greater than relief. I felt that He was listening to me, that He could hear me and would take my entreaty into account, that He would forgive both me and you, because He knows that if we did something bad, it was out of love and out of helplessness and desperation, but never out of wickedness. And all of a sudden I knew that He existed, that I wasn't abandoned, just as you are not abandoned, even at the moments of greatest trial.

God is with you, my dearest, and even if I can't be with you and maybe never will be again, that's not important. He will remain with you, just like my love, as long as you live.

Love, Bára